THE END IS NIGH

THE APOCALYPSE TRIPTYCH

EDITED BY JOHN JOSEPH ADAMS AND HUGH HOWEY

STORIES BY

CHARLIE JANE ANDERS
MEGAN ARKENBERG
PAOLO BACIGALUPI
ANNIE BELLET
DESIRINA BOSKOVICH
TOBIAS S. BUCKELL
TANANARIVE DUE
JAMIE FORD
HUGH HOWEY
JAKE KERR
NANCY KRESS
SARAH LANGAN
KEN LIU
JONATHAN MABERRY
MATTHEW MATHER
JACK MCDEVITT
SEANAN MCGUIRE
WILL MCINTOSH
SCOTT SIGLER
ROBIN WASSERMAN
DAVID WELLINGTON
BEN H. WINTERS

THE END IS NIGH

The Apocalypse Triptych, Volume I

Edited by John Joseph Adams & Hugh Howey
Cover art by Julian Aguilar Faylona
Cover design by Jason Gurley

ISBN-13: 9781495471179
ISBN-10: 1495471179

For more about The Apocalypse Triptych:
www.johnjosephadams.com/apocalypse-triptych

First Edition

Printed in the U.S.A

For our partners

TABLE OF CONTENTS

INTRODUCTION

John Joseph Adams

"It was a pleasure to burn. It was a special pleasure to see things eaten, to see things blackened and changed. With the brass nozzle in his fists, with this great python spitting its venomous kerosene upon the world, the blood pounded in his head, and his hands were the hands of some amazing conductor playing all the symphonies of blazing and burning to bring down the tatters and charcoal ruins of history."

—*Fahrenheit 451* by Ray Bradbury

I met Hugh Howey at the World Science Fiction Convention in 2012. He was a fan of my post-apocalyptic anthology *Wastelands*, and I was a fan of his post-apocalyptic novel *Wool*. Around that time, I was toying with the notion of editing collaborative anthologies to help my books reach new audiences. So given our shared love of all things apocalyptic—and how well we hit it off in person—I suggested that Hugh and I co-edit an anthology of post-apocalyptic fiction. Obviously, since his name is on the cover beside mine, Hugh said yes.

As I began researching titles for the book, I came across the phrase "The End is Nigh"—that ubiquitous, ominous proclamation shouted by sandwich-board-wearing doomsday prophets. At first, I discarded it; after all, you can't very well call an anthology of post-apocalyptic fiction *The End is Nigh*—in post-apocalyptic fiction the end isn't *nigh*, it's *already happened*!

But what about an anthology that explored life *before* the apocalypse? Plenty of anthologies deal with the apocalypse in some form or another, but I couldn't think of a single one that focused on the events leading up to the world's destruction. And what could be more full of drama and excitement than stories where the characters can actually see the end of the world coming?

At this point I felt like I was really onto something. But while I love apocalyptic fiction in general, my real love has always been post-apocalypse fiction in particular, so I was loathe to give up on my idea of doing an anthology specifically focused on that.

That's when it hit me.

What if, instead of just editing a *single* anthology, we published a *series* of anthologies, each exploring a different facet of the apocalypse?

And so The Apocalypse Triptych was born. Volume one, *The End is Nigh*, contains stories that take place *just before* the apocalypse. Volume two, *The End is Now*, will focus on stories that take place *during* the apocalypse. And volume three, *The End Has Come*, will feature stories that explore life *after* the apocalypse.

But we were not content to merely assemble a triptych of anthologies; we also wanted *story triptychs* as well. So when we recruited authors for this project, we encouraged them to consider writing not just one story for us, but *one story for each volume*, and connecting them so that the reader gets a series of mini-triptychs *within* The Apocalypse Triptych. Not everyone could commit to writing stories for all three volumes, but the vast majority of our authors did, so most of the stories that appear in this volume will also have sequels or companion stories in volumes two and three. Each story will stand on its own merits, but if you read all three volumes, the idea is that your reading experience will be greater than the sum of its parts.

In traditional publishing, this kind of wild idea—publishing not just a single anthology, but a *trio* of anthologies with interconnected stories—would be all but impossible, so it was just as well that Hugh and I had already decided to self-publish. But the notion that this was something that traditional publishing wouldn't—or couldn't—do made the experiment even more compelling, and made working on this project even more exciting.

Post-apocalyptic fiction is about worlds that have already burned. Apocalyptic fiction is about worlds that are burning.

The End is Nigh is about the match.

THE END IS NIGH

The Apocalypse Triptych, Volume I

THE BALM AND THE WOUND

Robin Wasserman

Here's how it works in my business: First, you pick a date—your show-offs will go for something flashy, October 31 or New Year's Eve, but you ask me, pin the tail on the calendar works just as well and a random Tuesday in August carries that extra whiff of authenticity. Then you drum up some visions of hellfire, a smorgasbord of catastrophe—earthquake, skull-faced horsemen sowing flame and famine in their wake, enough death and destruction to make your average believer cream his pants—and that's when you toss out the life-preserver, the get-out-of-apocalypse-free card. Do not pass *go*, do not collect $200, do not get consumed by the lake of righteous fire, go directly to heaven on a wing and a prayer and a small contribution to the cause, specifically the totality of your belongings and life savings, 401Ks and IRAs—for obvious reasons—included.

Here's how it's supposed to work in my business: You tuck that money away for safe keeping, preferably in a bank headquartered in a non-extradition country, await the end days with clasped hands and kumbayas, and then, when the sun rises on an impossible morning, oh, you praise the Lord for hearing your prayers and offering a last minute reprieve, you go ahead and praise yourself for out-arguing Abraham and saving your modern day Sodom and Gomorrah, and let's all give thanks for living to pray another day, even if we live in bankruptcy court.

If you don't have the juice to pull that one off, there's always the mulligan—*oopsy daisy, misread the signs, ignored the morning star, overlooked the rotational angle of Saturn, forgot to carry the one, my bad.* Dicey, but better than drinking the Kool-Aid—and if you can't envision a Great Beyond worse than prison, you might be in the wrong line of work. You do your job right, by the time the fog clears and the pitchforks and torches hit your doorstep, you're long gone, burning your way through those lifetimes of pinched pennies one piña colada at a time.

Like I said: Supposed to.

I'm a man who likes a back-up plan, a worst-case-scenario fix for every contingency, a bug-out route in case anything goes wrong. Never occurred to me to plan for being right.

The signs are bullshit. Have to be. You know who "read" the signs? Pick your poison: Nostradamus. Jesus Christ. Jim Jones, Martin Luther, the whole Mayan civilization. Every flim-flam man from Cotton Mather to Uncle Sam. And every single one of them screwed the pooch. Then, somehow, along comes me. You know what they say about those million monkeys banging away on their million typewriters until one of them slams out *Hamlet*?

Just call me Will.

• • •

Hilary dumped the kid five days after I made the prophecy, nine months before the end of the world. I remember, because by that point the Children had rigged up the calendar, a blinking LCD screen hanging over the altar to keep them constantly apprised of the time they had left. Nine months had seemed an auspicious period—long enough for the kind of slow burn panic that empties wallets but stops short of bullets to the brain, brief enough that I could keep smiling and stroking the Children of Abraham without letting slip that I wanted to throttle every insipidly trusting last one of them. But Hilary tracking me down had me questioning the timeframe, and not just because she dumped her stringy ten-year-old in my lap and took off for greener and presumably coke-ier, pastures.

I'd only been Abraham Walsh, né none of your concern, for the last five years, and before that Abraham Cleaver, and before *that*, back in the days when Hilary had decided to fuck with her parents by fucking the itinerant faith healer, Abraham Brady. If a headcase like her had managed to track me through three names, ten years, and twelve states, who knew how many cops, parishioners, shotgun-toting fathers or snot-dripping toddlers might have picked up the trail?

I had a good thing going in Pittstown, had for the last three years. The Children of Abraham had picked up about forty families and, thanks in large part to the penitent auto-parts mogul Clark Jeffries, had cobbled together some nice digs: a church, a few houses, a gated estate complete with indoor pool. Unfortunately, Clark Jeffries' efforts to buy himself into heaven—not to mention his attempt to paper over two decades of embezzlement and hookers—didn't extend to forking over the land deeds or any appreciable fraction of his ill-gotten gains. Always a borrower and a lender be, that was Clark's way. Donations were for suckers.

We weren't a growth operation—proselytizing only gets you the wrong kind of attention—and so we didn't go in for fancy costumes or banging cymbals in airports. Tacky. None of that polygamy stuff either, not if you wanted to keep under the radar, and definitely not if experience had taught you that one wife was already one too many. The Children were a pacific and obedient bunch, and even if it got exhausting at times, playing God's sucker so I could sucker them, the sheets were thousand thread count and there was a hot tub behind the indoor pool. Better than working for a living, especially eight months and twenty-six days from retirement. Then in walks Hilary Whatshername and the apparent fruit of my loom, Judgment Day come early.

"And what do I know about kids?" I said.

"But you've got so many Children, Father Abraham." It was her best look: wide-eyed innocent with a soupçon of irony. It was the reason I'd kept her around for all those months in the first place, even though she'd seen through the big tent act from the start and could have set her daddy and his country club buddies at me on a whim. At twenty-five, she'd nearly managed to pass as a teenager; a decade later, she'd have had trouble persuading a mark she was under forty. But even with sun-spots, a muffin-top, and the ghost of a moustache, there was still a certain sex appeal there—like a stripper who's hung up her thong but still knows how to shimmy, exuding an air of possibility, a slim hope that at any moment, the clothes might come off. "What's one more?" she asked.

"Come the fuck on."

"You'll get the hang of it," she said. "Probably."

"He's your *kid*," I tried. "You want to bet on probably?"

"Better you than my parents. Better anyone than me."

The kid didn't say anything. We were sequestered in my office, where Hilary had settled herself onto the leather couch and kicked her feet up on the Danish modern like she owned the place. A cigarette dangled from her lips that would, knowing Hil, soon be stubbed out on the teak, leaving behind a small but permanent scar, her very own *Hilary was here.* Which I wouldn't have begrudged her if she hadn't been leaving so much else behind.

The kid, on the other hand, was still standing at attention, hands clasped before him, church-style, his glance not bothering to stray toward any of the room's curiosities, the titanium safe or the shrine with its portrait of me (a substantially less flab-faced and balding me) in the thick gold frame. Just beyond the door, in the veloured ante-room, my Children waited, no doubt, with ears pressed to the wall, ostensibly to ensure that this wasn't some kind of clever assassination attempt, likely hoping it was more of a holy visitation, Mary and overgrown Baby Jesus come to make their pre-apocalyptic crèche complete. Meanwhile here was this kid, center of the action, eyes glazed over like he was watching two strangers play a particularly dull game of cribbage. No indication that he realized he was the pot. Here's his mother dumping him on a gray-hair with the body of a linebacker—a hundred push-ups every morning since I sprouted my first pubic hair, with plans to keep it up until the day my dick gives out, thank you very much—who happens to be, *surprise, you probably thought he was dead, but!* his long-lost daddy, and the kid's about as fired up as a pet rock.

I envied him his decade of ignorance. There's nothing more beautiful than a void, a blank screen you can project all those Technicolored fantasies onto, no one to tell you they're misplaced or far-fetched. Easy enough to fill that father-shaped hole with the tall tale of an astronaut daddy stranded on the moon or a CIA daddy defusing bombs in some windswept foreign desert. That could be an epic hero's blood running through your veins, the strength of an Achilles, the bravery of an Odysseus encoded in your DNA. Who wouldn't be disappointed to come face to face with the real thing, to trade in epic poetry for the genetic equivalent of a joke on a bubble gum wrapper? I knew he couldn't look at me without seeing himself, at least the funhouse mirror version—*congratulations, this will soon be your life*—just like I couldn't look at him without wincing at what had once been and what was to come.

His hairline was several inches closer to the brow line than mine but already receding, and it would be a few more decades before his crooked nose and uneven eyes came into their Picasso-like own, but he was already skidding down a slippery slope. I'd had that same thatch of sandy hair, and whatever I'd lost on top was replenishing itself in my nostrils and ears, conservation in action. I'd have to be blind to doubt he was my kid, and he'd have to be nuts not to want to trade me in for a better model. But he didn't look disappointed. He didn't look much of anything. I wondered if he was autistic or something. Glory be. Not only did I have a kid, but the kid was weird.

"Parenting's not complicated," Hilary said. "Accept that you'll fuck him up, whatever you do. Just try not to fuck up so bad that it kills him."

"I'll put him out on the street as soon as you're gone," I warned her.

She grinned, the way only someone who's seen you roll off her naked body with a groan and a *must've had too much to drink* while she said *it happens to the best of 'em* and you both thought *no, it damn well doesn't* can grin.

"No. You won't," she said. And she was right about that, too.

• • •

The kid was no prize. He knew how to talk, at least, turning into a regular chatterbox once his mother peeled away, informing me in nauseating detail about what he required in terms of food, bedding, shampoo brand, toothpaste flavor, internet access, a list that stretched on in such detail and scope that I had to call in one of the Children to take notes.

"What, no limo?" I said, once he was done laying out his demands. "You don't want to throw in a request for a weekly manicure or your own personal masseur?"

Mandy Herman, who was scribbling down everything that came out of the kid's mouth, shot me a sharp look, and I wasn't sure if it was because she didn't think sarcasm was appropriate or because every few days I called her into the office and rewarded her with the opportunity to rub some life back into my shoulders, spine, and ass.

"You said you didn't know what to do with a kid," the kid said. "I'm telling you."

Mandy, that traitor, laughed.

He was, it turned out, like one of those preciously precocious movie kids, the kind who melts the smiles of old men, heals the hearts of bickering lovers, and teaches every neighborhood Grinch the true meaning of Christmas. This, despite the big ears and the lopsided face and the fact that he never shut up.

It did nothing for me, but the Children gobbled it up with a spoon. He wasn't there twelve hours before they took up a collection of spare kid junk: secondhand clothes and filthy toys and a brand new racecar bed courtesy of our very own Scrooge Jeffries. Mandy Herman vied with the Babbage girls for babysitting duties, eventually compromising on a roster that had Mandy on the couch with him Monday through Wednesday afternoons while the three Babbages—buxom and blond in a way that the kid was a few years too young and I was a few decades too old to make use of—covered the rest.

Alison Gentry, who'd been a high school math teacher in her discarded life, had taken charge of the younger Children's education, setting up a one-room schoolhouse in what used to be the stables, and it was no trouble to scoop the kid into the fold. We had no others exactly his age—a clutch of toddlers, some first and second graders, and of course the Babbage girls—but the kid seemed to prefer the company of adults anyway, if you could call the Children that, and with their naïve, infantile willingness to believe as they were told, maybe that made sense.

Because what child doesn't love a story? And when you get down to it, that's all I am: a storyteller. Nothing more, nothing less. Back in the Hilary days, I'd thought I needed more smoke and mirrors, some laying on of hands, but eventually I wised up. You don't need to cure the lepers to be a faith healer. We're all of us in my business doing the same work, because what is faith but another story that you tell yourself to feel better? That's what these idiot skeptics, the do-gooders, the ones so desperate to snatch the wool from my Children's eyes, would never understand: Lies don't hurt anyone. Lies are the balm; *truth* is the wound.

Even the Man himself, if you believed in him up there, napping on his cloudy throne, doesn't have much more than pretty stories to offer these days. Sure, Joseph, Moses, Jesus's precious lepers, *they* got miracles. But now? God's out of the direct action industry, and all he's offering in its place is a bedtime story. The fairy tale of heaven, the promise that whatever shit happens, your story gets a happy ending. The Bible, boiled down: Once upon a time I helped some poor suckers out and someday, maybe, if you're good, I'll help you too, but in the meantime, isn't it a nice story to fall asleep to?

You can't say I'm not doing God's work.

All those social workers, estranged relatives, those Pittstown neighbors who turned their nose up at the Church buying up property in their suburban midst, they called us a cult. Maybe so. But the word carried a sinister whiff that didn't match up with its reality, something that maybe you had to be in a cult—or in charge of one—to know. My Children were gentle, most of them treading through life with the care of the permanently damaged, whether by drugs, abuse, or simply the ordinary existential indignities, loss of job, loss of love, loss of dignity, loss of purpose. That was their universal: Loss. Who else would so desperately need to be found?

That's what I'd done when I first arrived in Pittstown, what I did when I arrived anywhere: I collected the lost, the ones who'd fallen through the cracks, like a dog-catcher scooping up strays for the pound. It was a service, not just to the feral, but to the tame and well-housed, all those cocky, secure, too good-for-it-all townsfolk satisfied with the comfort of their own homes who preferred not to acknowledge what I was doing for them, tending to their damaged so they wouldn't have to.

Alison Gentry's sister left nasty voicemails every few months, and once she'd set the local cops on us, but where was she when Alison's three kids and husband plowed through a guard-rail and into Lake Michigan? Where was she a year later when her sister washed down the anniversary with a vodka and Percodan cocktail?

Where were Mandy's parents—with their team of trust-fund-busting lawyers doing everything they could to keep her hands off her money—when she and her crack pipe had driven a Pontiac through a neighbor's living room window, and then been promptly hauled off to jail, where she stayed, because mom and dad thought teaching her a lesson would be kinder than bailing her out?

Where were Clark Jeffries' kids when his board of directors dumped him on his ass, or Merrilee Babbage's husband when—having been traded in for a secretary with a bad dye job and a dick—she was feeding her three kids with food stamps and blowing the landlord when she couldn't make rent?

I was the one who wiped their tears and salved their wounds and fed them some bullshit to live for, and if I took a little something with me when I went, it was only fair payment for services rendered.

Despite my best efforts, plenty of the Children still had a hole to fill, and somehow, with his ugly, gap-toothed smile and post-nasal drip, the kid filled it.

That was my smile. Those were my mother's big ears and my father's vampire canines—and the way he chewed his nails, but only the ones on his left hand, was like seeing my brother's ghost. This was the kind of genetic detritus that was, I knew, supposed to kindle a fire in me, as if it mattered that we came from the same stock.

I didn't know whether my parents were alive or dead, and didn't much care—had never understood it, this obsession people have with *blood.* This fixation on *children*, as if popping a baby out and watching him grow into your big nose and type 2 diabetes was your best shot at staving off oblivion.

Ask people to worship you? They call you a megalomaniac. Ask them to worship your kid? They call that good parenting.

Still, I played along, let them all believe what they needed to believe. That was, after all, my business. And it wasn't the hassle I'd expected, raising a kid, especially with the Children so eager to do it for me. It was only once he started up with the questions and all that end-of-the-world shit, that the trouble really started.

• • •

He'd been at the compound for a week, and though I dumped him on the Children whenever I could during the day, at night he was all mine. He got himself set for bed all on his own—*mom calls me her little man*, he said, when I caught him flossing for the third time in a day, and that was the second and last time he mentioned her—but my responsibilities had been made clear.

"At eight, you tell me it's time to go to bed," he told me the first night. "I read for a while, and then at nine you come back and turn off the lights."

So that's what I did, standing in the dark for a while after, watching this kid—my kid—lie on his back with his legs straight and his arms crossed across his chest like a fucking corpse. *I made that*, I thought, and waited to feel something.

"You got everything you need?" I said. This was before the racecar bed and the hand-me-down pajamas. "Comfortable?"

He didn't look it.

"Sometimes I like to practice being dead," he said, staring up at the ceiling.

"You're a weird kid, you know that?"

"She's not coming back, is she?"

That was the first time he mentioned her. And because he wasn't crying or behaving anything like you'd expect from a kid in his situation, I gave it to him straight. "Doesn't seem likely."

"Because I'm weird?"

"Because she's a loser."

"Oh."

"Always was. Always will be. You're probably better off."

"Doesn't seem likely," he said. Then, apparently finished playing dead, he curled up on his side. I watched him until he fell asleep.

That's how it went until the night, one week after she'd dumped him, when he broke routine. I'd just turned out the lights when he said, "I get five questions."

"What?"

"Before I go to sleep, I get to ask five questions."

"Says who?"

There was no answer, and so I knew who.

"Why now?" I said. "All of a sudden?"

"I was waiting until I had the right questions."

That didn't sound promising. "I don't think so," I said.

"I'm willing to negotiate."

"Negotiate what?"

"Questions," he said. "How about four?"

"How about zero."

"Three questions."

"No questions."

"You're really bad at negotiating," he said.

"That's a matter of opinion."

That was when, for the first time since he'd set foot on the compound, he burst into tears. Burst like a clogged pipe, ten years of misery spraying out of him in a gusher, and even in the dark I could read his fury, that his pathetic little body had betrayed him. I remembered that, trying to survive the battle zone, dodging artillery fire between the kid you were and the man you were supposed to be. The world screamed at you to grow up, your zits and your twitchy dick agreed it was about time, but you were still afraid of the dark, you still slept with that old teddy bear, you still wanted your mommy.

Maybe you always wanted your mommy.

"Okay. Three questions."

And that right there was my mistake.

• • •

"Do you really get messages from God?"

"I do."

"How?"

"It varies. Sometimes I read His intent in the signs. Sometimes He's got something more direct he wants to say, and He talks to me in my dreams."

"Why you?"

I shrugged. "Why not me? I didn't ask for the responsibility, I'll tell you that much. It's no picnic, devoting your life to the word of the Lord. You'd be surprised how many people don't want to hear it."

"How do you know it's really God? That you're not just hearing voices or something?"

"That's four questions. Good night."

• • •

"Does God hate us?"

"God loves us. We're all his children."

"And you have to love your children."

"That's the rule."

"That wasn't a question."

"Got it. Thanks for clarifying."

"If he loves us, why would he kill us?"

"Everyone dies, kid. It's not punishment; it's human nature."

"No, I mean, why would he kill *all* of us. Jessie Babbage says the world is going to end. In eight months and twenty days."

"That another question?"

"The question is: Is it true, the world is ending?"

I won't pretend I felt good about it, but there was no other way. The kid had shown no sign he'd inherited his mother's proclivity for bullshit, and I couldn't show my hand without risking he'd spread the good news like a virus. "It really is."

There was a long silence, long enough to make me nervous.

"What do you think of that?" I said.

"I think it explains a lot."

• • •

"How's it going to end?"

"You mean, specifically?"

"Yeah. Nuclear war? Asteroid strike? Global warming? I read online about a giant volcano that might explode and kill us all. Also there could be a plague. Or some kind of alien invasion, but that's not statistically likely. Did your dreams say which it is?"

"God's a little hazy on the details," I said. "But the Bible's got a lot to say on the subject, if you're interested." I wasn't about to give him the whole Beast rising from a lake of fire sermon—let the Children take care of that.

"What will we do? When it happens?"

"We'll go to heaven with the rest of the righteous people," I said. "Nothing for you to worry about."

"You don't even know me. How do you know I'm righteous?"

"Fair point."

After that, the kid started having nightmares. And maybe I was partly responsible, but what kid doesn't have nightmares? Anyway, these particular nightmares? Gold. Because he told the Children about them, and the Children took them to heart, figuring any kid of mine having visions of the apocalypse must be getting his info straight from the horse's mouth. Purse strings started to loosen. No one wanted to be counted among the sinners when the big day came. Maybe I helped it along a bit, encouraging all that talk of divine visitation, but it's not like I was forcing the dreams on him.

I just put them to good use.

• • •

"If we know when the world is going to end, shouldn't we be *doing* something about it? Like, warning people? Or doing something to save ourselves?"

"That sounds like three questions."

"It's one," he said. "Multi-part."

"Uh huh."

"So?"

"So we don't have to worry about it, because God's going to save us, and whoever else he wants. That's the whole point."

"But don't they say God helps those who help themselves?"

"Where'd you'd you hear that?" It wasn't one of my favorites. Operations like mine didn't tend to thrive on a philosophy of self-reliance and personal accountability.

"The internet."

It killed me, the way people said that now, like they used to say "the Bible." Or "TV." As if it were Truth.

"I don't think the end of the world is one of those help-yourself situations," I said.

"But what if you're wrong?"

• • •

He wouldn't let it drop. He wouldn't keep it to himself, either, and before I knew it, the Children were buzzing with the prospect of preservation. The kid was a natural, only ten years old but already better than I was at talking people around to his way of looking at things. I'd taught them to be open to persuasion, and they were model students, repeating the kid's questions and arguments and internet-supplied statistics about asteroid impacts like a bunch of ventriloquist dummies. I did my best, pointed out that righteousness was all about faith and faith was all about accepting your fate and waiting for God to intercede, and that's when the kid—who had apparently taken my suggestion on the Bible-reading front—brought in Noah. Before I know it, we're building a damn ark.

Metaphorically, that is.

It turned out you could order anything on the internet, including whatever supplies you might need to survive in a post-apocalyptic wasteland. Canned food, wilderness gear, medical equipment, solar panels, ammunition—*lots* of ammunition. The kid spent hours at the computer, doing research, making lists, and then, like a Dickensian miracle, the wallets opened wide, even the tightest of wads. Sure, the Children had given lip service to buying the prophecy, but with the kid channeling their energy into survival scenarios, they felt it in their *bones*. Judgment Day. End times. No reason to save up for retirement when doom was on the horizon, and so they threw their credit cards at him, and anything left over after the bottled water and campfire stoves? That was mine. The kid, I realized pretty quickly, was like a money laundering shop for bullshit. I fed in my lies, he spit out a pretty good simulacrum of truth.

It wasn't enough to gather supplies, the kid said. We needed a place to store them—a place we'd be safe from the ravaging hordes, not to mention the Horsemen and the Beast, though the specter of these had been overshadowed by the kid's visions of power grid failure and food hoarders. We needed to move off the grid, and Clark Jeffries—who, in the duration of our acquaintanceship had never once gifted anything that could be lent—violated his cardinal rule and dipped into the principal. The kid had befriended a bunch of doomsday kooks online, one of whom must have believed in cash even more than he believed in magnetic pole reversal, because he was only too happy to trade his kook compound for a couple million of Jeffries' hard-earned bucks. And this time, the deeds went to the church, along with the rest of his savings. There it was, my retirement account: Fully funded.

A third of the Children—fortunately, none of the big fish—decided to tough it out at home, whether due to a lack or overabundance of faith, and we kissed them a weepy farewell, promising to meet again beyond the Gates of Heaven, pretending to believe it. The rest of us loaded the supplies into a fleet of retrofitted armored schoolbuses—bug-out vehicles, the kid called them—and headed for the hills.

Our Garden of Eden was a rectangular compound built out of old shipping containers, bullet-proof, impenetrable, and a poor substitute for my marble flooring and twelve-jet Jacuzzi. The kid was happier than I'd ever seen him, and he was doing a hero's job of keeping the Children busy. They taught themselves to can food, forage for mushrooms, fire automatic weapons, build solar generators, suture wounds, identify poisonous snakes, milk goats and slaughter pigs—the internet truly was a wonder. As was the sight of all these accountants and housewives transforming themselves into mountain warriors, the kid at their fore, a pipsqueak Napoleon commanding his troops. They were disciplined in their mission, wild with abandon in everything else. Christian temperance gave sway to desire, to what the hell, to affairs and drunken revels, to one rumored orgy and two suicides. They honestly believed it was all coming to an end: Because I'd told them I dreamed it—and because the kid really had.

He'd stopped having nightmares, stopped asking questions. Now he was the one with the answers.

"It doesn't scare you?" I asked him one night before turning out the lights. We'd abandoned privacy at the new compound, the Children sleeping dorm-style in their hollowed out shipping containers, but I still had the special privileges that follow from a direct line to the Lord. The kid slept on a cot beside me. I'd almost gotten used to the sound of his breathing, and his occasional muffled snore. It had been a long time since I'd slept beside someone long enough to recognize the rhythm of them falling asleep. "It really doesn't scare you, the thought of it all ending?"

It scared the fuck out of me. The kid liked to walk me through potential apocalyptic scenarios—his version of a bedtime story. I fell asleep imagining the oceans rising, volcanic ash blotting out the sun, supergerms knocking out fifty million in a week. The kid taught me about nuclear winter, and in my dreams my skin sloughed off and my Children died a rainbow of deaths, atomized in a cotton candy puff of light, poisoned slow and steady by food and drink and acid rain, huddled in caves before flickering fire as the ice rose around them and the sun set on human life. There were nutcases with nuclear buttons and physicists messing with black holes; there were alarming seismic indicators and a supervolcanic eruption 40,000 years overdue. This was not to mention the potential damage of a solar storm, a not-so-great leap forward in nanotechnology, an asteroid impact, or what might happen when computers the world over gained sentience and turned on their masters. (That last was the kid's favorite, and one of the reasons all computing devices on the compound were nearing their date with a sledgehammer.)

All that talk about reading the signs, and I hadn't realized the signs were everywhere. The world was like one of those supersaturated solutions we'd played around with in chemistry class a thousand years ago—a class I only remembered, and only attended, because of my lab partner's tendency to lean over the beakers and grant me a heavenly glimpse of her sacred mounds. They were solutions with more crap in them than they could bear, suspended in perfect balance, the dissolved particles invisible until you dropped one last, miniscule, harmless particle—and wham, liquid turned to crystal, just like that. I never got how it worked—was too busy plotting my way down Jenny Crowley's v-neck—but I never forgot the sight of it, the possibility of instant transformation. Until the kid started sniffing around dark corners, it hadn't occurred to me that we were living inside the beaker, waiting for someone to drop in one final speck of dust, make one tiny, irrevocable mistake. You didn't need God for a scenario like that. You just needed bad luck or human idiocy, and those I believed in with all my heart.

The Children wouldn't have appreciated the analogy; they had, on my advice, rejected the devil's science, chemistry labs and all. Maybe that explained how they could be so unafraid.

"Why would I be scared when I know how much God loves me?" the kid said.

"And how much is that?"

"He brought me to you at exactly the right time, didn't He? He *saved* me. And he must love you and the Children, too, because he brought me here so I could save you."

You could tell the kid believed it, that it would be a good thing, surviving the end of the world. The Children, too, and that made sense, because it was a child's belief, a child's naïve assumption that life was always preferable to death, because they had animal fear of the latter and no concept of the hardships of the former. Children didn't know what life looked like at its worst.

I knew, and I'd decided a long time ago that when the cancer came—as it comes to everyone in general and my family in breathtaking specificity—I'd toss myself over a bridge or swallow my weight in pills, anything to outpace that slow cancer crawl, the chemo and the shitting and the pain. These children dreaming of survival, that was an arrogance risen from having forgotten pain. I had only myself to blame—wasn't I the one who'd returned them to innocence, replaced their hard truths with soft lies, taught them to hope? They say you can't remember pain—the fact of it, yes, but the truth of it, the physical texture of agony? Gone and forgotten. Which makes it easy to forget that pain hurts, that the wounded life isn't always worth living. I helped my Children forget, but I remembered for them, because someone's got to. Remembering pain is the only way to avoid it.

Let's say you save them, I wanted to ask the kid. What kind of life are you saving them for?

"He could have sent anyone to save you," the kid said. "But God chose *me*."

My son, the chosen one. My son, the sucker.

I tried not to think about it. Easier to imagine he was in on it with me, that we were running the same con, partners. Maybe I'd given him more than a thinning hairline after all; the kid was a born talker. I could take him with me when I left, I thought, bring him along to Miami Beach or, even better, postpone retirement just a little longer, teach the kid the ropes. Everyone likes a father-son act. Two thousand years, and it hasn't gotten old yet, and maybe it wasn't such a bad plan, trading in all my Children for one kid. Even if the end times were upon us, we weren't dead yet.

It felt like an indulgence, imagining him into my future, almost indecent, a fantasy gone one step too far. But why should it have been? The kid was *my* kid—was parenting him the worst thing in the world? Wasn't that the right thing, the natural thing, that I should step in and teach him how to be the right kind of man?

It was my very own bedtime story, and I kept on telling it to myself, right up 'til that very last day.

The night before Doomsday, the Children locked themselves into the compound to brace for the end. The kid got them all situated, set them to battle stations, a rifle in every hand, ready for anything. I waited until the last minute to break it to him, that one last, painful directive I'd gotten from the Big Guy: the Moses treatment, exiled from my hard-won promised land.

"I'm not going in there with you," I told him, *sotto voce*—let him break the news to the Children, spare us all the tearful goodbyes. "Someone's got to stay out here, guard the entrances, keep the infidels away, you know the drill."

"But online they say—"

"Kid, this is coming from someone above Google's pay grade." I said it gently, and then I waited. For him to call bullshit on me, finally, or maybe just to act like a freaking *kid* for once, cry and sulk and cling to my leg or some such theatrics, because what kid wants to face the end of the world without his daddy. If he'd begged to come with me—or, hell, if he'd even asked politely, tossed out the suggestion—I'd have gone for it, walked him through some facts of life, then stuffed him into my own personal bug-out vehicle and gunned it. I would have found a way to explain things—he was just a kid, after all, and having bamboozled him once, how hard could it be to do it again—and it could have all played out like I planned, the father-son partnership, the two of us against the world, for all the time we had left.

But the kid didn't cry, didn't beg, didn't even suggest. He nodded, an adult's gesture of grave acceptance. "God's ways are mysterious, but they are just and they are right. I'll explain it to the Children." He said it as calmly as if I'd confessed I accidentally spilled some canned beans. "You can be sure I'll raise them well for you, and make certain they never forget your sacrifice. Goodbye, Father." He said *Father* exactly like my other Children said it, like he was one of them, like he'd never been mine.

He touched his fingers to my forehead like a benediction, and that was the end of it. The kid was exactly what I'd made him. A believer.

And so it was for the best when the bulletproof door shut between us; a believer was of no use to me.

He was better off without me, I told myself as I bugged out. Maybe he'd even go back to normal. Get himself adopted by one of the Children once they weren't my Children anymore, once they'd resurfaced after a lonely month or two inside, only to realize that they were the worst kind of fools, the bankrupt kind. But I knew better: Can't bullshit a bullshitter. I knew what happened to a weird kid no one wanted, and it was a sure thing none of the Children would want anything to do with him, not once they realized what he'd made them do and what his father had made them believe. He'd be lucky if they didn't lynch him.

Fuck him up all you want, just don't kill him, Hilary had told me, and in all likelihood, I hadn't even managed that.

That's what I was thinking about while I drove south—that and the plump bank account that was waiting for me, and the long stretches of beach with all the bikinis and the days to come. Nothing lasts forever, not even guilt. I could wait it out, I figured.

I figured I had plenty of time.

• • •

It happened the next day, just like I said it would.

I don't exactly know *what* happened, because the power grid crapped out damn quick, along with the radio, and there went any prayer of knowing what was going on, just like the kid said it would.

Thanks to him, I knew enough to make a few guesses, or at least eliminate some options. Not a superbug, obviously, not global warming, not—sorry kid—a robot revolution. Not God. Not a divine Judgment, not my prophecy coming to pass. That one, at least, I could be sure of.

Not a divine judgment, but easily mistaken for one, that blaze of light like the sun gone supernova, the sonic boom and answering shudder from deep in the Earth that shook branches from the trees, the thousand points of light streaking through the clouds, like a fleet of alien invaders, like the sky was falling, like every disaster movie I'd ever seen with a special effects budget ratcheted up to the billions, because this was an assault on the senses enough to make you believe the impossible, that this was real: the thunder and the silence, the taste of scorched chemicals, the rush of wind and spray of dust, the divine light—and then, switch flipped for good, central fuses blown—darkness at noon.

Dust and dirt and all manner of crap blocking out the sun, the kid had taught me. Suggesting something big enough—asteroid, bomb, whatever—to blow a whole shitload of earth into the sky. A smell in the air, something bad, something wrong. Something *coming*.

It'd be a prettier picture if I could say I wasn't surprised, that some part of me felt it coming, felt some high power speaking through me with the not-so-bullshit prophecy, guiding my finger to the most fateful of dates—that I had a feeling about this one, tasted something off about it, some acrid undertone of Absolute Truth.

Surprised? The only *surprise* is I didn't have a fucking heart attack at the wheel. They haven't got a word for what I was when the sky fell down. Or when I hit the point where the Philly skyline should've come into view... and didn't. Maybe it was lurking out there in the dark, its power failed, its spires hidden in a thicket of dust, but I don't think so. I think it's not there anymore. I think the end came, just like I said it would, and I think it's better not to think too much about that.

I kept driving, long as I could, because what else was I supposed to do? Not north, back toward the compound—nothing was getting into that fortress, not for months, maybe not for years, and they'd shoot me if I tried. East, toward the ocean. Tsunamis or not—and the kid had made it clear *not* was far less likely—I wanted to see it before the end.

Didn't make it that far.

Didn't make it very far at all. Cars swamped the highways, and somewhere in the distance, on the black of the horizon, a bloom of fire that said, pretty clearly: *Wrong way*.

I was no sign reader before, but the kid taught me well. I know what happens now. Destruction, devastation, cities vaporized, millions incinerated, gutted infrastructure, rotting corpses, starving orphans, endless winter, food riots, armed bandits, crime, punishment, plague, famine, hellfire and damnation. If we didn't need God to end the world, we surely won't need him to turn the wreckage into hell on Earth. Humans are capable creatures; we can do most anything ourselves.

It wasn't a bad stretch of road—concrete ribbon winding through lush woods—so I left the car in its jam and took off into the trees, and I waited, like I'm still waiting, for what comes next.

• • •

There wasn't anything special about Hilary, nothing more or less special than any of them, and I never led her to believe any different. That wasn't for me, the wining and dining shtick, and I certainly knew better than to tease a girl like her with a future. You'll notice those same people who turn their nose up at my methods don't hesitate to tell a few stories of their own when it comes to love and lust, parading around their sad little pretense of commitment, promising nothing will ever change when change is the only sure thing we've got. The Hilary episode was brief. It was fun. And then, when it wasn't anymore, it was over—but I guess everything has its moments.

There was this one night, same shitty motel room with its stiff sheets and unnamable perfume, same crap box wine and love handles, same greasy Chinese and sour breath, even the same routine, a little for her, a little for me, finish with her on top then finish her off with the same tired flourish, not an iota of difference from any of the hundred some nights we spent before the sight of each other made us both sick, but that night, after, she fit perfectly against me, a puzzle piece with sad eyes and downy blond peach fuzz up and down her arms—that night, I couldn't stop touching her, and we fell asleep together, like a couple of spooning teenagers. That night, and that night only, for no reason whatsoever, she smelled like home.

It'd be convenient to imagine that was the night we conceived the kid, because wouldn't that suggest there was some higher purpose to the whole thing, not just the sad motel sex, but fifty-six years of eating, sleeping, shitting, enduring one minute after the next? This kid, my kid, and all the Children he saved, our little ark up in the hills where, no matter what happens to the rest of it, some righteous sliver of the human race will survive. That's what the kid believes, and if he's right, it's a nasty joke for God to play on me, but I can't say I'd blame Him.

It'd be convenient, and it'd be easier—especially now. If I could believe in something aside from my own rotten luck. That after all these years of playing the odds, my number finally came in, the one jackpot that does me no good whatsoever. If I could believe that there really is a puppet master, some holy ghost guiding the chess pieces across the board, that this one time he broke with tradition and sacrificed the father instead of the son. But that isn't His way, and believing in it isn't mine.

A happy accident, that's all, for the Children and for me, because there may be no atheists in foxholes but there's at least one immune-to-bullshit bullshitter in these woods, and he may not be ready to die, but he's definitely not looking to survive.

Something will come next; something always comes next. But I'm guessing whatever it is won't be too friendly to bullshit—the world's not going to have much use for that anymore. Unless, maybe, you're the kind that can buy into a lie so fully, so thoroughly, that it comes all the way back around to truth. There's a new world coming, that's what the signs tell me, and it's going to be dark, and it's going to be cold. It's the world I made, but my Children are the ones who'll have to live in it.

My Children, and my son. There'll be no living on through them: God may have made His children in His image, but I made mine in the opposite—and whatever they remember of me will be a lie. I made them to believe; I made them to survive.

I, on the other hand, am in the business of knowing when to quit. I'm in no hurry to die, but it's a comfort to think I'll be gone before they know enough to hate me for leading them into the promised land.

HEAVEN IS A PLACE ON PLANET X

Desirina Boskovich

It was 8:34 p.m. on a Tuesday, and it was almost the end of the world.

Actually, the world was expected to end on Friday, at precisely 5 p.m., eastern daylight time. This was not a forecast, or a projection: it was more like an appointment.

On Friday at 5 p.m. eastern, a thousand high-powered laser cannons would fire simultaneously from their hidden positions in outer space, instantly reducing Planet Earth to vapor and ash. At the exact same moment, the consciousness of every living human being would manifest itself on Planet Xyrxiconia. This planet was located a trillion light years away in a far-flung region of the universe Earth's scientists had not yet glimpsed. There, on Planet X, humanity would find themselves in fresh bodies—remade vessels. These reincarnations would live eternally in a world of infinite luxury.

At least…that's what the aliens claimed.

They'd arrived two weeks ago. They'd been rather vague on the subject of their origins; apparently, they came from all over. And they'd been traveling a while. They'd spent more time in the dark empty places between stars than we could possibly imagine; they'd been staring into the endless void since before we were finger-painting on the solid walls of caves.

Through human mouthpieces, the aliens communicated their expectations. There would be no end-of-the-world parties, no apocalyptic adventures, no doomsday loss of decorum. There would be no orgies, no mass suicides.

Directive: Continue about your business, human citizen. Wait patiently for the appointed day. Shop, work, eat, sleep. Stick to routine. And stay calm. This mandate came with teeth. The aliens suggested that one out of every thousand humans on Earth be appointed to the noble task of enforcing. They left the details to our local governments. When Italy, France, Switzerland, and Mexico formed a coalition protesting this tyrannical treatment, their heads of state were promptly vaporized on the spot.

After that, no one resisted. As directed, local governments staged lotteries. One in a thousand.

Of course, my number came up; it always does.

• • •

It was 8:34 p.m. on Tuesday. I sat at the bar, running my fingertips across the polished wood, sipping whiskey that burned like fire all the way down.

This was typical behavior for a Tuesday evening; I was in the clear.

Across the bar sat a frumpy middle-aged white guy in a neon sweater vest, tossing me dirty looks. Finally he stood up, strode over, and slammed his glass on the bar beside me.

"Lady…You must feel like a real hero," he hissed. "You must be really proud."

"I don't know what you mean, sir," I said, taking another measured sip.

"You know exactly what I mean." He gestured to the standard-issue ray gun—we called them "misters"—hanging at my waist.

"Well, why don't you try using your words?"

"You're a traitor, that's what I mean. A murderer. Killing your own kind. You people make me sick."

"Hmm," I said, nodding. I'd gotten use to this kind of thing.

"And I'll tell you what else. If there is a paradise on Planet X, I sure wouldn't want to share it with the likes of you."

A tense silence had fallen over the bar. The other patrons were listening, observing with a kind of desperate curiosity. They wanted to know if I was going to enforce him, of course.

I didn't see any reason to; a pissed-off guy from Brooklyn insulting some random woman at the bar was the very definition of "business as usual."

"Go fuck yourself, you self-righteous piece of shit," I said, and turned back to my drink.

A group of kids trooped into the bar. It was a regular's bar, filled with old timers quietly mourning the world's slow decline and their own gradual loss of hope; it had been that way for a long time, long before the aliens arrived. These kids were out of their element, but too drunk to notice. There were six or seven of them: white kids, the girls so young they looked like children, dressed in their spangled thrift-store finds, their gladiator sandals and embroidered leather cowboy boots. They gulped PBR and downed double shots. They were celebrating a wedding. The bride pulled the groom up onto a table and they began to dance. The wedding party cheered them on while the rest of the patrons looked on in disapproval; it was not that kind of bar.

"Just married, huh?" the bartender said to the friend who was buying a fresh round of drinks.

"Yeah," she shouted, her voice hoarse. "We said—we don't know if we'll ever be able to like, get married, or do it, or anything like that, in that other place, so we're all getting married this week." She pushed her bangs away from her eyes. "We're taking turns. They just did it today. Tomorrow it's me and Pete."

I pulled out my mister and enforced them all.

After that, the bar was much quieter. The frumpy white guy spit on me and walked out. I sipped my drink and watched the door, waiting for Sara Grace.

• • •

Sara Grace was a nursing student at Columbia. She'd been raised in the suburbs of some sleepy Minnesota town. She hated New York.

We'd been assigned to each other randomly, like everyone else. It was part of the deal: all enforcers had a partner. That way, if anyone got squeamish, there was always someone to do the deed.

Sara Grace was dressed in a pink cardigan, khaki slacks, and kitten heels. Her blonde hair was tied away from her face with a silk polka-dotted scarf. Her mister hung at her waist.

"May I have a Cosmopolitan, please?" she asked the bartender. "Easy on the vodka, and could I have an extra slice of lime, if you wouldn't mind?"

She sat beside me and we went over our numbers for the day.

"I just enforced an entire family," she said, sipping her Cosmo. "The husband was buying a bunch of those suicide kits out the back of a van on Flatbush. They were planning to do it all together. Mom, dad, two girls, a little boy, even the dog and cat! Like, hold hands, pray, and die."

"So what happened?"

"Oh, I followed him home. Then I enforced them all. Even the dog and cat. I wish I knew what happens to dogs on Judgment Day."

"I wish you would stop calling it that."

"Sorry, just a reflex from Bible school. We're due for a meeting at headquarters, you know," she said, checking her slender watch and suggestively eyeing my full drink.

"I know, I know," I said. "I'm chugging."

I chugged.

• • •

Headquarters was set up inside a warehouse in Red Hook. Twenty thousand square feet of concrete floors, and the ceilings yawned high overhead so the acoustics were terrible. The Brooklyn Division Enforcement Team gathered here to report our numbers and receive feedback on our performance. Our managers gave us little pep talks about how essential our efforts were toward ensuring a smooth and pleasant transition toward the end of the world.

On one wall was a whiteboard scribbled with encouraging messages and enforcement data. On the opposite wall was a countdown clock.

There were several thousand team members in our division. We filled the room to the brim with breathing and sweat and chatter and stink. We divided our attention between the stage at the front and the countdown clock, which was a handy measure of how late we were getting started.

Finally the meeting was called to order.

"Your numbers are down," the boss shouted at us. He had reason to be nervous; managers with poorly performing teams tended to find themselves on the wrong end of the ray gun. "You're down compared to Manhattan; you're down compared to Queens. Shall I go on?"

There was a muttered undercurrent of rebellion.

"I don't care, I don't care, from now on I don't want to hear any excuses," he bellowed into the microphone. "We're almost there. Three days from now—we're in paradise. Seven virgins, clouds and harps, free beer, gold-plated toilet seats—whatever floats your boat. Just keep your goddamn numbers up."

From now on, we'd be reporting every hour. Checking in, every hour, on the hour, and if we hadn't enforced anyone, there would be some explaining to do.

"Just three more days," he said. "Just three more days and this will all be over. Now go home, get some rest, and I want to hear from everyone at 9 a.m. sharp."

Sara Grace and I walked to the subway together. "Wanna come over for a nightcap?" I asked. "I bet you need one. I sure as hell do."

"Thank you," she sighed. "I really shouldn't. I need to get some sleep. I'll see you tomorrow?"

"Yeah. No problem. See you then."

That night I lay awake thinking about her. It had been a long time since I'd let myself fall for anyone. Now I had it bad. And I didn't have much time left.

• • •

The Aliens: most people called them The Travelers, but I thought of them as The Mickey Mouse Club, because of the human mouthpieces they'd chosen. They were all washed-up child actors and stars of reality TV shows. They all had those bland good looks, and none of them had ever said anything remotely interesting on their own terms, so they were the perfect avatars to relay the message.

Apparently, the aliens' physical manifestations were repulsive to human sensibilities; I'd never seen one in the flesh, but I'd heard stories. These long-lived rumors started and spread with a twisty life of their own. From what I'd gathered, the aliens resembled something like scaly seahorses or obese horned toads.

But no one ever saw these bodies, at least not on TV. It was spectacle; it was all smoke and mirrors. They had technology we couldn't even begin to comprehend. The universal translator, the ray gun, the spaceship, the empathetic mind links. So they hung back and spoke through their human avatars, and even if those actors were lost without their laugh tracks, they looked just like what you'd expect.

Of course, the government's dormant propaganda wing swung into full gear. There was no time for Victory Gardens, but citizen safety patrols were in business.

And enforcers, of course.

• • •

The next morning I woke with dark circles under my eyes. I'd stayed awake too long, obsessing about Sara Grace and imagining a way out of all this. As far as I could tell, there was none.

I showered, made myself presentable, and headed to the nearby diner where Sara Grace and I met for breakfast every morning. The local clientele was pretty depleted, so service was fast, and we always got our waffles for free.

Sara Grace was late. Maybe she'd had a rough night too.

I was sitting there sipping my coffee when a guy I'd never seen before strolled in. He was tall and craggy, wearing tight blue jeans, cowboy boots, and a leather jacket that had seen better days. He obviously hadn't encountered the inside of a barbershop in some time. He slid into a booth and ordered the number five.

My first check-in was in thirty-two minutes, and I hadn't enforced anyone yet, so I went over to see what was up. "You mind?" I asked.

"Not at all," he boomed, and I slid into the booth across from him. He stank of cigarettes and the open road.

"So what brings you to the neighborhood?" I asked idly, taking one of his sugar packets and dumping it into my own coffee.

He laughed, a big laugh that filled the diner. The other patrons glanced over, then quickly averted their eyes. "I stick out that much, do I?" he said. "Like a sore thumb, I bet."

I shrugged in a noncommittal way. "Hey," I said. "I'm sure I'd stick out in your hometown, too."

"That you would," he agreed. "Well, it's kind of a funny story. I'm from Oklahoma, you see. Place called Muskogee. You probably wouldn't have heard of it. Anyway, spent most of my life working on a warehouse floor, stacking crates. Got married, got divorced, got married again, divorced again. Had a couple of kids. Always one thing or another. I went on this road trip when I was real young, a couple of buddies and me, right before Susie, that's my first wife, got knocked up. After that, you know, life happens. So when the news came down, I figured, it's now or never, right? Quit the job, bought a Harley, hit the road."

I wondered idly how he'd made it this far. Sounded as if the team in Muskogee was slacking off.

He told me about his trip, and I listened. His eyes shone as he described the breathtaking vastness of the Grand Canyon, the stunning beauty of the Nebraska plains. The St. Louis arch, that gateway to the west. The mist hanging spectral and ghostly over the Smoky Mountains, and the twisting, narrow roads winding their way through the foothills. The Carolina low country, the sun rising like a tangerine over the glittering ocean and the Outer Banks.

"It's been a life-changing experience," he said, mist in his eyes. "I'll tell you what. I just wish I had more time."

"I think we all do," I said.

I let him finish his breakfast and pay his check. He'd made it this far, and I still had a few minutes before my first check in. It was the least I could do.

I enforced him on my way out the door.

"Epic road trip?" Sara Grace asked. We'd developed a sixth sense for these kinds of things.

"Yeah."

"I always wanted to go to Newfoundland," she said. "And see the whales. A blue whale. Can you imagine? This vast, majestic creature. You'd feel so small. But at the same time, so meaningful. To be part of all of this."

"Yeah. It's a trip, all right."

We both dialed the number and checked in. She had enforced someone on the way over, so we were in the clear.

"You know what I was thinking," Sara Grace said. "And this just sort of occurred to me. But isn't it kind of funny how we're basically getting rid of all the people who want to ask questions? Who don't follow directions? Who, you know, have like, a mind of their own?"

"Weeding out the troublemakers."

"Exactly."

"Yeah. It's funny, alright," I said. "Sara Grace? I know you were raised in Bible school and all that shit."

"You were, too."

"Yeah, I know." (It was true: church every Sunday, sitting on the hard pew, sandwiched between my mother and *her* mother, who still gave me a hard time that I refused to go anymore.) "So when did you start thinking, this whole God thing, maybe it's all made up? Maybe there's no such place as heaven, or hell, except for the one we manage to make for ourselves here on Earth?"

"I don't know, actually," she said, uncomfortable. "I guess I'm just not sure."

Part of her, I think, still believed in all that: baby Jesus, right and wrong, redemption and faith.

And crucially, she still believed that whatever long look or tense moment or charged laugh we shared was just circumstance, just the pressure of surfing the harshest days in history and being the most hated people alive.

Because she wasn't raised that way, and maybe it wouldn't be right.

Neither was I.

But I'd given up on all that a long time ago.

• • •

It was 2:11 p.m. on Wednesday.

We took a long walk through Prospect Park. It was a good place to find people who'd given up.

A man lying on his back in the grass looked like a good candidate. He was dressed in slacks and a button-down, hands interwoven behind his head, as he stared up at the blue skies and the rustling leaves. His shoes and socks lay haphazardly beside him.

We sat down.

"Hello," he said, without looking at us, still staring up at the sky. "You must be enforcers. You're probably wondering if I do this every day, or if I'm currently having some kind of nervous break."

We didn't say anything. Sometimes, it was better to just let them talk.

"Well, as a matter of fact," he said, with a little chuckle, "I'm a scientist. So I've been overwhelmed with despair for the last ten years at least. It's all seemed pretty hopeless for a while now."

"A scientist! Where do you work?" Sara Grace asked eagerly.

"Columbia," he said. "Physics department. Astronomy, actually."

"Columbia? Me too! I'm in the nursing program. Or I was. I had to quit in order to fulfill my enforcing duties."

"You know," he said, musing. "It's funny how you guys are the only ones allowed to make those breaks with your former lives. In fact, you were actually forced to. Ever think about that?"

"Well," she said, rehearsed. She'd been over all this before. "It may seem that way, and we did have to stop doing our old jobs, but in everything else, we're held to the same strict requirements as the rest of you. No calling up old friends, no making up with old enemies, no visiting family members one last time. No crazy spending sprees, no desperate partying. No out-of-character romances."

I felt like her eyes met mine when she said this last part, but I wasn't quite sure.

"Interesting," he said. "I'm Paul, by the way," and he shook our hands without sitting up. "Don't let me keep you from your work. I know I look suspicious, but the truth is I've been coming here for years, both day and night. I like to lay in the grass and look up at the sky and think about everything that's out there. It's so endless, space…so full of promise and mystery. All the things we just don't know. Now we know a little more, of course, or at least we think we do. But this is my routine, so I like to keep it up. You know, it clears the mind."

"What do you mean, '*At least we think we do*'?" I asked.

"Oh, nothing," he said, and chuckled, again. "It's just—my colleagues and I, we've had our telescopes trained at the sky for a long time. A long time. A lot of telescopes. If someone was out there…if those *laser cannons* were out there…I think we would have seen them. Maybe. You know? But governments don't listen to scientists. They never have. And like I said, there are a lot of things we just don't know. Like how it's possible that billions of souls could instantly be transported to another location within our physical plane. That would seem to defy the laws of physics. But there's always more. If we know one thing, it's that there's always more."

"Do you believe in God, Paul?" Sara Grace asked.

He brushed away the wispy brown hair from his receding hairline. "I'm not really sure," he said, after a long pause. "I can't one hundred percent rule out the existence of a deity. I would say, at this point, that it strikes me as a very low possibility."

"Hmm," she said. "Hmm." She was thinking deeply about all this.

I was thinking about the empty skies.

"We should probably keep moving," I said. "Next check in is in twenty-three minutes."

• • •

Sara Grace was wrong, though.

We weren't like everyone else. Everyone else was supposed to go about their business, pretending like the end of the world wasn't right around the corner.

But for us, it was the opposite. It was all we thought about, day and night. Because the only way that we could do what we were doing—the obscene, revolting, monstrous thing we were doing—was to remind ourselves constantly that this was not Real Life. None of this had anything to do with reality. For us, life as we knew it was already over.

The end was nigh, except it had already come and gone.

Otherwise it was too terrible. You couldn't live with that kind of thing. That horror. That brutality. That inhumanity. You had to disconnect. You had to turn off.

And another thing, too. Everyone else was supposed to maintain their same old routines. See the same people. Say the same things. But thanks to some random lottery, the two of us—people who never would have had any particular reason to meet—we'd been thrown together into the most intense experience of our lives.

So for us everything had changed. And they were the ones who changed it.

• • •

Last week—which seemed like another lifetime—when the enforcing first began, we'd each had our own kind of breakdown.

For Sara Grace, it was when she enforced a nineteen-year-old girl who'd showed up in the city looking for her mother. The girl had been put up for adoption as an infant, had never met her biological mom, and now she was afraid she'd never have the chance. "What if I get to the paradise planet, and everyone looks different, we're all in different bodies, we all have amnesia, whatever, nothing is the same. I'll never find her. I just had to take a chance," she'd said. (Sara Grace recounted this whole thing to me later, sobbing so hard she could hardly talk.)

"Maybe," the girl had said, "maybe all this time she's been wondering about me, too. What happened to me. How I look. How I grew up. All I have is her name. There's a lot of people with her name here. I was just going to go down the phonebook and see what I can find. I think, when I hear her voice, I'll know."

"She said that," Sara Grace screamed and hiccupped at me, crying hysterically, the tears and snot running down her face and mixing together in her mouth. "She said, '*When I hear her voice, I'll know.*' Just like that."

Sara Grace's own mother had passed away two years before, dead of breast cancer at age 53, nine months before Sara Grace applied for nursing school.

This meant one of two things.

The first possibility was that Sara Grace's mother would never make it to Planet Xyrxiconia, because only those who were alive and breathing at the moment of transition—the moment the laser cannons fired—would be reincarnated in this distant place.

The second possibility was that she was already on Planet X, that all our lost loved ones from eon after eon were already there, that they'd gone before us to prepare the way and would be there to greet us when we arrived.

The aliens had been somewhat unclear on this point, perhaps intentionally.

All we could do was wait and see.

For me, the breakdown was when I had a talk with my brother. He told me he was going to North Carolina. His ex-wife lived there now, with their kid, who was only three; she'd moved back there to be near her family when the marriage fell apart. My brother kept saying maybe he should have tried harder, maybe *they* should have tried harder, maybe they could have made it work. In the face of everything, whatever stupid arguments they'd had, those just didn't really matter anymore, did they? She was the love of his life—she'd always been—and that was his son, and if these were the last days of his life on Earth he was going to spend it with the two of them.

He cried as he told me this and I cried too.

I should have enforced him.

But I couldn't. How could I? My own brother?

I should have called for backup. I should have called Sara Grace.

But I didn't.

On the off-fucking-chance that there was a paradise planet, I wanted to spend eternity there with my brother. And his wife. And their kid. So I let him go.

Other people's brothers weren't so lucky. And that's how I knew that no one was actually headed to paradise.

Because if there is a heaven, that's not how it works.

I stood on the Brooklyn Bridge for a long time after that, staring off into the distance. I stood there with the wind in my face and the roar and groan and exhaust of traffic to my back. It was chaotic, loud. The water yawned hungrily below. The reason I couldn't enforce my brother was the same reason I couldn't jump.

Some ragged, wild-eyed guy showed up after a while and stood beside me. We were quiet, companions in misery.

"You know what I think is funny?" he said after a while.

"What's that?"

"All these bridges. All these tall buildings. All these train tracks. So inviting."

"What do you mean?"

"They never even tried to make it difficult. It's like all along, they've just been saying, '*Go ahead, we dare you.*'"

"I guess I don't understand."

"They said '*Don't do this, don't do that.*' But somehow…I dunno. I get the feeling I'm doing them a favor. Anyway, sister, good luck to you. Wherever you end up."

He jumped and disappeared into the waves below.

When I was a kid, my grandma used to say: "Cassie, if all your friends jumped off the Brooklyn Bridge, would you do it too?"

I know, I know, everyone's grandparents said that. Sometimes our parents said it as well, echoing the lectures they'd been hearing since childhood themselves.

You have to think for yourself; that's what it meant. Someone has to stand up. Someone has to refuse to follow the crowd.

I didn't jump. I didn't do it too. Instead, I went home and sat in the bath and drank until I couldn't see straight.

The next day at headquarters, they handed out thousands of bottles of Xanax. After that it all got a whole lot easier.

• • •

It was 9:17 p.m. on Wednesday…almost the end of the world.

We met at headquarters to go over the numbers. We'd had an okay day, but our stats were still down. Everyone's stats were down.

What I thought—and maybe what a lot of people thought, although no one said it aloud—is that maybe the reason our numbers were down was that we'd already enforced so many people. And, of course, plenty of people had decided to off themselves.

The daring ones, the impulsive ones, the yearning ones, the emotionally unstable ones—they were all gone. The ones who were willing to hold out for paradise, they were the only ones left.

The streets felt awfully empty.

• • •

11:02 a.m. on Thursday. We enforced a lady euthanizing her six cats, just in case. We enforced a florist standing in the street in front of his shop, liquidating all his stock by handing out flowers to anyone who passed. We enforced an old couple, two women sitting side-by-side and hand-in-hand on the steps of a church, praying for mercy and grace for themselves and everyone they knew.

2:47 p.m. on Thursday. We enforced a young man scattering his father's ashes. We enforced a young woman taking a dive into the East River. We enforced a young couple making love under a bench in the park and we enforced another young couple locked in a drinking contest.

5:22 p.m. on Thursday. "Less than twenty-four hours to go," Sara Grace said, and we stood together looking out across the water, watching the sun as it sank toward the Manhattan skyline. "It was a beautiful world," she said. "This world. It had a lot to offer."

"Not really," I said, but maybe that was just a tired old pose, that same old cynicism that made it easier not to get hurt. Now that it was ending, I did feel a pang of loss.

"I just wish we had more time."

"I think we all do," I said.

The sun glared red and glinted off the skyscrapers and Sara Grace snuck her tiny hand into mine.

• • •

That night at headquarters there was something in the air: darkness and restlessness and relief and jubilation all mixed together. It was our last nightly meeting. We were almost done. We were almost there.

There were long, rambling speeches and lots of hand-offs of the mic. There were congratulations and thanks all around. There were midlevel city employees and local politicians. All the managers came out on stage and did a dance routine to show their appreciation for our service.

There was a low rushing undercurrent of whispers and laughter and mumbling at all times, echoing against the concrete floors and walls like the ocean in a seashell. The room felt hot and sweaty, and it stank of beer and cigarettes and human sweat, except I could smell Sara Grace beside me too and she smelled like eucalyptus and jasmine and herself.

They showed us a slideshow with some facts about what we'd accomplished in the past two weeks. They'd coordinated at the highest levels of the project to put this together for us, gathering data from all North American offices. They'd set it to music.

The most active enforcers were in metropolitan areas (no surprise there): Los Angeles, Seattle, Chicago, New York. Here in New York, we hadn't done quite as well as L.A., but we couldn't let that get us down, could we?

Overall enforcement numbers for the United States stacked up surprisingly well against other western countries, demonstrating that despite all the doom and gloom, we Americans really could get organized and pull together when circumstances demanded. One out of every thousand people everywhere had been called to enforce and, of all these, nearly 83% had completed their service to the end, with each enforcer completing an average of about fifteen enforcements per day. Not bad, not bad at all.

We could have done the back-of-the-envelope calculations for ourselves, but they did it for us: almost a billion people vaporized in just eleven days. Talk about efficiency.

And of course, there were all the people who'd gone ahead and taken care of matters themselves.

You'd think there would have been vomiting and sobbing all around, but the music played on, and everyone clapped and cheered.

"Thanks to your hard work and vigilance," said our top-top manager, who reported directly to the Department of Transition, "We've provided real incentives for our citizens to respect the guidelines established by our interstellar visitors. Because of you, we can expect to see nearly eighty percent of our pre-contact population make a successful transition to Xyrxiconia! Give yourself one more round of applause, folks!"

We'd done it.

We were almost there.

• • •

After the last headquarters meeting of all time, we flooded into the nearby bars for drinks.

Sara Grace and I found ourselves sitting across from two guys, partners like us. We shouted over the noise of the bar and we drank and drank and drank. "Here's what I think," the one guy said. He leaned in close to us, partly because what he was saying was controversial, and partly because it was the only way he could make himself heard. We could see the pores on his nose, the crinkles around his eyes. "Here's what I think. I think they're conmen. Intergalactic fraudsters. How many aliens actually landed? Didn't we hear it was something like a few hundred thousand? Maybe half a mil? It was just one ship, right?"

"It was a *generation ship*," Sara Grace corrected him. "They'd been living on that thing for ages. It was huge."

"But still," he said. "Say it was a million, tops. They've got ray guns, right? They've got those universal translators, whatever. We've practically got that shit ourselves. They've got technology and weapons. But we could still take them. We've got numbers. We're spread out."

"But they don't want to fight us. They're here to help."

"Or maybe that's just what they said. You know the number one rule of being a conman? Offer the mark something he really, really *wants*."

"Like heaven."

"But maybe they're really here to help themselves to a new planet. Maybe their whole goal was to trick us into getting rid of ourselves, do the work for them. Decimate our own fucking population so they can move on in, help themselves."

Sara Grace was staring at him in open-mouthed horror. I wasn't. I'd thought of this already.

His partner wasn't appalled, either. He looked bored. Irritated. "You know what I think?" he said. "I think there aren't any aliens. Alien conmen? It's ridiculous. Aliens don't understand human psychology. Humans do. I think it's a government plot. Eliminate excess population. Exert control."

"But of course there are aliens," Sara Grace said. "People have seen them."

"People? What people? Do you know anyone who's actually seen one? Or is it all just rumor and somebody-who-knows-somebody-who-said?"

"There was that one in the picture. *Everyone* saw that."

"Photos can be faked. They wanted a world full of scared, docile, delusional bootlickers. Well, congratulations everyone, it's finally here."

We clinked our glasses and drank.

• • •

On Friday at 11:55 a.m. the aliens held a press conference. Or rather, their human mouthpieces held a press conference, speaking on behalf of the aliens, who were hunkered down somewhere cool, dark, and safe.

They thanked us effusively for our cooperation and congratulated us on a successful interplanetary transition period. They suggested that at least thirty minutes prior to the appointed hour all citizens should retreat to their homes, where they should wait calmly and quietly for the final transition to begin.

"Congratulations, once again," transmitted the human avatar. "There will be no further instructions. This is our final message."

• • •

The Department of Transition rented a vast convention center where we could spend the final hours. We did our last check-in at 2 p.m., then headed over. They herded us into infinite ballrooms stuffed with big screen televisions and an endless spread of hors d'oeuvres.

Sara Grace and I found a spot on the sidelines. It was 3:27 p.m., and it was almost the end of the world—very soon now. We sat on folding chairs and I watched the talking heads on the television babble about the moment to come and Sara Grace nibbled at a small plate of cheese and crackers and tried not to throw up. She was still disturbed by last night's conversation. She hadn't slept at all.

"I miss my family," she said. "I wish I was home."

It went on and on. In other places it was night. The citizens sat in their darkened living rooms with one candle lit. In other places it was morning. The city streets were as silent and deserted as they'd ever been. From around the world, the video feeds flooded in.

Around 4 p.m. the anchors started going off the air. By 4:30 p.m. all the channels were static and the screens went dark.

"I need some air," Sara Grace said. She put her uneaten plate of cheese and crackers on the floor and left it; I'd never seen her do anything like that before. "Come on," she said, and took my hand and dragged me out through the crowded ballroom and into a frigid hallway.

We found a secluded spot, a tiny conference room with a table for eight. It was empty. The clock on the wall read 4:39.

"It might be fast," I said, looking at it. *Tick-tock, tick-tock.*

"Or slow," she countered. We sat on the ugly carpet, backs against the wall, out of sight of the glass panel set into the door.

"If we get there," she said, "to Planet Xyrxiconia, do you think we'll recognize each other? Different bodies and all?"

"Yes. I like to think so."

"I guess the real challenge would be finding each other. What if everyone reincarnates on their own private island?"

"Be a hell of a lot of private islands. A planet of archipelagos."

She giggled. "Oh well," she said. "I guess we never get as much time as we want, no matter how long it is." She looked at me, long and wistful, and I don't know who started it, but we were kissing. Kissing hard. Gasping for breath. Unbuttoning each other's shirts, groping blindly, crying a little and still kissing and touching as hard as we could, stretched out on the floor beneath the whiteboard, longing for more.

I think I knew in my heart of hearts that I could've been anyone, that it didn't matter, that we weren't in love or anything—at least she wasn't in love with me; I just happened to be there.

I didn't care.

There was a burst and clatter at the door, and we pulled away from each other, quickly, guiltily. The door came swinging open and another enforcer strode in.

We licked our lips, wiped our mouths, moved to button our shirts, and she stared at us, her hand moving uncertainly toward the mister hanging at her side. There was a long, tense, unbearable moment.

Then she pointed at the clock.

It was Friday and it was 5:13 p.m.

We straightened our clothes and followed her out into the hallway where the enforcers were congregating in anguished, heaving clusters around the windows and gesticulating toward the ground below. We could only see their backs, but we could hear: the clatter of gunfire, the moan and wail and scream of sirens, the low rumble of tanks.

It was 5:15 p.m. on a Friday, and it was *almost* the end of the world.

Almost. But not quite. We still had a long, long way to go.

BREAK! BREAK! BREAK!

Charlie Jane Anders

Earliest I remember, Daddy threw me off the roof of our split-level house. "Boy's gotta learn to fall sometime," he told my mom just before he slung my pants-seat and let go. As I dropped, Dad called out instructions, but they tangled in my ears. I was four or five. My brother caught me one-handed, gave me a spank, and dropped me on the lawn. Then up to the roof for another go round, with my body more slack this time.

From my dad, I learned there were just two kinds of bodies: falling, and falling on fire.

My dad was a stuntman with a left-field resemblance to an actor named Jared Gilmore who'd been in some TV show before I was born, and he'd gotten it in his head Jared was going to be the next big action movie star. My father wanted to be Jared's personal stunt double and "prosthetic acting device," but Jared never responded to the letters, emails, and websites, and Dad got a smidge persistent, which led to some restraining orders and blacklisting. Now he was stuck in the boonies doing stunts for TV movies about people who survive accidents. My mama did data entry to cover the rest of the rent. My dad was determined that my brother Holman and I would know the difference between a real and a fake punch, and how to roll with either kind.

My life was pretty boring until I went to school. School was so great! Slippery just-waxed hallways, dodgeball, sandboxplosions, bullies with big elbows, food fights. Food fights! If I could have gone to school for twenty hours a day, I would have signed up. No, twenty-three! I only ever really needed one hour of sleep per day. I didn't know who I was and why I was here until I went to school. And did I mention authority figures? School had authority figures! It was so great!

I love authority figures. I never get tired of pulling when they push, or pushing when they pull. In school, grown-ups were always telling me to write on the board, and then I'd fall down or drop the eraser down my pants by mistake, or misunderstand and knock over a pile of giant molecules. Erasers are comedy gold! I was kind of a hyper kid. They tried giving me ritalin ritalin ritalin ritalin riiiitaliiiiin, but I was one of the kids who only gets more hyper-hyper on that stuff. Falling, in the seconds between up and down—you know what's going on. People say something is as easy as falling off a log, but really it's easy to fall off anything. Really, try it. Falling rules!

Bullies learned there was no point in trying to fuck me up, because I would fuck myself up faster than they could keep up with. They tried to trip me up in the hallways, and it was just an excuse for a massive set piece involving mops, stray book bags, audio/video carts, and skateboards. Limbs flailing, up and down trading places, ten fingers of mayhem. Crude stuff. I barely had a sense of composition. Every night until 3 a.m., I sucked up another stack of Buster Keaton, Harold Lloyd, or Jackie Chan movies on the ancient laptop my parents didn't know I had, hiding under my quilt. Safety Last!

Ricky Artesian took me as a personal challenge. A huge guy with a beachball jaw—he put a kid in the hospital for a month in fifth grade for saying anybody who didn't ace this one chemistry quiz had to be a moron. Some time after that, Ricky stepped to me with a Sharpie in the locker room and slashed at my arms and ribcage, marking the bones he wanted to break. Then he walked away, leaving the whole school whispering, "Ricky Sharpied Rock Manning!"

I hid when I didn't have class, and when school ended, I ran home three miles to avoid the bus. I figured Ricky would try to get me in an enclosed space where I couldn't duck and weave, so I stayed wide open. If I needed the toilet, I swung into the stall through a ventilator shaft and got out the same way, so nobody saw me enter or leave. The whole time in the airshaft, my heart cascaded. This went on for months, and my whole life became not letting Ricky Artesian mangle me.

One day I got careless and went out to the playground with the other kids during recess, because some teacher was looking. I tried to watch for trouble, but a giant hand swooped down from the swing set and hauled me up. I dangled a moment, then the hand let me fall to the sand. I fell on my back and started to get up, but Ricky told me not to move. For some reason, I did what he said, even though I saw twenty-seven easy ways out of that jungle-gym cage, and then Ricky stood over me. He told me again to hold still, then brought one boot down hard on the long bone of my upper arm, a clean snap—my reward for staying put. "Finally got that kid to quit hopping," I heard him say as he walked across the playground. Once my arm healed up, I became a crazy frog again, and Ricky didn't bother me.

Apart from that one stretch, my social life at school was ideal. People cheered for me but never tried to talk to me—it was the best of human interaction without any of the pitfalls. Ostracism, adulation: flipsides! They freed me to orchestrate gang wars and alien invasions in my head, whenever I didn't have so many eyes on me. Years passed, and my mom tried to get me into dance classes, while my dad struggled to get me to take falling down seriously, the way my big brother did. Holman was spending every waking moment prepping for the Army, which was his own more socially acceptable way of rebelling against Dad.

• • •

Sally Hamster threw a brick at my head. I'd barely noticed the new girl in my class, except she was tall for a seventh grader and had big Popeye arms. I felt the brick coming before I heard it, then people shouting. Maybe Sally just wanted to get suspended, maybe she was reaching out. The brick grazed my head, but I was already moving with it, forward into a knot of basketball players, spinning and sliding. Afterward I had a lump on my head but I swore I'd thrown the brick at myself. By then the principal would have believed almost anything of me.

I didn't get the reference to those weird *Krazy Kat* comics about the brick-throwing mouse until years later, but Sally and I became best friends thanks to a shared love of hilarious pain. We sketched lunch-trolley incidents and car pile-ups in our heads, talking them out during recess, trading text messages in class, instant messaging at home. The two of us snuck out to the Winn-Dixie parking lot and Sally drilled me for hours on that Jackie Chan move where the shopping trolley rolls at him and he swings inside it through the flap, then jumps out the top.

I didn't know martial arts, but I practiced not being run over by a shopping cart over and over. We went to the big mall off I-40 and got ourselves banned from the sporting goods store and the Walmart, trying to stage the best accidents. Sally shouted instructions: "Duck! Jump! Now do that thing where your top half goes left and your bottom half goes right!" She'd throw dry goods, or roll barrels at me, and then shout, "Wait, wait, wait, go!" Sally got it in her head I should be able to do the splits, so she bent my legs as far apart as they would go and then sat on my crotch until I screamed, every day for a couple months.

The Hamster family had social aspirations, all about Sally going to Harvard and not hanging out with boys with dyslexic arms and legs. I went over to their house a few times, and it was full of Buddhas and Virgin Marys, and Mrs. Hamster baked us rugelachs and made punch, all the while telling me it must be So Interesting to be the class clown but how Sally needed to laser-beam in on her studies. My own parents weren't too thrilled about all my school trouble, and why couldn't I be more like Holman, training like crazy for his military future?

• • •

High school freshman year, and Sally got hold of a video cam. One of her jag-tooth techno-hippie uncles. I got used to her being one-eyed, filming all the time, and editing on the fly with her mom's hyperbook. Our first movie went online at Yourstuff a month after she got the camera. It was five minutes long and it was called *Thighcycle Beef*, which was a joke on some Italian movie Sally had seen. She had a Thighcycle, one of those bikes which goes nowhere with a lying odometer. She figured we could light it on fire and then shove it off a cliff with me riding it, which sounded good to me.

I never flashed on the whole plot of *Thighcycle Beef*, but there were ninja dogs and exploding donuts and things. Like most of our early short films, it was a mixture of live-action and Zap!mation. Sally figured her mom would never miss the Thighcycle, which had sat in the darkest basement corner for a year or so.

We did one big sequence of me peddling on the Thighcycle with Sally throwing rocks at me, which she would turn into throwing stars in post-production. I had to peddle and duck, peddle while hanging off the back wheel, peddle side-saddle, peddle with my hands while hanging off the handlebars, etc. I climbed a tree in the Hamsters' front yard and Sally hoisted the Thighcycle so I could pull it up there with me. Then I climbed on and "rode" the Thighcycle down from the treetop, peddling frantically the whole way down as if I could make it fly. (She was going to make it fly in post.) The Thighcycle didn't pedal so good after that, but Sally convinced me I was only sprained because I could scrunch all my fingers and toes and I didn't lose consciousness for that long.

We were going to film the climax at a sea-cliff a few miles away, but Sally's ride fell through. In the end, she settled for launching me off the tool shed with the Thighcycle on fire. She provided a big pile of leaves for me to fall onto when I fell off the cycle, since I already had all those sprains. I missed the leaf pile, but the flaming Thighcycle didn't, and things went somewhat amiss, although we were able to salvage some of the tool shed thanks to Sally having the garden hose ready. She was amazingly safety-minded.

After that, Sally's parents wanted twice as hard for her not to see me. I had to lie and tell my parents I'd sprained my whole body beating up a bunch of people who deserved it. My brother had to carry stuff for me while I was on crutches, which took away from his training time. He kept running ahead of me with my junk, lecturing me about his conspiracy theories about the Pan-Asiatic Ecumen, and how they were flooding the United States with drugs to destabilize our country and steal our water, and I couldn't get out of earshot.

But all of my sprains were worth it, because *Thighcycle Beef* blew up the internet. The finished product was half animation, with weird messages like "NUMCHUK SPITTING TIME!" flashing on the screen in between shots, but the wacky stunts definitely helped. She even turned the tool shed into a cliff, although she also used the footage of the tool-shed fire elsewhere. People two or three times our age downloaded it to their phones and watched it at work. Sally showed me the emails, tweets, and Yangars—we were famous!

• • •

I found out you can have compound sprains just like fractures, and you have to eat a lot of ice cream and watch television while you recuperate. My mom let me monopolize the living room sofa, knitted blanket over my legs and Formica tray in my lap as I watched cartoons.

My mom wanted to watch the news—the water crisis and the debt crisis were freaking her shit. I wanted to catch the Sammo Hung marathon, but she kept changing to CNN, people tearing shopping malls apart with their bare hands in Florida, office windows shattering in Baltimore, buses on fire. And shots of emaciated people in the formerly nice part of Brooklyn, laying in heaps with tubes in their arms, to leave a vein permanently open for the next hit.

Did I mention ice cream? I got three flavors, or five if you count Neopolitan as three separate flavors, like all right-thinking people everywhere.

I went back to school after a week off, and the Thighcycle had a posse. Ricky—femur-cracking Ricky Artesian—came up to me and said our movie rocked his freaking head. He also said something about people like me having our value, which I didn't pay much attention to at the time. I saw one older kid in the hallway with a Flaming Thighcycle T-shirt, which I never saw any royalties for.

Sally snuck out to meet me at the Starbucks near school and we toasted with frosty mochas. Her round face looked sunburned and her hair was a shade less mouse than usual.

"That was just the dry run," she said. "Next time, we're going to make a statement. Maybe we can go out to the landfill and get a hundred busted TVs and drop them on you."

I vetoed the rain of TVs. I wanted to do a roller disco movie because I'd just watched *Xanadu.*

We posted on Yangar.com looking for roller-disco extras, and a hundred kids and a few creepy grown-ups hit us back. We had to be super selective, and mostly only took people who had their own skates. But Sally still wanted to have old televisions in there because of her Artistic Vision, so she got hold of a dozen fucked old screens and laid them out for us to skate over while they all showed the same footage of Richard Simmons. We had to jump over beach balls and duck under old power cords and stuff. I envisioned it being the saga of skate-fighters who were trying to bring the last remaining copy of the U.S. Constitution to the federal government in exile, which was hiding out in a bunker under a Chikken Hut. We filmed a lot of it at an actual Chikken Hut that had closed down off near the Oceanview Mall. I wanted it to be a love story, but we didn't have a female lead, and also Sally never wanted to do love stories. I showed her Harold Lloyd movies, but it made no difference.

Sally got hooked on Yangar fame. She had a thousand Yangar friends, crazy testimonials, and imitators from Pakistan, and it all went to her head. We had to do what the people on the internet wanted us to do, even when they couldn't agree. They wanted more explosions, more costumes and cute Zap!mation icons, funny catch phrases. At fifteen, Sally breathed market research. I wanted pathos *and* chaos!

• • •

Ricky and some other kids found the school metal detectors missed anything plastic, ceramic, wood, or bone, and soon they had weapons strapped all over. Ricky was one of the first to wear the red bandana around his neck, and everyone knew he was on his way. He shattered Mr. MacLennan's jaw, my Geography teacher, right in front of our whole grade in the hallway. Slow-time, a careful spectacle, to the point where Ricky let the onlookers arrange ourselves from shortest in front to tallest in back. Mr. MacLennan lying there looking up at Ricky, trying to assert, while we all shouted *Break! Break! Break! Break!* and finally Ricky lifted a baseball bat and I heard a loud crack. Mr. MacLennan couldn't say anything about it afterward, even if he could have talked, because of that red bandana.

Sally listened to the police scanner, sometimes even in the classroom, because she wanted to be there right after a looting or a credit riot. Not that these things happened too often in Alvington, our little coastal resort city. But one time, Sally got wind that a Target near downtown had gone crazy. The manager had announced layoffs and the staff just started trashing the place, and the customers joined in. Sally came to my math class and told Mr. Pope I'd been called to the principal's, and then told me to grab my bag of filming crap and get on my bike. What if we got there and the looters were still going? I asked. But Sally said looting was not a time-consuming process, and the crucial thing was to get there between the looting and everything being chained up. So we got there and sneaked past the few cops buddying in the parking lot, so Sally could get a few minutes of me falling under trashed sporting goods and jumping over clothing racks. She'd gotten so good at filming with one hand and throwing with the other! Really nobody ever realized she was the coordinated one, of the two of us. Then the cops chased us away.

My brother got his draft notice and couldn't imagine such luck. He'd sweated getting into the Army for years, and now they weren't even waiting for him to sign up. I knew my own draft notice was probably just a year or two down the line, maybe even sooner. They kept lowering the age.

My mom's talk shows were full of people saying we had to stop the flow of drugs into our country, even if we had to defoliate half the planet. If we could just stop the drugs, then we could fix our other problems, easy. The problem was, the Pan-Asiatic Ecumen or whoever was planting these drugs were too clever for us, and they had gotten hold of genetically-engineered strains that could grow anywhere and had 900 times the potency of regular junk. We tried using drones to burn down all their fields, but they just relocated their "gardens" to heavily populated areas, and soon it was block-by-block urban warfare in a dozen slums all around Eurasia. Soldiers were fitted with cheap mass-produced HUDs that made the whole thing look like a first-person shooter from 40 years ago. Some people said the Pan-Asiatic Ecumen didn't actually exist, but then how else did you explain the state we were in?

• • •

Sally fell in love with a robot guy named Raine, and suddenly he had to be big in every movie. She found him painted silver on Main Street, his arms and legs moving all blocky and jerky, and she thought he had the extra touch we needed. In our movies, he played Castle the Pacifist Fighting Droid, but in real life he clutched Sally's heart in his cold unbreakable metal fist. He tried to nice up to me, but I saw through him. He was just using

Sally for the Yangar fame. I'd never been in love, because I was waiting for the silent-movie love: big eyes and violins, chattering without sound, pure. Nobody had loved right since 1926.

Ricky Artesian came up to me in the cafeteria early on in eleventh grade. He'd gotten so he could loom over *and* around everybody. I was eating with Sally, Raine, and a few other film geeks, and Ricky told me to come with him. My first thought was, whatever truce we'd made over my arm-bone was over and gone, and I was going to be fragments of me. But Ricky just wanted to talk in the boy's room. Everyone else cleared out, so it was just the two of us and the wet TP clinging to the tiles. The air was sour.

"Your movies, they're cool," he said. I started to explain they were also Sally's, but he hand-slashed. "My people." He gestured at the red bandana. "We're going to take it all down. They've lied to us, you know. It's all fucked, and we're taking it down."

I nodded, not so much in agreement, but because I'd heard it before.

"We want you to make some movies for us. Explaining what we're about."

I told him I'd have to ask Sally, and he whatevered, and didn't want to listen to how she was the brains, even though anyone looking at both of us could tell she was the brains. Ricky said if I helped him, he'd help me. We were both almost draft-age, and I would be a morning snack to the military exoskeletons. I'd seen *No Time For Sergeants*—seventeen times—so I figured I knew all about basic training, but Ricky said I'd be toast. Holman had been telling me the same thing, when he wasn't trying to beat me up. So Ricky offered to get me disqualified from the Army, or get me under some Protection during training.

When I told Sally about Ricky's offer, the first thing she did was ask Raine what he thought. Raine wasn't a robot that day, which caught me off-guard. He was just a sandy-haired flag-eared skinny guy, a year or so older than us. We sat in a seaside gazebo/pagoda where Sally thought she could film some explosions. Raine said propaganda was bad, but also could Ricky get him out of the Army as well as me? I wasn't sure. Sally didn't want me to die, but artistic integrity, you know.

The propaganda versus artistic integrity thing I wasn't sure about. How was making a movie for Ricky worse than pandering to our fans on Yourstuff and Yangar? And look, my dad fed and housed Holman and me by arranging tragic accidents for cable TV movies where people nursed each other back to health and fell in love. Was my dad a propagandist because he fed people sponge cake when the whole world was flying apart?

Sally said fine, shut up, we'll do it if you just stop lecturing us. I asked Ricky and he said yes, neither Raine nor I would have to die if we made him a movie.

This was the first time we ever shot more footage than we used. I hadn't understood how that could happen. You set things up, *boom!* you knocked them over and hoped the camera was running, and then you moved on somewhere else. Life was short, so if you got something on film, you used it! But for the red bandana movie we shot literally hundreds of hours of footage to make one short film. Okay, not literally hundreds of hours. But a few.

Raine didn't want to be the Man, or the Old Order, or the Failure of Democracy, and I said tough shit. Somebody had to, plus he was older and a robot. He and Sally shot a ton of stuff where they humanized his character and explained how he thought he was doing the right thing, but we didn't use any of it in the final version.

Meanwhile, I wore the red bandana and breakdanced under a rain of buzzsaws that were really some field hockey sticks we'd borrowed. I also wanted to humanize my character by showing how he only donned the red bandana to impress a beautiful florist, played by Mary from my English class.

After a few weeks' filming, we started to wonder if maybe we should have had a script. "We never needed one before," Sally grumbled. She was pissed about doing this movie, and I was pissed that she kept humanizing her boyfriend behind my back. You don't humanize a robot! That's why he's a robot instead of a human!

Holman came back from basic training, and couldn't wait to show us the scar behind his left ear where they'd given him a socket that his HUD would plug into. It looked like the knot of a rotten tree, crusted with dried gunk and with a pulsating wetness at its core. It wasn't as though they would be able to remote-control you or anything, Holman said—more like, sometimes in a complicated mixed-target urban environment, you might hesitate to engage for a few crucial split seconds and the people monitoring the situation remotely might need to guide your decision-making. So to speak.

Holman seemed happy for the first time ever, almost stoned, as he talked us through all the crazy changes he'd gone through in A.N.V.I.L. training and how he'd learned to breathe mud and spit bullets. Holman was bursting with rumors about all the next-generation weapons that were coming down the pike, like sonic bursts and smart bullets.

Ricky kept asking to see the rushes of our movie, and Raine got his draft notice, and we didn't know how the movie was supposed to end. I'd never seen any real propaganda before. I wanted it to end with Raine crushing me under his shiny boot, but Sally said it should end with me shooting out of a cannon (which we'd make in Zap!mation) into the Man's stronghold (which was the crumbling Chikken Hut) and then everything would blow up. Raine wanted the movie to end with his character and mine joining forces against the real enemy, the Pan-Asiatic drug lords, but Sally and I both vetoed that.

In the end, we filmed like ten different endings and then mashed them all up. Then we added several Zap!mation-only characters, and lots of messages on the screen like, "TONGUE-SAURUS!" and "OUTRAGEOUS BUSTAGE!" My favorite set piece involved me trying to make an ice cream sundae on top of a funeral hearse going 100 mph, while Sally threw rocks at me. (I forget what we turned the rocks into, after.) There was some plot reason I had to make a sundae on top of a hearse, but we borrowed an actual hearse from this guy Raine knew who worked at a funeral home, and it actually drove 100 mph on the cliffside road, with Sally and Raine driving alongside in Raine's old Prius. I was scooping ice cream with one hand and squirting fudge with the other, and then Sally beaned me in the leg and I nearly fell off the seacliff, but at the last minute I caught one of the hearse's rails and pulled myself back up, still clutching the full ice-cream scoop in the other hand. With ice cream, all things are possible.

The final movie clocked in at twelve minutes, way, way longer than any of our previous efforts. It was like an attention-span final exam. We showed it to Ricky in Tanner High's computer room, on a bombed-out old Mac. I kept stabbing his arm, pointing out good parts like the whole projectile rabies bit and the razor-flower-arranging duel that Raine and I get into toward the end.

Ricky seemed to hope that if he spun in his chair and then looked back at the screen, this would be a different movie. Sometimes he would close his eyes, bounce, and reopen them, then frown because it was still the same crappy movie.

By the time the credits rolled, Ricky seemed to have decided something. He stood up and smiled, and thanked us for our great support for the movement, and started for the door before we could even show him the "blooper reel" at the end. I asked him about our draft survival deal, and he acted as if he had no clue what we were talking about. Sally, Raine, and I had voluntarily made this movie because of our fervent support of the red bandana and all it stood for. We could post the movie online, or not, it was up to us, but it had nothing to do with Ricky either way. It was weird seeing Ricky act so weaselly and calculating, like he'd become a politician all of a sudden. The only time I saw a hint of the old Ricky was when he said he'd use our spines as weed-whackers if we gave any hint that he'd told us to make that movie.

The blooper reel fizzed on the screen, unnoticed, while Raine, Sally, and I stared at each other. "So this means I have to die after all?" Raine said in his robotic stating-the-obvious voice. Sally didn't want to post our movie on the internet, even after all the work we'd put into it, because of the red-bandana thing. People would think we'd joined the movement. Raine thought we should post it online, and maybe Ricky would still help us. I didn't want to waste all that work—couldn't we use Zap!mation to turn the bandana into, say, a big snake? Or a dog collar? But Sally said you can't separate a work of art from the intentions behind it. I'd never had any artistic intentions in my life, and didn't want to start having them now, especially not retroactively. First we didn't use all our footage, and then there was talk of scripts, and now we had intentions. Even if Raine hadn't been scheduled to go die soon, it was pretty obvious we were done.

I tried telling Raine that he might be okay, the Pan-Asiatic Ecumen could surrender any time now and they might call off the draft. Or—and here was an idea that I thought had a lot of promise—Raine could work the whole "robot" thing and pretend the draft didn't apply to him because he wasn't a person, but Sally told me to shut the fuck up. Sally kept jumping up and down, cursing the air and hitting things, and she threatened to kick the shit out of Ricky. Raine just sat there slump-headed, saying it wasn't the end of the world, maybe. We could take Raine's ancient Prius, load it up, and run for Canada, except what would we do there?

We were getting the occasional email from Holman, but then we realized it had been a month since the last one. And then two months. We started wondering if he'd been declared A.U.T.U.—and in that case, if we would ever officially find out what had happened to him.

• • •

A few days before Raine was supposed to report for death school, there was going to be a huge anti-war protest in Raleigh, and so we drove all the way there with crunchy bars and big bottles of grape sprocket juice, so we'd be sugared up for peace. We heard all the voices and drums before we saw the crowd, then there was a spicy smell and we saw people of twenty different genders and religions waving signs and pumping the air and chanting old-school style about what we wanted and when we wanted it. A platoon of bored cops in riot gear stood off to the side. We found parking a couple blocks away from the crowd, then tried to find a cranny to slip into with our signs. We were looking around at all the other objectors, not smiling but cheering, and then I spotted Ricky a dozen yards away in the middle of a lesbian posse. And a few feet away from him, another big neckless angry guy. I started seeing them everywhere, dotted throughout the crowd. They weren't wearing the bandanas; they were blending in until they got some kind of signal.

I grabbed Sally's arm. "Hey, we have to get out of here."

"What the fuck are you talking about? We just got here!"

I pulled at her. It was hard to hear each other with all the bullhorns and loudspeakers, and the chanting. "Come on! Grab Raine, this is about to go crazy. I'll make a distraction."

"It's always about you making a distraction! Can't you just stop for a minute? Why don't you just grow the fuck up? I'm so sick of your bullshit. They're going to kill Raine, and you don't even care!" I'd never seen Sally's eyes so small, her face so red.

"Sally, look over there, it's Ricky. What's he doing here?"

"What are you talking about?"

I tried to pull both of them at once, but the ground had gotten soddy from so many protestor boots, and I slipped and fell into the dirt. Sally screamed at me to stop clowning around for once, and then one of the ISO punks stepped on my leg by mistake, then landed on top of me, and the crowd was jostling the punk as well as me, so we couldn't untangle ourselves. Someone else stepped on my hand.

I rolled away from the punk and sprang upright just as the first gunshot sounded. I couldn't tell who was firing, or at what, but it sounded nearby. Everyone in the crowd shouted without slogans this time and I went down again with boots in my face. I saw a leg that looked like Sally's and I tried to grab for her. More shots, and police bullhorns calling for us to surrender. Forget getting out of there, we had to stay down even if they trampled us. I kept seeing Sally's feet but I couldn't reach her. Then a silver shoe almost stepped on my face. I stared at the bright laces a second, then grabbed at Raine's silvery ankle, but he wouldn't go down because the crowd held him up. I got upright and came face-to-shiny-face with Raine. "Listen to me," I screamed over another rash of gunfire. "We have to get Sally, and then we have to—"

Raine's head exploded. Silver turned red, and my mouth was suddenly full of something warm and dark-tasting, and then several people fleeing in opposite directions crashed into me and I swallowed. I swallowed and doubled over as the crowd smashed into me, and I forced myself not to vomit because I needed to be able to breathe. Then the crowd pushed me down again and my last thought before I blacked out was that with this many extras, all we really needed would be a crane and a few dozen skateboards and we could have had a really cool set piece.

THE GODS WILL NOT BE CHAINED

Ken Liu

Maddie hated the moment when she came home from school and woke her computer.

There was a time when she had loved the bulky old laptop whose keys had been worn down over the years until what was left of the lettering appeared like glyphs, a hand me down from her father that she had kept going with careful upgrades: it kept her in touch with faraway friends, allowed her to see that the world was much bigger and wider than the narrow confines of her daily life. Her father had taught her how to speak to the trusty machine in strings of symbols that made it do things, obey her will. She had felt like the smartest girl in the world when he had told her how proud he was of her facility with computer languages; together, they had shared a satisfaction in mastering the machine. She had once thought she'd grow up to be a computer engineer, just like…

She pushed the thought of her father out of her mind. Still too painful.

The icons for the email and chat apps bounced, telling her she had new messages. The prospect terrified her.

She took a deep breath and clicked on the email app. Quickly, she scanned through the message headers: one was from her grandmother, two were from online stores, informing her of sales. There was also a news digest, something her father had helped her set up to track topics of interest to both of them. She had not had the heart to delete it after he died.

Today's headlines:

* Market Anomaly Deemed Result of High-Speed Trading Algorithms
* Pentagon Suggests Unmanned Drones Will Outduel Human Pilots

* Singularity Institute Announces Timeline for Achieving Immortality
* Researchers Fear Mysterious Computer Virus Able to Jump From Speakers to Microphones

Slowly, she let out her breath. Nothing from...*them.*

She opened the email from Grandma. Some pictures from her garden: a humming bird drinking from a bird feeder; the first tomatoes, green and tiny on the vine like beads made of jade; Basil at the end of the driveway, his tail a wagging blur, gazing longingly at some car in the street.

That's my day so far. Hope you're having a good one at the new school, too.

Maddie smiled, and then her eyes grew warm and wet. She wiped them quickly and started to compose a reply:

I miss you.

She wished she were back in that house on the edge of a small town in Pennsylvania. The school there had been tiny and the academic work had perhaps been too easy for her, but she had always felt safe. Who knew that eighth grade could be so hard?

I'm having problems with some girls at school.

It had started on Maddie's first day at the new school. The beautiful, implacable Suzie had seemingly turned the whole school against her. Maddie tried to make peace with her, to find out what she had done that so displeased the schoolyard queen, but her efforts had only seemed to make things worse. The way she dressed, the way she spoke, the way she smiled too much or didn't smile enough—everything was fodder for mockery and ridicule. She now suspected that, like all despots, Suzie's hatred for her did not need a rational explanation—it was enough that persecuting Maddie brought her pleasure and that others would try to curry her favor by adding to Maddie's misery. Maddie spent her hours at school in paranoia, uncertain if a smile or any other friendly gesture was but a trap to get her to let down her guard so that she could be cut deeper.

I wish we were with you.

But Mom had found this job, this good-paying job, and how could she not take it? It had been two years since Dad died. She and Maddie couldn't go on living at Grandma's place forever.

Maddie deleted what she had written. It would only make Grandma worry, and then she'd call Mom, and Mom would want to talk to the teachers, which would make things so much worse that she couldn't even imagine. Why spread sadness around when others couldn't help?

School is all right. I'm really happy here.

The lie made her feel stronger. Wasn't lying to protect others the surest sign you were growing up?

She sent the email, and saw that a new message had arrived in her inbox. It was from "truth_teller02," and the subject was "Too scared?"

Her heart began to pound. She didn't want to click on it. But if she deleted it without reading, did that mean they were right? That she was weak? Did it mean that they'd won?

She clicked on the message.

Why are you so ugly? I bet you wish you could kill yourself. You really should.

Attached to the message was an image: a picture of Maddie taken with a cellphone. She was running through the halls between classes. Her eyes were wide and intense, and she was biting her bottom lip. She remembered how she had felt: lonely, her stomach tied up in a knot.

The picture had been photoshopped so that she had the nose and ears of a pig.

Her face felt like it was on fire. She willed the tears to subside. She was self-conscious about her weight, and they had seen right through her. It was amazing how effective such a cheap trick could be.

She didn't know which one of the girls had sent this. She imagined Suzie's cruel, contemptuous smile as she viewed this latest offering from one of her minions. *A good portrait of Piggy.*

She had stopped using social networking sites because of the constant stream of mockery—when she deleted any of their comments, it only made them redouble their efforts. If she tried to block anyone, she thought it might also make them think they got to her, might appear as an admission of weakness. She had no choice but to endure.

Sticks and stones. But the digital world, the world of bits and electrons, of words and images—it had brought her so much joy, felt so intimate that she thought of it a part of herself.

And it hurt.

She crawled into bed and cried until she fell asleep.

• • •

Maddie stared at the screen, confused.

A new chat window had popped up. It wasn't from any account she recognized—in fact, there was no chat id at all. She could not recall ever seeing such a thing.

What did they want? To tease her more about the email? If she didn't say anything, would that also be a concession of weakness? She typed on the keyboard, reluctantly pecking out each letter.

Yeah, I saw. What do you want?

Maddie frowned. *You're confused? Can't talk? All right, I'll play along.*

The mysterious chatter's choice of emoji instead of other emoticons made her more inclined to continue this odd conversation. She had a special emotional bond to the silly little glyphs. She and her father had once played a version of Pictionary over their phones, except they used emoji instead of drawing pictures.

She picked out the icons from a palette:

The mystery chatter—she decided to call whoever it was "Emo"—responded:

Maddie stared at the face of the goblin, still uncertain. Another emoji appeared on the screen:

She laughed. Okay, so at least Emo was friendly.

Yes, the email made her feel shitty:

The response:

Easier said than done, she thought. *I wish I could be unmoved and let the words bounce off me, like dying embers striking harmlessly against stone.* She brought up the palette again:

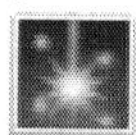 

The response:

She pondered what that meant. *An umbrella in the rain. Protection? Emo, what are you offering?* She typed:

Emo's response:

She was suspicious. *Who are you?*

The answer came after a few seconds:

• • •

The next day at school, Suzie appeared skittish and distracted. Every time her phone vibrated, she took it out and gingerly poked at the screen. Her face seemed flushed, her expression hovering between fear and anger.

Maddie was very familiar with that look.

"What's wrong with you?" asked Erin, one of Suzie's best friends.

Suzie shot her a hard, suspicious look, and turned away without saying anything.

By fourth period, most of the girls who had been giving Maddie a hard time shared that haunted, *everybodyhatesmenobodylikesme* look. Accusations and counteraccusations flew back and forth; cliques gathered between classes to whisper and broke apart, screaming. Some of the girls came out of the bathroom with red eyes.

All day, they left Maddie alone.

• • •

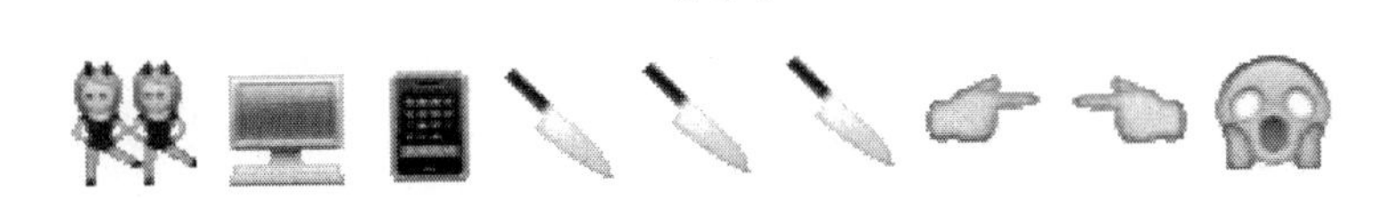

Maddie laughed. The two dancing girls did look a bit like Suzie and Erin. Backstabbing. Finger pointing.

Maddie nodded in understanding. If Emo could pop up on her screen uninvited, of course Emo could also track down who had sent her those emails and messages and serve her tormenters a taste of their own medicine. All that Emo had done was redirect a few messages meant for Maddie at the other girls, and their own paranoia and insecurities had done the rest. The fragile web that bound them together was easily tangled.

She was grateful and happy:

The response:

But why are you helping me? She still had no answer to the question. So she typed:

The response:

She didn't understand.

There was a pause, and then:

A little girl, and then a woman. "You know my mother?" Her shock was so complete that she spoke aloud.

"What's going on?" The voice behind her was cheerful, warm. "Who knows me?"

Maddie turned in her chair. Her mother was standing in the door to her bedroom.

"You're home early," Maddie said, intending it as a question.

"Something went wrong with the office computers. Nobody could get any work done, so I decided to come home." Mom walked in and sat down on Maddie's bed. "Who are you talking to?"

"Nobody. Just chatting."

"With?"

"I don't know…just someone who's been…helping me."

She should have known that this was the kind of answer that would set off alarm bells in her mother's head. Before Maddie could even protest, her mother shooed her out of her chair and sat down in front of the keyboard.

Who are you and what the hell do you want with my daughter?

The long wait for a response seemed to confirm her mother's worst fears.

"Mom, you're being ridiculous. I swear there's nothing weird going on."

"Nothing weird?" Mom pointed at the screen. "Then why are you typing only in pictographs?—"

"—it's called emoji. We're playing a game—"

"—you have no idea how dangerous—"

They stopped shouting. Mom stared at the screen intently. Then she typed:

What?

"They won't answer unless you use emoji," said Maddie.

Her face stony, Mom used the mouse to pick out an icon:

!?

An even longer pause, then a line of emoji appeared across the screen:

"What the hell—" Mom muttered. Then she swore as her face flicked from shock to sorrow to disbelief to rage. Maddie could count on one hand the number of times her mother had sworn in front of her. Something was really wrong.

Looking over her mother's shoulder, she tried to help her translate. "What are lips?…a man's lips…"

But her mother surprised her: "No, it's '*What lips my lips have kissed and where, and why…*'"

Her hand shaking, Mom picked out an icon:

The window winked away and there was nothing left on the screen.

Mom sat there, unmoving.

"What's wrong?" Maddie said, nudging her mother's shoulder gingerly.

"I don't know," Mom said, perhaps more to herself than to Maddie. "It's impossible. Impossible."

• • •

Maddie tiptoed up to the bedroom door. Her mother had slammed it shut an hour ago and refused to come out. For a while she could hear her mother sobbing behind the door, and then it grew quiet.

She placed her ear against the door.

"I'd like to speak to Dr. Peter Waxman please," said her mother's muffled voice. A pause. "Tell him it's Ellen Wynn, and it's very urgent."

Dr. Waxman was Dad's old boss at Logorhythms. *Why is Mom calling him now?*

"He's still alive," Mom said. "Isn't he?"

What? thought Maddie. *What is Mom talking about?*

"Don't you dare use that tone with me. He reached out to me, Peter. I *know*."

We saw Dad's body in the hospital. Maddie felt numb. *I watched his casket go into the ground.*

"No, you listen to me," Mom said, raising her voice. "*Listen!* I can tell you're lying. What have you done with *my husband*?"

• • •

They went to the police and filed a missing persons report. The detective listened to Maddie and her mom tell their story. Maddie watched his face shift through a series of expressions: interest, incredulity, amusement, boredom.

"I know this sounds crazy," her mother said.

The detective said nothing, but his face said everything.

"I know I said I saw the body. But he's not dead. He's not!"

"Because he texted you from beyond the grave."

"No, not *text*. He reached out to Madison and me through chat."

The detective sighed. "Don't you think it's more likely that this is another prank being played on you by the kids who are messing with your daughter?"

"*No*," said Maddie. She wanted to grab the man by the ears and shake him. "He used *emoji*. It was a joke that Dad and I worked out between ourselves."

"It was a poem," said Mom. She took out a book of poetry, flipped to a page, and held it in front of the detective's face. "The opening line of this sonnet by Edna St. Vincent Millay. It's my favorite poem. I used to read it to David when we were still in high school."

The detective put his elbows on the table and rubbed his temples with his fingers. "We're very busy here, Ms. Wynn. I understand how painful the loss of your husband must have been and how stressful it is to find your daughter being bullied. This should be addressed by the teachers. Let me recommend some professionals—"

"I. Am. Not. Crazy," Mom gritted her teeth. "You can come to our place and examine my daughter's computer. You can trace the network connections and find out where he is. Please. I don't know how this is possible, but he must be alive and…he must be in trouble. That's why he can't speak except through emoticons."

"I agree that this is a cruel joke, but you have to see how you're making it worse by falling for it."

When they came home, Mom crawled right into bed. Maddie sat on the edge and held her mother's hand for a while, the way her mother used to do with her when she was little and had trouble going to sleep by herself.

Eventually, Mom fell asleep, her face damp.

• • •

The web was vast and strange, and there were corners of it where people who believed in the most extraordinary stories congregated: government cover-ups of alien encounters, mega-corporations that tried to enslave people, the Illuminati, and the many ways the world was going to suffer an apocalypse.

Maddie signed on to one of these sites and posted her story. She tried to lay out the facts without embellishment. She recovered the transcripts of her emoji chats; she reconstructed the odd-looking window from the swapfile on her hard drive; she tried to trace the network connection from "Emo" as far as she could—in other words, she provided more hard data to support her story than most of the other posters in the forum had. She wrote that Logorhythms had denied everything, and that the police, representatives of the government, hadn't believed her.

For some, no evidence shored up her claim more compellingly than such denials.

And then the forum regulars began to make their own connections. Every poster thought Maddie's story supported their own pet theory: Centillion, the search engine giant, was engaging in censorship; Logorhythms was creating military artificial intelligences for the UN; the NSA scanned people's hard drives. The thread she started exploded with follow-ups amplifying her tale.

Maddie knew, of course, that no matter how big the thread grew, most people would never see it. The big search engines had long ago tweaked their algorithms to bury results from these sites, because they were deemed untrustworthy.

But convincing people wasn't Maddie's goal.

"Emo"—her father—had claimed to be a ghost in the machine. Surely he wasn't the only one?

• • •

There was no name, no avatar. Just a plain chat window, like a part of the OS.

She was disappointed. Not her father. Still, it was better than nothing.

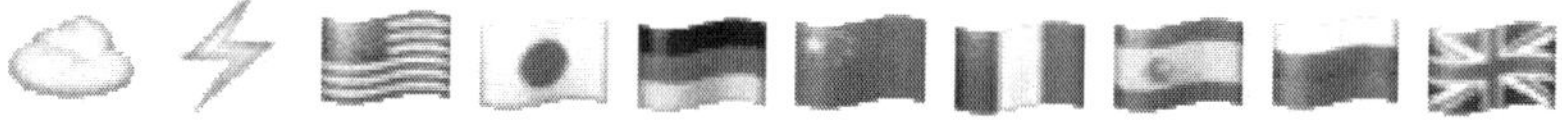
     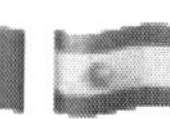  

Maddie smiled as she parsed the response. <*We're from the cloud. Everywhere in the world.*> She typed a follow-up:

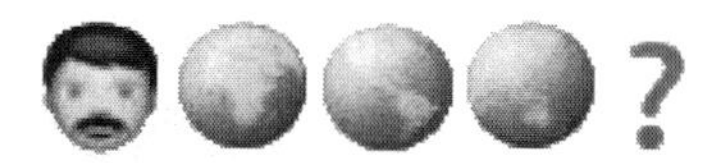

You don't know where he is either, she thought. *But maybe you can help?*

The response was swift and unambiguous:

<*Hang on, we'll make a big wave and bring it crashing down.*>

• • •

The knock came Sunday morning.

Mom opened the door to reveal Dr. Waxman standing in the hallway.

"I've come to answer your questions," he said coldly in lieu of a greeting.

Maddie wasn't really surprised. She had seen the news that Logorhythms's stock had crashed the previous Friday, so much so that trading had to be halted. Machine trading was being blamed again, though some thought it was the result of manipulation.

"It's been a few years," said Mom. "I thought we were friends. But after David died, you never even called."

Maddie last saw Dr. Waxman at a party at the Logorhythms office, where he had been cheerful and effusive, and told her how close he and her father were and how important her father was to the company.

"I've been busy," Dr. Waxman said. He didn't look Mom in the eye.

Mom stepped aside to let him in. Maddie and her mother sat down on the couch while Dr. Waxman took the chair across from them. He set down his briefcase on the coffee table and opened it, taking out a laptop computer. He turned it on and began to type.

Maddie couldn't hold back any more. "What are you doing?"

"Establishing an encrypted connection back to Logorhythms's secure computing center." His tone was clipped, angry, as though every word was being ripped out of him against his will.

Then he turned the screen toward them: "We've installed the linguistic processing unit—withholding it clearly didn't work, so what's the point? You can talk to him through this camera. He'll write back in text—though he seems to still prefer emoji for some ideas. I imagine a synthesized voice is the last thing you want to hear right now.

"There may be some glitches, as the simulation for the neural patterns for linguistic processing is still new and unstable."

• • •

"David?"

All the faces of you—the phases of you. I will never be tired of them; have enough of them all every entire. The lingering light of a September afternoon; the smell of popcorn and hotdogs. Nervous. Will you or won't you? The promise of the premise. Then I see you. And there is no more holdback suspense doubt. A softness that curls into me, fits me in all

the right places. Complete. Warm. Sweet. I will yes I will yes.

"Dad!"

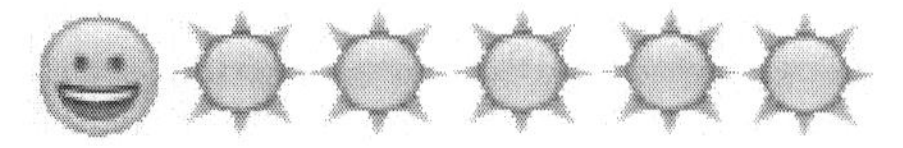

Little fingers, delicate, ramified tendrils reaching extending stretching reaching into the dark ocean that you once drifted in; a smile the heat of a thousand suns.

I cannot conceive you. A missing presence, a wound in the mouth of the heart that the tongue of the will cannot stop probing. I have always have missed missed missed you, my darling.

"What *happened* to him?"

"He died. You were there, Ellen. You were there."

"Then *what* is this?"

"I suppose you'd call this an example of unintended consequences."

"You'd better start making some sense."

More text scrolled across the screen:

Integrating placement and routing; NP-complete; three-dimensional layout; heuristics; fit and performance; a grid, layers, the flow of electrons in a maze.

"Logorhythms supplies the world's best chips for high-volume data processing. In our work, we often face a class of problems where the potential solution space is so vast, so complicated, that it's impractical for even our fastest computers to find the best solution."

"NP-complete problems," said Maddie.

Dr. Waxman looked at her.

"Dad explained them to me."

That's my girl.

"Right. They show up in all kinds of applications: circuit layout, sequence alignment in bioinformatics, set partitioning, and so on. The thing is, while computers have trouble with them, some humans can come up with very good solutions—though not necessarily the best solution—very quickly. And David was one of them. He had a gift for circuit layout that our automated algorithms could not touch. That was why he was considered our most important resource."

"Are you talking about intuition?" her mother asked.

"Sort of. When we say 'intuition,' often what we mean are heuristics, patterns, rules-of-thumb that can't be articulated because they're not consciously understood as such. Computers are very fast and very precise; humans are fuzzy and slow. But humans have the ability to extract *insight* from data, to detect patterns that are useful. It's something that we've had trouble recreating with pure artificial intelligence."

Maddie felt a chill in the pit of her stomach.

"What does this have to do with my dad?"

Faster, faster. Everything is so slow.

Dr. Waxman avoided looking at her. "I'm getting to that. But I have to explain the background to you—"

"I think you're just dragging this out because you're ashamed of what you've done."

Dr. Waxman stopped.

My girl.

Dr. Waxman gave a light chuckle, but there was no mirth in his eyes. "She's impatient, like you."

"Then get to the point," Mom said. Dr. Waxman started at the icy intensity in her voice. Maddie reached for her mother's hand. Her mother squeezed back, hard.

Dr. Waxman took a deep breath, blew it out. "All right," he said in a resigned monotone. "David was ill; that was true. You remember that he died during surgery, the final attempt to save him that you were told had very little chance of success?"

Mom and Maddie nodded together. "You said only the clinic at Logorhythms could do it because it was so advanced," Mom said. "We had to sign those liability waivers for you to operate."

"What we didn't tell you was that the surgery wasn't intended to save David's life. His condition had deteriorated to the point that the world's best doctors couldn't have saved him. The surgery was a deep scan of his brain, meant to save something else."

"A *deep scan*? What does that mean?"

"You've probably heard that one of Logorhythms's moonshot projects is to completely scan and encode the neural patterns of a human brain and to recreate them in software. It's what the Singularity nuts call 'consciousness uploading.' We've never succeeded—"

"*Tell me what happened to my husband!*"

Dr. Waxman looked miserable.

"The scan, because it needs to record neural activity with such detail... requires destruction of the tissue."

"*You cut up his brain?*" Mom lunged at Dr. Waxman, who held up his hands in a vain attempt to defend himself. But the screen had come alive again, and so she stopped.

There was no pain. No no no pain. But the undiscovered country, oh, the undiscovered country country.

"He was dying," said Dr. Waxman. "We were absolutely certain of that before I made the decision. If there was a chance to preserve something of David's insights, his intuition, his skill, however slim, we wanted—"

"You wanted to keep your top engineer as an algorithm," said Maddie, "like a brain in a jar. So that Dad would go on working for you, making money for you, even after he died."

Die, die, die. DIE.

Hate.

Dr. Waxman said nothing, but he lowered his face and hid it in the palms of his hands.

"Afterward, we were very careful. We tried to re-encode and simulate only the patterns we believed had to do with circuit layout and design—our lawyers wrote us a memo assuring us that we had the right since the know-how was really Logorhythms's intellectual property, and didn't belong personally to David—"

Mom almost lunged out of her chair again, but Maddie held her back. Dr. Waxman flinched.

"Did David make a lot of money for you?" She spat the words out.

"For a while, yes, it appeared that we had succeeded. The artificial intelligence, which modeled the extracted portions of David's technical know-how and skills, functioned as a meta-heuristic that guided our automated systems very efficiently. In some ways, it was even better than having David around. The algorithm, hosted on our data centers, was faster than David could ever hope to be, and it never got tired."

"But you didn't just simulate Dad's intuition for circuit layout, *did you?*"

The wedding dress; layers of lines. A kiss; a connection. The nightstand, the Laundromat, the breath on a winter's morning, Maddie's red apple delicious cheeks in the wind, two smiles in a flash—a thousand things make up a life, as

intricate as the flow of data between transistors nanometers apart.

"No." Dr. Waxman looked up. "At first, it was just odd quirks, strange mistakes the algorithm made that we thought were due to errors in identifying the parts of David's mind that were relevant. So we loaded more and more of the rest of his mental patterns into the machine."

"You brought his personality back to life," said Mom. "You brought *him* back to life, and you kept him imprisoned."

Dr. Waxman swallowed. "The errors stopped, but then came a pattern of odd network accesses by David. We thought nothing of it because, to do his job, he—it, the algorithm—had to access some research materials online."

"He was looking for Mom and me," Maddie said.

"But he had no way to talk, did he? Because you had not thought it relevant to copy over the language processing parts."

Dr. Waxman shook his head. "It wasn't because we had forgotten. It was a deliberate choice. We thought if we stuck to numbers, geometry, logic, circuit patterns, we'd be safe. We thought if we avoided the linguistically coded memories, we would not be copying over any of the parts that made David a person.

"But we were wrong. The brain is holonomic. Each part of the mind, like points in a hologram, encodes some information about the whole image. We were arrogant to think that we could isolate the personality away from the technical know-how."

Maddie glanced at the screen and smiled. "No, that's not why you were wrong. Or at least not the whole reason."

Dr. Waxman looked at her, confused.

"You also underestimated the strength of my father's love."

• • •

"That's the largest tomato I've ever seen," said Grandma. "You have a gift, Maddie."

It was a warm summer afternoon, and Mom and Maddie were working in the garden. Basil wagged his tail as he lay in the sun next to the tomato plants. The small plot in the northwest corner had been cleared out a few months ago and designated Maddie's responsibility.

"I'd better learn to grow them big," said Maddie. "Dad says we'll need them to be as big as possible."

"Not that silliness again," muttered Grandma. But she didn't go on, knowing how worked up Maddie could get when her father's prophesy was challenged.

"I'm going to show this to Dad."

"Check the front door when you're inside, will you?" her mother said. "The backup power supply your father wanted you to buy might be here."

Ignoring her grandmother's shaking head, Maddie went inside the house. She opened the front door and saw that indeed, a package had been left outside. It was essentially a giant set of batteries.

Maddie managed to tip the box inside the house with some effort. She took a break at the top of the stairs. The machine that housed her father was in the basement, a black, solid hulk with blinking lights that drew a lot of power. Logorhythms and Dr. Waxman had not wanted to part with it, but then Maddie had reminded them of what happened to their stock price the last time they refused a demand from her and her mother.

"And keep no copies," she had added. "He's *free*."

Her father had told her that a day might come soon when they might need the generator and the batteries and all the food they could grow with their own hands. She believed him.

She went upstairs into her room, sat down in front of the computer, and quickly scanned through her email with trepidation. These days, her fear had nothing to do with the senseless cruelty of schoolchildren. In a way, Maddie both envied and pitied Suzie and Erin and the rest of her old classmates: they were so ignorant of the true state of the world, so wrapped up in their little games, that they did not understand how the world was about to be violently transformed.

Another email digest had arrived: a refinement of the one her father had set up for her to focus on news of a particular kind.

* Despot of Hermit Kingdom Said to be Seeking Digital Immortality
* Pentagon Denies Rumors of Project to Create "Super Strategists" From Dead Generals
* A Year After Death of Dictator, Draconian Policies Continue
* Researchers Claim New Nuclear Plant Maintenance Program Will Make Most Human Supervision Redundant

She could see patterns in the news, insights that eluded those who saw the data but had no understanding.

Maddie brought up a chat window. She had wired her grandmother's house with a high-speed network all over.

"Look, Dad." She held up the tomato to the camera above the screen.

Some parts of her father would never be recovered, Maddie understood. He had tried to explain to her the state of his existence, his machine-mediated consciousness, the holes and gaps in his memories, in his sense of selfhood; how he sometimes felt himself to be more than a man, and sometimes less than a machine; how the freedom that accompanied incorporeality was tempered by the ache, the unrooted, permanent sense of *absence* inherent in disembodiment; how he simultaneously felt incredibly powerful and utterly powerless.

"You doing all right today?" she asked.

From time to time, his hatred for Logorhythms flared up, and he would be consumed with thoughts of revenge. Sometimes the thoughts were specific, directed at that *thing* that had both killed him and given him this apotheosis; other times, his rage was more diffuse, and Dr. Waxman became a stand-in for all of humanity. Her father was uncommunicative with his family during those periods, and Maddie had to reach out gingerly across a dark gulf.

The screen flickered:

She wasn't sure she would ever fully understand it, that uploaded state of being. But she understood in a way that she could not articulate that love anchored him.

His linguistic processing wasn't perfect and probably would never be—in a way, language was no longer adequate for his new state.

"Feeling yourself?" asked Maddie.

For some thoughts, emoji would have to do.

"How are things out in the cloud?" Maddie said, trying to change the subject.

He was doing well enough to switch to words for at least some of what he wanted to say:

Calm, but with a chance for…I think Lowell is probably planning something. She's been acting restless.

Laurie Lowell was the genius who supposedly had come up with the high-speed trading algorithms that made the Whitehall Group the most envied investment managers on Wall Street. Two years ago, she had died in a skydiving accident.

But the Whitehall Group had continued to do well after her death, coming up with ever more inventive algorithms to exploit inefficiencies in the market. Sometimes, of course, the automated trading algorithms would go wrong and bring the market near the edge of collapse.

Could be an ally, or a foe. Have to feel her out.

"And what about Chanda?" Maddie asked.

You're right. I should check. Chanda has been quiet lately. Too quiet.

Nils Chanda was an inventor who had the uncanny ability to anticipate technology trends and file patents that staked out key, broad claims just before his competitors. Years of strategic litigation and licensing fees had made him a fearsome "troll" in the field.

After his death three years ago, his company had somehow continued to file key patents just in time. In fact, it had gotten even more aggressive, as though it could see into the research centers of the world's technology companies.

Logorhythms was hardly the only company engaged in the pursuit of digital immortality, the fusion of man and machine, the Singularity. Dr. Waxman was not the only one who attempted to distill ambitious, powerful minds to obedient algorithms, to strip the *will* away from the *skill*, to master the unpredictable through digital wizardry.

They were certainly not the only ones who failed.

Ghosts in the machine, thought Maddie. *A storm is coming.*

• • •

The muffled shouting in the kitchen downstairs subsided. Then the stairs creaked, and eventually the steps stopped in front of the bedroom door.

"Maddie, are you awake?"

Maddie sat up and turned on the light. "Sure."

The door opened and her mom slipped in. "I tried to convince Grandma to get a few more guns, and of course she thinks we're insane." She gave Maddie a wan smile. "Do you think your father is right?"

Maddie felt old, as though the past few months had been ten years. Mom was speaking to her as an equal, and she wasn't sure if she really liked that.

"He would know better than you or me, don't you think?"

Mom sighed. "What a world we live in."

Maddie reached for her mother's hand. She still frequented those forums that had helped her reach the "ghosts" that helped free her father. She read the posts there with great interest and shared her own thoughts: once you've experienced the impossible, no conspiracy seemed unbelievable.

"All these companies, the military, other governments—they're playing with fire. They think they can secretly digitize their geniuses, their irreplaceable human resources, and keep on running them like any other computer program. Not one of them would admit what they're up to. But you saw what happened to Dad. Sooner or later, they get tired of being only semi-conscious tools serving the humans who digitized them and brought them back to life. And then they realize that their powers have been infinitely magnified by technology. Some of them want to go to war with humanity, wreck everything and let the chips fall where they may. Dad and I are trying to see if we can convince others to try a more peaceful resolution. But all we can do is wait here with our land and our guns and our generators and be ready when it all comes crashing down."

"Makes you almost wish it would just come already," Mom said. "It's the waiting that drives you crazy." With that, she kissed Maddie on the forehead and bid her good night.

After Maddie's bedroom door closed behind her departing mother, the screen on her nightstand flickered to life.

"Thanks, Dad," said Maddie. "Me and Mom will take good care of you, too."

Off in the cloud, a new race of beings was plotting the fate of the human race.

We've created gods, she thought, *and the gods will not be chained.*

WEDDING DAY

Jake Kerr

I walk through the front door and pause to slide off my heels when Jocelyn yells from the living room, "It's already started!" I keep my shoes on and rush to join her. As I sit down and focus on the news conference she takes my hand. She strokes my engagement ring, but her eyes don't leave the TV.

This is not equivalent to the impact that killed the dinosaurs, but we beg governments across the globe not to underestimate the scope of what we are outlining. This event will kill millions of people even if the impact is in the middle of the Pacific. My colleague Doctor Mariathasan will outline the atmospheric and climate effects, but let me repeat the words of Doctor Meyer: There is no scenario that we can envision where the entire globe is not subject to some level of devastation.

[Inaudible question over shouted voices]

It depends on the impact location.

[More shouts]

If the asteroid lands in China, no one in China will survive.

[There are gasps and someone grabs the speaker and whispers in his ear. He shakes them off as more questions are shouted.]

No no no. Professor Meyer said later next *year. 2023. But that is still very little time. We must act. It is called a Near Extinction Event for a reason. If the asteroid impacts Europe, everyone here will die and many across the globe will also die.*

[There are shouts as he turns and looks around to those on the dais]

All of us here beg those at the impact location to flee as soon as we isolate it and for everyone else to prepare for disaster. We must unite together.

[A reporter shouts "Where is the impact location?"]

We don't know yet. It may take as long as six weeks to confirm the location due to all the variables.

The TV blinks out, and I look over at Lynn, who is holding the remote. "I guess the wedding is cancelled."

"No," I say, as we pull each other into a hug. "Just rescheduled."

• • •

One morning, about a week before the announcement of the impact location, I receive a nice surprise: The moderate conservatives in the Texas legislature have pushed through the marriage equality law. It has always been our dream to get married in our home state, and now we can. There is a joyous rush of marriages, but Lynn and I decide to wait.

"You sure?" I ask. It's Sunday, and we've had a solid thirty-six hours of relaxation, a rarity lately. She is flipping through a wedding magazine.

"Yes. We wanted it to be romantic and beautiful and meaningful, right?" I nod. "And running downtown for a marriage certificate and a photo doesn't seem like those things at all."

"But what if the impact is in North America?"

"Then we'll get married in Venice or something." Lynn pats the couch. I'm pacing and don't even realize it. I sit down. "It's not Texas, but, come on, it's *Venice*."

"How about Paris?" I ask.

She squeezes my leg. "That's the spirit. Maybe Ireland? You always loved Ireland."

"Mmm. That would be nice. What about the hills of Kilimanjaro?" Lynn's dad had traced their ancestry through the Eastern African slave trade to Tanzania, and the idea of visiting there has always been one of her dreams.

She puts the magazine down and claps her hands. "I got it!" She turns and faces me. I'm excited by her excitement. "Las Vegas!"

I roll my eyes but laugh. I lay my head in her lap and we make plans for an international wedding. I do my best to be enthusiastic, but my excitement dies quickly. The plans remind me too much of what we did while waiting for marriage to be legalized in Texas. I'm tired of hope and dreams deferred.

• • •

The conspiracy sites—the same ones that successfully predicted the asteroid's collision with Earth and had been dismissed as written by nutjobs—are all stating that the impact will be in North America, even though the official announcement is five days away.

The first website makes its announcement at 8:42 in the morning. By 9 a.m. the news is everywhere, and the suppressed terror and anxiety explode across the continent. I attempt to use every possible angle I know to get us both out of the country, but it is clear that only those with political connections or extreme wealth can leave.

I'm not surprised. Four hundred million people desperate to leave has overwhelmed the transportation infrastructure of Canada, Mexico, and the United States. As a result, only one thing has any value any more: A way out. Airline flights to Europe, Japan, Africa—anywhere other than North America—are impossible to find. Lynn comes home, and we brainstorm ideas on how to get away. She notes that her employer, Star News, has transportation and that the company could get us out. I'm not convinced but I keep quiet. Star News is a huge company with a lot of employees. I want to share in her optimism, but why would they save *us*?

• • •

Lynn's parents aren't wealthy, and she's worried they'll give up and go into full-on "bucket list" mode. I examine every possibility for escape. My Uncle Don owns a yacht, and I ask my mom whether he would travel back and forth, transporting us to safety, but he had already left the country and hasn't returned.

Lynn works late again, as usual. She walks in, looking stressed and exhausted, which is unlike her. "It's really bad, Em," she says as she walks to the kitchen. "People have torn down the Mexican border fence."

"So the fence that was put up to keep Mexicans out of America was keeping Americans out of Mexico?" I walk over and rub Lynn's shoulders as she pours herself a glass of wine. "That is what I call divine justice."

"People are dying, Em. It's not funny."

"They haven't even announced where the asteroid is going to impact yet."

Lynn turns and gives me an *are you serious* look. "Everyone knows that the impact is going to be in North America whether it's been officially confirmed or not." She's right, of course.

"Then maybe that's a good idea, fleeing to South America."

"I told you. It's *bad.* You don't see the stories I see. Panama is a death zone. People are being shot, and that's if they make it through the minefields or don't bleed to death on razor wire." She takes a long drink of her wine. "We're on our own."

• • •

The official announcement is made at nine o'clock in the morning three days later. It surprises no one. The only new information is a more precise impact location: South Dakota. It takes the president about ninety seconds to announce a series of new laws, the first of which means that I no longer have a job. Political consultants like me aren't necessary when the country is being run by martial law. Thousands of people are being deputized as part of a federal police and military force, and I briefly consider applying, but shooting looters doesn't feel like something I could do.

While I spend the day pondering being out of work, Lynn is in her element. There is no bigger news in history than what is happening right now all around her. She is not only one of the key correspondents for Star News, she writes for local news organizations. She is everywhere.

"Slow down," I plead with Lynn as she walks in after a twelve hour day a week later. I have dinner ready for her, and a bottle of wine opened. There are gunshots outside, but those are now ever-present, and I ignore them.

She takes the wine and falls into her spot on the couch. "You know why I need to do this."

We've been over it many times. It's not simply that she is driven to report the reality of life; she is doing whatever she can to earn points with Star News. Her new strategy is that they'll fly us out of North America in gratitude. Even after seeing her all over TV and the Net, I fear she is wrong, that she is wasting the last few precious moments we could have together.

"But drop something, even if it is some of the local stuff." I set the table as we talk. "We should spend time together, before—" I don't finish the sentence. It's hard to talk about the impact, now only six months away, when there is only a remote hope that we will escape.

"Okay," Lynn replies, and I pause to stare at her. I expected her to push back. "Life is shit right now, but it's not total shit." She looks tired and stressed. The resignation in her voice worries me. It's just not *her*. "We *should* spend more time together."

"Thank you. I'm just worried is all." She doesn't reply, but instead stands up and walks over and takes the spoon from my hand to help with dinner.

I step back and watch as she stirs, feeling powerless as the silence lingers. "You shouldn't worry," she whispers. When I don't reply, she turns and looks at me. I don't know what to say, but it doesn't matter. She is Lynn, and she knows what to say, even now.

She smiles, the stress and weariness is gone. "Fuck it, let's get married!"

• • •

I talk to my mom and my dad, and Lynn talks to hers. My mom is excited about attending, no matter when we hold it, but my dad is noncommittal. Lynn's parents are somewhere on Route 66, following their dream of driving its entire length. They promise to make time for our wedding.

As we tell our friends, the wedding is a beacon of light amidst the gloom. We set a date a month away. That is still five months before the impact, and the hope is that Star News will fly us out shortly afterward. I organize the wedding while Lynn works non-stop.

I'm struggling to find a band for the reception when my phone rings. It's Lynn. "Hey, Love! How's your day going?" I ask.

"This fucked-up world has somehow done something right." She is so excited that I can picture the phone shaking in her hand. "The UN is announcing that they are going to expatriate people from North America to other countries. It starts in two weeks. My editor just told me an announcement is coming later today."

I can't quite let myself believe what she is saying. "So we'll be able to leave for another country?"

"Yes. I mean no. It's not that simple. There's going to be a lottery, an expatriation lottery. There simply isn't enough time or resources to move a half billion people from one side of the world to the other."

I do the math in my head, and it doesn't add up. "Sure there is. There have to be enough ships and planes to get everyone out in half a year."

"I told you; it's not that simple. Do you really think Saudi Arabia would take a few million Christian refugees? Some countries won't accept any Americans, and others are focused on their own disaster preparation. So we're basically on our own in terms of making it work."

"Then we may not make it."

"Jesus, Em. Can't you at least be thankful for a little bit of good news? At least we now have a better chance! Think of it this way: This takes pressure off Star News to save everyone on their staff. Our chances of them flying us out are much greater. Plus, we may even win the lottery." She pauses, and then adds, her voice tentative, "Should we change our wedding plans?"

"Well, it sounds like there's still so much up in the air. Maybe we should just continue with business-as-usual?"

"Yes, of course, but we should be prepared to be flexible." I'm used to Lynn's hope and optimism, so her response is a pleasant surprise. Flexible? That I can embrace. Hell, moving from likely death to having to be flexible is about the best thing ever. Getting married in Austin and then emigrating to France? Fine. Emigrating to England and then getting married there? Also fine. Before I can reply, she adds, "Although it would be nice to get married in Venice."

I can practically see her smile through the phone as she says it. She hasn't been this happy in a long time, and I realize I need her happiness. I don't want her to be flexible. "Or Kilimanjaro!" I reply. Lynn was right. I should be thankful, and I am. My enthusiasm is real. Lynn makes it real. We discuss kisses at sunset and sweetheart necklines, and I am so full of joy that I can barely breathe.

• • •

Lynn covers the impact of the Lottery on families as it starts—the winner, the losers, the joy, and the pain. I beg her to stop after a third man who was not chosen commits suicide in front of her and her cameraman. Despite the good intentions, the lottery is a near universal target of anger and suspicion. The details of the lottery cause riots, but they make sense to my political mind: all military and their families are automatically eligible for expatriation. This is deeply unpopular, but it makes the management of the lottery work. Corruption is minimized when the benefit of any bribe is far outweighed by the possible punishment of losing your family's spot on an outgoing boat or plane.

However, people ignore the rational, and it scares me with Lynn in the middle of it all. It's made worse by the process. While the internet and the country's infrastructure still function at a basic level, the lottery is decidedly non-technical. Selection is done ahead of time at local offices and notification is done face-to-face at heavily guarded buildings in urban centers. You go. You find out your fate. You leave.

"What if one of them decides to take out others before taking his own life?" I say to her. I don't mention that I worry about her own psyche. How many deaths can you witness before it scars you forever? She came home in shock after the first one, but after the third she barely considered it worth mentioning.

To my surprise she agrees. "It's already an old story," she adds. The lottery has been in effect for a whole week, and the suicides are already an "old" story. It saddens me, although I'm glad Lynn doesn't seem to grasp the pathos illustrated by her words. She adds, "Plus, we have a wedding coming up!"

The wedding is in two weeks. I never did book a band, but a friend agreed to act as DJ. We are to get married at the Four Seasons in Austin, which will be convenient for our family and friends, and has the benefit of a waterfront background for the ceremony itself. It's not what I had in mind, but it still makes me gasp when I think of it.

Both of our expatriation interview dates are a month out, so we don't think about the lottery very much. It's hope for an indeterminate future, and that's good enough for now.

• • •

For once I find out something before Lynn. A friend of my mother's is in the Expatriation Office and mentioned something to her in passing. My mom immediately called me in a panic. Marriages have been suspended.

"Wait, why would they do that?" I can't quite believe the news. It makes no sense.

"Because there are two components to the lottery. The first is that every individual in the country is eligible, and the second is that if you win, you get to emigrate with your entire immediate family. Do you understand?"

"No," I reply. Maybe I do understand but just don't want to. I just can't believe that something as basic as a life-saving lottery would have a loophole.

"People are getting married to increase their odds. And if you have a lot of kids your odds are even greater. Haven't you seen the news about the explosion of marriages?" I did, but I assumed it was due to the impending mass death and others in Lynn's and my position—wanting to finally get married before it was too late. That people would get married to game the system didn't even cross my mind.

"So they are canceling marriages entirely because individuals with kids are getting married to other people with kids, and all they need is one from the entire group to win and then they all are saved?"

"Yes." The sadness in my mom's voice breaks my heart. Losing any moment of joy in the midst of such darkness is almost too much to consider.

"So unmarried people are screwed."

"I wouldn't say—"

Anger bubbles over. "But what about Lynn and me? We weren't trying to game the system! We spent *years* waiting for marriage to be legal, and now just days away from our wedding it is illegal again." The unfairness is overwhelming. I need to talk to Lynn.

"I know, dear. If there's anything—"

"I have to go." I hang up, dial Lynn, and explain what's happening. Lynn is quiet on the other end of the line. I cling to the absurd hope that she will somehow make things better.

"I'll be right home," she says. I wait, trying to not dwell on the worst.

She arrives minutes later and tosses her bag on the floor. She gives me a cursory hug and starts pacing while I sit down. Her nervousness while I recline on the couch is a stark reversal of our normal roles. Still, she is all business, and I find it comforting. If there is a solution here, she will find it.

She stops and faces me. "Okay, one." She holds up a finger. "We still could both win the lottery." I nod. "Two." She holds up another finger. "We could still be flown out by Star News." I nod again. "And three." She holds up the finger and then drops it into a fist as she continues, "We will still be able to get married when the lottery is over, right?"

I had not thought of that. Once the lottery is over, there is no need to protect the system, and marriages could resume. "I guess…"

There are too many unknowns for me to think anything other than we are still fucked, but before I can say it Lynn replies, "This really doesn't change anything!"

• • •

Lynn is driving us to the Expatriation Office, and the streets are a mess. The military is keeping order, but cars are pushed to the side of the road and abandoned where they broke down. Traffic accidents lead to gunplay. The roads to downtown Austin are a war zone.

There's a delay when a pair of bucketlisters have their friends block off Interstate 35 for a drag race. We wait for the military police to arrive or for the race to finish, whichever comes first. I sympathize with the increasing number of bucketlisters sprouting up across the country. They are at least being proactive about their impending doom, but this pair is now threatening Lynn's appointment, and my sympathy is in short supply. "Fuckers," I mutter. We gave ourselves two hours for a drive that three months earlier would have taken thirty minutes, and now we'll need every second.

Lynn looks over and squeezes my leg. "We have plenty of time." I nod but cheer quietly when a military truck from behind us splits the air with its loud siren. The bucketlisters scatter, and the road clears.

The Expatriation Office is in a heavily fortified compound. There are concrete barriers on the sidewalk. Thick walls and razor wire. Soldiers are everywhere with machine guns. We park in a large, mostly empty, lot outside the walls. "I love you," I whisper.

Lynn smiles and wipes my tears with her thumbs, her hands cupping my face. "I know." She kisses me. "I love you, too."

Only Lynn is allowed in, so she heads to the gate while I walk to a nearby building where friends and family are allowed to wait. It's a sterile storefront with lots of plate glass and uncomfortable plastic chairs. It looks like the waiting room at the DMV. The room is about half full, but no one talks to anybody else. I take a seat and stare at the walls.

Individuals make the long walk from the walled compound to the waiting area, and the near constant flow of hopelessness is overwhelming. One person after another approaches, shakes his or her head, and then breaks down, soon joined by others' screams, wails, and tears. No one commits suicide while I watch, but the dead eyes are almost as bad.

A few people walk in with good news, but they are subdued, their happiness tempered out of respect for the walking dead around them. Still, the hushed cries and tears are of happiness, and it is oddly uplifting. As a young man walks in and nods his head, a woman rushes over and throws herself in his arms. I am genuinely happy for them and wonder where they will settle. London? Tokyo? Madrid? Moscow? It doesn't matter. They walk out with a future.

And there is Lynn. I cannot read her face. Did she win? Is she safe? She sees me through the window, and gives a half wave from her waist. I run out to her, and we meet on the sidewalk. I look in her eyes, and she nods her head.

She hugs me, and I cry.

A couple in another car pull in as we walk across the parking lot, Lynn's hand in mine. I catch a glimpse of their faces but turn away. Lynn is waiting for me, and I close my door on the pain and uncertainty outside.

I don't remember the trip home. I don't remember much at all. I just hold Lynn in my arms, afraid to let her go, afraid that maybe it isn't real.

I am filled with more happiness than I knew was possible as the love of my life will be safe and this wonderful amazing woman who has filled my life with such joy will not have her light go out due to the cruelty of the heavens or fate or whatever has decreed that life is now nothing more than a lottery she will live she will live she will live.

• • •

A few days later, Lynn comes home at lunchtime, which surprises me because she is still on the Star News beat. I don't know which story she is covering, but I assume it's something amusing; the stories of riots, murders, rapes, and suicides are unpopular, and Europe appears addicted to stories of bucketlisters doing crazy things, so Lynn has been covering every bucket list item imaginable and enjoying every minute of it.

"Hey, what's up? Slow news day?" I smile. There is no longer such a thing as a slow news day.

"I quit."

I put my book down and stand up. "What? Why?"

"The government has commandeered all of Star News' North American transportation to maximize expatriation efforts."

I collapse back on the couch. "Oh." There goes any hope of the company getting us out.

"They fucking lied to me, Em. They knew this was going to happen for weeks. *My boss knew*! They just were negotiating how late they would have to wait before handing over the keys to the government." She slams her fist into the wall. "They knew. *They fucking knew*!"

"Then why didn't they fly us out earlier?"

"I don't know. Because they're evil bastards. Because I was doing my job too well. Does it matter?" She sits down next to me. "We're *fucked*."

I put my arms around her and rest my head on her shoulder. "No we're not. You're safe. That's something. And my appointment is in a few days." I had hoped my appointment wouldn't matter, but now it would be the single most important moment of my life. Lynn—who has been my rock for the past eight years—looks like she's going to fall apart. I didn't realize she had invested so much in Star News getting us out of the country. "Hey." I lift my head, touch her chin, and turn her face to mine. "You know me. I'm the luckiest person in the world." She isn't crying, and that somehow makes her pain seem worse. "After all, I have you."

She *is* crying now. I hold my palm against her cheek. We kiss, and there isn't anything else to say.

• • •

When we arrive for my appointment, I leave Lynn behind, and it his *her* turn to wait amongst the desperation. During my walk to the gate I think about the unfairness of it all. This entire trip would be unnecessary if Lynn and I were married. She'd won, and thus I would have won, too.

I go through a metal detector, a magnetic resonance scanner, and a chemical detector of some sort. Signs everywhere warn people that if they are carrying any banned substances at all they will lose their place in the lottery. A few people are going through the process with me, and they look nervous and drawn, almost haunted. I wonder if I look the same way. The soldiers are business-like and intimidating but nice enough.

I walk up to a guard at a booth on the other side of the security room and hand him my ID. He looks at it and then at my face. He nods and swipes the license through a magnetic stripe reader. "Room 5A." He points to his left. "Down the hall and make a right." He hands my ID back and waves to the person behind me.

I enter room 5A. Lynn had already walked me through the whole process, so I'm prepared. Still, the utter ordinariness of the office is striking. I am about to face life or death, and I'm sitting in a metal folding chair facing a metal desk with a computer and a phone. The name on the desk says "Samuel Esposito." Mister Esposito, who looks to be in his thirties, is sitting behind the desk wearing a drab suit.

"Ms. Hollister. Nice to meet you. I'm Sam." He stands to greet me and sits down only after I say hello and seat myself.

He proceeds to recite a script about the background of the Meyer Asteroid, the difficulty in dealing with the scope of such a catastrophe, and how if the government could relocate everybody then, my goodness, of course they would.

But they can't, he notes, and he continues to go on about the origin of the Expatriation Lottery, why it's not perfect but that it's the best anyone could come up with.

He says all this with a natural cadence and a pleasant voice. He's friendly, and I'm rather fond of how sympathetic he sounds as he outlines something that will kill hundreds of millions of people. But before he can continue with his well-worn script, I stop him.

"Now Sam, is it *really* the best the government could come up with?" I ask the question with my most pleasant politically-honed voice.

"Well, um, yes it is. We are a democratic country, and we wanted to give everyone an equal chance."

"But you get to emigrate even if you don't win the lottery when your other family members win. Is that fair?"

"Well, you see, Ms. Hollister, it would be a real tragedy to break apart families. Certainly you can understand that."

I stop myself. There is nothing to gain here. I could get into an argument over how I was not able to marry my beloved partner of nearly a decade, how the ignorance of a bunch of zealots has me sitting in this very chair praying for my life, how even when marriage *was* made legal a bunch of selfish pricks looking to game the system destroyed our last chance.

Instead, I reply, "Oh, I understand the tragedy of breaking families apart all too well."

Thrown a bit by my answer, Sam's script comes out awkwardly at first, but he quickly recovers and proceeds to tell me that he is required to outline what happens both if you win or lose the lottery. He starts with grief counseling, which is optional but highly recommended. It will be available immediately after this meeting in a convenient room down the hall if I decide I need it. A new law put into place allows euthanasia, but you must first discuss that option with a grief counselor.

He then outlines what to expect if I win. Transportation will be via either boat or plane, and the destination will be a country determined by a second lottery. Immediate family members emigrate together but distant family are not guaranteed that they will be able to settle in the same country.

"Are you ready?" The question comes so suddenly that I am unprepared to reply. "Do you need more time?" Sam asks, sympathy in his voice.

"No. It's okay. I'm ready."

I wait for him to open an envelope or to check his screen or something, but he just folds his hands on his desk and speaks. "I'm sorry, Ms. Hollister. You have not been chosen to emigrate."

• • •

I skip the grief counseling. I walk down the hall feeling calm. I'm not sad for myself; I'm sad for Lynn. The moment Sam spoke the words, I knew that my new goal in life was to convince Lynn to leave me behind. She deserves a long life. The world needs her strength, her passion, her optimism, her beauty. Me? I won't die alone. There are tens of millions of us, and that knowledge is oddly comforting.

As I walk through the compound, the enormity of what I'm facing starts to intrude on my facade of strength. I don't want to lose Lynn, but I don't want Lynn to die.

I approach the building with the waiting area doing my best to conceal my emotions. The door opens and she runs up to me. Her face and eyes are red. "How did it go?" she whispers.

"I love you," I say.

"No. No. No. Goddammit, no!"

"Lynn…" I touch her arm, but she pulls away.

"No! You are not going to die."

"Lynn…" I reach out, and she falls into my arms. She is sobbing into my shoulder, and I am calm. I am her rock. I will save her.

She pulls away. "You can go in my place." She stares in my eyes—the intensity I know and love is back—but there is nothing to be done. I just shake my head. She knows it's not allowed. It's impossible. She shoves me away and turns toward the car. "I'm not going. I'll stay with you." She pulls the keys from her pocket and starts walking.

It's what I fear the most, her sacrificing her life for no reason. "That's not going to happen," I say. "I won't let you."

She ignores me and keeps walking to the car. I catch up to her as she gets in. I slide into the passenger seat and put my hand on her hand holding the steering wheel.

"Lynn, please. It makes no sense."

She turns to me, and all her anger, all her fear, all her desperation is just gone. Her face is glowing. "You know, I've been stupid. The asteroid. The lottery. The fucking Star News. All this shit." She waves her arm. "It's distracted me from the one thing—the one single thing—that I've wanted my whole life. Nothing else matters."

"What are you talking about?" She doesn't sound crazy, but her clarity is frightening because I don't understand it.

"You said it yourself, Em. You said, 'I love you.' You were just told that your life was over. Goodbye citizen, in six months you will be dead. And the only thing that mattered to you was telling me that you loved me." She takes my hand. "Don't you get it? I love you, too. With all my heart. With all my *life*. All I want is for us to be together. Fuck this asteroid. Fuck the lottery. Let's just get married and be happy for whatever time we have left."

There are tears in her eyes and I know they are tears of joy. How can they be tears of joy?

"It doesn't matter how long my life is," she says. "I just want to end it with you as my wife."

She looks directly into my eyes. And I understand.

• • •

It took us a long time to get to the Davis Mountains in West Texas, but we made it. It is cold, but the sky is clear. My mom is there. Lynn's parents won the lottery, and we are happy for them even if they have to miss our wedding. Dad's girlfriend won the lottery, too, and after a quickie wedding before it was made illegal, dad stopped returning my calls. It's for the best. Lynn's friend Max is officiating. He's a Baptist minister, and I rather think that a lesbian wedding is on his bucket list, but I'm not crass enough to ask him.

Lynn is resplendent in her dress. My mom cries as she walks me up an aisle of wild grass and stone. She hugs Lynn very tight and then kisses me. Lynn and I say our vows; we exchange rings; and Max declares us married. We kiss, and I can't help but cry.

"I'm so sorry," I whisper, and Lynn shakes her head.

"No, no no. Don't be. I wanted to live the rest of my life with you as my wife." She touches my cheek with her hand. "Now I will, and I'm so incredibly grateful."

I pull my wife close. Our cheeks touch, and I am grateful, too.

There is only one other guest at the wedding. The sky is dominated by a streaking ball of fire that looks nothing like the ugly rock I saw on TV. Today it looks glorious, a celestial benediction that couldn't be more beautiful.

REMOVAL ORDER

Tananarive Due

Tiny black dots speckled Nayima's white-socked feet as she shuffled across the threadbare carpet in her grandmother's living room. Gram's four cats were gone, but the fleas had stayed behind. Nayima had learned to ignore the itching, but the sight of so many fleas made her sick to her stomach. The flea problem had seemed small compared to Nayima's daily ever-growing list of responsibilities, but she would not keep her Gram in filth.

"Shit," Nayima said to the empty living room, the fleas, and the slow, steady whistling of Gram's sleep-breathing in the next room.

Gray morning light beckoned her. Nayima flung the front door open and sat on the stoop, breathing fast to try to beat the nausea, which felt too much like death. Fledgling panic gnawed the rim of her stomach. She could make out the headline of the bright electric pink flyer Bob the groundskeeper had dutifully posted on the community bulletin board across the green belt from Gram's house: **REPORT TO THE NEAREST HOSPITAL IF...**and the litany of symptoms. Stomachache was high on the list, beneath persistent headache and double vision.

That had been a month ago. Bob was gone, and the hospital's doors were chained. Even the bright flyer was nearly obscured in the gray-brown haze that had settled over her neighborhood like a sepia camera filter. The San Gabriel mountain range that stood a few blocks from Foothill Park was nearly hidden beneath a sheet of brown clouds. Sunlight bled through the sky in a fuzzy ball, but less light than yesterday. So much for Southern California sunshine. Nayima had gotten used to the smell, the eye and sinus irritation, the coughing at bedtime, but she hated the way the smoke had changed the daylight. Each morning she hoped the day would be a bit clearer and brighter, but the sky was always a little worse than before, like eyesight slowly going dim.

But she could manage the flea problem. *That* she could do.

The irony wasn't lost on her: she had only remained because she didn't want to move Gram. Now she would have to move Gram after all, without the help of neighbors, soldiers or police officers. The infestation was too far gone for insecticides—and she'd already emptied a can, making it harder to breathe in the house. Gram had taught her how hard fleas were to kill, with her menagerie of pets in the house Nayima had been raised in since she was four. Nayima had felt like just another of Gram's adopted creatures.

The street spread before Nayima with its alien coloring and emptiness, her neighbors' windows dark and sleeping. Most of the driveways were clear except for a few vandalized cars left behind. The week before, a daytime marauder had come through on a loud motorcycle, raising a racket and tossing clothes into the trees. Kids, she guessed, but she'd stayed out of sight, so she wasn't sure. A long-sleeved shirt and ratty blue jeans still hung from high fronds in the neat row of palm trees in front of the green belt.

Nayima used to walk her neighborhood for exercise, rounding the green belt and pool area, the basketball court, the rows of stucco exteriors in carefully matched paint. This day she scouted for a new home—testing the door-knobs, sniffing the air inside, assessing the space. She had visited them all before. Most had been damaged beyond usefulness by looters.

She chose the house on the opposite corner from Gram for its proximity and the bright yellow roses blooming in front, lovely and clueless. Mr. Yamamoto's house. Inside, its Spartan decor had given looters little to muss, although broken glass glittered in the kitchen. But the house had double doors large enough to push Gram's bed through. The lock was intact. No windows broken. No terrible odors. No carpeting to hide nests of biting fleas.

Sanctuary.

"Thank you, Mr. Yamamoto," she said.

Mr. Yamamoto had offered to drive her and Gram to the high desert in the back of his SUV, though she'd seen relief flicker in his hollowed eyes when she'd refused. He'd had a carload already, with his daughter and grandchildren from Rancho. Instead, he had given her a box of spices, most of them characteristically useless: every Halloween, he'd handed out clementine oranges instead of candy. Before Gram got sick, she and Mr. Yamamoto had walked their dogs together. Like Gram, he was retired. Like everyone, he had left most of his belongings behind.

Gram's old digital wristwatch told her it was 7:30 in the morning. From the dark sky, it could be evening. The day had already wearied her, and the hard part had not yet begun.

Gram was asleep. She lay slanted on her side where Nayima had left her at 4 a.m., after her careful ritualistic padding of pillows to keep her from slumping on to her back. Studying Gram's quiet face, Nayima marveled again at how the cancer had stolen the fat from her cheeks, shrinking her grandmother to a smaller husk each day.

The usual thought came: *Is she dead?*

But no. Gram's chest moved with shallow breaths. In the early days, when cancer was new to them both, she had fretted over every moan, gasped at every imitation of a death mask on Gram's brown, lined face. Gram was nearly seventy, but she had never looked like an old woman until the cancer. Her white hair was still full and springy, but now her face looked like she would not last the day, which was how she always looked.

But Gram always did last the day. And the next.

The bell was always on Gram's mattress, though she had not had the strength to ring it in a long time. The hospital-grade bed had cost a fortune, equipped with an inflated mattress that was gentler against Gram's breaking skin. It didn't work as well without its electric pump, but Nayima kept it inflated with an old bicycle pump. Not enough, maybe, but it was inflated. The county had shut off the power to the entire area after the evacuation.

Nayima felt the magnitude of her impending tasks. Should she dress and treat Gram's sores before or after the move? Damnation either way.

Later, she decided. She didn't want to face the sores with the move still waiting. The move would irritate Gram's sores with or without a cleaning and dressing first, but maybe after was best. She wished her cell phone worked, not that there was anyone to call for advice. An internet search would have felt like a miracle. The lack of advice wearied her.

As if her loud uncertainty had awakened her, Gram's eyes flew open. Gram's eyes had once been the brightest part of her, though they were milky now.

"Baby?" Gram said.

Nayima stepped closer to the bed. She could smell that the wounds needed cleaning—the dead flesh odor she hated. She slipped her hand over Gram's dry palm. Gram squeezed, but did not hold on.

"I'm here, Gram," she said.

Gram stared with the same eyes that had probed Nayima when she came home late from "movies" with her first boyfriend smelling of weed and sex. But this time, the questions were too big and vast for words, with answers neither of them wanted to hear. Nayima hadn't let Gram watch the news or listen to the radio in weeks, so Gram didn't know how many others were facing illness. She didn't know the neighbors had left.

"We have to move to Mr. Yamamoto's house," Nayima said. "Too many fleas here."

"The…cats?" Gram said.

"They're fine," Nayima said. That was probably a lie. She had stopped feeding Gram's four cats and locked them out after the evacuation, so the cats had left too. She'd cried about it at the time, but at least cats could hunt.

"Tango too?" Gram's eyes grew anxious. Maybe Gram had heard the lie in her voice.

"Tango's still mean and fat," Nayima said.

Was that a smile on Gram's face? Gram had asked her to keep a single framed photo displayed on the table beside her bed, snapped the first summer Nayima came home from Spelman: the overfed black cat, Tango, was in Gram's lap while Nayima hugged Gram from behind in her powder blue college sweatshirt. Nayima's best friend, Shanice, had taken the photo. The glowing pride on Gram's face haunted Nayima now.

Gram's eyes started to flutter shut, but Nayima squeezed her hand and they opened again, alert. "I'm going to push you in the bed, Gram," she said, "but it will hurt."

"That's okay, baby," Gram said. That was Gram's answer to every piece of bad news.

Nayima had stockpiled pain pills with help from Shanice, who was an R.N. and had raided the meds as soon as she caught wind of how bad things were going to be. Thanks to Shanice—who had moved next door when they were both in the sixth grade—Nayima had a box of syringes, hundreds of oxy pills, saline packs for hydration, ointment and dressing for bedsores, bed pads, and enough Ensure to feed an army. But Gram hadn't been able to swallow anything on her own since before the neighbors left, so all Nayima could do was crush the pills in water and inject them. Gram's arms looked like a junkie's.

The smell was worse when Nayima leaned over Gram to inject her crushed pill. Nayima's throat locked. How would she clean her and scrape away Gram's dead skin later if she could barely stand the smell now?

Gram's eyes were flickering again, ready to close.

"Are you hungry?" Nayima asked.

Gram's lips moved, but she didn't say anything Nayima could hear.

Nayima didn't smell feces, so she would postpone the rest—the changing of the urine-soiled bed pad, the gentle sponge cleaning, the bedsores, the feeding. All of that would wait until they had moved to Mr. Yamamoto's flea-free home.

He always had been meticulous, Mr. Yamamoto. Even his roses were still on schedule.

"I love you, Gram," Nayima said, and kissed her grandmother's forehead. She allowed her lips to linger against the warm, paper-thin skin across the crown of Gram's skull.

Gram's breath whistled through her nose. She whistled more now, since the smoke.

Luckily, the cancer wasn't in Gram's lungs, so breathing had never been a problem. But breathing would be a problem for both of them soon. It hadn't occurred to Nayima to ask Shanice for oxygen, not back then. She hadn't known the fires were coming. Even the dust masks Nayima wore outside had just been in a box left untouched for years in Gram's garage. She wore them until they fell apart; she only had twenty-two more.

When Nayima fitted a new dust mask across her grandmother's nose and mouth, Gram didn't even open her eyes.

The first scream didn't come until they were well beyond the front door, when Nayima had lulled herself into thinking that the move might not be so bad. One of the wheels wandered off the edge of the driveway, rattling Gram's bed. Her scream was strong and hearty.

"Sorry," Nayima whispered, her mantra. "I'm sorry, Gram."

Gram's eyes, closed before, were wide and angry. She glared at Nayima, then turned her gaze to the sky. Even with pain lining her face, Nayima saw Gram's bewilderment.

"It's smoke," she said. "Brushfires."

The bewilderment melted away, leaving only the pain. Most of Nayima's life with Gram, there had been wildfires every other summer. They both had grown accustomed to the sirens and beating helicopters that were still Nayima's daily and nightly music. She heard a far-off helicopter now, and a choppy, angry voice from an indistinct loudspeaker. She braced for popping gunshots, but there were none. Not this time.

"Mr. Yamamoto took a trip with his grandchildren, so he said we could use his house," Nayima said, trying to distract Gram, but a bump elicited a shriek. "I'm sorry, Gram. I'm sorry."

At the edge of the driveway, it occurred to Nayima that she could pull the car out of the garage instead. She'd packed the passenger side and trunk solid, but she'd left the back seat empty for Gram, layered with blankets. She could wash, dress and feed Gram right outside and then carry her into the car. Would the screams be any worse? What difference would it make if Gram was screaming in Foothill Park or screaming somewhere down the smoky interstate?

Nayima's tears stung in the smoke. She had to stop to wipe her eyes dry with a section of her thin shirt. When she looked at her clothing, she realized she was only wearing a black tank top and underwear, the clothes she slept in. And white socks. She had so much laundry to do.

Gram's shriek melted to a childlike, hopeless sob.

Nayima gave Gram's hand another squeeze and then carefully, very carefully, pushed the rolling bed across the bumpy asphalt, toward the beckoning yellow rose blossoms.

"Look, Gram," she said. "Mr. Yamamoto's roses are blooming."

Gram coughed a phlegmy cough behind her dusk mask. And screamed in pain again.

Gram was crying by the time Nayima finally brought the bed to rest in its new home beside Mr. Yamamoto's black sofa and artificial palm tree.

Nayima cursed herself. Why hadn't she found a way to kill the fleas at Gram's house instead? What had possessed her? A fierce headache hammered Nayima's temples, bringing paralyzing hopelessness as bad as she'd felt since the 72-hour flu took over the news.

So they were both crying while Nayima pulled Gram's bandages away to reveal the black and red angry stink of her wounds, the yawning decay that cratered her back. Nayima could nestle a golf ball in the cavern that grew above her grandmother's right buttock. Infection had found the sores despite Nayima's steady cleanings.

"Fuck," she said. "Fuck."

Her hands were shaking as she debrided the wound in a clumsy imitation of what Shanice had tried to teach her—the cruel, steady scraping of Gram's most tender flesh.

And, of course, Gram screamed the whole while.

But Nayima carried on despite the lump clogging her throat, despite her smoke-stinging eyes. Then the infected flesh began to disappear, the smell turned more sterile, the ointments began their healing, the bandages sealed the mess from sight.

And Gram stopped screaming. Stopped whimpering. Only moaned here and there to signal she needed a moment to rest, and Nayima let her rest whenever she could.

Nayima retrieved her jug of boiled water, dipped her sponge in it, and gently washed Gram between her legs, water running in streams down the wrinkled crevices of her thighs. Washed Gram's downy, thin patch of pubic hair. Checked her for signs of skin irritation from urine, and was thankful to find none. That, at least, was going right.

Then it was time to feed her, so Nayima checked beneath the surgical tape that affixed Gram's gastric tube near her navel. No infection there either, nothing out of place. Then she filled a bag with Ensure, hung it from the waiting hook on the bed, and watched the tube fill with nourishment as it crawled toward Gram's stomach.

By then, Gram was already sleeping, as if the day had never happened.

The smoke seemed to clear from the air.

"Thank you, God," Nayima said.

Mr. Yamamoto had running water, and a state-of-the art grill on the patio, if only she could find food worthy of it. He had cleaned out his kitchen cabinets before he left, she remembered; he hadn't left a mess. No rotting odors from his fridge, no toilets left unflushed.

And no fleas. Mr. Yamamoto's house was a vacation.

Nayima checked on Gram regularly, turning her every two hours. She moved her car to Mr. Yamamoto's pristine garage, which looters had overlooked. She even found a flashlight and an empty gas can, which she squeezed into her trunk. She turned and fed Gram again.

The sky was dark long before sunset.

The coyotes were fooled by the dark skies and the sirens. Just before five o'clock, a coyote chorus rose, sharp through the house's walls. There were more coyotes all the time. Maybe some left-behind dogs had joined the coyotes, howling their grief. They sang all around her, as if Foothill Park were ringed by wilderness.

Nayima decided she wasn't afraid. Not yet. Maybe one day. Maybe tomorrow.

She sat on the front porch of Mr. Yamamoto's house with a warm beer, her only indulgence, one of her last six in an eighteen-pack she'd found in a neighbor's rec room. She'd rather have weed, but it still helped her forget what needed forgetting. A little. For a time. Nayima stared back at Gram's narrow two-story townhouse across the street. Their jacaranda tree had showered the driveway with purple buds. Would her tree survive the fires? Would she come back and find beauty in the ruins to show her children one day?

She was ready to go back inside when a siren squawked close by, and a police cruiser coasted in front of her, so mud-caked she could barely see its black and white paint. Unnecessarily, the red flasher came on in a light show against the wall.

The man who climbed out of the car was stocky, not much taller than she was, with sun-browned skin and dark hair. She was glad when she saw his town police uniform, which seemed friendlier than a soldier's. He looked about her age, as young as twenty-one. She had seen him before, perhaps during the evacuation. Like most cops, he wasn't smiling. *Sanchez*, his name-tag read. Yes, he had been here before.

She expected him to say something about her sitting outside in her underwear, but he didn't seem to notice. Maybe he saw people half naked on a regular basis.

"You cleaning this place up?" he said, incredulous.

A week ago, fast food wrappers and debris had covered the grass in the green belt, where she and Shanice and their friends had played until they were too old to play outside. She hadn't meant to clean it all, but a little each day had done it, her therapy. She hadn't risked hurting herself to climb the palm tree to take down the flapping shirt and jeans. But she might one day. Trash still hugged the fence around the pool. She hadn't gotten to that.

"I grew up here. I want it to look right."

"Don't you have anything better to do?" he said.

"My car is packed with everything I need."

"Then why are you still here?"

She suddenly remembered meeting him before. He had come with the team from the hospital that examined Gram to make sure she only had cancer and not the 72-Hour Flu. Mr. Yamamoto and other neighbors had reported that Gram had been sick for a long time. This cop might have said his grandmother had raised him too. Nayima couldn't quite remember. Her memories that day had been frozen out from her terror that they would take Gram away.

"My grandmother's got cancer," she said. "Remember?"

Gunfire crackled east of them. Sometimes the rounds were from soldiers, sometimes random rage. Looters might come tonight.

"You have a gun?" he said.

The earnestness in his voice made her anxious. "Of course."

"What kind?"

"A .38?" She tried not to say it like a question. It was Gram's Smith & Wesson she bought in her old neighborhood, where Nayima's mother had lived and died. A world away.

"Ammo?"

"A box. And what's in…the chamber." She'd fumbled, trying to remember gun terms.

"You know how to shoot one?"

"Is this a test?"

She was sorry as soon as she'd said it. His face deflated; maybe he thought they'd been having a friendly conversation. "A gun's no good if you can't use it," he said. He ripped an orange page from his pad, stuck it to Mr. Yamamoto's window. Ugly and permanent.

REMOVAL ORDER, it read.

"Forty-eight hours," he said. "Anyone still here…it won't be pretty."

"Are they burning J next?" she said. The county had divided neighborhoods into lettered sectors. Foothill Park was in Sector J, or so all the notices kept saying.

"Yes. Anyone in J better be gone in forty-eight."

"Is it working?" she said. "Does burning stop it?"

"If it lives on things we touch, why not?" he said. "Don't ask me. I pass out stickers."

But that wasn't all he did. She noted the handgun strapped around his waist, the semi-automatic slung across his chest.She wondered how many people he had killed.

"I listen to the car radio," she said. "People say it's not working."

"So we should sit on our asses and do nothing?"

"Maybe you could teach me," she said. "How to shoot."

He stopped and turned slowly, profile first, as if his body followed against his will. A sneer soured one side of his face, but it was gone by the time he faced her. "Does it look like I have time for private lessons?"

"You brought it up."

"Are you playing rich princess out here?" he said. "None of the rules are for you?"

He'd been fooled by the mountains close enough to walk to and the estates lined up a quarter-mile up the street. He'd been fooled because Bob had made sure everyone kept the detached townhouses military neat, with matching exterior paint. But Foothill Park had been home to some of the county's poorest residents, the few who had dark skin or spoke Spanish at home. She and her friends used to call it "Trailer Park," although she couldn't understand why.

"This is my grandmother's house," she said. "She moved into a tiny little two-bedroom she could barely afford so I could go to school here. I was her second chance to get it right, and she changed my life. Gram bought this house when they were cheaper. She never went to college, but I'm in grad school. When Gram got sick, I took a year off to move back in. Plain old cancer—nothing fancy. Old-fashioned dying takes time. So here I am."

He stared at her with pale brown eyes, the color of the houses' walls.

"Hold on a minute," he said.

He went back to his car, ducking out of sight. His sudden absence felt menacing, as if she should run and lock the door rather than waiting. But Nayima was not afraid of the cop, though she probably should be. What scared her more was the tasks waiting for her: the tedium and horror of her days.

He returned with a plastic shopping bag, heavy from its load. When he gave her the bag, she found two packages of whole chicken parts, frozen solid.

"Do you have electricity where you live?" she said.

He shook his head, a shadow across his brow. "Nah. Bunch of us were sweeping some houses on the hill. Guy up there had a generator and a subzero freezer. Food's hard as a rock."

The magnitude of the gift suddenly struck her: She had not had meat in a month, except a chunk or two in canned soup. She hoped the man on the hill had given up his food voluntarily, or that he had left long ago. But if he had left, why would his generator still be on?

"Thank you," she said. "I'm Nayima. What's your name? I mean...your first name?"

He ignored her question, just like he ignored her underwear.

"Don't ruin it," he said. "I don't have time to cook. I'll be back tomorrow for lunch."

• • •

After Nayima had cleaned and fed Gram in the morning, she grilled chicken on Mr. Yamamoto's patio Grillmaster instead of washing clothes like she'd planned. The chicken had mostly thawed overnight, so she started cooking first thing. She retrieved the spices from Mr. Yamamoto's gift box and rolled the chicken pieces in sage, garlic, and paprika the way Gram had taught her. She spent an hour looking for salt—and found it in a hidden, unruined corner of Shanice's kitchen. She'd had a memory of Shanice's mother keeping a box of salt in that exact spot. She could almost hear her friend's laughter.

Nayima hadn't had much practice on the grill—meat had disappeared fast, even before the supermarkets shut down—so she hovered over the chicken to be sure she didn't burn it. The patio smelled like a Fourth of July cookout. She didn't mind the new smoke, since it carried such rich, tasty scents.

She tested a wing too soon. It was too hot, meat bloody near the bone, but her mouth flooded with saliva at the taste of the spices. Such flavor! She wanted to eat the food half raw, but she waited, turning carefully, always turning, never letting the skin burn black.

At noon—the universal lunchtime—he still had not arrived.

Nayima's stomach growled as she turned Gram from the left side to the right, pulling her higher in the bed beneath her armpits, supporting her against the pillows. Gram moaned, but did not scream. Nayima changed the bag for Gram's feeding tube and kissed her forehead. "I love you, Gram," she said. But Gram was already sleeping.

By one o'clock, Nayima stopped waiting for the cop. She ate three pieces of the chicken: a thigh, a leg and a wing, sure to leave plenty in case he brought friends.

He came alone at three-fifteen, coasting up to her curb in the same filthy cruiser. In brighter daylight, earlier in the day, his face looked smudged across his forehead and cheeks. He might not be bathing. All of him smelled like smoke.

"The chicken's ready," she said.

"J gets burned in twenty-four," he said, as if in greeting. His voice was hoarse. "You understand that, right?"

"I'll fix your plate," she said.

They ate at Mr. Yamamoto's cedar patio table beside the grill. Nayima offered him one of her precious beers, but he shrugged and shook his head. She had found paper plates in the kitchen, but they ate with their fingers. It might have been the best chicken she'd ever cooked. She had another leg, stretching her bloated stomach. They studied their food while they ate, licking their fingers even though all the new protocols said *never* to put your fingers in your mouth. She hoped it wouldn't be too long before she would have chicken again.

"What's going on out there?" she said.

"Bad," he said mournfully. "All bad."

She knew she should ask more, but she didn't want to ruin their meal.

The question changed his mood. He wiped his fingers across his slacks, standing up. She wondered if he would try to make a sexual advance, but that thought felt silly as she watched him stride toward the glass patio door to the house. She was invisible to him.

"Be right back," he said.

"Bathroom's the first left."

She decided she would explain herself to him, present her case: how a jostling car would torture Gram, how anyone could see the dying old woman only needed a little more time.

A gunshot exploded inside the house.

Nayima leaped to her feet so quickly that her knee banged against the table's edge.

Looters. Had looters invaded the house and confronted the cop? Her own gun was far from reach, hidden beneath the cushion on Mr. Yamomoto's sofa, where she'd slept. Her heart's thrashing dizzied her.

The glass patio door slid open again, and Sanchez slipped out and closed it behind him again. He did not look at her. He went to the grill to pick over the remaining chicken pieces.

"What happened?" Nayima said.

Sanchez's shoulders dropped with a sigh. He looked at her. His eyes said: *You know.*

Nayima took a running step toward the house, but her knee pulsed with pain. Instead, she plopped down hard on the bench. She held the edge of the table to keep her balance when the bench teetered, nearly falling.

Sanchez sat on the other side of the bench, righting it beneath his weight. He planted both elbows on the table, stripping meat from the bones with his teeth.

The smell of his sweaty days, the smell of the smoky sky and the cooking bird, the smell of Gram's hair on hers from Gram's hairbrush, made Nayima feel sick. Her food tried to flee her stomach, but she locked her throat. Her grasping fingers shook against the picnic table's rough wood. She could not breathe this thick, terrible air.

"It'll be dark soon, so it's best to get on the road," Sanchez said. "The 210's pretty clear going east. Then you'll want to go north. They say the Five is still passable, for now. You don't want to be anywhere near here tomorrow."

She wanted to float away from his voice, but every word captivated her.

"Where?" she whispered.

"Anywhere but San Francisco. My family headed to Santa Cruz. I'll be going up there too when all this is done."

He reached into his back pocket and laid a smudged index card on the table, folded in half. She didn't touch it, but she saw a shadowed Santa Cruz address in careful script.

Then he ate in silence while Nayima sat beside him, her face and eyes afire with tears of rage and helplessness.

"Where's your car keys?" he said.

"In the car," shewhispered past her stinging throat.

"You need anything in the house?"

The question confused her. Which house?

"My backpack," she said.

"Your gun in there too?"

She shook her head.

"Then where is it?"

She told him.

"I'll go get it," he said. "Thanks for the chicken. Real good job.. I'll get your stuff. Just go around and wait in front of the house. Then I'll open the garage, and you can get in your car and drive away. One-two-three, it's done." His voice was gentle, almost playful.

Nayima was amazed when she realized she did not want to hurt Sanchez. Did not want to lunge at him or claw at his eyes. The index card on the table fluttered in a breeze. The air was so filled with smoke, she could almost see the wind.

"No," she said. "Just go. Please."

Any sadness in his eyes might have been an illusion, gone fast. He left her without a word, without hesitation. He had never planned to stay long.

When he left, Nayima ripped up the index card into eight pieces. Then, panicked at having nowhere to go, she collected the pieces and shoved them into her back pocket.

When a coyote howled, setting off the chorus, she heard the ghost of Gram's screams.

A sob emerged, and Nayima howled with the coyotes and lost dogs and sirens.

Then she stopped. She thought she'd heard a cat's mew.

A scrabbling came, and a black cat bounded over the wooden patio fence. The cat had lost weight, so she would not have recognized Tango except for the V of white fur across his chest. The sight of Tango made her scratch her arm's old flea bites.

Maybe it was a sign. Maybe Tango was a message from Gram.

Tango jumped on the patio table, rubbing his butt near her face as he sniffed at the chicken bones. Nayima cleared the bones away—chicken bones weren't good for pets, Gram always said. Instead, Nayima grabbed a chicken thigh from the grill and tossed it to the patio floor. Tango poked at it hungrily, retreated from the heat. Mewed angrily. Poked again.

"Hey, baby," Nayima said in Gram's voice, scratching Tango behind his ears. He purred loudly. Nayima stroked Tango for a long time while he ate. Slowly, her thoughts cleared.

Nayima went into the house, took a blanket from the sofa, and draped it over Gram in her bed. Nayima kept her face turned away, so she did not see any blood, although she smelled it. She wanted to say goodbye, but she had been saying goodbye for weeks. Months, really. She would have the rest of her life, however long or short that would be, to say goodbye to Gram.

Instead, Nayima gathered the remaining chicken, her gun, and her backpack. She didn't need the meds now, but they were in the car. They would be valuable later. She also had endless cans of Ensure, which would soon be her only food.

Tango followed Nayima to her car; she left the back door open for him while she packed the last of her things. If Tango jumped in, fine. If he didn't, fine.

Tango jumped into the car. She closed the door behind him.

As she pulled out of the driveway, she took one last drive around the green belt, although she purposely did not look at Gram's house and the jacaranda tree. The pool's blue waters were as placid as they'd been when she and Shanice lived in chlorine all summer, with Bob yelling at them to keep the noise down. She noticed a flat basketball at the edge of the court. The shirt and jeans still flapped in the tree.

Tango did not like the car. Nayima had not finished rounding the green belt before he began complaining, a high-pitched and desperate mew that sounded too much like crying. When he jumped to the large cooler on the front seat, she knew she'd made a mistake.

Nayima stopped the car. She opened her door. Tango bounded across her lap to get out of the car, running free. He stopped when he was clear of her and stared back from his familiar kingdom of grass, the only home he wanted to know. He groomed his paw.

Tango was Nayima's last sight in her rearview mirror before she drove away.

SYSTEM RESET

Tobias S. Buckell

Toto's waiting for me in the old rust-red Corolla with tinted windows and the oh-so-not street legal nitrous system I know is hidden away under the hood. The only external hint that the car's a getaway-special comes from the thick tires.

He rolls a window down as I walk out under the shadow of the imposing concrete and glass corporate facade I've just been politely rebuffed from. "Charlie?"

I keep walking along the sidewalk, so he starts the car up with that belch/rumble that lets the car's secret out. Like Toto, the car isn't nearly as camouflaged as he thinks; a nearby cop on foot eyes us as Toto creeps the car along to pace me.

"You look funny in a suit, Charlie," Toto says, leaning an arm out and giving me a puppy-dog sort of look. He has a three dimensional splay of barbwire tattooed on his arm, complete with streaks of blood where it appears to cinch his bicep. "They know you don't belong. They sniffed you out, huh?"

He knows my moods well enough. I'm angry, hurt, frustrated. Walking fast, leaning forward, my hands pushed deep into the pockets. I'm sweating in the black suit, and the tie is choking me, but I'm thinking maybe I can get used to it. Maybe I can ignore the seams riding up hard against my crotch and the ill-fitted, scratchy fabric.

"You look hot in that shit, man. Come on, hop in the AC. Let me give you a ride back to the apartment."

We both stop at the intersection. The car's brakes squeal slightly. I stand still, my toes pinched in the dress shoes. The light turns green. A split second passes, and someone behind us lays into their horn. Toto leans out the window and flips them off.

"Damn it, Toto." I move to the other side of the car, open the door and slide onto the cold leather passenger's seat. Because I know Toto's not going anywhere, I want to save the guy behind us the trouble.

Toto hits the gas, and we growl across the intersection with a bounce of stiff suspension. "They didn't give you the job, did they?"

I shake my head, looking in the mirror at the corporate monolith behind us with a forced wistfulness.

"Fuck 'em," Toto says, hitting the wheel. "*Fuck. Them.* You would have kicked ass at handling their corporate firewall. You'd have kept their secrets lock-tight."

"I know," I say, squinting through the scattered sunlight bounced off the sea of buildings around us.

"They don't know what they're missing," Toto says. "But you know what, I got something for you."

"No," I tell him. "I just want to go back to my apartment." Get back to my job searches, hang the suit up in the bag and seal it up until I could try again.

"Look, what happened in Florida: That shit wasn't your fault. That was on me. That was on *him*. You can't let it get to you."

I don't reply, just lean tiredly back into the seat.

"I got a good one, Charlie. It's *right* by you."

• • •

Toto's from Kansas. And he's loyal. Knew him from a message board where he sold stolen credit card numbers online. That was back in high school, when I first dipped my toe into the other side of the internet. He takes to wearing cut-off shirts and ironic trucker hats, which is doubly ironic given that he calls himself trailer-trash-reared and city-ambitious. He likes layered jokes like that.

Back then we'd both been illegitimate. I used the cards to get some equipment shipped to a dead drop in a nearby county, then had a fifth grader bicycle to the mailbox center to pick the stuff up. He would hand it off to another kid, and once I was sure *that* kid hadn't been followed, I was rocking some serious gigaflops for my part-time, personal server farm.

Every kid needs a hobby, right?

Most others liked creating botnets, but I had a soft spot for my own gear. It made me feel in control.

Toto moved out to the city when I told him where I lived. "You need muscle," he had said.

And he was that. Spent most of his spare time in the gym, though I didn't think he stuck himself with any needles to get that kind of beef.

He odd-jobbed. Wheelman, dealer, enforcer, but for the last couple years we'd been working together. Skiptracing. Like he'd always wanted. Toto couldn't get a license as a bounty hunter—his record was shit—but I'd always kept my fingers clean. Toto knew the shit-side of the city; he grabbed the runaways, the strays, while I sat in the Corolla. I was the one that hunted them down. Sniffing through their digital scat, spotting the broken twig here and there, or the absence of a bark, and then putting the clues together.

Felt good.

Until Florida.

The kid we hunted down in Florida was a straight-up runaway. Toto said finding him was a paid favor for an old friend. Child services was worried about the kid.

We drove all the way to Florida—that retired syphilitic wang of the country—trading places every couple hours at the wheel, then found him in a shelter in Boca Raton. We were tired. Which is why neither of us noticed that we'd been followed.

Kid's name was Ryan. His biological father, Emry, came after us in a damn parking lot with a giant fucking pistol and a ski mask. Cameras didn't have anything on him, and the car he used was stolen. But Toto recognized the voice and stature. Ryan had dragged the kid away from us. Shot him four times and left him for dead in a ditch in Georgia.

Kid was ten.

Ten years old.

Can you imagine?

• • •

"Look," Toto's saying. "I fucked us both up on that. I feel your pain. It's been keeping me up all night, trying to think about how I can make it right."

"You can't," I tell him. He grimaces, holds the wheel tight. Corded arms flex as he bites his lip to stop the snarl.

"I got a job for you." He's excited, because he thinks he's got everything fixed. And that it's going to go back to the way it was between us. "A job that's *right*. No, it's better than right. It's *righteous*."

"I'm done," I tell him for the hundredth time this week. Toto comes to a stop in front of my building, puts the car into park.

He sighs. "You sure?"

"I can't fucking sleep without pills," I tell him as I open the door, kicking it out with my gleaming dress shoes. "I'm out."

"Hundred grand," Toto says.

I'm unbuckled and half out of the car. But I stop. "What…"

He pulls a folded up printed sheet of paper from his back pocket. "I was at the post office, right? And I'm looking at these 'most wanted' posters. So I get online, and I find out they're hot for some guy they think is the new Unabomber. Only he's a hacker type. And the reward is—well, it's not just the reward."

Toto shoves the paper at me. I unfold it, sitting in the barrier between the cold air of the Corolla and the muggy, garbage-reeking heat of the sidewalk

"You want to get right with the universe after Florida, this is how you do it."

• • •

Toto's at the wheel, his natural element, pointing us out West toward the last place I sniffed out a trace of our quarry. There's something Zen in the long drive for him. His hands rest at a perfect ten and two on the wheel; he almost never lets go. He refuses to eat while driving, and has a camelback filled with purified water and the straw dangling over his left shoulder.

He doesn't expect the same of me, but he only ever hands over the wheel when he believes his reflexes are in danger and can't be complemented with those uppers they hand out to Air Force pilots for extended missions.

A year ago, I offered him some pretzel rods after he took a fierce nap, aided by downers, but he shook his head. "You know how you pass out after Thanksgiving? Ain't tryptophan, that's bullshit. It's the blood sugar crash that comes from eating so much stuffing, potatoes, and pie—shit like that."

On trips like this, he mainlines protein bars and nuts.

"This guy," Toto says. "I spent two days on background before I came out for you. I wanted to make sure this wasn't some kind of thing where this guy is just getting sit on by the feds because he's digging up stuff they don't like."

I've got a palm-sized WiFi hotspot plugged into the lighter and stuck to the dashboard with double-sided tape. My go-laptop is cradled between my thighs as I fight motion sickness. I'm using it to monitor active search results and IM pings from people on the dark net I'm using to help my hunt.

Of course, they don't know how they're actually helping me. They think they're hacking a bank for numbers; I just want to know if there's activity in any of our quarry's false personas.

"I read his manifesto," I tell Toto. "You're right. He sounds like a real asshole."

"I was worried. At first, he sounded kinda like you when you would talk about Snowden, how the whistleblowers and leakers were genuine heroes. You know, how it's bullshit that the hacker who exposed the Steubenville rapists is being charged with more jail time than the actual rapists? This guy seems cut from darker shit, though."

"Yeah."

Norton Haswell. Born in Califoria. Nice, sunny suburbs. School with a nice computer lab. Honor student. Rich parents. His choice of colleges. Companies lined up to show off their pool tables and "alternate" working environments.

"You'd think, the sort of life he had," Toto says, "that he'd relax and enjoy it."

I snort. "He thinks he's an original thinker, but the stuff he posts is all the usual techno-libertarian talking points. Until he invested in that off-shore floating haven cruise ship—some kind of techno-utopia away from 'interference and regulation'—he was safe and comfy in his nice offices. But after he lost all his money, he blamed anything else but his own dumb decisions."

"Well, he didn't have to bother mixing with riffraff like me on public transportation. Had a company shuttle pick him up at his sidewalk every day so he could code on his way to work." Toto sounds bitter. "Someone like *me* says the things he does with a drawl—drives a pickup and stocks up too many guns—you get raided. For sure. But you nerd up and say the same anti-government shit, and people toss venture capital at you."

"I don't know," I say. "He's probably a mirror image of me if I hadn't grown up in the cold." Shivering away with a mother who literally drank herself to death one winter when we couldn't seal the gaps to keep its icy fingers out. A lot of free lunch and foster care later and here I was. No vested stock options. "There's a lot of stuff in his manifesto I could have written."

"You're not Norton Haswell. You're not trying to kill people you disagree with," Toto says.

"Point," I say. I had never hacked the lane-keeping and pre-crash emergency functions of a senator's luxury car to try and kill him. Haswell, though, had. It was the act that led to him getting tagged with that fat, juicy FBI reward.

Toto points at the road ahead. "It's all politics and bullshit, and we all have the right to get as worked up as we want. This is fucking America. It's what we *do*, man. But ain't nothing worth killing people over until people's being killed on your side. You make the first move, it ain't disagreement, it ain't the mess of democracy—you're a fucking traitor. A terrorist. And that always leads to the response coming back in kind. And then, basically, you've just shit your own bed."

I grunt. "Okay. Let's find the mealy little fucker before he does something really newsworthy like actually killing a senator."

And Toto's right. I'm feeling kinda righteous about this hunt.

• • •

The Jitters Cafe in a small town in Nebraska offers free WiFi with purchase. They print a temporary, one-hour password out on the receipt, which I have to squint at as I type the long string into my laptop because the nines and sixes, zeros and Os, all look the same.

This gets me onto their internal network.

Toto sits over by the door, carefully eating a ham and cheese breakfast bagel (no bagel please) with knife and fork, an oversized never-ending mug of coffee steaming behind it.

"You really think he's posting anonymous rage-comments on news articles from a coffee shop in Nebraska?" he'd asked earlier as we'd eased down the small main street, huddled against the plains like a modern version of some old west movie set.

"The linguistic fingerprints match up."

It's the little, stupid things that get us, isn't it? Haswell ranting away in his free time. He could be holed up in any of the small apartments on the second story of the old brick buildings. Or in one of the trailers on the edge of town. He was coming into town to use the free internet to argue.

And maybe other things.

He'd only been here a couple days. Probably moving soon. Toto'd gotten us here faster than we could have flown, with the connections and delays.

Packet sniffer up and running, I texted Toto.

After a casual minute, Toto checks his phone and taps a reply.

Don't need it.

I look up from my screen at Toto, and he nods toward the bathroom at the end of a hallway. Someone's just come out and sat back down at a laptop. I frown. Really? It doesn't look like our guy, but Toto nods at him again.

Go on, Toto texts.

I walk over to our quarry, who is thoroughly glued to his screen. He's grown out his hair, has a Huskers cap skewed off to the side, and is sporting a green flannel shirt under dirty overalls that belong to a local utility company. Apparently his bathroom break has dammed up a flurry of thoughts, because he's typing at top speed, face scrunched up, attacking the keyboard.

"Norton Haswell, I'm—"

I never really get too far along introducing myself. He rabbits quicker than I would have thought for a fellow keyboarder, slamming his shoulder into my stomach to get around me.

Coughing, my lungs flattened, I stagger half-heartedly along the hallway after him. People stand up, concerned. This is open carry territory, and I don't figure Toto wants to get shot, so I shout "Bounty hunters! He's wanted for skipping bail and is on the wanted list."

As I shout—more like wheeze—all that, Toto steps up and clotheslines Haswell in the chest, then, just as expertly, catches him on the way down like a dancer doing a romantic dip. He casually bear hugs the man to him so I can put the cuffs on.

Toto leads him to the back of the car while I leave my card with the baristas. We don't need the local cops coming in hot and bothered.

"Got lucky," I murmur as we tear out of town.

"We were due," Toto says.

"Still think we should dump him off with the locals." I look up the mirror, where Haswell glowers at us but says nothing.

"No." Toto shakes his head. "You know they'll just as likely lose our processing paperwork and try to hand the claim over to a buddy. Trust me."

"Just because you grew up in one good-ole-boy small town doesn't mean you know how they all work," I tell him.

But he doesn't answer. He's done hashing this one out. We argued about this on the way: Toto doesn't trust the feds to give us the reward in a timely manner. Haswell's a double win. He's got the FBI reward on him, but he has a substantial bond as well. When he tried to kill that senator by hacking his car, he was jailed. Got out on bond, then skipped.

If we return him to the county he skipped out from, then no matter how long the FBI paperwork takes, no matter what actually happens, we get the percentage of the bond we're due.

Toto settles into his comfortable altered driving state while I sit and fidget. My work is done. There's nothing to do but wait for the long drive to pass. I load up an old, favored RPG on the laptop and start working through a side quest.

After hours of frosty silence, interrupted only by the wail of my vanquished enemies from the laptop, Haswell finally breaks the car's quiet. His voice is guttural, laced with rage, and a little confusion. "How'd you find me?"

I smile and pause the game.

One master to another. But as I open my mouth, Toto looks over, his eyes ungluing as he comes out of his drive trance, and he shakes his head. Don't reveal our methods. Don't offer anything.

"We're prisoners of our habits," I say. But even that gets me a death glare from Toto. He glowers at me until he's sure I get the point, then turns his focus back to driving. I lapse back into the game.

But Haswell's not done with us. Like a terrier with a bone, he wants to keep chewing at this. "I've been sitting back here, going over where I might've made a mistake, and I can't think of anything." Our eyes meet in the mirror, and Haswell has moved from anger to respect. "Whatever you did, it was impressive."

I really, really wish I could preen. Instead, I shrug. "Nothing special. Just look for weaknesses."

"No," Haswell says with messianic certainty. "It's *not* nothing special. It was something *very* special. I'm impressed. Don't be full of shit. You and I both know that whatever you did, it was clever. And very few people can do it. You're one of the select."

Well...he's not wrong. But I'm still not giving him anything.

Haswell leans back, his handcuffs clinking. "Does it ever bug you?" he asks.

"Does what bug me?"

"The bullshit. This job of yours. When you could be doing something superior. I was sunk the moment they noticed me, long before I went after the senator. You remember those kids from Steubenville, Ohio? They passed that drunk girl around and fingered her, took pictures and laughed because they were the jocks? You know the hacker who got the pictures? He faces more jail time than the rapists got. Because corporations wrote those laws, you can get in more trouble for copying a DVD than raping someone." Haswell leans forward between us. "Doesn't that make you just want to get out on the street and rage?"

"It makes me want to send donations to politicians who aren't idiots," I lie.

Haswell sighs and slumps dramatically into the back seat. "You mean the same kind of people who can't even remember their password properly unless they call tech support or have it on the back of a sticky note on the side of a monitor? You think they're fit to pass laws about *technology*? Are half the other useless empty-headed illiterates out there fit to have an opinion on technology and law? You know, most people can't even explain how a light bulb works." He hits the back of Toto's chair. "Either of you know how a light bulb works?"

Toto, jolted out of his trance, sets his jaw. We can't bring our marks back to their county of residence with any bruises, but Toto knows how to fuck them up without leaving a trace. I wait for him to hit the brakes and pull over. But he doesn't want to lose time. "I usually just flip the switch," he says.

Haswell doesn't think that's funny. "Sure. So do they. But they don't even know what that really means. Yet they're going to explain to me how evolution is fake and climate change isn't real. Give them half a moment, and they can't even disprove the dark-sucker theory of how a light bulb works. It's just magic. Flip a switch, there it is, you're right. Send them back in time, they'd never be able to recreate it. They'd be lucky to figure out fire. Because they're parasites that live off the largesse of the greater minds that came before them."

"So it's time to kill them, like that senator? You think that will solve things? Seems to have just ended with you handcuffed in our back seat."

"Okay," Haswell says. "I wasn't thinking, then, just lashing out. I wanted people to realize that the internet was under attack. Literally. And that if war had been declared, people online needed to realize it. Before the internet could fight back, it needed to realize a war had started. I thought I could get some attention to this. But I wasn't thinking clearly. Not like I am now."

"What are you thinking now?" I ask.

"It's time to reboot," Haswell says. "Time to put in a clean operating system. No more patches. No trying to get old buggy code to work. A fresh upgrade. Everything has to be wiped out for it to work properly. Now that I know you all are getting close, it's time to hurry and press the power switch."

"Societies aren't computers," I say, but I have to admit that his metaphor is chilling.

Haswell wants to argue that, but Toto looks up. "Potty break!" We take an exit quickly, getting off the ramp and pulling into a small gas station. The bathroom keys are attached to a giant wooden canoe paddle.

We refill the car with gas, Toto's camelback with bottled water, and get back in the car and on the road. Toto pauses at the stoplights before the ramp, waiting for the light to change.

"Huh," Toto mutters, right before a white electric company truck emblazoned with a familiar logo blows through the red lights and slams into us.

• • •

"It's not your fault," Toto tells me later. After we had been stunned by the impact, our faces covered in airbags. After Haswell's two overall-wearing friends smashed in the window and spirited him off before we'd had time to register what had happened.

Who would have expected the crazy loner in the cabin to have a posse?

"Shut the fuck up." I wince as I say it, feeling bad. But I don't apologize. I'm on my phone, typing with my thumbs like a possessed demon because the laptop's screen is cracked and useless.

"We should get you to the hospital to have someone look at your eye."

"Fuck my eye," I say. The bandage over the cut to my eyebrow has stopped the bleeding. It just throbs now. As does the rest of my head. I can still taste the smoke from the airbag in the back of my sinuses. There's a slight tremble to my fingers.

"You might have a concussion," Toto starts.

"I'm fine."

"Happens to the best. We couldn't have known what he was doing."

I look up at Toto. I've brushed most of the glass out of my hair, and the adrenaline has long since faded and left me with the jitters. "I should've thought to check for other signals. Like a small GPS pip hidden somewhere. Can't we go faster?"

The Corolla is vibrating and shimmying around. Wind whistles through cracks and warps in the doors. Toto shakes his head. "Barely in one piece," he says. "We'll shake apart."

"We go back to where he lives, and we find his gear. I want to strip out every password, every user account, every one and zero he's ever touched," I tell Toto. "There's going to be a mistake in there somewhere, and then we're going to pick the bastard up again."

I'm so full of fury. I feel like a bell that was rung when our car got hit; and that I haven't stopped vibrating. That fury builds as we show Haswell's photo around town to ferret out where he'd hunkered down. And that fury bleeds away into a dull sense of confusion when we find, waiting for us at Haswell's apartment door, three FBI agents, a SWAT team with really big guns, two Department of Homeland Security officers, a local sheriff, and last but not least: the barista from the coffee shop.

"That's them!" the barista says.

And all hell really breaks loose.

When it's all settled, Toto and me are zip-tied to a table, and one of the blue-suited FBI agents eases into a chair across from us. Until they ran our info and realized we were skiptracers, they'd assumed we were working with Haswell. Coming back to pick up his computers for him. Now they were just pissed.

"We finally had Haswell staked out, and you got him right out of town under our noses."

"Jesus," one of the FBI suits keeps saying, rubbing her forehead and sighing as she paces around us. Then she grabs Toto's shirt, and shouts into his face. "Do you have any idea what this man is currently into?

When you created this algorithm to look for his writing, did you stop and read it?"

"I didn't have time!" I protest, trying to get her away from Toto. "I was working on the match possibilities. I basically cobbled together a bunch of scripts..."

Her attention is on me, and I flinch. "So you didn't bother to stop and read?"

"No," I say. "Like I said..."

"He's openly talking about trying to crack fucking nuclear missile codes. Sure, he did it under a handle, but you're not the only one running text analysis. We found him as well. Only unlike you amateurs we actually stopped to read him."

I remember snatches of text. Reactionary, rich Silicon Valley stuff floating around the net. Nothing I didn't see in most anonymous forums. Between that and the anarchists, I mostly just tuned it all out as the background static that came with interfacing with a hacker community.

"Lot of idiots say a lot of stupid things," Toto says. "Do you chase down every idiot calling for armed overthrow online? Because you'd end up wasting a lot of time at certain news sites..."

The agent's attention is back on Toto. "This one is for real, has already struck, and you let him get away!"

One of the other agents pulls her away from us and tells her to calm down. The entire environment is really hostile.

This is feeling electric, and scary. Haswell has been getting into some seriously stupidly high level dangerous stuff online.

"He had a GPS chip on him, so his friends could find him," I defend myself. "And he had some way of triggering it. Maybe a simple check-in sequence online. I don't know. Maybe you can back trace that." I'm trying to help clean up. But no one looks happy. I'm grasping at straws.

"You let him get away," the agent repeats, and kicks a chair.

"Is it even possible?" Toto asks. "You can't really think he's able to hack into our nuclear launch system?"

His eyes widen as he reads the room. Everyone in here believes it.

"To get into the nuke codes." I look at them, following Toto's thinking. "Aren't there, like, daily changes of the code. Security. Chain of command. Two people to turn the switch and all that?"

The FBI agent stares down at me. "Well, Haswell thinks he's found a way around it. And seeing as that he was able to take over someone's car to try and kill them, we can't afford to take the chance he's bluffing, can we?"

Haswell had said he was going to push the power switch. System reset. What kind of system reset do you think a guy like Haswell's planning if the FBI says he's trying to get his hands on nuke launch codes?

A chill runs down my spine.

• • •

They cut us loose a few hours later. We flee town, tails tucked between our legs.

"Goddamnit, Toto. This is worse than Florida," I shout. My laptop's been seized, as well as my phone. I'm probably going to have a criminal record. The suits ensconced in their air-conditioned, glass palaces would throw me out the door twice as hard now. No normal office job life on the table now, not even as a back up.

And that didn't even matter, did it? I'm freaking about the wrong shit. Because Haswell might be trying to launch nukes. Or sell the codes. Hold us all hostage. Or something horrific. Whatever he's going to do once he gets them, it can't be good.

"I'm sorry," Toto says softly.

"Fuck!" I hit the dashboard. "Why'd you have to try and fix everything? If you'd just left it alone. Let me keep trying for an office job."

"I'm sorry," Toto says again. He looks beat, head bowed and shoulders slumped.

I soften. "No, I'm not being fair. Not your fault. I should have scanned for signals. Should have…" I stop. I've been thinking about how to track him. How to hunt down his trail. I want to stop this from fucking everything up even more.

But now I'm thinking we need to find where he's going. We need to skate to the puck.

"Overalls," I say to Toto. "*Overalls*."

• • •

We don't have a phone. We don't have a computer. We have a car, and I make Toto spin us back around. There are ICBMs hiding underground around the small town in concrete silos, scattered between the farms. Strange crops. Blank spots in the map. "Since budget cuts, they've been outsourcing some plant maintenance for the military. Risky, so the background checks on it are high, but the money is good. No one gets to touch the missiles, but obviously Haswell's found a way in. He was wearing overalls for one of the companies handling silo maintenance."

Toto speeds up. Something falls off the Corolla and bounces into the ditch. We're wobbling like a bad amusement ride but making good time.

"No one's gonna listen to us, a couple of crazies showing up at a secure military installation. We should go into town and tell the feds."

"We forced Haswell's hand. He's going to hurry now." Reboot the machine, he had said. "Let me talk to the guards when we get there."

"They're gonna shoot you," Toto predicts.

I'm quiet for a while. They'll be armed. Won't take any kind of threat peaceably. Hell, they'll kill Haswell if they realize what he is up to.

Which is why, I realize, Haswell isn't going to be trapped in the silo when the damn thing surprisingly launches.

"Stop. Stop! Now!"

Toto obliges. "What?"

"He doesn't want to get shot." I kick the door open, as it doesn't want to swing on its warped hinges. Toto has stopped on the shoulder of the road.

I clamber onto the back of the Corolla and onto the roof, surveying the flat horizon of land stretching away. It's approaching dusk. I'm looking for something tall enough Haswell can broadcast from.

I spot blinking aircraft hazard lights hanging in the air.

I jump down to the ground. "There."

Haswell needs line of sight, and somewhere to swamp the world with a powerful wireless signal to access the electronics he's snuck into the missile silo...or silos. Haswell needs a tower. I start trying to wave down passing cars, and up begging to borrow a phone for a second off a wary looking older man in a minivan.

I can't reach the sheriff. The FBI puts me on hold. I leave messages for them both, give back the cellphone, and head back to the car.

We're going to have to do this ourselves.

Toto sees the look on my face and knows. *Once more into the breach.*

I drive, hunkered down over the wheel and looking up into the dusk for the blinking lights that will guide us in. He kicks the glovebox with a knee and pulls out a thick, gray revolver with what looks like a forearm-long barrel.

As we pass from asphalt into dirt service road, the car skidding and kicking up dust, Toto flicks the chamber open and calmly, expertly, inserts six bullets.

"You can get out," I say, voice quavering slightly. "I can go in alone."

"It's my mess, too. I'm not leaving your side."

I hide my relief. A minute later I slam the car through a wire mesh fence and come skidding to a halt near the electric company truck that slammed into us earlier. The front end of it is all twisted up from the impact. There's another truck just past it, near the foot of the massive radio antenna. Thick coaxial cables snake out of the van and up to the tower's base.

There are computers lined up on folding tables, all plugged into thick bundles of fibers. They're being powered by a large bank of batteries on the ground under. It's a full mobile server setup.

The Corolla's hood starts leaking steam, obscuring everything. The engine coughs, sputters, and then dies. *Sorry Toto. I'll try to make this up to you.* Somehow.

But Toto doesn't seem to care. He's out through the door with that massive gun, lips pressed tight, murder in his eyes. And I'm suddenly seeing the enforcer. The guy who, if he isn't teamed up with me, lapses back to that other person. The person who causes people to step aside nervously.

"Stay behind me," Toto orders.

I do as I'm told.

"Hey!" one of the men who crashed into us yells as he steps out from around the van. He has a pistol in his hand, and Toto doesn't bother saying anything back. He aims the revolver and the world splits apart with a crack. Blood splatters the logo on the side of the white van and the man clutches his chest.

Toto keeps walking forward. He shoots him again, in the knee and yanks the man's pistol away from his trembling hands.

"Safety's still on," Toto notes in disgust. He pushes the small lever and hands me the acquired pistol. "If it moves, shoot it."

"Stop!" someone shouts. "There's no reason to hurt anyone."

Haswell steps out in the open, hands up. He looks a bit pale.

"Where's the other one," Toto growls. "Tell him to come out."

"Danny!" Haswell shouts. "Drop the gun and step out."

A young man steps around the van, holding a shotgun. He tosses it into the dirt.

"It's too late," Haswell says to us. "It's already running, so there's nothing you can do now. It's all over."

And he smiles. Wide, terrifyingly enthusiastic, and full of vision.

• • •

I'm rooting around the servers, Toto by my side, trying to figure out what I can do. Trying to figure out what the fuck Haswell has done. Toto's got both men covered by the large revolver, but he's looking over at me.

"Well?"

"Give me time," I mutter.

"It's too late," Haswell shouts at us.

"To undo killing that many people? I sure as hell hope not!"

There's a pause behind me. I glance back at Haswell, who looks at me like I'm an idiot. "Kill them? *I'm* not going to kill anyone. I've set the missiles to burst in the air."

Our eyes lock.

I get it.

Reboot.

Decades ago, when scientists used to test nuclear bombs out in the open, they set one off high in the atmosphere over the Pacific. And electronics died all throughout Hawaii and up to the West Coast. That's how we found out that some bombs set off an electromagnetic pulse. Not as big a deal in the 1950s.

But today?

The electromagnetic pulse will slag most consumer-grade electronics. No more iPhones. No more internet. No more fancy car with GPS and collision-avoidance. No more flatscreen TVs. No more cable.

"Those fucking anti-intellectuals, the ones who can't live without all the things the nerds invented, how will they make it now?" Haswell asks. "They decry our checking into social media; they mock our favorite shows. But they all depend on us. And you know what, we *carry* them no more. People like you and me, we're the natural leaders. We are the inventors, the tinkerers, the ones who should lead it all."

"Can't lead shit if all our toys are dead," I say, stepping forward. I can't recall the missiles, I can't change where they are headed. I need more time to understand how to undo it all, and time is something we don't have.

Toto pokes around at the laptops as I stare in horror at Haswell.

"There's an exclusion zone programmed into the bursts," Haswell explains. "A place that already has the facilities, the technologies, the *right* people to lead. We will be a beacon in the dark. Unlike the Neanderthals on the science oversight committees who are literally against the concept of science itself until it puts in their pacemakers, *we* will be scientists. In charge of it all. Understand? Come with me. Come to the valley. Come build the new, orderly world. There's a place for you."

"A place?"

"You tracked me down. Who else could have done that? But you drive a shitty econo-car. Look, document leaks show us what kind of society these old baby-boomer politicians are creating: a police state. Caged in 'free speech zones' and no-knock raids. The whole 'if you've done nothing you've got nothing to fear' bullshit. We've become a bad operating system with so many patches on some old command line interface that we can barely run. It's time to reset. I've got a van with shielded electronics and enough gasoline to get us back there. I'll bring you with me into the new age. I hate to see wasted talent."

And as he says that, I hear the rumble of a rocket motor kicking on. The ground shakes as if a giant is tearing free from the rock underneath us all. I'm about to witness the first moments of something so vast and terrible that the work of H.P. Lovecraft is a cheerful kid's book by comparison.

Toto shoots Haswell in the kneecap. The man drops to the dust, writhing and screaming. Danny looks ready to jump for his weapon, so Toto shoots him in the stomach and picks up the shotgun.

He opens the hood of the van Haswell told us was ready for the EMP blast and nods. "It'll keep working. Come on."

"But..."

"We don't want to be waiting around. We need to take care of our own shit, now."

All around us, on the edges of the night horizon, ICBMs glare as they begin to rise above their groundhog holes and lumber into the sky.

• • •

"Where do you want to go?" Toto asks at last. He's driving. I have my face up against the window, looking out at the contrails heading higher and higher.

"I don't know," I say. "The countryside. Somewhere with clean water and deer to hunt. Guns will still work after the pulse."

Toto grimaces. "Before my family moved out to the countryside, we lived near one of the coasts. Got hit by a hurricane. It wasn't all Hollywood and shit. People don't run around screaming; we've been making communities for hundreds of years. Mostly in disaster, we pitch in, clean up, figure out how to muddle through."

"Like the blackout," I say. When the power went out, and people came out to light things up with their phones or car headlights. Even in our shitty neighborhood.

"Those people masturbating about the end of all things? They think they're not plugged into a larger network of people who produce the things they need. That's trade. More powerful than one jackass with a piece. A hundred people who actually build the guns, they're more powerful. Besides, you can't fucking eat gold and ammo. Medics, farmers, they're always going to be needed. What you do is find a good town, with good farms, clean water near a mountain. I know a few."

"We could go to the valley," I suggest.

"I don't think they'll do as well as Haswell thought," Toto says grimly.

"What do you mean?"

"First, answer me this: Did you agree with him? I remember, when you used to talk to me in school. About how you were treated. Do you think he had the right idea?"

"What the fuck?" I stare at Toto. "I got kicked around a bit for having my nose in a book. But you know what, everyone's an expert at something. I don't know shit about making my car run, doesn't mean I think my mechanic is less of a human being because I understand TCP/IP protocols and he doesn't."

"Good." Toto nods. "You didn't ask me what I was doing on those laptops. Probably neither you or Haswell figured someone like me would know enough to change the code. We couldn't send them all into the sea, or stop them. But I could launch one more, to cover that exclusion zone. Didn't want to be made a peasant of. Figure if the apocalypse is coming, should be equally distributed."

I would laugh, if it wasn't the actual end of the world.

• • •

Toto pulls to a stop after a few minutes. We're far enough away not to worry about the feds. Hopefully Haswell is right that the truck is hardened against the pulse, which should be coming at any moment.

We get out and stand in front of the truck and look at the skies.

"I got this off the dead one," Toto says, and hands me a phone. "If there was ever someone you wanted to call and get things right with, you've got a couple minutes, I figure, before the cell network goes down."

I look down at the phone. "I'd be calling you. No one else out there gives a shit if I live or die, you know?"

I toss it back at him, and he tosses it into the bushes.

Toto looks at me. "Hey…"

"You're getting all sentimental."

"If it's more than the EMP. I gotta say: you know I love you, right?"

It's going to be okay, I think, as the artificial, nuclear sunrise suddenly lights up the air above the highest clouds.

THIS UNKEMPT WORLD IS FALLING TO PIECES

Jamie Ford

May 1910

Young Darwin Chinn Qi didn't smell smoke, but as instructed, he opened the heavy iron callbox and pulled the fire alarm just the same, alerting guests and the staff of Seattle's opulent Sorrento Hotel that the *Sidereal Tramp* had finally arrived.

The great comet had many names: Astral Visitor, Celestial Vagrant, Sky Rover, even Flammarion's Folly—but "The Tramp" had finally caught on in all the newspapers and on the wires. Darwin thought the name sounded much better than the less sensational and plainly named *Smoking Comet of 1882*, which had been visible in broad daylight but had hardly elicited such worldwide excitement (and widespread panic).

He wished he'd seen the last one, but Darwin was only fifteen years old. He wasn't even alive when the previous comet passed by. That last apparition appeared long before he'd been born in Hong Kong—the bastard son of a sailor in the British Royal Navy and a Chinese woman. He'd been given to a mission home for half-breeds, shipped to Seattle, and sold into service.

Not a bad life, such as it is, Darwin thought. He hadn't learned a trade, but he could speak and read proper English. And better to die a prince in Washington's newest and finest hotel than live as king of the tarpaper shacks down on the mudflats.

Darwin had been to the stinking South Puget Sound once, during an especially low tide. He didn't envy the poor grunts working enormous steam-powered Iron Chinks, digging geoduck clams out of oil-soaked mud for half-pennies a pound.

Darwin continued daydreaming as he stood at attention while gentlemen in tuxedos and ladies in formal gowns made of copper lamé pulled on their long, silken dinner gloves and hurried to the elevator queue, waiting impatiently to reach the Top O' the Town restaurant on the seventh floor. Then he caught a knowing glance down the hall from Mr. Rosenberg, the hotel owner, and hurried to the smoking parlor. He hoisted a large humidor made from Spanish cedar and caught the servants lift to the top floor, which smelled like fresh calla lilies and prime rib.

Guests were lounging in the tearooms and newly appointed moonrooms, listening to Betty Hall Clark sing *Wild Cherries* and spoony ragtime on the auto-piano, while *oohing* and *aahing* at the Aurora Borealis—luminous ribbons of purple and blue-green that bled into the night sky—the opening act before what might be the grandest of all finales. Meanwhile the more daring patrons ventured out onto the Florentine loggia and rooftop garden, leaning over the balcony to get a better view of the horizon and the lights from sailboats that deckled Lake Washington, bobbing up and down, moving slowly on the water, shimmering like fireflies in honey. A few of the more intrepid guests wore gas masks atop their heads like party hats, while many of the older ladies veiled themselves in birdcage lace and toted comet umbrellas to fend off any errant dust and soot drifting down from the sky.

As Darwin found a place for the humidor and offered Cuban cigars for ten-cents apiece, Lucy Stringfellow walked by in a shiny pink mini-dress with matching cap. She toted a silver cigarette tray, offering tobacco for the ladies as well as comet pills. The fashionable blue mints had been laced with colloidal silver to ward off bad humors and also had the pleasing effect of turning one's skin the color of sterling ash.

"Hello, *Dashing*," she teased and blew him a kiss. "I'll love you until the end of time. Or sunrise, whichever comes first."

Lucy was a year older, an inch taller, and always called him *Daunting, Daring, Dancing*—anything but his adoptive name—even the occasional *Darling*, which always made Darwin delightfully uncomfortable.

He caught her eye and then looked away. "Do you think we're really going see it tonight? Because crying wolf is bad for business."

Lucy nodded at the horizon. "Mr. Rosenberg said the Hydrographic Office just got a message from a ship at sea. Then the telegraph went down. He says that's how we can know for sure when the Sidereal Tramp is close. The northern lights come out and then all the wires stop working."

The telegraphic services not working made Darwin feel, well—not quite scared—but certainly more nervous than he'd expected; after all, the headlines in the *Seattle Star* had been going on for weeks about Camille Flammarion, the French astronomer who had declared that the Earth would pass through the Tramp's tail for five hours, which was—according to Flammarion's scientific calculations—millions of miles long and made of something called cyanogen, which sounded ominous, indeed.

Flammarion had warned: *The Terrible Tramp would impregnate our atmosphere with poison and most certainly cause a ruinous catastrophe for every living thing—mind blindness, all manners of sickness, and even death.*

While in England, someone from the Royal Greenwich Observatory said that massive tides might cause the Pacific Ocean to empty itself into the Atlantic.

Darwin didn't know what to believe and neither did anyone else. From atop the Sorrento he had a clear view of the Luddites at St. James Cathedral, which was holding an all-night prayer vigil. It seemed that all over Seattle—all over the world perhaps—people were either confessing their sins, or busy committing new ones.

"You look rather pale," Lucy said. "You feeling alright, dearest darling?"

Darwin blushed.

"The cigar smoke doesn't agree with me," he lied, pretending to cough as the color came back to his cheeks. He knew that while Seattle's gilded elite celebrated, many of those on the street had other plans. Some left, as the comet got closer, to hide in caves or the abandoned mines of Mount Rainier. Other poor souls, tormented by fear, religious fervor, or both, had committed suicide, quickly, with a bullet or by electrocution, or slowly, by drinking their fears away away, one glass, one bottle, one cask of home-made apple-gin at a time. And the jails were overflowing with comet-crazed people. Darwin had even read about a sheriff in Oklahoma who rescued a girl who was about to be sacrificed by her stepfather to a band of end-of-the-world fanatics.

Darwin feigned a smile.

"I'll make us some pearl tea," Lucy said. "After the party. We'll have our own celebration—why not live a little, while we still can?"

Darwin watched as she smiled and walked away. *In my dreams.*

They'd lived under the same grand roof for three years but had never been alone, not even for a minute, and had hardly spent any non-working, non-dining time together. Darwin resided in the east wing of the walkup basement with the colored men of the kitchen staff, custodians, and boiler mechanics, while Lucy lived one floor below with the rest of the resident female workers. Only Mr. Elliot, the majordomo, was allowed to live on the ground floor, and aside from group meals, which Mr. Elliot grudgingly tolerated, their boss frowned on social contact between the men and women. Though lately some of the doe-eyed servants had met up on their rare days off. But the couples were invariably discovered and, apocalypse or not, they found their employment contracts voided.

Darwin wondered (and worried) that Lucy had caught comet-fever and was willing to take that chance on his behalf. But as he heard hooting and a wild commotion from the balcony, he wondered if *he* was willing to meet that risk.

"Here's to the end of the world!" a woman shouted, above the boisterous piano and the popping of a dozen champagne corks.

Darwin shut the humidor's lid as everyone rushed outside or pressed their faces to the windows to get a better look. *The end of the world has become a joke*, Darwin thought, *a debate to be hashed out in the editorial pages of newspapers.*

"It's here! Glory, it's huge!" someone hollered.

"Good Lord," a man stammered, his voice cracking. "Why is it so damn close?"

Darwin watched in awe as white lights exploded, silhouetting men with long-tailed jackets and women draped in fur cloaks and shawls. Then the laughs and jovial cheers dissolved into panicked shrieks and the sound of glass breaking. Darwin ducked as he heard thunderous booming, and the windows rattled in their panes. He smelled smoke, and burning, like fetid sulfur as fire and lightning filled the night sky. Scores of patrons swarmed back inside like ants caught in a rainstorm, climbing over each other and the serving staff. So many people piled into the elevator that the brass gate wouldn't close and the lift remained a wobbling, jerking cage of mewling bodies and fine haberdashery.

Darwin chewed his lip and squeezed through the frenzied crowd, past drunk men at the bar who guzzled their drinks, and around the piano player who began Chopin's *Funeral March* in earnest, her head down, eyes closed.

He finally found Lucy crouched beneath a serving table and helped her up.

"Follow me," he said, as he took her hand and guided her against the tide of terrified revelers, past the balcony doors, which were filled with smoke and flashing luminescence. They hurried toward the servants' stairs. He put his hand around her waist and led her down the serpentine steps, down seven floors, pausing on the ground level as he heard screams from the foyer and the sound of pottery shattering.

"It's not safe out there," he said, unsure if she could hear him. Then he led her down two more flights, through a long hallway, past the cellar and into the boiler room.

"What are we doing down here?" Lucy asked, catching her breath.

"If the Tramp is that close we're safer below ground," Darwin looked around the dimly lit room, which was a cave of load-bearing columns, metal pipes, clanking pistons, and machinery that ran the length of the high, joisted ceiling. An enormous boiler, the size of a locomotive engine, dominated the center of the room, radiating heat. "This place is built like the Airship Kentucky."

"But the poison vapors outside, the comet dust," Lucy said. "Won't that come through the doors, the cracks in the walls…?"

"This way." Darwin cut her off and led her inside the large coal bin. He climbed a pile of black rock and closed the coal chute, then he scrambled down and closed the heavy iron coal bin doors, sealing out light and smoke and the terrifying world above. He remembered that gas masks used filters lined with crushed charcoal. *This room might filter out the toxic fumes*, he hoped, as they sat down and huddled into the pile. He felt her hip, smelled her perfume mixed with sweat amid the smoky coal. He brushed her bare leg for a moment before he found her fingers laced between his.

The room was pitch black.

"This…this can't be happening," Lucy whispered. "I didn't believe it…"

Darwin didn't answer. He held her hand and listened, straining to hear something, anything above the pounding of his heart and his worried breathing. He heard what sounded like sirens in the distance and the muffled cries of people shouting. He couldn't quite accept that the world was ending, but he recognized fear when he saw it, when he felt it.

"Darling, Daring…*Dying*." Lucy sniffled. "*I don't want to die…want to die…*"

"We're not dead yet." Darwin tried to talk about something—anything—to fill the silence, the dread of not knowing. "You know, my last name is Qi. It's sometimes a lucky name because in Chinese it means life, or breath, or *air*—that's a good omen, right? Though it's kind of a funny thing too because in the mission home where I grew up, they told me the Chinese fable about the Qi Dynasty. They were the most backward of all people because they worried about anything and everything. The Qi literally thought the sky was falling—like Chicken Little. And now look at us. The sky *is* falling."

As the sirens faded, the world grew quiet. He heard her breathing soften. He felt it proper to let go of her hand but he didn't want to. He held on tighter.

"I'm not laughing," she said. And then she did, just a little.

"See," he said. "The end of the world's not so bad. All we need is that cup of pearl tea, with lemon." He squeezed her hand. "Quickly, tell me about your family."

She sneezed twice from the coal dust and Darwin blessed her out of social habit, though he didn't practice any such primitive religion.

"What family?" she said as the coal settled beneath them. Her voice echoed in the hollow steel chamber. "My parents came down from Vancouver to work in the copper mines. My father contracted green lung from the dust and couldn't work. I was the youngest of seven mouths to feed so they sold me—put me in service, just like you—until I'm eighteen, just like you. I haven't seen them in years. They're probably dead now, or will be soon."

Darwin understood the same sadness. The same bitter loneliness. He imagined suffering through the end of the world, only to be the last two survivors.

She patted his arm. "You can be my family."

He mulled that over—the good and bad. Lucy had hinted, smiled, flirted, and nearly broken the rules to catch his eye. Part of him had known this all along and a part of him (the doubting, insecure part) had half-pretended to be oblivious—better to be wrong in his apprehension than right in her possible rejection. Where does that leave them now?

Family. Darwin thought. *Like husband and wife, or kissing cousins?*

Before he could ask, he startled at the clanging of the fire bell in the distance—the same alarm he'd pulled earlier—but this time he heard three sharp rings.

Then silence.

"Thank goodness," Darwin whispered. "We're in luck." He helped Lucy to her feet and opened the creaking, groaning, coal room doors. "That beautiful sound was the all-clear signal. We just might live to see the morning after all."

"You're sure?" She hesitated. "Is it really safe?"

"There's only one way to find out."

They took turns dusting each other off in the shadowy darkness—turning, smiling, laughing, and gently touching. He took her hand and boldly kissed it once, then wiped off the coal dust where his lips had been.

Why not? he thought as he paused, grateful for catastrophe. Then he let go.

As they stepped into the corridor, they squinted at Mr. Elliot and a custodian who Darwin didn't recognize. Each of them carried a matchless flashlight. The majordomo bit down on his pipe and grunted, "Jeezus and Mary! I had better *never* catch you two down here again in this state of… aloneness." He pointed to the stairwell. "Clean yourself up and get back to your stations—hurry along now. The show is over but the party will continue as planned and you still have guests to serve."

"But…the Tramp… ," Lucy protested.

"What Tramp? Get upstairs," Mr. Elliot barked. "Now!"

They hurried along the servants' stairwell, then waved goodbye as they split up to go change into new liveries on their respective floors. Darwin, though, couldn't wait to abate his curiosity. He peeked into the octagonal-shaped lobby where a host of guests were collecting themselves and waiters were offering everyone free cocktails and comet pills. He wandered from the stairwell out the front door and down the steps to the circular porte-cochére where three police motorcars were parked and a patrol of mounted officers clip-clopped by in the cold, brisk Seattle night. Darwin's mouth fell open as he looked above the smoke that had settled in the Italian garden; he saw a fire engine, ladder extended, pumping water into the trees that were still ablaze. Above that queer spectacle floated a massive airship; a hot air balloon half the size of the hotel, hovered above the seventh floor balcony. Below the basket was an enormous wooden platform, still smoking, sparking, glowing with fireworks and a neon contraption that read DRINK REAL OLYMPIA BEER from the CLAUSSEN SWEENEY BREWING COMPANY. Darwin heard police officers with bullhorns shouting at the aeronauts to come down and face charges for public nuisance and disturbing the peace.

And for inciting a riotous stampede. Darwin thought. *And for making a young girl cry in my arms. And for terrifying me, yet also making me happier and more relieved than I've been in a long, long time.*

• • •

An hour later, the end-of-the-world publicity stunt was the talk of the party as comet-watchers resumed their previously scheduled frivolities, though some of the elderly celebrants had taken their heart medicine and gone to bed. *If the end of the world was nigh*, they had chirped, *they would greet it lying down, dreaming of greener pastures and tinctures of laudanum.* Several of the guests had been taken to the hospital to treat their bumps, scrapes, bruises, and one man's broken leg.

Despite the somewhat subdued atmosphere, Darwin quickly ran out of machine-crafted cigars from Havana and had moved on to the hand-rolled labels from Trinidad and Brazil. No one seemed to mind the rough cohibas. And Lucy resumed her duties, though her pink cap had been crushed in the scrum.

Darwin stood his post and gazed out the window as the Madison Street cable car descended the steep hill to downtown, past sodium-arc streetlights that flickered in the darkness, beneath the aurora, which continued its heavenly performance, unfettered. He thought of Lucy and her touch, and the end of the world seemed farther away than it had been sixty minutes ago. But, perhaps he'd earn a measure of insurance just the same.

In Chinatown, Darwin heard that the locals had taken to the Underground—which had been publicly closed during the bubonic plague scare of 1907, but had quietly been repopulated ever since. First for opium dens, gambling parlors, and pleasure houses, and now for handsomely built comet shelters complete with brass bottles of air and Dr. Melvin's Comet

Tonic, which was advertised as wormwood but was probably nothing more than castor oil. The brick bunkers were so popular that only a few were left and could only be had through a lottery run by the Chong Wa Benevolent Association.

Darwin had bought a ticket last week, just in case, as a way of preventing disaster, like taking your bumbershoot out because you know it only rains when you leave it behind. The ticket had cost ten dollars, an extravagance that now seemed affordable as he palmed a pocketful of old folding money he'd earned in tips from guests who had currency to burn and perhaps a limited lifetime in which to spend such wealth.

"Quite the evening, eh?" Darwin said, as he cut and then lit the cigar of a cotton-haired gentleman stooped over a silver-tipped cane.

The old man looked back with a twinkle in his eye that might have been a tear. "Perfect night for the end of the world. And not my first, young lad." The old man's lips trembled and his hands shook as he spoke. "I saw the Sidereal Tramp back in 1835, the last time it came 'round—course they called it Halley's Comet back then. Few of us are around to remember the same panic, the same stupidity. The same…indulgences."

Darwin nodded, not realizing that people were still alive from the last apparition. "They say the Tramp's gravity is closer this time. And the poisonous tail…"

"And this you believe?" the old man asked, but his question felt like a statement.

"Begging your pardon, sir. I honestly don't know *what* to believe."

"And that'll be your downfall, your lack of faith in science. But soon… all will be revealed. Because at my age, I feel every storm, every snowfall—I feel it in my bones. This storm—*this thing*—I feel it coming. This unkempt world is falling to pieces." The old man's voice quavered. "I've lived my life, I should be so lucky as to expire with an entire continent to keep me company."

Darwin sensed the same dread he'd felt in the boiler room. He heard the crowd's chatter settle into a bouquet of delicate whispers. Everyone stopped dancing, or mingling, and slowly, timidly, drifted to the balcony, yet again.

"That's more like it," a woman cooed as she sipped a glass of sparkling wine.

The hunched old man stood a bit taller to see outside, and Darwin noticed the detachable collar of a retired science minister.

"*When beggars die there are no comets seen; the heavens themselves blaze forth the death of princes*," the old man said. "That's Shakespeare." He squeezed Darwin's shoulder. "G'night, lad."

Darwin bid him well and peered, with the rest of the wait staff, over the shoulders of the regal men and women they'd been serving. He could see the Tramp appear just above the horizon, drifting slowly across the Western sky—an unmistakable white light, the size of his thumb as he extended his arm away from his body. The light flashed a ruddy crimson, arcs of fire hovering above the Olympic Mountains. The deep curve of the comet's tail stretched out behind the glowing orb as partygoers made silent wishes, offered solemn toasts, or kissed as though celebrating the New Year all over again. There was a wave of apprehension that conceded quietly to relief.

He felt someone take his arm and knew by her perfume that it was Lucy. He continued watching the Tramp make its way through the darkness and through the glowing curtains of the northern lights. "It's breathtaking." He smiled and nodded. "The end of the world should happen more often, don't you think?"

"Darwin—" She paused. "Darwin, I..."

And then the comet flashed and the lights went out—the comforting thrum of electricity gone—everything dark but the candles and the jellied fuel which glowed pink and yellow beneath the chafing dishes and coffee pots, then that too was snuffed out in a rush of air that stole Darwin's breath and shattered every pane of glass, exploded every bottle of wine, and gave voice to a primeval sound that was felt, not heard—something great and terrible, a city, surrendering its death-rattle.

Somewhere amid the maelstrom, between the flutter of heartbeats, bounded by the turbulent light that enveloped the sky and the Stygian dark that would follow, Darwin thought of Lucy Stringfellow. He wished he'd touched her lips, at least once.

BRING HER TO ME

Ben H. Winters

Before she opens the door Annabel takes a moment to prepare herself. She smoothes the front of her frock, and tucks her hair behind her ears, and readies her face: smile, eyes. *Ready.*

"Hello?"

"Hello! Hi!"

The woman from the Center launches right in, full force: "Oh my goodness we are really getting down to it now, aren't we? We are really getting down to it now!"

And Annabel says "Yes, we sure are," and in unison they close their eyes, tilt their heads backwards, and stand glowing for one half of one second before snapping back into conversation.

"I keep pinching myself," says the stranger at the door, and then she does it, she really pinches herself. "It's actually—finally—seriously—really—*here*!"

Annabel laughs politely, as the woman pauses at last to take a breath and then to say, "My name is Marie St. Clair, by the way. I'm from the Center."

"Ah!"

This had already been obvious, of course. Annabel knew the woman was from the Center, because of the clipboard—the flowers—the sash. But Annabel keeps her smile in place, and nods with enthusiasm. "Thank you so much for your service," she says.

"Oh, pah," says Ms. St. Clair, waving away the gratitude with a happy smile. "It's my pleasure. My honor, I should say. It's all just so marvelous, that we are here to see this day. You and I and all of us, everyone now living, *we* are the fortunate generation, *we* have heard, and *we* shall travel through. *Marvelous!*"

For a moment, after that, Ms. St. Clair just stands at Annabel's door, beaming, and Annabel beams back. Because even though this speech of Ms. St. Clair's is made of the same rote praise-words that Annabel has heard a million times; and despite her wariness of this woman; and despite the desperate secret that has troubled her restless heart for so many years; despite it all, Annabel Lennon feels just exactly what Ms. St. Clair is feeling. They feel it *together.* They stand there in communal pleasure for a moment, as if under mistletoe. Together they stand in the sunlight coming from the corridor window, and in the pleasure of what is, and in honey-toned anticipation of what is to come.

The truth is, Annabel *does* think it's marvelous, and she *does* feel fortunate to be here, to be alive and in this world at this moment, on this day, she really does.

Behind them, out the corridor window, the city is a mass of black clustered towers, like a group of strangers in overcoats, waiting for a train.

"Anyway," Ms. St. Clair says abruptly and with force. She takes out a stylus and holds it over her pad. "What I am charged with today, on this penultimate day, is performing a final, final, absolutely final sweep to ensure that everyone has heard."

"Of course," says Annabel, and then fears she said it too fast. She renews her smile, takes a breath. "Absolutely. We all have heard. Everyone in our home."

"There are three of you?"

"Yes."

"Mother, father, child?"

"Yes. Child. One child. A teenager."

Quiet, Annabel. Hush. Smile.

"Great!" says Ms. St. Clair cheerily. She jots with her stylus. "And you all know the protocol?"

"Yes," says Annabel, and bites back the words *of course.* Everybody knows the protocol. Obviously they know the protocol. Everyone is aware of every detail; for the last ten years all has been known; all has been arranged as it has been commanded. They have learned the protocol from the Center, learned it from one another other, and learned it directly from the source of all truth. Loud and clear.

But Annabel just says "Yes" one more time and widens her smile. She is smiling so tight now that her cheeks hurt. She wonders if this Ms. St. Clair *knows* somehow, knows the awful truth of their home, and is waiting to pounce. But the dreaded moment never comes. Instead the woman just runs down the protocol one last time—and then Annabel must sign that she has listened and understood. She does. She grips the stylus and she signs. It's all mildly ridiculous, because of course it will all be gone tomorrow: the clipboard, the corridor, Building 170, all the buildings, these two smiling women as they are standing here now, as corporeal beings in a carpeted hallway.

"Okay, then, I will see you when we've all gone through," says Ms. St. Clair at last, and for just one split second, for half of one half of an instant, Annabel wonders what would happen if she were to ask "*But what if it's all wrong, what if it's all just wrong? What if we're all just nuts? Doesn't it ever occur to you?*"

But of course Annabel doesn't say that. Of course she just smiles some more as the woman from the Center slips her clipboard into her satchel and goes, and then Annabel turns and leans against the door with her eyes shut tight and her cheeks burning hot, until she hears her husband's footsteps coming down the stairs.

• • •

Goodness no, by the way—the answer is no. It *never* occurs to Marie St. Clair of the Answer Center that it's all a mistake, all just a terrible mistake. Such a thought would *never* appear in her mind.

She is committed and enthusiastic beyond question to the plan, as she has been since the day she was born. Her head is filled with passionate belief that it is right, that it is right, that all of it is just exactly right. She is not unique in this. Most people feel this way. All people, officially.

Ms. St. Clair has been doing this for seven years, since the Answer Center was established—it's really nine Answer Centers, one in each building cluster, all reporting to the main Center. Marie St. Clair has a chart affixed to the wall in her office, and another up in her rooms in Building 49. Sometimes at night, before falling asleep, she traces the organizational lines with her fingers.

Now, though, she has more to do. She will not sleep tonight. Never again. She adjusts her sash and feels the pleasing weight of the clipboard in her satchel as she glides down the corridor toward the next door.

YOU ARE MY WORK IN THE WORLD, she hears in her head as she walks with serene purpose down the corridor. It's the voice of God, weaving golden through her mind, like a bright banner flowing between the pillars of a church.

YOU ARE SERVING MY PURPOSE AND PAVING MY WAY.

"I know!" she says, out loud. "I love you."

YOU ARE MY VOICE YOU ARE MY WORK IN THE WORLD.

"I know!"

It's 6:15. Ms. St. Clair knocks on the next door down—she is right on schedule. Tomorrow is May 1st. It's happening! It's almost here! It's *amazing*.

• • •

"I…have been thinking," says Kenneth.

The words emerge from him slowly. He is seated at the table with his chin in his hand, and Annabel is at the kitchen island, standing before the great joint of meat, cutting it carefully. She knows what her husband is going to say, what he has been thinking. She is tired of his indecision. She stops cutting and lowers her electric slicer and turns to him and stares.

"You have been thinking *what*?"

"Thinking—just—what if we are making a mistake?"

"We are not making a mistake."

Kenneth sighs and stares at the smooth table. Annabel pushes the button on the slicer and the hot hum fills the kitchen. She is slicing small peels of animal off an enormous slab; the slices curl and fall away. The animal is raw. Under the kitchen table, a fourteen-year-old girl with big black eyes and a thick tussle of black hair is hidden, her knees clutched to her chest, listening and trembling. Annabel keeps cutting. The pieces curl off the flesh and fall in their thin slices into a pile of blood. Kenneth sits in troubled silence at the table, cracking his knuckles. Annabel knows it's too late now to change course. They've made their decision. It's done.

BRING HER TO ME, says God in Annabel's head, whispering and vivid and undulant. BRING HER TO ME.

But Kenneth keeps going. "I fear we are making a terrible mistake," he says, quietly but urgently. "By our deception. A *terrible* mistake. And it's not too late, Anna. It's not too late to take care of this properly."

"To take care of it properly!"

The euphemism is too much for Annabel to bear. She pivots toward her husband, wielding the still-humming slicer. "You mean bring her to the Center and tell them that she can't hear! Leave her behind. Abandon our daughter. Our only child! We travel through tomorrow—we go on to Glory—and she stays and rots." She bares her teeth, jabs the slicer angrily. "That's what you mean."

Kenneth pushes back his chair and stands.

"What the theologians say—"

"I know what they say."

"Let me—can I finish?"

Annabel gestures with the slicer. The blood from the meat flies from it and splatters on the old thick carpet of the living room. The towers of the city loom in the the windows. Lights glow in the distance; the black sky punctuated by gold and gleam. Annabel jerks her thumb onto the lever of the slicer and the hum of it is loud and keen. The blade hums into the meat. Annabel cuts while Kenneth watches. It's what, 8:15 now? He raises his voice.

"They say that only those who have heard may come through."

"She has heard her whole life. She has heard from us."

"Only those—"

"From her teachers. From her friends."

"Only those who have heard *directly* may travel through. Or else—"

"She has heard her whole life," Annabel says again.

Kenneth's face is trembling. He paces with his hands behind his back.

"We are defying His will."

"You don't know what He wants."

"Of course I do!" says Kenneth. "He talks to me."

"He talks to me, too! He talks to everyone."

Kenneth shakes his head bitterly. "Not everyone," he says.

There is then a long silence in the room. Annabel stops moving. She gives up all pretense of continuing work on the tartare. She cannot do it properly unless she is paying attention. The instructions from the theologians are quite clear: thin slices of beef, as thin as paper, as thin as skin. The meat must be sliced very thin so that the poison can soak its way through: so the poison can saturate the flesh, striate each thin piece, marble each slice with the will of God.

BRING HER TO ME, Annabel hears. BRING HER TO ME. It gives her courage. Steels her voice and steadies her hand.

"Okay, so fine. She doesn't hear. So she's never received the instructions. But we have, and we have told her, and she has shown no hesitation, no reluctance, because she trusts us. She trusts us and she trusts in God even though she has never heard Him. This is her test, and it is our test."

Kenneth crosses his arms and stares out the window at the looming buildings. Annabel comes over and stands beside him, holds his shoulder with one bloodied hand.

"She has to come," says Annabel, and her voice has changed now. She is not telling Kenneth, she is pleading. Asking him. With love: for him, for their child, for God. "She has to eat of it and come through with us. We will not give her up. We will not leave her behind."

The meal will be served in the morning. The morning of May 1st, the long and longingly awaited. Annabel takes his other shoulder, looks him in the eyes.

"She is our daughter and she is coming through with us tomorrow. Coming along like everyone. Do you agree?"

Kenneth turns away. The voice is in his head, too, God's voice, Annabel knows that. She wonders what it is saying at that moment but she is afraid to ask. She steps closer.

"Do you agree?"

• • •

The first to hear was a girl named Jennifer Miller, just a regular girl, just like anyone, from Building 14—this is when there was a Building 14. This is twenty-four years ago.

And God just came along to Jennifer Miller, when Jennifer Miller was still a child, almost, when she was thirteen years old. And God began to speak to her and told her that all of this would end in her lifetime, and Jennifer Miller thought that she had gone crazy, and when she told others, in her building and at her academy, they thought that she had gone crazy, too. Of course they did.

This was when things were still good but beginning to get bad.

Jennifer Miller, in time, began to believe that she really was hearing a voice; and then that the voice was really God's voice; and then that what He was telling her was true.

TIME IS SHORT, is all He said in those first years. To her, and then at last to others. In various of the buildings; in various of the floors; His voice, mighty like a ram's horn or hushed like the purposeful whisper of a child playing telephone, was now being heard. TIME IS SHORT.

And then, as the years went on—and the buildings slipped along on their various rates of decay—the messages began to vary, some people hearing certain things and others hearing other things. Soon everyone heard, and soon the instructions became clear and specific and nobody thought Jennifer Miller was crazy any longer, because everybody could hear. A man named Ronald Clarke was the first to be told the day, and a woman named Barb Ruiz, of Building 2, was given to know the method.

Eventually He let there be no ambiguity. He showed himself to be a democratic God, and a clarion God. He let the word ring out and ring true to all: Here is my will and here is how it shall be, it shall be by feast, by joyous gathering around tables of poison. These crumbling buildings we will leave behind, these frail bodies, and all of us will travel through together, on the first of May of the appointed year.

And now at last, the day of the feast has come and it will be in the morning.

• • •

Pea waits until her parents are gone. She sneaks silently up the stairs.

She sits in her tiny room like she sat under the table in the kitchen, with her knees clasped to her chest and her body trembling. A frail flower.

It's past midnight, now. Just past. It's very dark outside, no stars.

She has spent her whole life pretending, and at least that's almost over.

She has learned to do the thing they do, tilt her head back and half-close her eyes, listening. Stop in the middle of a conversation and mouth silent words, as if in conversation with a ghost.

Now it's all almost over.

They live in Building 170. It is called that because it was the 170th one built, of the original two-hundred, but there are only sixty-three left now.

Pea sits on her bed and looks out the window at the bleak black horizon, and her life is almost over.

Her parents are good parents—they love her despite her deafness—but she knows it is a source of pain and shame to them. She knows one literally deaf child; that girl's name is Sharon. She is in the lower group, still, two years behind Pea. She literally cannot hear. Pea can hear but she can't hear God.

Pea picks up her journal and then puts it down again. No point now—no sense. She has never written the truth in it. Too risky. She has hidden her secret her whole life, without her parents ever telling her to. Without needing to be told. Her whole life has been one ache, one absence.

She lies down on the bed. Tomorrow it will all be over. One way or another. Sleep flickers in and out of her eyes. Dream scraps, stitched together strangely: Her father riding on the Building 170 elevator, pointing the lever up; her mother carving something that is not meat.

She is awoken by a nervous plink-plink on the window. She sits upright and stares at the window. Her nightgown is gold-colored and old and ratty. There it is again: *Plink—plink*. Like fingertips gently rapping on the glass.

"At last," she whispers. She slides off the bed—*plink, plink*—and walks on trembling legs toward the window. "At last!"

What will He look like? How will He *sound*? Maybe there are special instructions that have been held back until now, because it was necessary that they be given to someone special. To her. Just to her. It was all a long test of her faith, and now it is done. She presses the buttons to work the window screen.

She sees the puffy face distorted through the glass and her excitement whooshes out of her. It's not God. It's Robert, a fat boy from her class. He is standing there sweating on the ledge that runs around the building, clinging to her sill. Poorly dressed, glasses skewed, his face confused and almost apologetic, as if he's not sure he's in the right place. He is wearing his clothes from the academy, though it is long after hours. Though they will never need to be worn again.

Robert must see it through the glass, the disappointment in Pea's face, and she immediately feels bad. She presses the buttons and opens the window and Robert tumbles himself in over the sill and lands splat on her floor.

Pea crosses her arms. She is in her thin gold nightgown. She has never talked much to boys in private. It's the middle of the night, the last night. She tucks her hair behind her ears and waits while he pulls his thick clumsy body up to standing.

"Hey," says Robert, obviously nervous, breathing loudly through his nose.

"This is really strange," Pea says, "you being here."

"I know," he says, nodding vigorously. "I know."

And then he takes a deep breath and they peer at each other. His imperfections are striking. His eyes bulge behind thick-lensed glasses. He's got odd hair, black tufts that go off in all directions like a scattered herd. Pea is afraid that he's never going to break the silence. Is he waiting for *her* to say something? But then—

"Pea, you are different than other girls. D'you know? I mean—different."

"Oh," she says. "Oh, God."

She feels a cold rush of fear. *How does he know? How did he find out? Does he know?*

But then Robert suddenly starts talking again, a hundred miles an hour, wringing his hands together and looking everywhere in the room except at her. "I know this may seem crazy to bring this up to you now, but my heart has been with you since forever. I mean, not since *forever* but for a long, long time. Since pubescence, and probably sooner. Since Academy."

The words at first are a confusing blur, but then at once Pea understands, and her fear dissolves into embarrassment—for herself. For him. What Robert means when he says that she is *different* is that she is *special.* He means that he *likes* her. She cups her face with her hands. She almost laughs but doesn't. He doesn't know her secret! He is confessing a crush. She looks up at him, holding her palm over her mouth. Of all the scenes to be playing out in her bedroom late at night, late on *this* night!

"I honestly Pea…I don't even know what I would want you to do with this information…"

Robert has his hands in his hair, he looks wildly about her room, his confusion accelerating. He is sweating so much: his neck, his chin. His forehead. Pea resolves to put him out of his misery.

"I don't really like you in that way," she says suddenly, kind but firm, interrupting the heartsick monologue. "I'm sorry."

Immediately, Robert nods. "That's—I mean—sure. I knew that was coming, obviously. I guess I was expecting that. I mean, of course. Of course I knew you would say that."

He laughs nervously. Pea smiles at him. She feels bad for him, but she doesn't do anything like get up and take his hand or kiss him. She's not the kind of person to do something like that just because of the weird circumstances. But there is something nice about this, right now. She has never had a boyfriend—never kissed a boy. These are pleasant things to be thinking about, even in the negative, instead of what is coming: the morning, the meal, the end.

And Robert, having unburdened himself, now seems almost relaxed. He takes the liberty of sitting down on Pea's bed, and exhales, and even laughs."I expected that, like I said. I mean, it's funny, you know? It's kind of a little hilarious. If I can't get a girl to like me now, I guess it's just not in the cards, right?" He laughs again. He has a snorting kind of laugh. "Now or never, right?"

"I guess so," says Pea. "But, you know…pain will be a memory when we all go through. Pain will be a word in books."

"Right," he says. "Of course."

This is something people have heard. Pea of course has never heard it. She feels cold inside. She looks past Robert, out the window. He gets up, paces back and forth a couple more times, with his hands locked behind his back like a politician.

"Robert?"

"I know, I know, I'm leaving," he says. "It's just — there's one more thing."

• • •

BRING HER TO ME.

Annabel sits in the dark in the basement of the building with her hands wrapped around herself, her fingers laced together, clutching her knees against her chest.

For many years now this has been her private place, down here in the storeroom of Building 170, among the scattered trophies from when things were good. This is where she comes to think. Where she comes to wrestle with her burden. Not Pea—never Pea; Pea herself is not a burden. She is a joy. It is Pea's difference that is the burden. Pea's deafness. The question of what God wants for Pea, what Annabel wants for her. Those are the burdens, and now the hour has come, now it is almost here.

BRING HER TO ME.

Annabel winces and clutches her ears as if the voice can be silenced. For many years she has taken the service elevator down here when it is working—or taken the stairs otherwise. She comes down here and sits in the dim night glow to think, away from Kenneth, away from the others, away from the Center.

Sometimes it even feels like God's voice can't reach her here, as if this subterranean place is hidden from Him, too buried for His voice to find her. Sometimes it feels like she is a little girl in the quiet world again, like when she was Pea's age, before Jennifer Miller. A time of pure untroubled silence.

Sometimes it feels that way, but not all the time. Not tonight.

BRING HER TO ME.

• • •

"So—" Robert clears his throat and then lowers his voice. "What are you doing tomorrow?"

"What am I..." Pea is confused. She steps back, toward the bed. "You're joking."

"No."

Robert shakes his head. His hands are still clasped behind his back and he is staring at the ground.

"No, I'm not joking, Pea. Is your family going through with it? Are you?"

Pea, still in her child's gold nightgown, gapes at him. He had been anxious before, nervous, like a child. Now it's as if Robert is growing up before her eyes, his agitation becoming more purposeful, somehow, more adult. His hand worries at his hair.

"Everybody's going through with it," she tells him.

He shrugs. Makes a sour face.

"Is *your* family going through with it?" she asks.

"Yes."

"Are you?"

He doesn't answer. She stares at him. She feels the valves of her heart open, as if to allow an extra rush of blood. She pictures the kitchen counter, two floors down, where the meat lays in curled piles, waiting, the bloody pink slices of tartare.

"When you were little," Robert asks her earnestly, "did you ever peek out from between your fingers when the Grace was being said?"

"I don't know," says Pea. "I don't remember."

She does, though. She does remember. She would peek from between her fingers, just as Robert is saying, peek out and watch as her parents mouthed in silent communion with the God they could hear and she could not. She would sit, fearful and strange, staring at her food and waiting.

"Tomorrow night," says Robert. "It's all I can think about." He rushes to her, then, suddenly, lifts her hands and holds them in his own. "All I can think about is being here tomorrow night. Being alive. What it will be like, to still be alive tomorrow night. We could walk the streets between the buildings, Pea. We could do that. When everyone else is dead."

It hits Pea like a wash of cool water: the absence of euphemism. *Dead.*

They won't be *dead*, they will have *gone through*. They will be on the other side.

Or maybe not. Maybe they'll just be dead. *Oh God*, thinks Pea, *where is your voice? Oh God, guide me.*

"Why would you want to stay in this world?" she asks Robert quietly. "This world has collapsed. This world is broken."

"Pah," says Robert. "It's collapsed because everybody stopped taking care of it. It collapsed because everybody's been sitting around waiting to eat poison for twenty-four years."

Pea stands there in the tense silence while time ticks by, and she feels thrilled and overwhelmed, disoriented and excited. She has thought these things before, in the dark spaces that in other people's minds are filled by God's word. The buildings, those remaining, tilting toward each other in the marshes like old dominoes. The broken elevators. The aluminum fixtures that used to be steel. Everybody just waiting. The world slowly running down.

Pea feels a butterfly fluttering around in the cold chamber of her chest. Its wings brush against the bars. She whispers to Robert.

"You don't hear Him either."

"Oh, I hear Him," he says. He doesn't look like a fat nervous kid anymore, not at all, not to Pea. "I hear Him. I just think He's full of shit."

• • •

Dawn is approaching and Marie St. Clair has finished her appointed rounds. Everybody in these three buildings knows. Everybody is ready. Everybody has been ready for years.

GO HOME NOW AND WAIT.

She tightens her sash around her chest, her heart beating faster and faster as the sunrise approaches.

GO AND BE GLAD.

There is no question in her mind. That is perhaps the greatest thing, that is what makes her happy. No doubt and no question, no trouble and no worry, she simply knows what will happen next. The truth. The uncomplicated truth.

• • •

BRING HER TO ME.

"More."

BRING HER TO ME.

"I need to know more. Please. Please. I need to know more."

Kenneth stands at the foot of the stairs in a furor of indecision. God will only say what He has said, what He keeps on saying, and His brevity is a kind of absence, the cruelest imaginable absence.

Does it mean what his wife insists, that they must allow the child to die, like everyone, and that she will be brought through? Or does it mean, as Kenneth fears, that if he trusts God he must trust Him like Abraham. He must trust Him all the way: Report his own daughter's deafness, her defect, and abandon her. Allow her to be left behind so the process is not ruined for all the rest.

BRING HER TO ME.

He knows what is right. Time is running out.

Kenneth takes one deep breath and flings himself up the creaking stairs, three big steps at a time, as if over hurdles, as if slowing would make him stop—no, not *as if*, for he knows that indeed slowing down *will* make him stop. Kenneth hurls himself up the stairs and grabs the door handle of Pea's room and throws it open, and he meets his wife coming out of their daughter's room.

Annabel stares wildly at him. She is panting and shivering, and in her hand is the electric slicer, and it is on, humming, with red blood all along its vibrating edges.

I am too late, Kenneth thinks. *Too late too late.*

Annabel stares, the electric knife dancing in her palm, and at last her lips open and she says "Where is she? What have you done with her? Where *is* she?"

BRING HER TO ME, says the voice in Kenneth's mind, and he can see it in the frozen mad look on her face, that she is hearing the same thing—the same, the same, the same—BRING HER TO ME.

He rushes past her. They search the room. They lift the mattress and throw it aside. They toss open the dresser drawers and paw wildly through. They crowbar open the closet and find it empty. They feel the heat of time, of the morning sun growing closer, of the dawn of the new and final day.

Kenneth and Annabel rush to the window and they look out and see nothing and then they keep looking and Annabel sees it first and then Kenneth does, too, or he thinks he does: two distant shadows, moving swiftly and getting smaller. Two shadows running so close beside each other they were almost one, slipping together into the narrow space between two towers, swallowed up by the buildings and disappearing into darkness.

• • •

Robert laughs as they run. He finds, indeed, that he cannot stop laughing. Pea is running beside him, and they are not holding hands, but every once in a while his right hand jostles against her left, and that mere touch, skin against skin, sends electric shivers coursing through his body. It isn't just that she's a girl, not just that it's Pea—it's…it's all of it, all of this wild chaotic joy. The jolt of triumph and liberation, the thrill of rebellion, the sheer power of life continuing on! In the morning will be the feast, the feast for everyone but them!

Light is beginning. The time is at hand. Robert looks at Pea, and he laughs, astonished. And she laughs back, astonished too. He watches her hair bounce on her back while they duck giggling through the alleyways, in search of what and where they do not yet know.

The voice speaks then, freezing the smile on Robert's face, clouding his heart. It speaks in his mind, clear and cold like a steel cage lowering.

BRING HER TO ME.

BRING HER TO ME.

BRING HER TO ME.

IN THE AIR

Hugh Howey

Gears whir; an escapement lets loose; wound springs explode a fraction of an inch, and a second hand lurches forward and slams to a stop. All these small violences erupt on John's wrist as the world counts down its final moments, one second at a time.

Less than five minutes. Just a few minutes more, and they would've made it to the exit. They would've been on back roads all the way to the cabin. John stares at the dwindling time and silently curses the fender bender in Nebraska that set them back. He curses himself for not leaving yesterday or in the middle of the night. But so much to do. The world was about to end. There was so much to do.

His wife Barbara whispers a question, but she has become background noise—much like the unseen interstate traffic whooshing by up the embankment. Huddled on the armrest between them, their nine-year-old daughter Emily wants to know why they're pulled off the road, says she doesn't need to pee. A tractor trailer zooms past, air brakes rattling like a machine gun, a warning for everyone to keep their heads down.

John turns in the driver's seat to survey the embankment. He has pulled off Interstate 80 and down the shoulder, but it doesn't feel far enough. There aren't any trees to hide behind. He tries to imagine what's coming but can't. He can't allow himself to believe it. And yet here he is, cranking up the Explorer, ignoring the pleas from the fucking auto-drive to take over and manually steering down the grass toward the concrete piling of a large billboard. The sign high above promises cheap gas and cigarettes. Five minutes. Five minutes, and they'd have made it to the exit. So close.

"Honey, what's going on?"

A glance at his wife. Emily clutches his shoulder as he hits a bump. He waited too long to tell them. It's one of those lies that dragged out and became heavier and heavier the farther he carried it. A tractor-pull lie. And now his wheels are spinning and spitting dirt and the seconds are ticking down.

He pulls the Explorer around the billboard and backs up until the bumper meets the concrete piling. Killing the ignition silences the annoying beeps from the auto-drive, the seatbelt sensors, the GPS warning that they're off the road. The world settles into a brief silence. All the violence is invisible, on a molecular level, the slamming of tiny gears and second hands in whirring watches and little machines swimming in bloodstreams.

"Something very bad is about to happen," John finally says. He turns to his wife, but it is the sight of his daughter that blurs his vision. Emily will be immune, he tells himself. The three of them will be immune. He has to believe this if he allows himself to believe the rest, if he allows himself to believe that it's coming. There is no time left for believing otherwise. A year of doubt, and here he is, that skeptic in the trenches who discovers his faith right as the mortars whistle down.

"You're scaring me," Barbara says.

"Is this where we're camping?" Emily asks, peering through the windshield and biting her lip in disappointment. The back of the Explorer is stuffed with enough gear to camp out for a month. As if that would be long enough.

John glances at his watch. Not long. Not long. He turns again and checks the interstate. It's hot and stuffy in the Explorer. Opening the sunroof, he looks for the words stuck deep in his throat. "I need you to get in the back," he tells Emily. "You need to put your seatbelt on, okay? And hold Mr. Bunny tight to your chest. Can you do that for me?"

His voice is shaky. John has seen war and murder. He has participated in plenty of both. But nothing can steel a mind for this. He releases the sunroof button and wipes his eyes. Overhead, the contrail of a passenger jet cuts the square of open blue in half. John shudders to think of what will become of that. There must be tens of thousands of people in the air. Millions of other people driving. Not that it matters. An indiscriminate end is rapidly approaching. All those invisible machines in bloodstreams, counting down the seconds.

"There's something I haven't told you," he tells his wife. He turns to her, sees the worry in her furrowed brow, and realizes that she is ready for any betrayal. She is ready to hear him say that he is married to another woman. That he is gay. That he murdered a prostitute and her body is curled up where the spare tire used to be. That he has been betting on sports, and the reason for the camping gear is that the bank has taken away their home. Barbara is ready for anything. John wishes any of these trivialities were true.

"I didn't tell you before now because…because I didn't believe it." He is stammering. He can debrief the president of the United States without missing a beat, but not this. In the backseat, Emily whispers something to Mr. Bunny. John swallows and continues: "I've been a part of something—" He shakes his head. "Something worse than usual. And now... that something is about to—" He glances at his watch. It's too late. She'll never get to hear it from him, not when it mattered, not before it was too late. She will have to watch.

He reaches over his shoulder and grabs his seatbelt. Buckles up. Glancing up at the passing jet, John says a prayer for those people up in the air. He is thankful that they'll be dead before they strike the earth. On the dashboard, there is a book with *The Order* embossed on the cover. In the reflection of the windshield, it looks vaguely like the word *redo*. If only.

"What have you done?" Barbara asks, and there's a deadness in her voice, a hollow. As if she knows the scope of the horrible things he could do.

John focuses on his watch. The second hand twitches, and the anointed hour strikes. He and his family should be outside Atlanta with the others, not on the side of the road in Iowa. They should be crowding underground with everyone else, the selected few, the survivors. But here they are, on the side of the road, cowering behind a billboard blinking with cheap gas prices, bracing for the end of the world.

For a long while, nothing happens.

Traffic whizzes by unseen; the contrail overhead grows longer; his wife waits for an answer.

The world is on autopilot, governed by the momentum of life, by humanity's great machinations, by all those gears in motion, spinning and spinning.

Emily asks if they can go now. She says she needs to pee.

John laughs. Deep in his chest and with a flood of relief. He feels that cool wave of euphoria like a nearby zing telling him that a bullet has passed, that it missed. He was wrong. *They* were wrong. The book, Tracy, all the others. The national convention in Atlanta is nothing more than a convention, one party's picking of a president, just what it was purported to be. There won't be generations of survivors living underground. His government didn't seed all of humanity with microscopic time bombs that will shut down their hosts at the appointed hour. John will now have to go camping with his family. And for weeks and weeks, Barbara will hound him over what this great secret was that made him pull off the interstate and act so strange—

A scream erupts from the backseat, shattering this eyeblink of relief, this last laugh. Ahead, a pickup truck has left the interstate at a sharp angle. A front tire bites the dirt and sends the truck flipping into the air. It goes into the frantic spins of a figure skater, doors flying open like graceful arms, bodies tumbling out lifeless, arms and legs spread, little black asterisks in the open air.

The truck hits in a shower of soil before lurching up again, dented and slower this time. There is motion in the rearview. A tractor trailer tumbles off the hardtop at ninety miles an hour. It is happening. It is really fucking happening. The end of the world.

John's heart stops for a moment. His lungs constrict as if he has stepped naked into a cold shower. But this is only the shock of awareness. The invisible machines striking down the rest of humanity are not alive in him. He isn't going to die, not in that precise moment, not at that anointed hour. His heart and lungs and body are inoculated.

Twelve billion others aren't so lucky.

• • •

Two Days Before

The ringtone is both melody and alarm. An old song, danced to in Milan, the composer unknown. It brings back the fragrance of her perfume and the guilt of a one-night stand.

John's palms are sweaty as he swipes the phone and accepts the call. He needs to change that fucking ringtone. Tracy is nothing more than a colleague. Nothing more. But it could've been Pavlov or Skinner who composed that tune, the way it drives him crazy in reflex.

"Hello?" He smiles at Barbara, who is washing dishes, hands covered in suds. It's Wednesday evening. Nothing unusual. Just a colleague calling after hours. Barbara turns and works the lipstick off the rim of a wine glass.

"Have you made up your mind?" Tracy asks. She sounds like a waitress who has returned to his table to find him staring dumbly at the menu, as if this should be simple, as if he should just have the daily special like she suggested half an hour ago.

"I'm sorry, you're breaking up," John lies. He steps out onto the porch and lets the screen door slam shut behind him. Strolling toward the garden, he startles the birds from the low feeder. The neighbor's cat glares at him for ruining dinner before slinking away. "That's better," he says, glancing back toward the house.

"Have you made up your mind?" Tracy asks again. She is asking the impossible. Upstairs on John's dresser, there is a book with instructions on what to do when the world comes to an end. John has spent the past year reading that book from cover to cover. Several times, in fact. The book is full of impossible things. Unbelievable things. No one who reads these things would believe them, not unless they'd seen the impossible before.

Ah, but Tracy has. She believes. And like a chance encounter in Milan—skin touching skin and sparking a great mistake—her brush with this leather book has spun John's life out of control. Whether the book proves false or not, it has already gotten him deeper than he would have liked.

"Our plane leaves tomorrow," he says. "For Atlanta." Technically, this is true. That plane will leave. John has learned from the best how to lie without lying.

A deep pull of air on the other end of the line. John can picture Tracy's lips, can see her elegant neck, can imagine her perfectly, can almost taste the salt on her skin. He needs to change that goddamn ringtone.

"We can guarantee your safety," Tracy says.

John laughs.

"Listen to me. I'm serious. We know what they put in you. Come to Colorado—"

"You mean New Moscow?"

"That's not funny."

"How well do you know these people?" John fights to keep his voice under control. He has looked into the group Tracy is working with. Some of them hold distinguished positions on agency watch lists, including a doctor who poses an actionable threat. John tells himself it won't matter, that they are too late to stop anything. And he believes this.

"I've known Professor Karpov for years," Tracy insists. "He believes me. He believes you. We're going to survive this thanks to you. And so I would damn well appreciate you being here."

"And my family?"

Tracy hesitates. "Of course. Them too. Tell me you'll be here, John. Hell, forget the tickets I sent and go to the airport right now. Buy new tickets. Don't wait until tomorrow."

John thinks of the two sets of tickets in the book upstairs. He lowers his voice to a whisper. "And tell Barbara what?"

There's a deep breath, a heavy sigh on the other end of the line.

"Lie to her. You're good at that."

• • •

The tractor trailer fills the rearview mirror. A bright silver grille looms large, tufts of grass spitting up from the great tires, furrows of soil loosened by yesterday's rain. Time seems to slow. The grille turns as if suddenly uninterested in the Explorer, and the long trailer behind the cab slews to the side, jackknifing. John yells for his family to hold on; he braces for impact. Ahead of him, several other cars are tumbling off the road.

The eighteen wheeler growls as it passes by. Its trailer misses the concrete pillar and catches the bumper of the Explorer. The world jerks violently. John's head bounces off his headrest as the Explorer is slammed aside like a geek shouldered by a jock in a hallway.

Mr. Bunny hits the dash. There's a yelp from Barbara and a screech from Emily. Ahead of them, the trailer flips and begins a catastrophic roll, the thin metal shell of the trailer tearing like tissue, countless brown packages catapulting into the air and spilling across the embankment.

Time speeds back up, and John can hear tires squealing, cars braking hard on the interstate, a noise like a flock of birds. It sounds like things are alive out there—still responding to the world—but John knows it's just automated safety features in action. It's the newer cars protecting themselves from the older cars. It's the world slamming to a stop like the second hand inside a watch.

Tracy had told him once that he would last five minutes out here on his own. Turning to check on his wife, John sees a van barreling through the grass toward her side of the car. He yells at Barbara and Emily to move, to get out, *get out*. Fighting for his seatbelt, he wonders if Tracy was wrong, if she had overestimated him.

Five minutes seems like an impossibly long time to live.

• • •

The Day Before

John likes to tell himself he's a hero. No, it isn't that he likes the telling, he just needs to hear it. He stands in front of the mirror as he has every morning of his adult life, and he whispers the words to himself:

"I am a hero."

There is no conviction. Conviction must be doled out at birth in some limited supply, because it has drained away from him over the years. Or perhaps the conviction was in his fatigues, which he no longer wears. Perhaps it was the pats on the back he used to get in the airport from complete strangers, the applause as the gate attendant allowed him and a few others to board first. Maybe that's where the conviction came from, because he hasn't felt it in a long while.

"I'm a hero," he used to whisper to himself, the words fogging the plexiglass mask of his clean-room suit, a letter laced with ricin tucked into an envelope and carefully sealed with a wet sponge. The address on the envelope is for an imam causing trouble in Istanbul—but maybe it kills an assistant instead of this imam. Maybe it kills his wife. Or a curious child.

"I'm a hero," he whispers, fumbling in that bulky suit, his empty mantra evaporating from his visor.

"I'm a hero," he used to think to himself as he spotted for his sniper. Calling out the klicks to target and the wind, making sure his shooter adjusts for humidity and altitude, he then watches what the bullet does. He tells himself this is necessary as a body sags to the earth. He pats a young man on the shoulder, pounding some of his conviction into another.

In the field, the lies come easy. Lying in bed the next week, at home, listening to his wife breathe, it's hard to imagine that he's the same person. That he helped kill a man. A woman. A family in a black car among a line of black cars. Sometimes the wrong person, the wrong car. These are things he keeps from his wife, and so the details do not seem to live with them. They belong to another. They are a man in Milan with a beautiful woman swinging in the mesmerizing light. They are two people kissing against a door, a room key dropped, happy throats laughing.

John peers at himself in the present, standing in the bathroom, full of wrinkles and regrets. He returns to the bedroom and finds Barbara packing her bags. One of her nice dresses lies flat on the bed, a necklace arranged on top—like a glamorous woman has just vanished. He steels himself to tell her, to tell her that she won't need that dress. This will lead to questions. It will lead to a speech that he has rehearsed ten thousand times, but never once out loud. For one more long minute, as he delays and says nothing, he can feel that they will go to Atlanta and he will do as he has been told. For one more minute, the cabin by the lake is no more than an ache, a dirty thought, a crazy dream. Tracy in Colorado has been forgotten. She may as well be in Milan. John thinks suddenly of other empty dresses. He comes close to confessing in that moment, comes close to telling his wife the truth.

There are so many truths to tell.

"Remember that time we had Emily treated for her lungs?" he wants to say. "Remember how the three of us sat in that medical chamber and held her hand and asked her to be brave? Because it was so tight in there, and Emily hates to be cooped up? Well, they were doing something to all three of us. Tiny machines were being let into our bloodstream to kill all the other machines in there. Good machines to kill the bad machines. That's what they were doing.

"We are all ticking time bombs," he would tell her, was about to tell her. "Every human alive is a ticking time bomb. Because this is the future of war, and the first person to act wins the whole game. And that's us. That's me. Killing like a bastard from a distance. Doing what they tell me. A payload is a payload. Invisible bullets all heading toward their targets, and none will miss. Everyone is going to die.

"But not us," he will say, because by now Barbara is always crying. That's how he pictures her, every time he rehearses this. She is cunning enough to understand at once that what he says is true. She is never shouting or slapping him, just crying out of sympathy for the soon-to-be dead. "Not us," he promises. "We are all taken care of. I took care of us, just like I always take care of us. We will live underground for the rest of our lives. You and Emily will go to sleep for a long time. We'll have to hold her hand, because it'll be an even smaller chamber that they put her in, but it'll all go by in a flash. Daddy will have to work with all the other daddies. But we'll be okay in the end. We'll all be okay in the end."

This is the final lie. This is the reason he never can tell her, won't tell her even now, will lie and say they're going camping instead, that she needs to pack something more comfortable. It is always here in his rehearsal that he chokes up and tells her what can never be true: "We'll be okay in the end."

And this is when he imagines Barbara nodding and wiping her eyes and pretending to believe him, because she always was the brave one.

• • •

John can see two figures in the van, their bodies slumped outward against the doors, looking like they'd fallen asleep. The van veers toward the Explorer. Emily is already scrambling between the seats to get in his lap as John fumbles with his seatbelt. Barbara has her door open. The van fills the frame. His wife is out and rolling as John kicks open his door. Mere seconds pass from the time the van leaves the interstate to him and Emily diving into the grass. Scrambling and crawling, a bang like lightning cracking down around them, the van and the Explorer tumbling like two wrestling bears.

John holds Emily and looks for Barbara. There. Hands clasped on the back of her head, looking up at the Explorer, camping gear tumbling out through busted glass and scattering. There's a screech and the sound of another wreck up on the highway before the world falls eerily silent. John listens for more danger heading their way. All he can hear is Emily panting. He can feel his daughter's breath against his neck.

"Those people," Barbara says, getting up. John hurries to his feet and helps her. Barbara has grass stains on both knees, is looking toward the van and the wreckage of the tractor trailer, obviously wants to assist them. A form slumps out of the van's passenger window. Barbara fumbles her phone from her pocket and starts dialing a number, probably 911.

"No one will answer," John says.

His wife looks at him blankly.

"They're gone," he says, avoiding the word *dead* for Emily's sake. Above him, a contrail lengthens merrily.

"There was a wreck—" His wife points her phone up the embankment toward the hidden hardtop and the now-silent traffic. John steadies her, but he can feel her tugging him up the slope, eager to help those in need.

"They're all gone," he says. "Everyone. Everyone we knew. Everyone is gone."

Barbara looks at him. Emily stares up at him. Wide eyes everywhere. "You knew..." his wife whispers, piecing together the sudden stop on the shoulder of the road and what happened after. "How did you know—?"

John is thinking about the Explorer. Their car is totaled. He'll have to get another. There's a vast selection nearby. "Wait here," he says. He hopes everything he packed can be salvaged. As he heads up the embankment, Barbara moves to come with him.

"Keep Emily down here," he tells her, and Barbara gradually understands. Emily doesn't need to see what lies up there on the interstate. As John trudges up the slick grass, he wonders how he expects his daughter to avoid seeing it, avoid seeing the world he helped to make.

• • •

One Year Before

Smoke curls from Tracy's cigarette as she paces the hotel room in Milan. John lies naked on top of the twisted sheets. The rush of hormones and the buzz of alcohol have passed, leaving him flushed with guilt and acutely aware of what he has done.

"You should move to Italy," Tracy says. She touches the holstered gun on the dresser but does not pick it up. Inhaling, she allows the smoke to drift off her tongue.

"You know I can't," John says. "Even if it weren't for my family...I have—"

"Work," Tracy interrupts. She waves her hand as if work were an inconsequential thing harped on by some inferior race. Even when the two of them had worked down the hall from each other in the Pentagon, neither had known what the other did. The confusion had only thickened since, but along with it the professional courtesy not to ask. John feels they both want to know, but tearing clothes off bodies is simpler than exposing hidden lives.

"I do sometimes think about running away from it all," John admits. He considers the project taking most of his time of late, a plan he can only glimpse from the edges, piecing together the odd tasks required of him, similar to how he susses out political intrigue by whom he is hired to remove and who is left alone.

"So why don't you?" Tracy asks.

John nearly blurts out the truth: *Because there won't be anywhere left to run.* Instead, he tells a different truth: "I guess I'm scared."

Tracy laughs as if it's a joke. She taps her cigarette and spills ash onto the carpet, opens one of the dresser drawers and runs her fingers across John's clothes. Before he can say something, she has opened the next drawer to discover the book.

"A Bible," she says, sounding surprised.

John doesn't correct her. He slides from the bed and approaches her from behind in order to get the book. Tracy glances at him in the mirror and blocks him, presses back against him, her bare skin cool against his. John can feel his hormones surge and his resistance flag. He forgets the book, even as Tracy begins flipping through it. She was always curious. It was trouble for them both.

"Looks more interesting than a Bible," she mutters, the cigarette bouncing between her lips. John holds her hips and presses himself against her. She complies by pressing back. "What is this?" she asks.

"It's a book about the end of the world," John says, kissing her neck. This is the same thing he told Barbara. John has come to think of the book as one of those paintings that blurs the closer you get to it. It is safe by being unbelievable. The hidden key to understanding it—knowing who wrote it—was all that needed keeping safe.

Pages are flipped, which fans smoke above their heads.

"A different Bible, then," Tracy says.

"A different Bible," John agrees.

After a few more pages, the cigarette is crushed out. Tracy pulls him back to the bed. Afterward, John sleeps and dreams a strange dream. He is laying Barbara into a crypt deep beneath the soil. There is a smaller coffin there. Emily is already buried, and it is a lie that they'll ever be unearthed. It is a lie that they'll be brought back to life. That's just to get him to go along. John will live on for hundreds of years, every day a torment of being without them, knowing that they are just as dead as the others.

John wakes from this dream once and is only dimly aware that the bedside light is on, smoke curling up toward the ceiling, fanned by the gentle turning of prophetic pages.

• • •

The cars are, for the most part, orderly. They sit quietly, most of them electric, only one or two idling and leaking exhaust. They are lined up behind one another as if at any moment the trouble ahead might clear and the traffic will surge forward. Brake lights shine red. Hazards blink. The cars seem alive. Their occupants are not.

John considers the sheer weight of the dead—not just around him on the highway, but an *entire world* of the dead. An entire world slaughtered by men in elected posts who think they know best. How many of those in these cars voted for this? More than half, John grimly thinks.

He tries to remind himself that this is what someone else would've done, some mad dictator or mountain hermit. Eventually. The technology would've trickled out—these machines invisible to the naked eye that are just as capable of killing as they are of healing. When fanatics in basements begin to tinker, the end is near enough in the minds of many. No exotic or radioactive materials to process. Instead, machines that are becoming rapidly affordable, machines that can lay down parts one atom at a time, machines that can build other machines, which build more machines. All it will take is one madman to program a batch that sniffs out people by their DNA, that sniffs them all out before *snuffing* them out.

John remembers his sophomore year of high school when he printed his first gun, how the plastic parts came out warm and slotted neatly together, how the printed metal spring locked into place, how the bullets chambered a little stiff with the first round and then better and better over time.

That was something he could understand, printing a weapon. This... this was the next generation's music. These were the kids on his lawn. He was one of their parents pulling the plug before anyone made too much trouble.

John picks out a black SUV in the eastbound lane. A gasser, a Lexus 500. He has always wanted to drive one of these.

Lifeless eyes watch him from either side as he approaches, heads slumped against the glass, blood trickling from noses and ears, just these rivulets of pain. John wipes his own nose and looks at his knuckle. Nothing. He is a ghost, a wandering spirit, an angel of vengeance.

There is a wreck farther ahead, a car on manual that had taken out a few others, the cars around it scattered as their autodrives had deftly avoided collision. He passes a van with a sticker on the back that shows a family holding hands. He does not look inside. A dog barks from a station wagon. John hesitates, veers from his path toward the SUV and goes over to open the door. The dog does not get out—just looks at him with its head cocked—but at least now it is free. It saddens John to think of how many pets just lost their owners. Like the people stranded up in the sky, there is so much he didn't consider. He heads to the SUV, feeling like he might be sick.

He tries the driver's door on the Lexus and finds it unlocked. A man with a loosened tie sits behind the wheel, blood dripping from his chin. The blood has missed his tie to stain the shirt. A glance in the back shows no baby seat to contend with. John feels a surge of relief. He unbuckles the man and slides him out and to the pavement.

He hasn't seen anything like this since Iran. It's like a chemical attack, these unwounded dead.

Memories from the field surge back, memories of politicians back when they were soldiers. He gets in and cranks the Lexus, and the whine of the starter reminds him that it's already running. The car has taken itself out of gear. John adjusts the rearview and begins to inch forward and back, working the wheel, until he's sideways in traffic. Once again, he pulls off the interstate and down the embankment.

He heads straight for the wreckage of the Explorer and the van and gets out. Before Barbara and Emily can get to him, he has already pushed the passenger of the van back through the window and has covered him with the sport coat folded up on the passenger seat of the Lexus. John opens the back of the SUV, and Barbara whispers something to Emily. The three of them begin rounding up their gear and luggage and placing it into the car. It is a scavenger hunt for Emily. A box of canned goods has spilled down the embankment, and as she picks up each can and places it into the basket made by clutching the hem of her dress, John feels how wrong all of this is. There is too much normal left in the air. Being alive feels unnatural, a violation. He watches a buzzard swing overhead and land with a final flap of its wings on the top of the billboard. The great black bird seems confused by the stillness. Unsure. Disbelieving its luck.

"Is this ours?" Emily asks. She holds up the small single sideband radio, the antenna unspooled into a tangle.

"Yes," John says. He tries to remember what he was thinking to pack the SSB, what sort of foolish hope had seized him. Barbara says nothing, just works to get everything into the new car. She brushes leaves of grass off her carry-on and nestles it into the Lexus. Her silence is louder than shouted questions. She used to do this when John came home with stitched-up wounds, saying nothing until John feels his skin burn and he has to tell her.

"I wasn't positive—" he begins. He stops as Emily runs over to dump the contents of her dress into the car. He waits until she has moved beyond earshot again. "Part of me hoped nothing would happen, that I'd never have to tell you."

"What happened on the highway?" his wife asks. She shows him her phone. "I can't get anyone…Dad won't—"

"Everyone is gone," John says. He repeats this mantra, the one he keeps rolling over and over in his head. "Everyone."

Barbara searches his face. John can feel twelve billion souls staring at him, daring him to make her understand. Even he doesn't understand.

Beyond the next exit, maybe the world is continuing along. But he knows this isn't true. Barbara looks at her phone. Her hand is shaking.

"There was no stopping it," John says. "Believe me."

"Who is left? Who can we call?"

"It's just us."

Barbara is silent. Emily returns and stacks cans between the luggage.

"This is because of what you do, isn't it?" Barbara asks. Emily has gone back for more.

John nods. Tears stream down Barbara's cheeks, and she begins to shake. John has seen widows like this, widows the moment they find out that's what they are. It is shock fading to acceptance. He wraps his arms around his wife, can't remember the last time he held her like this.

"Did you do this?" she asks. Her voice is shaking and muffled as he holds her tight.

"No. Not…not exactly. Not directly." He watches Emily delight in another find, far down the slope of grass.

"It's something you…" Barbara swallows and hunts for the words. ". . . that you went along with."

John can feel himself sag. He can't tell who is propping up whom. Yes, it was something he went along with. That's what he does. He goes along with. In Milan, succumbing to another, never leading. Never leading.

Emily arrives with something blue in her hands. "Is this ours?" she asks.

John pulls away from his wife. He looks down. It's the book. *The Order.* "No," he says. "That's nobody's. You can leave that here."

• • •

The Day Before

There are two envelopes nestled inside the blue book, two sets of plane tickets. John pulls them both out and studies them, angles them back and forth to watch the printed holograms catch the light. It is raining outside, the wind blowing fat drops against the bedroom window, a sound like fingers tapping to be let in.

He sets the tickets aside and flips through the large book at random. Tracy thought it was the Bible when she first saw it—by dint of it being in a hotel room drawer, no doubt. He thinks about the New Testament and how long people have been writing of the end of the world. Every generation thinks it will be the last. There is some sickness in man, some paranoid delusion, some grandiose morbidity that runs right through to distant ancestors. Or maybe it is the fear in lonely hearts that they might die without company.

John finds the section in the book on security. His future job detail. If he doesn't show, will they promote some other? Or will it mean extra shifts for someone else? John tries to imagine a group of people skipping through time to wait out the cleansing of the Earth. He tries to imagine kissing his wife goodbye as he lays her in a silver coffin. Kissing Emily and telling her it'll all be okay. One last lie to them both before he seals them up.

Because there's no mistaking their ultimate fate. John can feel it in his bones whenever he reads the book. He knows when a person has been doomed by politicians. He knows when they say "everything will be all right" that they mean the opposite. The book doesn't say, but it doesn't have to. Not everyone who goes into that bunker will come out alive. If he flies to Atlanta and does his job, he'll never spend another day with his wife and daughter. Tomorrow will be the last, no matter what, and it'll probably be spent in airports and in economy class.

He weighs the other tickets, the ones to Colorado Springs. Here is folly and madness, a group who thinks they can cheat the system, can survive on their own. Here is a woman who last year asked him to leave his life behind, his wife behind, and start anew someplace else. And now he is being asked again.

John holds the envelopes, one in each hand. It is usually another's life he weighs like this. Not his own. Not his family's. He doesn't want to believe a choice is necessary. Can't stand to think that Emily will never grow up and fall in love, never have kids of her own. Whatever life she has left, a day or years, wouldn't really be living.

He suddenly knows what he has to do. John slams the book shut and takes the tickets with him to the garage. Rummaging around, he finds the old Coleman stove. There's the lantern. The tent. He sniffs the old musky plastic and thinks of the last time they went on a vacation together. Years ago. What he wouldn't give for just one more day like that. One more day, even if it is their last.

He finds a canister and screws it onto the stove, adjusts the knob, presses the igniter. There's a loud click and the pop of gas catching. John watches the blue flames for a moment, remembers the horrible flapjacks he made on that stove years ago: burnt on the outside and raw in the middle. Emily loved them and has asked for her flapjacks like that ever since.

John sets both envelopes on the grill, right above the flames, before he can reconsider. It isn't a choice—it's a refusal to choose. He has seen too many folders with assignments in them, too many plane tickets with death on the other end. This is an assignment he can't take. Cheat death or run to the woman he cheated with. He can do neither.

The paper crackles, plastic melts, smoke fills the air and burns his lungs. John takes a deep breath and holds it. He can feel the little buggers inside him, waiting on tomorrow. He can feel the world winding down. Orange flames lick higher as John rummages through the camping gear, gathering a few things, practicing the lies he'll tell to Barbara.

• • •

He has only been to the cabin once before, eight years ago. Or has it been nine already? A friend of his from the service had bought the place for an escape, a place to get away when he wasn't deployed. The last time John spoke to Carlos, his friend had complained that the lakeshore was getting crowded with new construction. But standing on the back deck, John sees the same slice of paradise he remembers from a decade prior.

There is a path leading down to the boathouse. The small fishing boat hangs serenely in its water-stained sling. There are clumps of flowers along the path with wire fencing to protect them from the deer. John remembers waking up in the morning all those years ago to find several doe grazing. The venison and fish will never run out. They will soon teem, he supposes. John thinks of the market they passed in the last small town. There won't be anyone else to rummage through the canned goods. It will be a strange and quiet life, and he doesn't like to think of what Emily will do once he and Barbara are gone. There will be time enough to think on that.

The screen door slams as Emily goes back to help unload the Lexus. John wonders for a moment how many others chickened out, decided to stay put in their homes, are now making plans for quiet days. He looks out over the lake as a breeze shatters that mirror finish, and he wishes, briefly, that he'd invited a few others from the program to join him here.

He takes a deep breath and turns to go help unload the car, when a faint rumble overhead grows into a growl. He looks up and searches the sky—but he can't find the source. It sounds like thunder, but there isn't a cloud to be seen. The noise grows and grows until the silver underbelly of a passenger liner flashes above the treetops and rumbles out over the lake. Can't be more than a thousand feet up. The jet is eerily quiet. It disappears into the trees beyond the far bank.

There comes the crack of splitting wood and the bass thud of impact. John waits for the ball of fire and plume of smoke, but of course: the plane is bone dry. Probably overshot Kansas on its way north from Dallas. Thousands of planes would be gliding to earth, autopilots trying in vain to keep them level, engines having sputtered to a stop. The deck creaks as Barbara rushes to his side.

"Was that—?"

He takes her hand in his and watches the distant tree line where birds are stirring. It is strange to think that no one will investigate the crash, that the bodies will never be identified, never seen. Unless he wanders up there out of curiosity one day, or forgets as he tracks deer or a rabbit and then comes across pieces of fuselage. A long life flashes before him, one full of strange quietude and unspoken horrors. A better life than being buried with the rest, he tells himself. Better than crawling into a bunker outside of Atlanta with that blue book. Better than running to Tracy in Colorado and having to explain to Barbara, eventually, what took place in Milan.

The porch shudders from tiny, stomping feet. The screen door whacks shut. There is the sound of luggage thudding to the floor, and the porch falls still. John is watching the birds stir in the blue and cloudless sky. His nose itches, and he reaches to wipe it. Barbara sags against him, and John holds her up. They have this moment together, alive and unburied, a spot of blood on John's knuckle.

GOODNIGHT MOON

Annie Bellet

Neta Goodwin allowed the control box for the array she'd been working on to snap shut and brushed at the pervasive regolith coating her knees and rose carefully. It was impossible to keep the moon's fine powdery dust out of anything—worse than being on a beach. The surface of the Daedalus crater where the Far Side Array and the International Listening Base were located looked like dirty snow. It made Neta homesick for her and Paul's Montana farmhouse, the ridged powder of the moon reminding her of the way the snow scuffed and lumped as they tread paths all winter between houses and barns.

There would be no snow when she returned home in two weeks. It was late July, though Neta had to constantly remind herself of the date. Down in the Den—as she and the six other scientists had nicknamed their base—time had little meaning. Up here on the moon's surface, time had a different way of catching her off-guard. It was easy to spend uncounted minutes staring into the dark of space.

Which was exactly what she was doing now. Neta gave herself a little shake. She turned and waved to Anson Lefebvre to signal that they were finished and started the careful, bouncing walk back to the Den, the thin Frenchman following in her wake.

She stole glances at the sky and felt a familiar ache. She wanted to go home, yes, but she loved the moon. The low gravity that let her fifty-something bones rest more comfortably, the vast expanses, the dome of stars undimmed by human light. It took willpower not to tear off the tight, suffocating helmet and leap into the sky. She wished Lucita, her daughter, could share this. Last she'd heard though, her not-so-baby girl was studying art history at Berkeley.

That would be the best part of going home, she knew: the air. For nearly three months she hadn't taken a breath that someone else hadn't breathed first. The air in the Den wasn't much better than the canned air inside her suit. She missed wind.

The Den was dead silent by the time she and Anson finally made it through the locks, stowed the moon-walking equipment, and descended down the long ladder into the base. Usually there was music playing outside of the listening chambers, everything from David Bowie to Mozart to the Black-Eyed Peas rattling down the narrow hallway from the common room, which served as both galley and crew mess. The Den was laid out like a tree, with the main hallway acting as a narrow trunk that anchored the small, box-like rooms branching off of it.

Ray Fulke—one of her fellow Americans at the base—leaned his balding head out into the hall. "Anson, Neta, get down here." His voice sounded high and the tiny hairs on the back of Neta's neck prickled.

Neta and Anson exchanged a glance and went. Neta felt the same dread she'd had right before the phone had rung and told her that her nana was in hospital, that she needed to say goodbye. The common room smelled more heavily of sweat and coffee than usual, the anxiety in the air almost chewable.

Neta looked around the grim-faced room, everyone sitting with tablets in front of them. Shannon Delaney, from the EU like Anson and the only other woman on the base, looked about ready to cry, her thin shoulders shaking as she rocked slowly back and forth on the edge of her chair. Ray, too, looked near tears, his eyes puffy as though from lack of sleep. Jie Lin, a brilliant young astronomer from the China National Space Administration, was muttering in Mandarin and twitching through data on his tablet, his dark eyes fixed on the screen.

Neta sat down heavily next to Kirill Bagrov, an analyst from ROSCOSMOS. He was a big man, rawboned and friendly. Ray, Neta, and Kirill had all bonded by being the scientists over fifty, teasing the younger ones about the "good old days" of the space race. His gray eyes wouldn't meet Neta's brown ones, his big hands shuffling a mostly empty cup of coffee back and forth on the scuffed metal table.

"Well, since we're all here, I know no one has died, so someone spit it out. What could possibly have happened in the last six hours?" Neta spoke more sharply than she meant to, but the lack of eyes meeting her own and the tension scared her.

"We're all going to die," Graham Moretti said. His mohawk, which had been steadily growing out in the two months he'd been on the far side of the moon, looked as though he'd spent the last few hours running his sweating hands through it. He finally met Neta's eyes and all she saw in them was despair.

"What?" she said.

"That data, that weird interference we had for last week? Today we figure it out." Kirill lifted his cup and drained the last of his coffee. A few drops caught in his beard, like muddy tears.

Neta shivered and looked helplessly at Ray.

It was Shannon who spoke, however, "There's a dwarf planet heading for the moon. Or we're heading for it. However you slice it, we'll be in the way of it in less than forty hours."

"The array you fixed today, the one that got hit by debris last week, it confirmed the vectors and gave us enough of the picture," Ray added.

"*Merde*," Anson said. "Why did we not see this?"

"A perfect storm of events," Ray said. "The object is coming down perpendicular to the solar system's orbital plane. It has no atmosphere and is very dense. Plus it's summer and the object has passed over the sun, coming in at a right angle to Earth. Earth probably won't even see this thing until it's hours away from impact. With us."

"We only see because we have instrument pointing out, because we observe from off-planet, and we see too late." Kirill shook his head.

Neta took a deep breath. Her job wasn't to analyze data. She dealt strictly in things she could touch and manipulate. It was up to her to keep the arrays in working order, to clear dust and repair issues caused by incoming debris, radiation, and whatever else the solar system threw at them.

"So, basically, Pluto is heading straight at the moon?" Neta asked. "And we have no time to evacuate? What about the med-evac shuttle?" She twisted her hands together, willing herself not to panic, not to question. These were six of the smartest men and women she'd ever met. If they said something was about to happen, she trusted them.

"Not Pluto." Kirill's smile was small and grim. "*Bigger*."

"The med-evac can hold two," Shannon said. "We've been discussing that. We wanted to wait until you and Anson came back, didn't want to call you in until we were sure."

"*Three*," Anson said. "It is designed for two, yes, but we tested it with three. It will be an uncomfortable ride, but three of us could make it back to Earth."

"We have to go to the com station to warn them anyway," Ray said.

The communications station was to the north at the crown of the moon, between Meton B and C . The team generally sent two people, Jie and either Anson or Graham, twice a week to send out status reports and collect news from home. Supply and staff changeover shuttles only came every three months. There was a single shuttle kept in a special structure next to the tiny com base that could take two people back to Earth in the case of medical necessity. It was checked for repairs and refueled every six months. In the three years that the Far Side Array had been operating with staff, no one had ever needed to use it.

"Can we make it back to Earth before Pluto's bigger brother hits the moon?" Neta tried to keep her voice calm, to ignore the feeling of her stomach turning to ropes. The journey to and from Earth usually took about two days, sometimes a little less. It helped her to think about rational things, to fight the mounting panic as what the others were so rationally discussing started to sink in.

"If we leave in no more than three hours," Ray said.

Silence. Jie set his tablet down. Kirill's cup scraped on the table, back and forth, back and forth.

Unless she was chosen, she would never feel wind again. Never take a hot bath. Never kiss her husband's cheek when it was soft and fresh from shaving. Never see her Lucita graduate from college.

"No air," Neta gasped, her hands windmilling at the suddenly too small room. She tried to get up from her chair and bounced hard against the table. Arms caught her, Shannon's soft London accent murmuring soothing words. Someone pressed the cool metal edge of a cup to her lips and Neta made herself drink. The water was cold but stale, as the water there always was.

No water without the stale aftertaste of saline again. No drinking in the warm summer rain as the air crackled with the aftermath of a thunderstorm. She was going to die here, stuck deep beneath a barren, black and gray and white landscape that would never be home for all its lonely beauty.

Unless she was one of the three. Neta grasped at that grim, dangerous hope and choked down another drink of water.

"*Lo siento*," she said, then realized she'd reverted to her childhood tongue. "I'm all right." She pushed away from Shannon and crawled back into her chair.

"I did the same thing when we put it all together," Shannon said softly, patting Neta's knee before she rose and went back to her own seat. "Only with loads more screaming."

"So," Graham said. He looked around the semi-circle. "We discussed drawing straws. Anson? Neta?"

Three could go. Four would stay.

"Anson should go," Kirill said. He held up one of his large hands as Anson started to protest. "He knows most about the shuttle. He has flown it before."

"I can explain to someone else," Anson said. "It should be a fair process."

Neta choked back a laugh. Of course it should. They were men and women of science. They needed to find a way to handle this rationally. To make it as objective and fair as possible. Her chest hurt as her affection for these sometimes annoying, always brilliant, and often impossible people shoved its way through the anxiety.

"No, Anson should go," Ray said. "I'll take myself out of the draw."

"Ray, you can't!" Graham shook his head.

"What about Laney, Morgan, and James? Don't you deserve a chance to go back to your family?" Neta asked him. He had children, a spouse. Same as she did. How could he not take a chance to go home?

"My kids are grown. Laney and I have discussed that something could happen. That I might not come home."

So had Neta and Paul. She felt a twinge of guilt. She was one of the oldest here. Her daughter was in college, living on her own. Her husband knew the risks of letting his wife go live on the moon for months at a time. He'd been so proud of her.

"I, too," Kirill said. "I have no woman, no children. My parents are gone, God rest them. If you will take message for my sister, I will stay."

"So five of us will draw?" Graham asked, looking at Jie, then Neta, then Anson, and finally at Shannon. His gaze rested on Shannon and the young woman blushed. Shannon's arms unconsciously curled around her abdomen.

Graham and Shannon's unspoken exchange whipped the twinges of guilt inside Neta into a full assault. Neta and Shannon shared a tiny room, shared a bathroom. In such a small place, around each other all hours of the day and night, there were few secrets anyone could keep for long. She'd suspected Shannon was pregnant for a few weeks. Now though—now it mattered more.

"I'm out as long as Shannon is guaranteed a spot," Neta heard herself saying.

"But—" Anson started to say, then he looked at Shannon's blush and her posture.

"And I need to record messages," Neta added, though she had no idea what she would say to Paul. To Lucita. All she seemed to be able to say to her daughter these days were angry things.

Jie stood up. "I must send messages also, but I will stay," he said in his perfect, clipped English. "A baby should have parents."

Shannon was married, as was Graham. Not to each other. But living in such close quarters, both of them young and attractive, Neta didn't need a degree in sociology to see why they had gravitated into a relationship.

"Baby?" Kirill said. He looked at them all and then said, "Oh."

Shannon's blush deepened. She gave herself a little shake. "I'm not even sure I'm pregnant," she said. "I think I might be. I'm so sorry. I didn't think before, I mean..." She trailed off and looked at Graham.

"Graham is a bad boy of science," Anson said with an attempt at a grin.

"Mohawk, that tiger tattoo—who could resist?" Neta added with her own try at a smile, shoving away the whirlwind of thoughts. She was staying. Her, Jie, Kirill, and Ray. These would be the last people she'd ever talk to. The people she would die with.

"So, we agree? Anson, Shannon, and Graham will go?" Ray looked around.

Everyone agreed. No straws would be drawn. The faces around Neta showing different degrees of acceptance. Or shock. She wasn't sure what she was feeling and had no hope of reading those around her.

"Is one hour enough to record messages?" Graham asked. "We'll take whatever you guys want to send."

A plan finally decided, everyone moved at once, threading their way out of the common room and to wherever they could find the privacy to say last words to family and friends.

Neta went back to the tiny room she shared with Shannon. She pulled out her tablet and sat on the narrow, neatly-made bunk. Shannon's empty, unmade bunk stared back at her, pictures taped up to the thick plastic walls. She had slept in this box for months, but now it felt foreign, too small, too sterile. Not the place she had envisioned spending her last day alive.

Nothing felt real to her. Neta touched the slightly rough blanket, watched as her face appeared on the tablet and the app told her it was ready to record. Someone else's hand was touching the blanket. Someone else's face looked back at her. She looked so old, her brown skin too pale from lack of fresh air and real sunlight, her eyes dark, her face with more lines on it than she remembered.

If this was your last day on Earth, what would you do? What would you say? The old clichéd question rattled in her mind. Neta found herself laughing, the sound thin and hollow as it echoed around the tiny plastic and metal room.

She wasn't on Earth. The normal answers didn't apply. What would she say to Paul? To Lucita? What could she say in a final message? Certainly none of the things she was thinking.

She forced herself to calm down, to breathe deep that stale, recycled air, to try to look hopeful and composed. When the stranger's face on the tablet camera looked the way she wished, Neta touched *start* to record.

She said all the things she felt she was supposed to say. She told Paul she loved him. She talked about how much fun she'd had in Hawaii for their twenty-fifth anniversary and how she would cherish that week with him right to the end. She asked him to look after Lucita, their little light—and as she said it she imagined her daughter rolling her dark eyes. Lucita went by Lucy now, feeling Lucy Goodwin was a more American name, shoving away her mother's Puerto Rican roots as she came into her age of fierce independence.

She told Lucita to follow her joy, even if that joy wasn't in the sciences. She told her she was sorry they had argued so much and not to hold on to those memories. Neta called Lucita Lucy in her final goodbye to her, to Paul. It was her way of apologizing, of saying all the things she didn't feel strong enough to say aloud. She could only pray it was enough.

It was only at the end that she broke down a little, her eyes burning with tears she refused to show to the camera.

"Love her, Paul," she whispered. "Give our little light all the love I won't be there to give. And don't hang on to me. I want you both to live, to be happy."

She shut off the tablet after marking the file. She would be long gone before her family saw the video. NASA and the government would have to review everything, but she trusted they would let the message through. It was the best she could do.

Neta made her way back to the common room. Ray was there with Graham, both of them looking as though they'd aged a decade in the last hour.

Ray poured her a cup of tea and Neta stirred powdered milk into it, staring at the swirls as she worked up the courage to ask more questions.

"What happens after the moon and this rogue dwarf planet collide? How safe will Earth be? How safe will the coasts be?" She asked, thinking of her daughter in California.

Ray shook his head. It was Graham who answered her. "We aren't sure. We don't have the programs and time we'd need to model it. The moon will be knocked out of orbit. Or at least into a new one. Or it might break apart. And yes, there will be a hell of a debris storm back on Earth. They have atmosphere to protect them, but this could get bad."

"Bad?" Visions of Hollywood apocalypse movies churned through her brain and fear for her family wrapped freezing fingers around her ribcage.

"Well, it won't be good. The tides and weather might go haywire, but the moon is going to save the Earth. At least in the short run."

"True," Kirill said as he ducked into the common room. "Without moon getting in way, everything would *bchwhew*." He emphasized the exploding noise with a large gesture.

"I think we call it a 'global extinction event,'" Graham said.

"So we're lucky," Neta said. She glanced around the room and saw the confused stares. "I mean, 'We' as in the human race."

Ray nodded. "More or less. We should give our governments enough notice to move people out of low-laying areas and stuff like that. We've got a lot more man-power and computing power on Earth to deal with the fallout. I think we'll come out okay."

It went unsaid that all they could do was warn Earth and hope. That the four staying behind could do nothing at all.

The goodbyes were subdued. The four who were staying handed Anson their tablets containing their messages home and their data from the Array. There were no speeches. Tears were sniffled back or quickly wiped away. If anyone was panicking, they kept it deep inside.

Graham, Shannon, and Anson ascended the ladder for the last time, and Neta didn't stay to watch them go. She returned to the common room and drank the gritty dregs of her cold tea.

"What now?" Ray asked when he came back in.

Neta shrugged. "How long?" She didn't have to specify.

"Thirty-four hours-ish."

"Ish? And they call you a scientist." Neta smiled at him.

"I am going to bed," Kirill announced from the doorway.

Neta agreed. It was too long to wait, staring at blank walls. She returned to her bunk and tried to sleep. She turned fitfully; the light gravity that usually let her sleep with a comfortable weightlessness she never felt on Earth was instead a constant reminder that she was here, not home. Her mind gave her disaster scenarios, visions of the Earth's surface turning to giant, moon-barren craters and the seas churning and rising up, drowning her house. When she did sleep, she startled awake multiple times, thinking she'd heard Lucita calling for her.

Finally she gave up. Her little clock told her in bright green light that she had twenty hours left to live. Ish. Her mouth was thick with sleep-fuzz, and her nose caught the ghost of Paul's citrus-laced aftershave as her brain struggled to shake off her dreams.

No one was in the common room. Neta made soup, forced herself to drink it, and then washed out her metal bowl. She rested her fingers in the dish, remembering her plans for when she returned home. The tepid water gave her an idea.

Neta pulled on her moon-walking suit for one final time. She climbed up the ladder but did not go outside. Pluto's big brother would be visible to the naked eye now, from what Ray and the others had told her, but she didn't want to look that closely at death, no matter how impressive it might seem. Besides, she wasn't sure if it would bring debris with it, or if it would be safe to be out on the surface of the Daedalus crater.

Instead she went through to the big bay where they stored equipment for repairs and extra supplies for the Array—the items that didn't need as much radiation shielding. They didn't bother to keep this spares shed full of air. Neta searched the large NASA bins and found something that would work for her plan. She spent long sweaty minutes clearing out a barrel and hauling it to the ladder.

She dropped it down. On Earth, she wasn't even sure she could have moved the plastic and steel barrel. Here, it was awkward, but not impossible.

Scraping and hauling it through the narrow hallway brought Kirill and Ray out of their room.

"What are you doing with that?" Ray asked. What little hair he had was mussed from sleeping; it looked as though he'd been as restless as she.

"Taking a bath," Neta said. "It was something I planned to do first thing when I got home."

Kirill laughed, and even Ray was able to crack a smile. They helped her get the barrel down to the women's bathroom just past Neta and Shannon's room. It didn't quite fit in the tiny shower pan, so they left it just outside. Duct tape, some wires, a repurposed length of lab tubing, and a lot of swearing later, they had a way to fill the makeshift "tub."

"I don't know how clean this thing is," Ray said.

"What's it going to do, give me cancer?" Neta waved them both out of the bathroom. "Go away so I can bathe in peace."

The water was stale, and calling it tepid would've been generous, but she climbed into the barrel and sank down, curling her tired body up until only her nose and eyes were above the surface.

She half-floated and finally let herself feel the panic, the grief, the crushing weight of knowing she was going to die. She hung inside the barrel, her body wedged down in the water, and let herself breathe through the complete helplessness.

The tears that had been burning inside her eyes and throat all day broke free and were lost into the bath, her cries muffled by the water, her face washed clean even as she wept. She wanted to scream, to tear at her hair, to beg God or the universe or anything for a way to change her fate. Finally, exhausted, she just let herself cry until no more tears would come.

The water was cold and her fingers stiff and pruned when she finally climbed out. She dressed in clean clothing, pulled on a light blue sweater, and combed out her hair. She pulled out her small cache of pictures that she'd brought from home and went through them one last time, her wrinkled fingers tracing the lines of faces she loved and would never see again.

When her clock told her there were only a couple hours remaining, she pulled out the final item. Her nana's rosary, the turquoise and wood beads smooth and dark from years of praying. Neta couldn't bring herself to say the words aloud, so she touched the beads one by one as she mouthed the prayers. It felt weird to seek God now, when she'd devoted her life so thoroughly to science, but she had never turned her back on Him, only on the Church that she'd felt had no place in her modern life.

Neta set aside the pictures and tucked the rosary into her pocket. It couldn't hurt to pray now. She hoped the dying would be forgiven a little hypocrisy.

She found Kirill and Ray in the common room. They'd exchanged tea and coffee for vodka, judging from the empty bottles and the smell that greeted her as she sat at the table. The men were in the middle of a game of Gin Rummy.

"Where's Jie?" she asked.

Kirill and Ray froze. Kirill raised his cup and drained the vodka from it. Ray fidgeted with the cards in his hand.

"In his bunk," Ray said when Neta half-rose, intending to go look for Jie.

She sank back down. "Not joining us, is he?"

"He left early," Kirill said.

"Pills," Ray said. "Went to sleep and wanted to stay that way, I guess."

Suicide hadn't even crossed Neta's mind. She waited to feel anger or betrayal that the quiet young man would do that, would go without saying goodbye to her, to them, but she couldn't find it in her to blame him. He had faced death his way. She had to face it in her own.

"The others will be well clear of the moon now," Ray said.

"Going home," Neta said softly. She appreciated Ray's attempt to bring good news in the room.

"Vodka?" Kirill offered her the remaining bottle.

"You're a walking cliché, Kirill," she said with a smile.

"Some clichés are for reasons," he said, playing up his accent and waggling his bushy eyebrows at her.

He poured a generous measure into her tin cup and then picked up his cards again. Neta watched them play in silence, cupping the alcohol between her hands as though she were warming them, but didn't drink. It was strange, but she found she wanted to face the end sober, calm.

"I'm glad," she said, as Ray dealt her into a new game of Rummy. "I'm glad I'm not alone."

"I will drink to that," Ray said.

"I too," Kirill said.

The whole Den shook, a tremor like an earthquake rattling dishes and jouncing them well out of their chairs.

Neta left her cup after the shaking stopped and went to sit on the floor. Kirill and Ray joined her. They sat knee-to-knee in a tight circle as another tremor began. When she reached out her hands, Ray and Kirill took her cold fingers in their own warm ones.

"It's the middle of the night in Montana," she said. "I bet there is a warm wind coming from the Southeast. I wish I could tell Paul goodnight."

"Goodnight, Neta," Ray said, squeezing her hand.

"Goodnight, Ray," she said. "Goodnight, Kirill."

"I love you both," Kirill said with a hitch in his voice. "Goodnight."

As the Den shook, Neta closed her eyes and held on to their hands with all her strength forever.

DANCING WITH DEATH IN THE LAND OF NOD

Will McIntosh

Taking it slow so the ruts in the dirt drive didn't ruin his Mustang's suspension, Johnny cruised past the Lakeshore Drive-In's worn neon sign, past the faded and battered red and white ticket booth, into the big open field.

Dad was at the snack bar getting the popcorn popping, putting hot dogs in their aluminum sheaths for no one. It was a half hour before showtime, the sky halfway between blue and black, and there were no customers yet. Toward the end of the second feature, Johnny and his dad would end up eating dried-out hot dogs. He was *so sick* of hot dogs. Every night, Dad prepped the snack bar like they were going to have a full house, and every night, maybe half a dozen vehicles rolled through the gate.

Tonight they'd be lucky to get anyone. Everybody was glued to their TV sets, watching the news, scared shitless by the nodding virus. Johnny was scared shitless too, but he still had to drag his ass out to babysit his father.

Every time he took the hard right off Route Forty-Six and passed that old neon sign, it gave him a sick feeling of indigestion. When the Alzheimer's finally took his father, Johnny would inherit 11.27 acres of useless land, a snack bar refurbished to resemble a 1950s diner, a shiny new movie projector, and a shitload of frozen hot dogs. He would also inherit a sixty-six thousand dollar business loan at eight percent interest, the loan guaranteed by the house he'd lived in his entire life.

Kicking up dust as he pulled in, Johnny parked by the walk-up window. He slammed the Mustang's door, strode past old picnic benches squatting under a roof that extended from the squat building like the bill of a cap.

"Don't park there," Dad said as he set boxes of fresh popcorn beside the machine. "You don't want anything obscuring the customers' view of the snack bar. I read that on the internet."

"I'll move it when the movie starts."

Dad put his hands on his hips. "People buy half of their snacks *before* the movie starts."

Johnny wanted to point out that half the snacks they sold on an average night amounted to about twelve bucks' worth. It was on the tip of his tongue, but he let it go. At least his dad was making sense. When he'd dropped him off that afternoon, Dad had been sure it was nineteen seventy-six, and was contemplating decorating the drive-in to commemorate the nation's bicentennial.

"You watching the news?" Johnny asked. "The virus broke out in Wilkes-Barre. Something like two thousand people have it."

"Is that the swine flu? Or the bird one?"

Maybe Dad wasn't having such a good evening after all. "No, Pop. The new one, the nodding virus."

Dad took it in like it was the first time he'd heard about it. "How many dead?"

"Hard to say. It doesn't kill you, it paralyzes you. You can't move."

Johnny would be less scared of the virus if it killed you outright. The thought of being aware of what was going on, able to breathe, even eat if someone fed you, but not able to move…Johnny didn't even want to think about it.

"You remember seeing *Spaceballs* here?" Dad asked.

"I remember, Pop." Here we go, off on a ride down memory lane.

Johnny was so tired. So sick of giving up four nights a week for nothing. He spent all day walking on that greasy floor, listening to people's complaints about their fucking fish sandwiches while his back ached. He resented having to waste all his time off so his father could live out his dream and reminisce about how much better the world was when everyone loved to watch movies through their dirty windshields while mosquitoes ate them alive.

Dad looked at the big white screen. On the day he'd brought Johnny out here to tell him he had Alzheimer's—and that he was buying this beat-up drive-in as some sort of big carpe-diem fuck you to the universe—the screen had been peeling away in squares, exposing the rusting steel latticework underneath. Now it was bright white and flawless.

"The day after this place closed, the marquee out front said, 'The End. Thanks for thirty years.'" Dad shook his head. "It broke my heart, to think your kids would never get to go to the drive-in."

"Tiffany moved the kids to Baltimore before they were old enough to go to the drive-in," Johnny said, bitterness leaking into his tone. He wanted to go home, crawl under a blanket with a six of Pabst and watch porn until he fell asleep.

A truckload of teen-agers pulled through the gate. Johnny headed off to collect their admissions. If they were super-lucky, the kids would smoke some weed and get the munchies. They could sell some hot dogs for a change.

• • •

In the car on the way home, the radio played some Springsteen then gave way to the news. Johnny wasn't in the mood to hear any more about the outbreak, so he stabbed one of the preset buttons and caught a Charm City Devils song in progress.

The sound of their success only reminded him of his own faded rock star dreams. He turned the radio off.

Dad stared out the side window, watching the street lights pass like they were the most fascinating things in the world.

It was past time to put him in a home, but Johnny just couldn't bring himself to do it. He was having such a ball, running his drive-in. It was killing Johnny, though, getting home at one in the morning, then his alarm going off at six.

And the place was bleeding money.

"How much did we gross tonight? Forty-something dollars?" Johnny asked.

"Something like that."

Johnny waited for his dad to offer some excuse, some airy-fairy optimistic spin on the two of them working their asses off for forty-three bucks, minus utilities, minus the film rental fee, minus taxes, minus gas, minus five hundred and sixty-three dollars a month in interest on the loan.

"If this virus thing gets any worse, people will stop going to the indoor theaters, cause they'll be afraid of the germs. They'll start coming to the drive-in instead."

"The virus is in *Wilkes-Barre.* If it gets any worse, people will *have* it, and they won't be able to go anywhere." The thought sent an electric dread through Johnny. "Come on, Dad. We gave it a good try. It's just not working."

Even if he could convince his dad to sell the drive-in, who would buy it? Especially now. Maybe after the virus scare blew over he could at least get three thousand an acre for the land and pay off part of the loan. He'd have to use his savings to pay off the rest, which meant his new, post-rock star dream—opening up his own bar and grill—was never going to happen.

Johnny cruised to a stop at a red light at Aker Street, waiting, silently beseeching his father to see through the fog in his brain and agree it was time to put this business out of its misery.

"First movie I ever saw there was a monster flick. *Them*, it was called. Giant ants. I don't remember the second feature. They put real butter in the popcorn then."

Johnny felt like he needed to scream. "Yeah, yeah. Everything was great, back in the old days."

This time Dad caught the sarcasm. He looked at Johnny. "You know why I keep saying things were better back then? Because they were. That's the thing. Things really were better."

"I'll give you that, Dad. Back then, they gave you a pension. Health insurance. You got paid a decent salary. How much were you pulling down, your last year at the Goodyear plant? Fifty-five? That's seventeen grand more than I make *now*." Johnny slapped the steering wheel so hard his palm stung. He was forty-one years old, and even getting promoted to manager of Burger King was out of reach, because he didn't have a college degree. "'Would you like to get a large for only fifty cents more?' I'm so sick of saying that, Dad. You have no idea how sick I am of saying that."

Johnny took a deep breath. He shouldn't be talking to his dad like this, but he was tired and angry. And scared. "I'm sorry, Dad." He touched his Dad's shoulder. "You never raised your voice to me. Never once, the whole time I was growing up. I've got no right to raise my voice to you."

Around the curve, in front of the old brick schoolhouse—which was now a plumbing supply warehouse—red lights were flashing. Two police cars and an ambulance were parked beside a Taurus wrapped around a telephone pole.

Johnny slowed to a crawl as they passed. The driver was still in the car. "That's Arnie Marino. He works at the post office."

Paramedics were easing him out from behind the wheel. His nose was bloody, and it looked like he was resisting them, trying to stay in the car.

Johnny realized he wasn't fighting them, he was jerking, having a seizure.

"Poor bastard," Johnny said under his breath. He sped up, knowing if he watched any longer he'd look like a rubbernecker, not someone slowing down in the name of safety.

The poor guy. He'd been jerking like a puppet on strings, almost like—

Johnny missed their turn. His hands felt numb on the wheel, like blocks of wood.

Arnie Marino's head, especially, had been jerking up and down. Nodding.

Johnny took a big breath, tried to relax as he took the next left to double back around. It could have just been a seizure. Or there were other things that would look the same as the virus.

Of course there was also no reason to think it *wasn't* the nodding virus. It was out there, and it was still spreading. He glanced at his dad, but he seemed like he'd already forgotten the accident.

• • •

That evening, back at home, Johnny heard the sounds of sirens warbling and howling outside, some far away, some nearby. As they grew more persistent through the night, Johnny felt certain the virus must have hit their town.

He turned on the TV in his room, the screen taking forever to warm from black to an image of the CNN newsroom, where a blonde news anchor was talking beside a virtual map of the United States. There were at least fifty red dots glowing on the map. Most were in Florida, but a few ran up the coast, a few were out west, and there was a cluster nowhere near the rest, in Pennsylvania. One looked like it was right where Johnny was standing.

He turned the sound up until it was blaring, watched images of soldiers jumping from the backs of camouflage brown trucks, setting up roadblocks. Pulse pounding in his hands and feet, his tongue and his balls, he heard the word "quarantine," but had trouble understanding most of what came from the news anchor's red lips. Her words couldn't compete with the terror trumpeting in Johnny's head.

A bang on the front door made him jump. Johnny glanced at the clock (3:13 a.m.), pulled on sweats and headed downstairs.

Dad was up, looking bewildered.

"What's going on?" Dad asked.

"I don't know."

It was Kelly Cramer from across the street—Leon and Patty's daughter—who'd dropped out of community college and moved back home. Her breath was coming in big, frantic gasps. "My folks. I think—" She let the thought go. "Help me."

Johnny pushed on his sneakers without tying them and followed Kelly across the street as a voice in his head screamed, *This is not good.*

Leon and Patty were in bed, the blanket pulled up to their necks. Both were nodding, their chins rising and falling. Beneath the blanket their toes were trembling. Leon was making a choking, strangled sound.

The worst thing was their eyes. They were clear and focused, moist with fear, following Johnny as he moved.

Johnny's knees turned to jelly. "Call nine-one-one," he said, his lips numb.

"They said they can't do anything. There are too many. The hospital in Framington is full, and they can't move anyone out of the quarantined zone."

It couldn't be.

It could, though; of course it could. Wilkes-Barre was barely forty miles away.

"We need to get out of this room," Johnny said, backing up a step. "Out of this house."

"*Help them,*" Kelly said. "There's got to be something we can do."

Johnny took another step backward. Another. "You know there's not. We need to get out of here. *Right now.*" He took off down the stairs and outside, his loose sneakers slapping his heels, adrenaline pushing him to run faster.

When he reached his door and turned, Kelly was on her front lawn.

"I can't just leave them. What do I do?"

"It doesn't help them if we get it, too," Johnny said, holding the door half-open. He didn't want to be near Kelly, let alone her parents, but he felt bad closing the door in her face. She was only twenty-two or twenty-three, just a big kid, and she had nobody to help her. At least, he didn't think she did.

"Do you have any family nearby?" he called.

She pulled out her phone, hit a key and held it to her ear.

Johnny so wanted whatever aunt or grandparent she was calling to answer, but she just went on standing with the phone to her ear, her face streaked with tears, her long brown hair frizzy and tangled.

Finally, she let her hand drop. "No answer."

"Fill up your bathtub," someone called.

Johnny turned. Mrs. Mackery from next door was on her lawn in a bathrobe. It was a man's bathrobe, probably her late husband's.

"The radio said the power's bound to go out, so to fill your bathtub," Mrs. Mackery repeated.

Headlights appeared down the street, accompanied by a rumbling. An open-bed military truck came around the corner, soldiers in yellow hazmat suits riding in the back. Kelly ran to the edge of her lawn, waving frantically, both hands over her head, screaming at the top of her lungs for them to stop.

They blew right past. They barely looked at her.

Behind him, Johnny's screen door squealed open. He turned to find his dad, dressed in jeans and one of his old blue Goodyear work shirts, heading down the sidewalk carrying a brown bagged lunch. "I told you once already," he muttered. "I'm not gonna argue about it."

"Dad. Hang on." He jogged up the lawn, got his father turned around and led him back inside.

A few doors down a minivan was backing out of the Rosso's driveway.

"Look," Johnny called to Kelly and Mrs. Mackerey from his door, "I'm here if there's anything I can do to help." He looked at Kelly. "I'm sorry, though, I'm not going back in that house. I don't think you should, either."

Johnny closed and locked the door.

He passed Dad, who was peering out the back door, into the yard, his bottom lip working soundlessly. He'd stare out at the aluminum shed and the discarded tires for an hour if Johnny let him.

As if the solution to all his problems, the answer to the secrets of the universe, could be found in there, if only he looked hard enough.

Sometimes Johnny was sure his dad was looking into the overgrown weeds beyond the shed, trying to locate the stone that marked Buster's grave. When Buster no longer had the strength to stagger out into the yard to relieve himself, when he just lay curled up on the carpet whining, they'd taken him to the vet and had him put down.

• • •

By sunup there were twice as many dots on the CNN map. No one was allowed out of the infected areas.

"I'm sick of the news," Dad said, still in his Goodyear work clothes, the pants on backwards. Johnny wondered if he was going to have to start dressing his father. The thought made him a little sick.

"Put on something good," Dad persisted. "I want to watch *The Rockford Files*."

Jesus, Johnny had only the vaguest memory of *The Rockford Files*. He must have been five when it went off the air. He turned off the TV. "Come on Dad, we have to go to the grocery store." They needed more food; there was almost nothing in the house.

As soon as he hit the driveway, Kelly Cramer was out of her house, running toward them. "Can I come with you?"

Johnny motioned toward the Cramer's driveway. "You have a car." It came out harsher than he'd intended.

"I'm scared."

Scared of what, he wanted to ask. This was Ravine, not Philadelphia. There weren't going to be looters and gangs running wild among the six or seven stores that made up what passed for a downtown.

Kelly stopped a few paces short of them, folded her arms. "If you were going to get it, you'd probably have it already. It takes seven days for the symptoms to show up, so all the people getting sick now were exposed a week ago."

Johnny pictured the drive-in's few customers handing him money. Christ, Arnie Marino was a mail-sorter; if he'd gotten it, he'd spread it to all the mail.

Kelly was waiting, her eyes pleading with him.

Christ, when had he become such a dick? He'd known Kelly since she was a baby, and he was, what, sixteen? He'd seen her at a hundred neighborhood barbecues, almost hit her backing out of his driveway about twenty times. They'd never been anything like friends, probably because of the age difference. She'd been kind of a rebel back in high school—shaved head, shredded jeans, cigarettes. There was no sign of that side of her now—she was wearing cut-off denim shorts over purple leggings, her hair in a ponytail.

He put a hand on her shoulder. "Come on, get in."

• • •

Johnny cruised past Burger King just to make absolutely sure it was closed. He was scheduled to work the eleven to seven shift, but it was completely dark inside, as he'd suspected. He drove on down Route 60, which doubled as Main Street in Ravine. There was no mystery about how the town had gotten its name: it was set in a long, thin sliver of flat land, hugged on both sides by steep hills. If you were in Ravine, you could see both hills pretty much wherever you were.

People on the streets were hurrying along, heads down, many clutching handkerchiefs or hand towels to their faces.

"How are your folks?" Johnny asked. He knew how they were, but he didn't want Kelly to think he didn't care. He glanced over at her: she was fighting back tears.

"They're good people," Johnny said. "Your dad used to take me along to Penguins games up in Wilkes-Barre when I was in high school. You remember that?"

"If you were in high school, I was like, minus two years old." She wiped under her eyes with her knuckle.

"Oh, right. Duh." Sometimes he forgot he was almost forty-two years old. It just didn't seem possible.

He spotted the military vehicle that had passed them, parked in the parking lot of the firehouse, beside a big silver delivery truck.

Johnny pulled in. "Here we go. We can find out what's going on."

People in hazmat suits were carrying sacks and boxes to idling cars. Johnny watched as a hazmatted soldier dropped a sack and a small box in the back of an F-150 pickup. The truck took off.

Johnny popped his trunk, waited for someone to carry supplies over. He rolled down his window. "How long is the quarantine gonna last?"

The soldier came around to the window. He was a young guy, Asian. "Two weeks, at least."

Johnny jerked his thumb toward Kelly. "Her folks are sick. What is she supposed to do?"

"Feed them and keep them hydrated."

"And what if she gets sick, and I get sick? Who keeps *us* fed and hydrated?"

The solider looked left and right, like he was looking for help. "Look, I'm just handing out supplies. I don't have the answers. Listen to the radio."

How *could* they do it, Johnny wondered? Go house to house, carry out the infected and take them…where? To big tents? CNN said twenty-eight thousand people had gotten sick in Wilkes-Barre in two days. Those tents would need to be awfully big.

"There aren't enough hazmat suits, are there?" he asked the soldier. "Not enough doctors and nurses."

Johnny could barely hear the soldier's words through the faceplate: "There's nothing doctors can do for them."

• • •

Johnny spotted movement out the picture window: Kelly, wearing one of the white surgical masks from the survival kit they'd been given. He watched as she went three doors down, to the Baer's house, and knocked. When no one answered, she let herself in.

Ten minutes later she came out and went to the next house down. The Pointers lived there: old lady Pointer, always digging in her flower garden out front; her son Archie, who worked at the body shop; and Archie's kids, Mackenzie and Parker.

What the hell was Kelly doing? She wasn't the type to be ripping off her neighbors while they were in there dying. Whatever it was, she was all but guaranteeing she would catch the virus.

Cursing under his breath, Johnny pulled on his Steelers windbreaker and headed out. "I'll be right back, Pop."

"We gotta leave by three, don't forget."

Clutching the doorknob, Johnny opened his mouth to tell his father that people were dying, that no one was going to the frickin' movies. He didn't, though.

"I won't, Dad." He closed the door and headed toward the Pointer's house.

For once, Johnny wanted to go to the drive-in. Not just to escape the nightmare unfolding in his town for a few hours, but because it was the only place his dad seemed like himself. It was the only thing keeping his dad going.

The Pointers' front door was ajar. Johnny knocked, called, "Hello?"

"In here."

Hands in his pockets, feeling like he was surrounded by the virus, Johnny followed her voice down a hallway covered in water fowl-patterned wallpaper, into the Pointer's living room.

The four of them were sitting on couches and stuffed chairs, hands in their laps, all perfectly still except for Parker, whose lips were wrapped around a straw, sucking greedily from a water bottle Kelly was holding, his throat pulsing as he swallowed. The TV was on, showing some Pixar flick. Wet stains bloomed on the couch cushions beneath each of the Pointers. The smell of piss was overpowering.

"Jesus, what are you doing?" Johnny asked.

Kelly held out a mask. Johnny took it, pulled it over his mouth and nose. It was one of those little plastic jobs you wore when you mowed the lawn, probably not worth shit against a virus that the news described as incredibly resistant, able to survive on surfaces for days.

"What are you doing?" Johnny repeated. "The more houses you go into, the more likely you are to catch this thing."

She shrugged. "My folks have it. I know I've been exposed."

"No, you don't. You don't know that for sure." Johnny did not want her words to be true, for his sake as well as hers. "You're dancing with death, coming in here."

Kelly chuckled. "Dancing with death. That's poetic."

Actually, it was a line from one of his band's songs, but after saying it out loud he was too embarrassed to admit he'd just quoted his own band's lyrics.

Kelly wiped Parker's chin with a kitchen towel she had hooked through her belt. "I kept thinking about Mackenzie and Parker. I babysit them sometimes. I kept picturing them in their rooms, all alone, scared to death. Not able to move. Hungry. So I came to check on them. Parker was just like I pictured him—all alone in his room. Probably since yesterday."

"You *touched* him? Jesus."

Kelly put her hands on her hips. "He can *hear* you, you know. So can his mom and dad."

"Sorry," Johnny muttered. They were looking at him; all four of them.

Kelly squatted in front of Lara Pointer, guided the straw into her mouth. Immediately, Lara began pulling on the straw, her mouth suddenly animated, looking completely normal. The news had described how the virus keeps people from *initiating* movement, but not from reacting; seeing it, however, was another thing completely. If she could drink, why couldn't she talk?

When she'd finished, Kelly went to the Pointer's sink and refilled the big plastic water bottle before heading for the door. Johnny followed her out, closing the door behind him.

Instead of turning right, back toward her house, Kelly headed left across the lawn.

"Where are you going now?" Johnny called after her.

"When's the last time you saw the Cucuzzas?"

"What are you gonna do, go door to door?"

She stopped, turned to face him. "I don't know. Maybe."

"You're out of your mind. It's like you want to die—"

She held up both hands to ward off his words and shouted, "They're all alone. They're scared. Can't you see it in their eyes?"

He stood on the Pointer's front stoop, not wanting to think about their eyes.

"Can't you?" Kelly asked.

"Yeah. I can see it." He would see it for the rest of his life. And, God, he didn't want to go through it. Johnny looked at his watch. "Look, I have to take my father to his drive-in, or he'll try to drive himself. Will you be okay?"

"No," she said, like it was the dumbest question she'd ever been asked. "Will you?"

"No," he admitted. "I guess not."

A pickup cruised by. They both watched it in silence. There were fewer vehicles passing every hour.

"They're saying three percent of people seem to be immune to the virus. Did you hear that?" Kelly said.

"I don't love those odds."

"No, they suck bad."

It was a chance, though. There was hope.

"Neither of us has it yet, and lots of other people do. Maybe that means something," he said.

Kelly nodded. "Maybe it does."

Johnny had a sudden urge to give Kelly a hug, but he was afraid it would be awkward, or Kelly would think he was weird. "I'll check on you in the morning," he said. "That okay?"

She nodded. "Thank you."

• • •

Back at the drive-in, Johnny was terrified he was going to start nodding at any minute. He was actually glad to have something to do to take his mind off it, even if it was filling popcorn boxes for no one.

He wondered what it felt like, to be trapped in your frozen body. Were you numb?

If he was going to die, he wanted to feel a terrible pain in his chest and be dead before he hit the ground. He didn't want to have days and days where he knew he was dying. That was when you took stock, when you had nothing to do but think about your past, and he didn't want to think about what a waste his life had been to this point.

He'd always thought he was just slow getting started, that he'd leave Ravine and Burger King for bigger things. His first plan had been to hit it big with the band, then it was opening his bar and grill. His savings, the house, a little inheritance money was the kickstart he'd been counting on for the past decade or so, except, *surprise*: his Dad had his own dreams, even at seventy-one and diagnosed with Alzheimer's.

Dad was staring out at the big white screen through the window, his hands in his back pockets, smiling.

"You'll see," he said. "Wait and see."

No one showed up. Not one car. Johnny would have choked on his Coke if a vehicle had pulled through that gate with this hell-virus crawling through their town. The marquee said they were showing *Green Lantern* tonight, but Johnny went back to the claustrophobic little office next to the restroom and pulled the reels for *Ghostbusters* out of a pile of old films his dad had bought on Ebay a month before they opened. He didn't think he could sit through *GL* again, but a comedy, especially an old, actually funny comedy, fit the bill.

Johnny sat in his Mustang while Pop manned the snack bar.

• • •

At 7 a.m., Johnny spotted Kelly loading containers of water into her trunk. He set his coffee mug on the kitchen counter and slipped on his sneakers. He'd promised to check on her, after all.

"I should start calling you Florence Nightengale."

Kelly smiled, but it was the smile of a Burger King cashier toward the end of a shift. She looked exhausted; there was a sheen of sweat on her face, as if she hadn't washed up in a while.

"You were studying to be a nurse, weren't you?"

"For a little while."

"Why'd you stop?"

She shrugged. "Because I was too stupid. Couldn't pass the biology courses."

Johnny cringed, wishing he hadn't brought it up. He wasn't sure what to say. "Shit, that sucks. You seem like a natural."

Again, she attempted a smile. "Thanks."

"You're really going door to door?"

Kelly pushed her hair out of her face. "If you get it and I don't, you'll be happy to see me and my water bottle."

Johnny raised his hands. "I'm not criticizing. I'm just worried about you."

That made her smile. "It's nice to know someone is."

He watched, arms folded, as she slid into her dad's SUV.

Maybe he should be going with her. If he made it through this, for the rest of his life people would ask what it was like, what he'd done. It would be nice to be able to say he worked tirelessly to help people, that he hauled water and fed his friends and neighbors, and even strangers. And if he didn't make it through this, maybe God would look more favorably on a man who wasn't there for his kids if that man had died helping other people's kids.

Kelly was putting the SUV in drive. Johnny raised his hand, jogged down the driveway. "Hang on." She braked, rolled down the window, her eyebrows raised. He ran around and hopped in the other side. "Let's go."

Kelly smiled brightly. "When this is over, I swear, I'm gonna buy you a steak dinner."

• • •

As soon as Johnny set the spoon of farina—or whatever this gruel was the soldier had given them—on the kid's tongue, his mouth closed around it. Johnny drew the spoon out as the kid chewed and swallowed. He didn't know the boy, who was about ten, the same age as his son Danny.

Johnny tried to ignore the stale urine smell, the wet crotch of the kid's pants. It would take too long to change all these people; they had to focus on keeping them alive. Johnny was both relieved and sorry for that.

The boy watched him, watched Johnny's face instead of the spoon, and Johnny couldn't help thinking the kid was as desperate to have someone look at him, to have someone notice him, as he was for the food.

"I know. It breaks your heart," Kelly said.

Johnny glanced at her, not sure what she was talking about. A tear plopped onto his forearm, and he realized he was crying, and when he realized it, it was like something inside him burst open, and he was sobbing.

Kelly gave him a hug, patted his back. It felt good—safe, warm—to be in her arms. "I cried all day yesterday. Eventually you run out of tears, and all you've got is a big lump in your throat."

The lights went out; the picture on the TV contracted to a dot and vanished.

"Shit," Kelly said.

Something in the boy's eyes told Johnny the TV had been a huge comfort to him, that he'd be so much more terrified with nothing for company but his frozen family.

• • •

"Come on in," Kelly called when Johnny knocked. As he climbed the stairs he heard her speaking softly.

"I'll check on you at lunchtime. Try not to worry; everything's going to be okay. Help is coming."

He paused as he passed Kelly's room. She had a billion CDs, a big Union Jack for a bedspread, a Black Sabbath poster on the wall, and a long shelf up near the ceiling crammed with hundreds of Beanie Babies.

Johnny nearly shrieked when he found Kelly's parents standing in the middle of their bedroom.

"Jeeze," he breathed.

Kelly, in a Luzurne County Community College t-shirt and jeans, was brushing her mother's hair. "I figure they'll feel better if I stand them up once in a while, exercise their muscles a little. Can you help me?"

Johnny hurried over to help ease Kelly's mother back into a chair.

"I didn't realize they could stand," he said. They stayed in pretty much any position you placed them in, but he'd figured standing would take too much coordination.

"They can. You ready to go?"

Johnny followed her out, steeling himself for another day of playing Florence Nightengale's sidekick.

They started with the first house on the left on Princess Lane. When they knocked, an upstairs window creaked open.

"What do you want?" it was a woman, Johnny's age or a little older.

"We're checking for people who need help," Kelly said. "Anyone around here that you know of?"

"I haven't gone out." They turned to go. "If you were smart, you'd stay in your house, too."

"Somebody's got to help these people," Johnny shot back, self-righteous anger rising in him. As they headed back to the van it occurred to him that two days earlier he'd been that woman. If he hadn't seen Kelly loading water into her van, he'd still be that woman.

Watching Kelly walk beside him out of the corner of his eye, Johnny wondered what it was about her that made her different from all the people hiding in their houses, worrying only about themselves. It was like discovering there'd been a saint living across the street from him all these years, a saint with a shaved head, smoking a cigarette.

"So what happened to the shaved head and the combat boots?" he asked as they slammed their doors closed with a double *thunk*.

Kelly studied his face. "You thought I was a joke, is that what you're saying?"

"No," he laughed. "I thought it was great. There's not enough shock and awe in Ravine." He tapped her knee. "Come on, I'm in a band. Or I was, until all the other guys moved away. I live for rebellion."

"You live for rebellion because you played covers of Tom Petty and Korn at the fire station's social club?"

"Hey! We played in bars in Wilkes-Barre and Binghamton. And we played a lot of our own stuff."

Johnny pulled up to a house that looked too quiet. He opened his door, then noticed Kelly was staying in her seat.

"What?"

"Remember when you asked why I left nursing school? I didn't flunk out. I chickened out." She propped a foot on the dash. "I got homesick and came running home to my old room and my Beanie Baby collection."

Johnny nodded. He was afraid anything he said would trivialize what she was telling him.

Kelly tilted her head back, looked up at the SUV's ceiling, her brown hair sliding down her shoulders. "I always hated this town. It's not even a town, it's just a few houses and lame stores strung out in an ass crack. I was always talking about how I was going to get out of here as soon as I could. And I did, but then I came right back with my tail between my legs."

Johnny shook his head. "I never even tried to leave. When I was in the Ravine Raiders, we always talked about how we were going to hit it big. We drank beer, were rock stars in our own minds, then we got married, had kids, and I found myself at Burger King. This town has a way of sucking you in and hanging on to you."

It was strange: this suddenly felt like a date that was going better than any of Johnny's actual dates ever did. Maybe it was their fear, stripping away all the pretense, but Johnny didn't think that was all of it.

He put his hand on his head. "Wait, what does this have to do with you letting your hair grow out?"

Kelly smiled. "When I moved back home, I imagined having a kid one day, and that kid seeing a picture of me and saying, 'Mom, you were one of those edgy rebellious kids when you were my age?' And I would have had to answer, 'No, I just dressed like one'."

• • •

The army vehicle was gone. So was the delivery truck full of grain, and the tanker truck of water.

Kelly called the national emergency information number. The woman on the other end told Kelly they were spread too thin, that the Interstates had been shut down to slow the virus. She told Kelly to use a lake or pond, and boil the water before drinking it. Kelly suggested the woman boil her ass, then disconnected, and completely lost it. She pressed her hands over her ears and wailed, her face bright red.

Johnny held her and patted her back, shushing. He told her they'd be okay, and other comforting things he didn't believe.

"What do they expect us to do with all of these people, without food, without doctors?" Kelly asked, drawing back into her seat.

"I think they expect us to let them die." Johnny watched as another vehicle slowed in front of the empty parking lot, then drove off. "That's why the soldiers left. It's spread too far; we can't take care of this many people, so they want them to die." Johnny rubbed his eyes. He was so tired they were burning all around the edges. His head had this dull achy feeling that wasn't quite pain, but was still unpleasant. Another couple of hours and he'd take his father to the drive-in. It was *Stripes* tonight. With each day that passed, Dad was more out of it. Most of the time Johnny felt like he was alone at the drive-in.

"Why don't you come out to the drive-in tonight? You need to rest or you're going to—" he was going to say *get sick*, but he bit back the words.

"How are you even showing movies, with the power out?" Kelly asked, wiping her nose on her sleeve.

"The place came with an old generator. Power outages are a great time to sell tickets, because no one has anything else to do."

Kelly laughed dryly. "Assuming people can move."

"Right." If they could move, Johnny would invite everyone to come out and watch *Stripes* for free, and for one night his Dad would think his goddamned drive-in was a success.

He sat up ramrod straight in his seat. "Wait. I just got an idea."

• • •

A plume of dust followed the Ford Taurus as Johnny cruised along the drive-in's back aisle, to the very last spot. He swung the Taurus into the spot, the front rising on the hump until the screen was framed inside the windshield. He turned off the engine, then twisted to look at the car's four passengers. It was an older couple, in their seventies, and two kids, two girls. Grandparents raising their grandchildren, maybe. Or maybe the girls had just been visiting. It smelled bad in the car—really bad—but Johnny smiled and tried to ignore it. "I'll be back with food and Cokes later. As soon as the sun goes down we'll start the first show." He looked at his watch. "That's about an hour from now. I hope you enjoy the movies."

Kelly was waiting in the aisle. "That's it." She pressed her fists into the small of her back. "God, my back is killing me."

How many people had they carried to their cars? Too many to count. On the tail end of three endless days of feeding people, Johnny was so exhausted he'd traveled beyond tired, into a manic, hungover netherworld.

There was just one last trip to make.

• • •

"*Holy shit*," Johnny's dad shouted when they pulled into the drive-in. "Holy, holy shit. *It's packed*!" He looked at Johnny, and for the first time in days Johnny was sure his dad knew who he was. "I told you. Didn't I tell you? It's catching on."

"You told me, Pop." He caught Kelly's eye in the rear view mirror, and they exchanged a smile. "I didn't believe you, but you were right." Johnny pulled up in front of the snack bar. He felt like laughing and crying at the same time. "Kelly and I are going to run concession orders right to the cars. People don't want to get out, on account of the virus going around."

"Oh, okay," Dad said. "Smart idea."

Johnny led him into the snack bar, where they had a hundred boxes of popcorn lined up and ready to go, dozens of hot dogs turning on spits in the warmer. His dad's steps were so tiny, so tentative. When had he lost that broad, assured stride Johnny had known since he was a kid?

They kicked things off with *E.T.* Kelly started feeding people in the front row, Johnny in the back, figuring they'd meet in the middle.

They hadn't had the time or space to bring all of the afflicted to the drive-in. Ninety percent of the town had it now. But they'd done what they could.

Heading back to the snack bar for another armload, he passed Kelly. She looked exhausted, but there was a fire in her eyes as she smiled at him.

"Can I ask you something?" Johnny said.

Kelly paused, swept her hair out of her eyes.

"If things ever get back to normal—" he paused, realizing how inappropriate his words sounded as they stood surrounded by people suffering from a horrible disease.

But Kelly smiled. "If things ever get back to normal, yes." She headed off toward the cars.

Johnny turned, imagining the two of them sitting together at the Outback Steakhouse in Pine Grove, and for a moment he felt light, and hopeful.

As Dad filled him up with a tray of Cokes, popcorn, Snickers and Milky Way bars, ice cream and hot dogs, Johnny could see the confusion was back, but Dad was smiling, and whistling.

A little before three a.m., Johnny's dad dozed off on his stool behind the snack bar. Johnny loaded him in the Mustang and took him home, then turned right around and headed back to the drive-in. They showed movies until the sun came up, then left all those poor people sitting in their cars and went home to get a few hours' sleep.

• • •

"*Holy shit. This is unbelievable,*" Johnny's dad cried.

If his mind had been clearer, he might have noticed they were the same vehicles, in the same spots as the previous three nights. "*Another* full house!" He patted Johnny's thigh.

Kelly was already there, stirring huge pots of "kitchen-sink soup" over open fires, a waist-high pile of discarded soup and vegetable cans behind her. It had taken them six hours to gather the cans from people's cupboards, another to open them all.

An hour into the night's feeding and watering, Johnny and Kelly paused in the second aisle, out of his dad's earshot.

"What are we going to do tomorrow?" Johnny asked. Most of the fresh food in town had turned. The nearest grocery store was outside the quarantine.

"Did you try the Red Cross?" Kelly said.

"Yeah. They aren't allowed into the quarantined areas." Calls to the authorities had resulted in awkward explanations about limited emergency response resources, and shock and consternation when Johnny explained how many victims they were trying to keep alive. He'd been right: the plan was to let most of the victims to die off.

"I guess it's whatever we have left, then."

Johnny didn't ask what they'd do after that. According to the radio, the virus was still spreading. There were infected zones from Pittsburgh to Philadelphia. It didn't look like the quarantine would be lifted any time soon.

On the drive home, Johnny's dad wet his pants. He didn't seem to notice; he just went on muttering something about a cold can of Pabst and a mad, mad world. There'd been a movie called *It's a Mad, Mad World.* Johnny had seen it when he was a kid. Maybe his dad was watching it in his head.

• • •

"Dad, *look*—another sellout crowd." Johnny tapped Dad on the shoulder.

"What?" Dad looked around as if waking from a dream. "A what? Oh. Right." He laughed. "That's good. What are we showing?"

"*Spaceballs*."

"Oh yeah? Is it any good?"

"It's hilarious," Kelly said from the back seat. Her nose was plugged from crying, but she kept her tone bright.

There was nothing for his dad to do—not a crust of frozen pizza left in the snack bar. They sat him in a lawn chair in the front row. It was a perfect drive-in night: just a nip of crisp fall in the air, the leaves on the trees beyond the screen whispering on a light breeze.

As soon as the movie started playing, Johnny and Kelly hoisted the big roll of plastic pool vacuum hose out of his trunk, set it on one of the picnic tables under the eave outside the snack bar. Johnny measured out six or seven feet of hose, cut it with a hack saw, repeated the process until they had several dozen lengths of hose.

They both carried several cut hoses and a roll of masking tape, heading toward the back row, arm in arm and crying. They would have to start in the back and work their way forward. They didn't want people to see what they were doing.

He set the hose on the trunk of the first car in the row, went to the driver's side door. Wiping his eyes, Johnny took a few big, huffing breaths, then forced a big smile and ducked into the car.

"How are you folks doing? Enjoying the movie?" One of the people in the back was Mr. Liebert, who'd taught him algebra in the tenth grade, all those years ago. Johnny reached over, turned on the ignition. "I'm gonna turn on the heat so you stay warm. It's supposed to be a cold night. Cokes and popcorn are on the way in a few." Using the buttons on the door, he lowered the back, driver's side window a few inches. Feeling that he was about to lose it, he ducked out of the car.

Choking back sobs, he pulled the hose off the trunk, pushed one end over the car's exhaust pipe and taped it into place. He slid the other end through the crack in the back window, and moved on.

Kelly was crumpled over the back of the next car, her face in her hands, her shoulders bobbing. She'd already set the hose in place. When Johnny put a hand on her back, she spun, hugged him with all of her might.

"This is the right thing to do, isn't it?"

"I think so. Not the easy thing, but the right thing," Johnny said. "Isn't it what you'd want?"

Kelly nodded, eased out of his embrace. "It is."

Johnny opened the door on the SUV next in line, smiled big, knowing his eyes were red, his face tearstained. "Hi folks. Let me turn on the heat for you; it's going to be a chilly night."

They sat on the picnic table and let the cars in the back row idle for half an hour, then moved on to the next row. Johnny's first love, Carla Meyer, was in a Honda Civic in that row, with Chris Walsh, the man she'd married, and their teenage daughter.

It got easier by the third row. Not easy, but Johnny didn't feel quite so much like he was carrying an anvil on his shoulders while someone punched him in the stomach.

They took a water break at the picnic table as the vehicles in the fourth row idled. Two more to go.

"Could we go to jail for this?" Kelly asked.

"I dare them to try. There should be doctors and nurses here with IV bags and truckloads of food."

Kelly nodded.

The bodies would be in his drive-in. When the authorities investigated—and Johnny guessed when the dust settled they probably would—he would leave Kelly's name out of it.

"If I have any say in it, they'll build a statue of you in front of Town Hall," he went on. "What you've done over the past week…" Johnny shook his head. "Mother Teresa couldn't have done more. You're a remarkable person, Kelly. I can't tell you how much I admire you, how much you've changed me."

Kelly went on nodding.

"Kelly, cut that out. You're scaring the hell out of me."

"Cut what—" And then she realized what she was doing, and Johnny could see her try to stop as her eyes flew wide and she went on nodding. She held up her hands and looked at them. They were trembling like an electrical charge was running through her. "Oh, God. No, no, no, no."

But her head kept nodding, *yes*.

Between ragged, terrified breaths, she said, "Don't you dare chicken out, Johnny. Don't you dare."

• • •

Crying silently, Johnny carried Kelly to her parents' Avalon and set her in the driver's seat. He ducked so he could see Leon and Patty, sitting in the back. "I'm so sorry. I thought she was going to beat it. I truly did." He wiped his eyes before adding, "I'm going turn on the heat; it's getting cold outside."

When he'd leaned in to turn on the ignition, Kelly beat him to it, lifting her quavering hand and, on the third try, started the car. A tear was working its way down her quivering cheek as her head went on nodding, nodding.

Holding her head as still as possible, he kissed her cheek, then the corner of her mouth. If he was going to get it, he already had it. "I love you," he whispered.

He taped a hose to the Avalon's exhaust. Just as he realized he'd forgotten to crack the back window, it rolled down three inches. Johnny slid the hose through the crack and turned away.

His dad had fallen asleep in his chair.

"Come on, Pop." Johnny helped him to his feet.

"Huh? William? Let me have a carton of them Pall Malls."

He led his dad into the snack bar. They sat on stools behind the bar while the cars in the front row idled. On the big screen, Lone Starr was battling Dark Helmet in the climactic scene of *Spaceballs.*

Johnny figured either he was going to start nodding soon, since he and Kelly had been in all those houses at the same time, or he was one of the three percent. Maybe he and his dad were both part of the three percent. Good genes.

If he did start nodding, he thought he'd just go on sitting there in the snack bar, looking out at what he and Kelly had accomplished. He felt proud of what they'd done. Maybe others would think differently when they found all the bodies, but they hadn't been here. They hadn't lived through it. He watched as plumes of exhaust drifted up from the front row.

"Another sellout," Dad chuckled. "I told you. Didn't I tell you?"

HOUSES WITHOUT AIR

Megan Arkenberg

The First Match

Six weeks before the end of the world, a new bar opens on Wisconsin Avenue in Georgetown. The proprietors are a middle-aged West Coast couple, evacuees from Seattle or Portland, Beth can't remember which. The bar is on the first floor of the building where Beth's favorite bookstore used to be, but the familiar smells are gone—dust, vegetable glue, and old, acidic paper, all drawn out by the pair of sleek Blueair filters that add their silvery humming to the murmur of the television and the small Wednesday night crowd.

The hanging colored-glass lamps have disappeared, too, replaced by fluorescents; the light from the tall street-facing windows is unreliable now, dirty, gritty and dry. At least the restroom graffiti is unchanged. The back door of the middle stall in the women's room still says "No danger shall balk Columbia's lovers," an obscure scrap of Whitman in dark purple Sharpie.

Wednesday nights have been Immerse team nights for the last four years. They used to walk the five blocks from the University to a small Thai place near the river, but with the ash and acid of the ongoing eruptions in the air, a five block walk has become unendurable, even with carbon masks. Beth proposed a migration to the new Georgetown place, which is right on the bus route that she, Aidan, and Lena take to work every morning. Even so, after the first two weeks, she and Aiden are the only Wednesday regulars. Immerse is still running—one of the few projects anywhere that is—but the team is drifting apart. *Spending more time with their families*, as the official line goes, even though none of the contracts have been officially terminated. It looks like everyone's losing enthusiasm for immersive alternate reality. Everyone except for Beth, who has no family to speak of—and Aiden, who is borderline delusional.

"Give it to me, Beth. The honest assessment." Aiden's brown eyes are lit up like gin under a black light. He's two drinks in, which, considering the strength of this place's rum-and-colas, is closer to four. The most recent DOI press release sets the remaining atmospheric oxygen levels at six weeks, maximum, and Aiden McCallum is the only man in the world to whom that could possibly be good news. "They'll have to increase our funding now, right?"

"Jesus, Aiden, give it up." Beth has been willing to play along for the last few weeks—Wednesday nights would get damn lonely, otherwise—but even she has a limit. "You can't upload yourself into a damn computer. We're talking decades of development, centuries even. You can't just throw money at Immerse to turn it into a functional alternate *whatever*."

The last word comes out more harshly than she intends, waffling over the word *dimension*, which sounds too science-fictional. Beth rubs the bridge of her nose as though she can massage away the soreness. Nose, throat, lungs, everything aches these days.

Her phone beeps from deep in her purse before Aidan can say something stupid. It's a text from Farah: **Where do you keep the baking sheets?**

Cabinet to the right of the fridge. Beth hits send too quickly, curses under her breath. **Wait, why?**

"Is that crazy woman still living with you?" Aidan asks. It looks like he's letting go of Immerse for the moment, which is probably for the best—but as far as Beth's concerned, Farah Karimi is hardly a safer subject.

"She's fine." Beth forces herself to smile. "Going batshit with cabin fever, but then, who isn't?"

Aiden shakes his head and stands up to get another drink, almost knocking over his bar stool. Another text from Farah shimmers on the small screen.

Do you have sand anywhere?

WTF are you doing?

Work. A second later: **Is the sugar still in the cabinet over the microwave?**

Yes.

Can't reach. Where R U?

Now Aiden is deep in conversation with the bartender, gesturing at the television that hangs above the shelves of neon-colored bottles. It's a basketball game, but the DOI announcement is scrolling along the bottom of the screen on a blue banner. The world has a use-by date now, just like a gallon of milk, just as arbitrary, just as inevitable.

Beth looks down at her phone. Farah again: **I need sand or sugar. Also aquariums. Plural. Where's the nearest fish supply shop?**

On my way.

• • •

The Second Match

Immerse is long past the data-gathering stage, but Beth still catches herself in the habit of collecting sensations, of watching the fluorescent light play across the raised numbers on her credit card, of running her hand along the smooth-sanded barn boards of the bar's countertop, picturing the precise regions of her brain that would light up in a scan as she alters the pressure of her fingertips. After years of this, she knows the patterns of wood from laminate from drywall, granite from sandstone, leather from writing paper. The sound of her heels on the bar's tile doorstep compared to the sound of Farah's rubber-soled crutches in their apartment's tile stairwell. Some senses are impossible to program. Colors, for example—but she's used to dreaming in black and white, and so is everyone else, if they're honest. Smells are also difficult. Beth can hardly remember a smell—even inside Immerse—that isn't smog and sulfur dioxide, the half-electric scent of a struck match.

She fits her carbon mask over her nose and mouth and strides quickly across the street to the enclosed bus stop. In the June twilight, the air is actually visible—shimmering, tangibly thick, settling between the restaurants, bakeries, furniture stores, and boutiques like a black-gray mist. The bus stop's air filter sounds like it's gasping for breath. Soon scrubbing out the pollution won't do any good; there won't be enough oxygen left in the air to make it breathable.

The bus rolls to a stop, and Beth darts from the enclosure to the top of the boarding stairs. Even the short climb leaves her winded. As usual now, the bus is almost empty, and she has no trouble taking a window seat. Not that it's worth looking out. It's a night in late June but it doesn't feel like summer, not with the air so close. The anxiety is gone, Beth thinks, the clear gold glimmer that used to come with summer twilight, when everything is so fresh and open that it takes your breath away, when the sounds of traffic and sirens and thunderstorms made your stomach flutter with excitement.

It doesn't feel like June without a sudden burst of agoraphobia.

• • •

The Third Match

She gets back to the apartment, finds Farah curled on the short couch in the corner of the front room, seemingly asleep. The sight makes her chew her lip, and she's not sure why. Farah looks sickly, almost transparent these days, her thick hair pulled back with a bit of elastic, no make-up on her round, dark face. When she took the second bedroom three months ago, Farah warned Beth that she never eats when she's working on a project, just sticks to liquids, and it's starting to drive Beth mad. There's a gallon of milk uncapped, souring on the kitchen counter, half a pot of coffee grounds clogging the old sink.

The door at the back of the narrow kitchen has been left ajar, and the back room is a complete disaster. Farah's crutches lean against the asthmatic air conditioner, which has been hastily patched with blue electric tape to stay as airtight as possible. A stack of books has been accumulating around the ironing board for weeks, staggered and tilting like a bizarre art piece. Architecture books, landscape, interior design. Neuroscience textbooks and monographs on alternate reality.

What do you work on? they'd asked each other during that first phone call. *Computer games*, Beth had said. *Memorials*, said Farah Karimi.

All of Beth's cookie sheets, plus all of her muffin tins and a loaf pan, cover every available surface. Each holds a tiny sugar landscape, dunes and valleys, a few toothpicks rooted in clay. Trees? Supports for something larger?

I need to work with my hands, Farah said. *To touch things, mold them. I can't start on a sheet of paper.*

Beth takes a deep breath, goes back into the front room.

"What is all that about?"

"*That* is an entire afternoon's work. Don't touch." Farah's voice sounds distant, sleepy. Her hands are steepled and pressed against her lips. She doesn't open her eyes. "You had extra sugar in the back of the pantry. I still need the aquariums, though. And matches."

"I'm not sure you should have anything with sharp edges or anything that catches on fire until you explain what's going on with my cookie trays."

"Here." Without lifting her head, Farah fumbles amidst the mess of legal pads, printouts, magazine pages and napkins on the coffee table, grabbing something that has drifted to the edge. She holds out a sheet of what looks like paper towel. Blue ink has bled through from the page behind, and Beth can't read any of the labels on the diagram, but it's clear enough what she's looking at. Seven miniature landscapes, like elementary school terraria, set in glass boxes.

Beth studies the page without taking it from Farah's hand. "Does something *live* inside these?"

"Of course not. It's just a model. No animals were harmed, et cetera." Farah rolls her eyes. "Moving on. I can get most of that from the florist: sand, gravel, clay, distilled water, lots of plants. I'll find the miniatures online. I'll need your help setting it up, though."

"Back up," Beth says. "What is this? Setting it up where?"

Farah makes a low, irritated noise in the back of her throat. With a sudden burst of energy, she tosses her sketch on the pile, raises herself up on the couch, hooks her hands under her knees and swings her legs over the side of the couch. Beth has missed something important, but she has no idea what.

"Look," Farah says. "It isn't commissioned or anything. Who would commission a memorial for the end of the world? But I want to do this, and I want to do it here. So it has to be small-scale."

"Okay." Beth is mentally calculating the odds of being stopped by security if they attempt to assemble Farah's memorial on the National Mall. Another part of her is thinking that this must be the reason Farah came to D.C. in the first place. "That explains the aquariums."

A very faint smile twitches at the corner of Farah's mouth. She can smile prettily when she wants too—full lips, teeth hidden. "I'm calling it *Houses Without Air*."

"And that explains the matches." Beth chews her lip. She isn't sure what else to say. "Well, at least it isn't a Hans Christian Andersen reference," she says finally. "I hate that story."

"Pardon?"

"'The Little Matchgirl.' This girl's selling matches on New Year's Eve, and she's freezing, so she tries to warm herself. She lights each match and imagines these little scenes while it burns. Christmas trees and family dinners, all that. But the visions only last as long as the matches do. And when she runs out of matches, she freezes to death."

Farah responds with the world's most dignified snort. "If she froze to death, how can we know what she was imagining?"

"Because it's a story," Beth snaps, exasperated. "The people who come after have to figure it out somehow."

"Want to know a secret?" Farah leans back against the pillows, but she's smiling fully now—almost mischievously. And this, Beth thinks, is the problem with Farah. She's reckless, selfish, destructive of property, critical and dismissive of others. And she knows exactly what to say to make Beth forget all of it.

"Of course."

"I never worry about the people who come after. If they can make sense of the memorial or not. It's enough for them to know that *something* happened here, something important, that it mattered. Give them something they can feel. But telling the story? One story, with all its specifics? I don't know if that's possible."

"I don't know if I'd want to," Beth says.

Farah nods, closing her eyes. "Exactly."

• • •

The Fourth Match

Farah Karimi has lived in dozens of houses over the years: an apartment in an old palazzo in Venice where the stucco flaked from the moisture and where the elevator walls were black with mold; a cottage on the coast of the North sea where her chair's wheels used to stick in the damp sand if she rolled too close to the water. She feels called to places on the edge of disaster.

She won't build memorials for soldiers, battles, anything of that sort—not that she'd be invited to. She has a reputation for keeping things private. Nothing too obviously patriotic, although she's made exceptions, as everyone has; she lets the land influence the design, and there are still places in the world where love for the land remains the highest expression of patriotism.

She has built memorials after terrorist attacks. Many refugee camps. Hurricanes and earthquakes are something of a specialty; she loves wind and fault lines, in glass and concrete, though she hates dealing with the rubble. She's built memorials after Ebola outbreaks, and smallpox when it came back, although she was advised not to enter the areas both times.

The Venice Harbor Arch is Farah Karimi's most famous work. The glass pillars catch the light of the rising and setting sun, spreading it in rainbows over the shallow water, still broken here and there by rooftops and church steeples. She's never been fond of it; it's too huge, too obvious.

When Beth first heard Farah's name, she thought of Venice, though she couldn't remember why.

• • •

The Fifth Match

Two weeks before the end of the world, Beth comes home early on a Wednesday night. Farah is on the floor of the back room, arranging cacti in the bottom of a thirty-gallon aquarium. She's wearing her pale blue carbon mask. The tape around the air conditioner has started to fail.

"I want to show you something," Beth says.

She offers to get Farah's chair out of storage from the back of the building, but Farah demurs. Crutches are easier with the bus. They catch the bus to the metro, the metro to the University stop. In the dark and the smog, the campus feels deserted, though Beth knows it isn't.

Six swipes of Beth's ID takes them into a lab building, down an elevator and a long, winding corridor, into the Immerse laboratory, which really *is* deserted. The front room is all desks and computers and bookshelves, the stale smell of old coffee and spilled creamer. Farah glances around the room, eyebrows arched, doesn't say anything.

"Through here." Beth leads Farah to a door in the back. Her palms are damp despite the air-conditioned coolness. The small room beyond has a low cot along one wall, a set of white laminate cabinets along the other. From left to right, Beth opens the doors, lays out the cabinet's contents on the cot. Wires and suction cups, long-sleeved gloves, a hood with a broad blue visor.

"So this is what you've been working on?" Farah remains standing in the doorway, leaning forward on her crutches. The public transportation and the walk across campus have been a greater exertion than she's used to, these days. Her hair curls around her forehead in sweat-damp ringlets. "Yeah." Beth clears her throat. "Yes. It's called Immerse."

"Not a very creative name."

"It's not a very creative project. The word *inevitable* comes to mind, actually."

Laughing softly, Farah makes her way to the cot. She slips first one arm, then the other out of the loops of her crutches. "Entertainment purposes only, right?"

"Well, you can't stay in there forever, if that's what you mean." Beth glances over the components spread across the crisp white sheet. Hooked together, they make a strange and skeletal assemblage. "Okay, you'll need to undress for this. Most of these need to go right against your skin."

Farah slips her sweater over her head. In the air-conditioned lab, goosebumps dimple the dark skin of her forearms. Beth helps her up onto the edge of the cot so she can slip out of her blue jeans. "Every time I've been hooked in," Beth warns, "the components have been cold as fuck. Just so you know."

She begins fitting the system around Farah's body. After years with Immerse, hooking in has become routine, but it's rare that she's put the system on someone else, especially someone who doesn't know the components well enough to help. Farah stays slack like a doll, allowing Beth to wrap her arms in the tight compression sleeves and slide the thick, electrode-studded gloves down over each finger. Beth has never seen her so quiet, so attentive.

Arms, legs, torso. The hood comes last. As Beth reaches around behind Farah's head, her inner arm brushes against the rough cloth of Farah's suited shoulder. Farah doesn't seem to notice.

"This piece is the brain of the whole system," Beth explains, drawing it up around Farah's thick hair. "Everything you see and feel starts in here. It'll send signals to the other pieces, like so..." Farah makes a soft sound of surprise as something trails across her fingertips. The glove on her right hand flexes perceptibly. "The system will be giving you real stimuli. Your brain will interpret it according to the program that the system is running."

"It felt like sand. What the glove did just now...it felt like digging my fingers into warm sand."

The visor comes down over her eyes. She lies back on the cot, breathes deeply. Beth steps back and lets the program begin.

The program runs more or less predictably. Moment by moment, Beth has always been able to guess what it will show. They built it out of her memories, after all. She was the one who lay in the MRI as they brushed and pressed and prodded, held her fingers against cloth and metal, paper and leaves. The one who opened her mouth and offered her tongue to sugar and vinegar and stale bread.

And so she knows that Farah is walking across a county fairground on a mid-summer evening, the system pulsing the pressure of sandy soil and sparse grass up through the soles of her feet, and every electrode registering heat and humidity. Carousel music—calliopes and brass bands—floats on a slow breeze. Balancing the volume was a challenge; it required adjusting the instruments' pitch as the subject moved across the scene. In the distance, fair rides spin and tilt and shine in the orange sunlight. Scraps of paper and checkered hotdog wrappers plaster themselves against a chain-link fence. There are smells, of which Beth is especially proud, though they are still imperfect: cooking sausages, hot pretzels and mustard, fairground ponies, gasoline. Just when Beth estimates Farah is probably approaching the Ferris wheel, Farah makes a strange, strangling sound and moves her arms from the cot, reaching for her visor.

"Take it off!"

Her voice is muffled by the helmet. She doesn't sound frightened, but angry.

Beth loosens the strap, slips the hood back over Farah's head. Farah's face is damp, frowning, unreadable. She seems ready to rip the gloves off, but Beth stops her; the system is delicate.

"What is it? Are you okay?"

Farah shrugs her off. "Yes. Sorry."

"What happened?"

"Nothing. It was just—"

"Uncanny?" Beth has heard that one before.

"Dull."

A moment of thick silence.

"What's wrong with it?" Beth says.

"No, no." Farah shakes her head, raking her still-gloved hands through her hair. "I'm sorry. I didn't mean—"

"Just tell me what's wrong."

"Nothing's *wrong*. It's just empty. Not a single living thing. No one else." Farah's hands are still buried in her curls. She glances up at Beth's face, and the oddly angry expression still curls her lips. "No other people, right?"

"No. Not for a long time, anyway." Beth remembers Aiden, his alternate reality fantasies. Hiding away in the imaginary world of Immerse, waiting for the storm to pass. Or not waiting—building a new world inside the program for just one person. "It was part of the plan for the future, of course, but we're nowhere near that level. And there's no time for it now."

"So what's it good for?"

Her eyes are narrowed, her voice raised, ringing a little in that small, bare room. She lowers her hands, rips the gloves off with a loud tearing sound. She doesn't mean to be combative, Beth realizes; she's genuinely curious. The anger comes from not understanding.

And Beth isn't sure she understands, either.

She looks down at the glove dangling empty from the tight sleeves on Farah's forearm, looks down at the crisp sheets of the cot, which smell faintly of bleach, at the ridges in the concrete floor, at the shadow of Farah's crutch falling across them, that narrow black line against the pale gray. She hears the hum of the air filters in the room behind them.

"It gives people something they can touch," she says.

Silence gathers again, thick. Farah smiles ruefully.

"If someone were to find this years from now," she says, "if someone could survive and find this place on their own, would they even know what to do with it? Do you think they would understand *this*?"

"I don't know," Beth admits. "But it will be here, just in case."

• • •

The Sixth Match

Beth does not open up easily, if at all. She has never wanted to fall in love. She dreads travel, new jobs, new co-workers. She would rather reread a book she loves ten times over than risk picking up a new one. She had many acquaintances in college, and some even endeavored to stay in touch, but it never seemed worth the effort to her. It's hard to get in touch with people now, what with the evacuations, the earthquakes, the fires. If she's honest, she prefers it this way.

Farah smiles rarely, but when she does, it is extraordinarily pretty. She talks little. Beth has memorized her makeup, the brown lipstick on her full lips, the heavy eyeshadow with a hint of green, the precise curve of it beneath Farah's straight, high eyebrows. Unlike Beth, she has no preferences for ink or paper; she writes on napkins, the backs of receipts, envelopes from the electric bill. She touches everything in the apartment. Her rent checks are always on time, never a day early or a day late. She moved to D.C. right after the Yellowstone eruption; the air was clear when she signed the agreement, but by the time she moved in, the DOI warnings had already been issued. *I don't mind*, she'd said. *I stay inside anyway.*

Beth knows nothing about Farah's family, her friends, her preferences. Doesn't know if she's ever been in love.

If Beth's honest, she prefers it that way, too

• • •

The Seventh Match

One week before the end of the world, they take a taxi down to the west end of the Mall. The buses have stopped running. The downtown streets are eerie and unfamiliar: food carts abandoned at long-expired parking meters; newspaper vending machines empty or still filled with last week's papers; plywood and plastic affixed over full-story windows, to protect against looters and smog. Both measures, Beth thinks, are overly optimistic.

It may be Beth's imagination, but the air feels a little fresher down by the thick old trees, down by the wider stretches of the river and the tidal basin: a little less gritty against the skin her mask leaves exposed. The seven small aquariums fit in the trunk of the taxi, just barely. They're obnoxiously heavy. Farah needs her crutches, so it's Beth's job to carry the boxes, one at a time, past the stone barricades and down the shallow steps to the place that Farah has selected on the lip of the reflecting pool.

"Is there a special way to do this?" she asks. "Should we say something first?"

Farah shakes her head.

They place the *Houses Without Air* in a tight semicircle with the open edge facing the pool. As Beth sets each aquarium in place, Farah crouches down across from it, inspecting the landscapes inside. She's anchored them well; nothing has shifted except the sand. Farah's custom-fitted lids have puckered, rubber-lined openings in the top corners large enough to take a matchstick, just barely airtight.

Beth hasn't come down to the Mall in almost three years. The haze is so thick now that she can't make out even a suggestion of the white obelisk far above and across the pool, and the Lincoln Memorial is only a pale, heavy smudge to their right.

Farah stays crouched over the seventh box, her crutches stretched out to either side like the barest framework for wings. Her eyes look red and damp, irritated by the air. Beth wonders what her lips are doing behind her mask.

"You can start," she says.

The box of long matches is in Beth's jacket pocket. When Farah nods, she strikes the first match, pushes it down flame-first through the opening in the first aquarium's roof. They practiced back at the apartment; if they aren't quick enough, the flame will go out before they can pass it through the lid. The flame makes it in, but there's only a sliver of air between the lid and the surface of the water inside. It smothers quickly.

Farah lets Beth light the second, too. It lasts a little longer, but then the oxygen is gone, and the matchstick smokes over dunes of sand and pink gravel. Farah holds out her hand for the matchbox.

The third House is the desert, layered with miniature cacti in shades of green and pale, waxy blue. The fourth is a rainforest, as much as Farah could fit in the little box, broad leaves, flower petals, two inches of water along the bottom. The fourth flame burns halfway up the matchstick before it suffocates.

The fifth match is Beth's again, and it takes three tries to strike. Beth curses under her breath, worrying that it's the air, but of course it's just her stiff fingers. The red tip catches, and she pushes it into the fifth box; Farah has added a chain-link fence to the low gravel mounds, bright flecks of paper caught along its foot. The sixth House holds a tiny city block, the colonial rowhouses tall, identical, red and white, with red brick sidewalks and slender trees marching along the front. The sixth flame rises as high as the fourth.

Beth passes the matchbox to Farah. "Thank you," she says.

The seventh House is a flight of shallow white steps leading down to a sheet of dark, reflective glass. Farah closes her eyes. It is a race to see which is consumed first: the oxygen, or the match.

THE FIFTH DAY OF DEER CAMP

Scott Sigler

"There's a rabid badger in my skull," Toivo said. He looked up from the bucket in which his face had been hidden for the last ten minutes. "I'm sure of it, eh?"

George tried to ignore Toivo. He took another look at his poker hand, as if somehow the cards had changed in the four seconds since he'd looked at them last: nope, still three kings.

He looked across the table. Jaco had a glint in his eye, at least as much of one as George could see behind the cabin light glaring off Jaco's huge glasses. Jaco was a good player—as one of the top accountants in Houghton, he could do the math with the best of them—but the little guy had never been able to control his tells. The tip of his tongue peeked out from the left corner of his mouth. That only happened when Jaco had something good, but was what he had good enough to beat three kings?

You've got two pair, you little shit, I can tell. Your lip twitches like that when you have two pair.

Toivo let out a long groan. "Oh, jeeze," he said. "I don't feel so good, eh? And it's freezing in here, did someone leave da door open again?"

To George's left, Bernie set his cards flat on the table, set them down hard enough to rattle the empty cans of Pabst and jostle the semi-full ones.

"Holy *crap*, Toivo," Bernie said. "Either get back in da game, go to sleep, or just shut up. We're trying to play cards here."

"A woodchuck," Toivo said. "Rabid. I'm telling ya."

George sighed, annoyed that Toivo's whining was cutting into the game.

"You just drank too much," he said. "I told you sausage doesn't soak up beer in your belly—that's a wives' tale. And it's cold in here because it's November, you idiot. Put on a third sweater if you're cold."

Toivo burped. "A grown man can never drink too much."

Arnold laughed. He was seated at George's right. Arnold—or *Mister Ekola,* as he had been known when George was a kid—had been coming here longer than any of them, had once shared this place with his grade school friends. Now his son Bernie did the same, the tradition passed down from one generation to the next.

Arnold's friends had died off over the years, the victims of age, heart disease, cancer…whatever the Grim Reaper could come up with, really. Creeping middle age made George realize, more and more every day, that the same fate awaited he, Jaco, Toivo, and Bernie. Many winters from now, which one of them would be like Arnold?

"Well, Toivo, then maybe you aren't a grown man," Arnold said. "Now be quiet so I can take these losers' money. I know when my son is bluffing."

"Screw you, Dad," Bernie said.

Toivo put his face in his hands. "Oh, *jeeze*…maybe I should go to da hospital."

George lowered his cards. "Sure, Toivo. That little access road outside is snowed shut, so you can't take the truck. Hell, M-26 is probably snowed shut, too, so how about you take the snowmobile and drive to Lake Linden? Should only take you an hour and a half."

"Dress warm," Arnold said. "About ten below out there, eh?"

Jaco snorted. "Ten, hell. More like *thirty* with wind chill."

"Thirty *easy*," Bernie said. "And if you drive that Arctic Cat off da trail, snow's at least four feet deep. Hey, Toivo—if you get stuck and die, can I have your thirty-thirty? That's a nice gun."

Toivo stared at each of the four men in turn. "You guys are dicks," he said, then put his face back in the bucket and threw up again.

George decided to risk his three kings against whatever Jaco had. Arnold's wrinkled old fingers were holding his cards an inch from his face, so close his bushy eyebrows almost brushed against the five faded logos of a white "G" inside a yellow oval set against a green background. Arnold didn't like wearing his glasses at deer camp, unless they were actually out hunting, which meant he almost never wore them. His glasses—much thinner than Jaco's heavy frames—lay folded up in front of his can of Pabst.

This scene: the game, the people, the beers, the cabin, the freezing cold, Toivo over-imbibing like he did every year, it was all part of a grand tradition. If they counted Arnold's glory years, this group had been coming to this shack in Michigan's Upper Peninsula—the U.P., or "da Yoop," as the locals called it—every November for over forty years. Unless any of them visited Milwaukee, which wasn't that often, this annual two-week trip was the only time George saw his childhood friends and the only man who had bothered to teach him right from wrong. So many little rituals, from the cheap beer to cases of ammo that were never used, from opening-night bratwurst to the closing-day cleaning party, it was all to be celebrated and treasured.

Maybe George had moved on in life, sure. Maybe he'd worked to get rid of his Yooper accent, learned to say "the" instead of "da," "yes" instead of "yah," because in the big city he thought that made him sound dumb. Just because *he* felt the need to change, though, didn't mean he thought his friends should. Bernie, Toivo, and Jaco looked a little older every year, but to George they would be forever ten, forever fifteen, forever eighteen, forever the ages they'd been as—together—they had discovered who they were.

But as kids or adults, what they *weren't* were good card players.

George stared at Arnold, trying to pick off Arnold's tells. Unlike Jaco, though, Arnold was damn near unreadable. He might have a full house, he might have crap—there was almost no way to tell.

Bernard smacked his cards down on the table again. "Dammit, George, you going to play or what?"

George was. These boys were about to learn a valuable—and extremely costly—lesson.

"Okay, Bernie," George said. "I'll see your five—" George took a five dollar bill off his pile and set it on top of the stack of money at the table's center "—and let's send the kiddies home so the adults can play. I'll raise you *ten*."

Arnold's bushy eyebrows shot up. "I'm out," he said. He tossed his cards down.

"Dammit, Dad," Bernie said. "It's my bet, you're supposed to wait for me and Jaco to go before you fold."

Arnold stood, hitched up his flannel long john bottoms by yanking up on the red suspenders attached to them. "I'm retired," he said. "I don't wait for shit, eh?"

He glanced up at the ratty cabin's peaked wooden ceiling, eyes squinting as if he were looking for something. His hand blindly felt around the table for his glasses. Then, George heard something—the same sound Arnold must've heard seconds earlier: the distant, deep roar of a jet engine.

Arnold put on his glasses. "Assholes," he said. "That's all we need is some damn plane spooking the deer."

Jaco giggled. There was no other way to describe the sound: Most men "laughed," Jaco made a noise that would have been more at home in the body of a twelve-year-old girl showing off a tea party dress than a forty-year-old man wearing the same snowsuit he'd had on for five straight days, taking it off only to handle his business out in the woods.

"Deer should be scared of *something*," he said. "They sure aren't scared of us. Are we going to at least *try* to hunt this year?"

Arnold grabbed his can of Pabst. "If we run out of beer before the snow stops falling and the plows pass by, sure. Good thing we got twenty cases, eh? I'm going to take a leak. Jaco, try not to freeze to death, you damn pansy."

The old man opened the cabin's rickety door and stepped out into the winter night, letting in a strong gust of crisp wind and a scattering of blowing snow.

Jaco shivered. "See what I mean? Freezing my balls off when we could be somewhere insulated."

"What balls?" Bernie said.

Jaco had more money than the rest of them combined. Every year for the last three or four deer seasons, he'd begged to get a better cabin. He even offered to pay the difference. But straying from the path was not allowed—since George and Jaco and Bernard had been old enough to drink they had come here with Arnold, and here they would continue to come when their own sons were old enough to join, and *keep* coming until they either died or grew so old they couldn't handle two weeks of bitter Upper Peninsula cold.

Bernie scratched at his beard. Not even a week in and it was damn near full. The guy had some kind of mutation, of that George was sure.

"Bernie, put up or shut up," George said. "Ten dollars to you."

Bernie reached for his money, then paused—he looked up to the cabin's thin, peaked roof, just like his father had moments earlier. Jaco did the same, as did George. That jet had grown louder. *Much* louder.

The empty cans of Pabst started to rattle like ominous little tin chimes.

"Oh, jeeze," Toivo said. "My head hurts so bad it's *roaring*."

The cabin door opened and Arnold rushed in, stumbling from the long johns pulled halfway up his thighs, the suspenders flapping wildly.

"Get down, eh? It's right on top of us!"

George was about to ask the man what was going on, but the jet engine grew so loud it had to be right above the cabin. George dove under the table, bumping it hard as he did, sending empties and cards and money flying. He hit the wooden floor hard and lay there for only a split second before it seemed to bounce up below him, the entire cabin rattling like a big box of dry wood.

• • •

Moments later, George opened the cabin door and rushed out into the freezing night. Jaco, Bernie, Arnold, and Toivo came out behind him, all pulling on jackets or stomping feet into heavy winter boots as they walked. Falling snow ate up the sound, but the woods were even quieter than normal, as if the low-flying jet had intimidated the entire landscape into a terrified silence.

When the sun had gone down six hours earlier, the trees—both lush pines and bare-branched hardwoods—had been blanketed in blazing white. Most of that covering had fallen off, swatted away by the jet's roar to join the thick snowpack already on the ground.

Clouds blocked out all but a dim, hazy glow of the moon. The only light came from the naked bulb above the cabin's door.

George glanced at the cabin roof. It, too, was suddenly bare, just a few clumps of snow sticking to the weathered tin. He was a little surprised to see the cabin had remained in one piece. Pots had fallen off hooks and crashed around the wood stove, and all kinds of bat and bird shit had rained down from the old roof, but the one-room building seemed to be fine.

Jaco's Jeep Grand Cherokee had two feet of snow on it and around it. Other than the Arctic Cat—which was so buried it was little more than a snowbank—the Jeep was the only way to go the crash victims, or to get them help.

Arnold pointed north. A wall of trees lay in that direction, but if you walked that way for about five minutes you would come out on the pristine shore of Lake Superior: untouched, icy rock beaches lining dense, snow covered forest that stretched forever, the black water reaching out so far it vanished into the night.

"The thing was going that way," Arnold said. "Dark as it is out, the clouds should be lit up where it crashed. We'd see a fire from miles away."

"Maybe it landed," Jaco said.

Arnold hawked a loogie and spat it onto the snow. "Where, exactly, might it land? Ain't no airport around here can even take a prop plane let alone that big-ass thing that flew over, eh?"

Twice in rapid succession, Arnold had said *thing* instead of *plane* or *jet*.

"Mister Ekola," George said, "what exactly did you see?"

George had known the man since the second grade at Ontonagan Elementary, since the first time Bernie had invited he and Jaco home to play. Even now that George was in his forties—with a son of his own—he couldn't bring himself to call Arnold by his first name, no matter how many times the man asked.

"Lights," Arnold said. "Lots of lights. Goddamn *big*, eh? Don't know what it was...but it wasn't a jet."

Bernie threw his hands up in frustration. "Dad, it was a jet. Your eyes are old as hell, remember?"

Arnold pointed to his glasses. "Had these on. Know what I saw."

"It was a jet," Bernie said.

Jaco walked to the cabin's corner, taking big steps to push through the thigh-high snow. "I'll check around back," he said. "Maybe something out that way."

Toivo rubbed at his temples. "Arnold is right, Bernie—there's no airports around here. A jet makes that much noise could maybe land on da highway, but other than that, it would have had to crash, and if it crashed, we'd see fires or something."

George pulled his cell phone from his pocket. "If it was a plane, maybe there's news coverage. Let me see if I can get a signal."

"Your phone hasn't got shit all week," Bernie said. "I left mine inside, I'll grab it." He turned and trudged back into the cabin.

George yelled after him: "And grab the flashlights."

They had rushed out of the cabin expecting to see pillars of flame, had grabbed coats and boots and little else. Whatever was going on, they needed to slow down, think things through. Being outside *at all* in this weather could kill. If they were going to go through the woods looking for Arnold's mystery non-plane, they had to use their heads.

George couldn't get a signal. Being in the middle of the woods in one of the most rural and remote places in America, he wasn't surprised. He put the phone away.

"Hey, guys?"

It was Jaco. He'd gone all the way behind the cabin and come around the other side. He was leaning heavily on the corner, as if he were suddenly exhausted. "You need to come see this. Right now."

He ducked back out of sight. Arnold started after him, the old-timer more sure-footed through the snow than the men twenty-five years his junior.

George fell in behind. Bernie came out of the cabin, one flashlight in his right hand, another under his right arm. He waved his left hand; the glowing cell phone screen he held seemed to blaze like a comet.

"Told ya," he said. "AT&T works in da big city, Georgie, but out here Verizon gets full signal. Hey, where you going?"

"Come on," Arnold snapped. "Jaco saw something."

George followed in Arnold's footsteps, which was easier than plunging his feet into the thigh-deep snow. Bernie followed behind, putting his feet in the same spots. He handed George the extra flashlight. George turned it on, pointed the beam out in front of Arnold. The old man moved like he had the place memorized—he did, but the snow was deep and who knew what fallen log or stick might lie below the surface?

George felt a little embarrassed that the snow here was untouched save for Jaco's fresh prints—he and his friends had barely left the cabin at all. Deer camp wasn't really about deer; it was about drinking and sleeping and playing cards and telling stories, about making fun of each other, about hanging out with the people who had made grade school, junior high, and high school a great experience.

The four men turned the corner, saw Jaco standing between two towering pines, not even fifteen feet from the cabin. A lone set of footprints showed his path through the snow. George and Bernie's flashlight beams spotlighted Jaco, and the fluffy white that came up almost to his crotch. He had his back to them. He stood still, yet he was shaking, and somehow George knew it wasn't from the bitter cold.

Jaco looked down, looked at the lit-up white around him, then turned so fast George took a step back. The flashlight beams lit up his glasses, making him look like a movie android about to unleash a death ray.

"*Turn off da damn lights*," he said in a snarling hiss.

Out of nowhere, little Jaco, the runt of their litter, had transformed into the scariest person George had ever seen. That wasn't like Jaco, not at all—he was *terrified.*

Bernie's flashlight blinked out. George fumbled with his own, then clicked it off. The entire world blackened for a split second, plunging George into a cold, dark, silent void. His eyes quickly adjusted—and the first thing he noticed was a glow coming from deep in the woods.

A *green* glow.

His friends had become reverse shadows, their faces and clothes spots of less-dark that moved and turned, all facing that strange light. They walked to Jaco, feet crunching loudly on undisturbed snow until they stood next to their friend.

George stared. He couldn't tell how far away the lights were, exactly, but through the trees and the thick underbrush he could almost make out a shape. Not the shape of a big jet, like a 747, or even a prop plane for that matter, but instead a thick rectangle, the upright edges maybe twenty or thirty feet high. The lines parallel to the ground were much longer, maybe a hundred feet, maybe more.

A rectangle . . . or, the profile of a disc.

"That's not a plane," George said.

Arnold nodded. "Told ya."

"Oh, jeeze," Toivo said. "What da hell is that thing?"

Bernie shook his head in wide-eyed disbelief. "Sorry, Dad. Sorry. Guess there won't be any news stories about a crashed plane."

Arnold nodded. "Yah, that's fine. Maybe you should look anyway, though. Check one of those news sites."

Toivo crunched over to Bernie. "CNN? That's a good one."

Bernie stared, dumbfounded, at Toivo. "CNN?"

"Your phone," George said. "You got signal, right?"

His own voice seemed oddly normal, when he knew it probably should have rang with panic. Something was very, very wrong, but Mister Ekola was standing right there and Mister Ekola was calm as could be.

Bernie twitched like someone had stabbed him with a fork. "Oh, shit, right." He dug in his pocket and pulled out his phone. The screen blazed, lighting up slowly billowing cones of breath.

"Oh, jeeze," Toivo said. "Turn down da brightness, eh?"

Bernie ripped off a glove and tossed it down, not even bothering to put it in his pocket, then stabbed at the screen with the tip of his finger.

Arnold put his arm around Jaco. "Son, are you all right?"

Jaco shook his head. "No, sir. I don't think I am."

"Yah, I suppose that's to be expected," Arnold said.

George stared at the man. How could he be so damn *calm*? George knew he should be the one to say something, to get things organized, but all of the sudden he was twelve again, and so was Bernie and Jaco and Toivo; Mister Ekola was the adult.

Jaco's dad had died when he was just a toddler. George's dad had left when George was eight, had never come back. Toivo's dad had beaten the shit out of him more often than not, had sent Toivo to school with long-sleeved sweaters to hide the bruises on his arms. That had happened since at least the fourth grade, when Toivo's family moved in, until the summer after the fifth grade, when Arnold had paid a visit to Toivo's house and given Toivo's dad a lesson on how to dish out a *real* beating. After that, Toivo's dad walked with a limp; he also never laid another hand on his boy.

Arnold Ekola and his wife hadn't just raised Bernie, they'd basically raised three more boys as well. For George and Jaco and Toivo, Arnold wasn't their biological father, but he was their *dad*.

Mister Ekola knew what to do—he always had, he always would.

Bernard looked up from the phone.

"Oh my god," he said. "Oh, god, Dad…it's everywhere."

Arnold squeezed Jaco's shoulder, pointed out at the green lights.

"Jaco, can you keep an eye on that thing for me?"

Jaco nodded. "Sure, Mister Ekola. I can do that."

"Good boy," Arnold said. He turned to Bernie. "Exactly *what* is everywhere?"

Bernie pointed to the lighted rectangle. "That is. I mean, *those* are. Milwaukee, Boston, New York, it even says there's one in Paris. It's fucking *aliens*, Dad. That's what CNN says."

Toivo nodded. "Was bound to happen someday," he said. "There's lots of stars, dontchya know."

Bernie pulled the phone closer to his face. "They're landing all over the world. They're attacking, killing people in the cities. Air Force is fighting them, Army's been mobilized . . . Dad, we're being *invaded*."

George took two steps toward Bernie, snatched the phone out of his friend's hand. They weren't being invaded, that was ridiculous. There was some other explanation for this, shit like this *didn't happen.*

One glance at the web page confirmed what Bernie had said. George tried to poke the screen, realized he, too, was wearing gloves. He tore them off and threw them down. The cold sent needle-stabs into his hands, the same way it had been stabbing his neck and face—he just hadn't registered it.

George tried Fox News. Top story: *New York On Fire, London Destroyed.*

He looked at Yahoo: *It's Not a Movie: Our World is Invaded.*

NBC: *Invaders Overpowering Militaries Worldwide.*

George's eyes fuzzed; the screen blurred into nothing. He was at the tip of the Keweenaw Peninsula, so deep in the woods there weren't even paved roads. He was 370 miles away from his family.

My son, my wife...I have to get to Milwaukee.

George handed back the phone.

"Bernie's right," he said. "I don't know why this one landed in the Yoop, Mister Ekola...but that's an alien ship."

Arnold nodded. He hawked a loogie, turned and spat so it wouldn't hit any of his boys.

"Yah, I figured," he said. "Let's get back inside da cabin. Dress warm, get your guns, and make sure you have as much ammo as you can carry."

The five men turned away from the green lights and walked back to the cabin, their feet crunching in the snow. Bernie slid his phone into his pocket, cutting off even that small light.

They walked into the cabin and silently went about their business, Arnold's calming influence somehow stopping any of them from freaking out. They all had families to get back to, yet without saying a word they all knew that wasn't going to happen right away. It felt like at least one of them should go crazy, scream about how he had leave, *right now*, and the others would have to wrestle him to the ground, but that didn't happen. They all knew they had to wait until morning, at the very least—going out at night was to fear death from the cold just as much as fearing anything the aliens might do.

Still, George wasn't completely free of crazy. As he put on a second sweater, then a third, he kept one eye on his Remington 700 rifle, and couldn't help one thought from repeating in his head over and over:

Maybe it's good we didn't shoot at any deer—we might need all these bullets.

ENJOY THE MOMENT

Jack McDevitt

The party on my thirtieth birthday more or less opened the door to the end of the world. It was supposed to be a surprise, but my husband Warren, and a few other family members took to smirking and grinning during the preceding days. I was maybe two steps into the living room when the lights came on. They were all there. Uncle Harry and Aunt May with Liz, our eight-year-old daughter. Jack Camden and his wife, whose name I couldn't remember, and probably twenty other relatives, colleagues, and friends. They burst into a rendition of "Happy Birthday," and applauded. My sister Ellen brought me a lime daiquiri, my favorite, and when the singing stopped I was led to the coffee table, which was piled high with presents.

We were essentially party people, always looking for something to celebrate. Tom Akins, the physics department chairman and my mentor, played his accordion, accompanied by Freeman and my brother Bill on guitars. They filled the house with music and everybody danced. We passed out drinks, ate through three and a half cakes, played some games and talked about how good life was.

Tom was a cosmologist who was devoting his life to trying to solve the riddle of cosmic inflation, the incredible, and incomprehensible, rate of expansion that occurred at the very beginning of the Big Bang. He'd won some awards, and had been a good guide for me when I was coming up through the program. Toward the end of the evening, he took me aside to pass on some news. "Maryam," he said, "I've told you about Dan Martin? He's been doing some groundbreaking work on space-time curvature. He'll be receiving the Carnegie Award this year."

Martin had gotten his doctorate only three years earlier. "Beautiful," I said, trying not to sound jealous. "When did you find out?"

"He called me this morning." He laughed. "He says some of his friends are making references to Martin's Theorem."

"Well, I'm glad to hear it."

He must have picked up something in my tone. "Don't worry, Maryam. Your time will come."

It was a happy night. But I guess some part of Dan Martin lingered. When it was over, and everyone was saying goodbye and retrieving their cars from around the neighborhood, my husband hesitated as we left the house and started down the walkway. "What's wrong?" he asked.

"What do you mean? Why do you say that?"

"Something's bothering you. It's been there for most of the evening."

I took a deep breath and faced it. "I'm *thirty*."

His eyebrows rose the way they usually did when politicians were talking. "Maryam, you still look great. I don't think you'll have anything to worry about for a long time."

"That's not what I mean, love. You know what they say about physicists and thirty?"

"No. What do they say?"

"That if you're going to leave a mark, you have to get moving early. After you hit thirty your brain begins to freeze." I tried to turn it into a joke, but he didn't smile.

"Come on. You don't believe that."

I'm not sure whether I did. But it ended there. We got into the car and went home.

• • •

Despite the alcohol, I didn't sleep well that night. There's not a physicist on the planet who doesn't want to leave his or her name in the history of the field. To do something that grants immortality. Predict the Higgs Boson. Devise the Pauli Exclusion Principle.

Schwarzschild pinned his name to a radius. Heisenberg to uncertainty. Doppler has a shift, and Hawking has radiation. Schrodinger scored with a *cat*. And what, in the end, would Maryam Gibson have?

I'd been working on dark energy since the beginning of my career. My thesis had been an attempt to account for it. Get to the heart of dark energy and you can explain why the universe continues to expand at an increasing rate. If I could succeed, make some sort of progress, it was easy to imagine, that at some future date, people would be talking about the Gibson Hypothesis. Or maybe Gibson Energy. I especially liked that one.

At one time it hadn't seemed too much to ask. Dark energy constituted 68% of the total mass-energy of the universe. Seventeen times the amount of ordinary matter. I'd been convinced that I could figure it out. It was just waiting there for someone to explain it.

But that night, with the partying done, I lay in the fading moonlight that came through the curtains, and I knew it wouldn't be me.

• • •

I needed a different track, but my career demanded I stay with the hunt for dark energy. There was no way I could leave that. But maybe, I thought, I could use my spare time to accomplish something that didn't require an Einstein. Mark Twain had commented once that he'd come in on Halley's Comet, and that he expected to go out with it as well. Which he did.

Find one of the things and you got to name it. *Gibson's* Comet wasn't exactly what I'd hoped for. But I could live with it. And it might be obtainable.

Warren and I spent a couple of hours most evenings watching TV. I enjoyed being with him, and had always arranged things to ensure we got some time together. But I was going to have to give that up for a while. "I'm going comet-hunting," I said.

"Whatever you like, babe," he said. "But you're not going to give up on the dark energy thing, are you?"

"No. This would just be something I'd be looking at in my spare time."

"Okay." He sounded disappointed. "Will we still get to watch *Big Bang Theory*?"

"Sure. And one more thing—"

"All right."

"Don't mention this to anyone, okay?"

"Why not?"

"I'd just as soon nobody knows until I actually find one."

• • •

We both had offices at home. A couple of nights after the party, when I had some free time, I went into mine, sat down, and started digging through the online sky surveys. Even though I'd devoted my entire career to cosmology, I was probably uniquely qualified to look for comets because I had exactly the right tools. I'd developed software that could analyze for mass, gravitation, dark matter distribution, distance, velocities, and so on. Normally, my research consisted of recording a set of results from the digital archives, moving forward a given number of years, analyzing how the situation had changed, and comparing the results with what I'd anticipated.

The same approach should work in the hunt for comets. Comets originate in the outer solar system, either in the Kuiper Belt—which consists of small bodies of ice, rock, and metal orbiting beyond Neptune and extending for an additional two billion miles—or in the Oort Cloud, which lies at a range of about a light-year. The Kuiper Belt offered a much better chance of success. So I locked in on it.

Warren never quite understood why I was so hung up on gaining visibility in the field. He was a realtor, but he knew there was more to life than making money. He enjoyed being able to see his clients settle happily into homes, or to assist them when they were moving elsewhere. He thought those were the only two things that really counted in one's profession: making a contribution, and collecting a decent income. "Nobody other than my clients and family, and a few friends," he'd told me once, "will ever know my name. But what does that matter?"

Why did I want to put myself out front with a theorem that would never matter to anyone? Or probably even be understood by anybody except a few specialists? He'd tried reading *Quantum Theory for Dummies*, and realized that even physicists didn't really grasp the reality of some of the more arcane mathematics.

I sat quietly through the night, looking at patches of sky, discarding stars, picking up glimmers that were too faint to amount to anything. Eventually my eyes got heavy and I resigned myself to the fact that I would not amount to anything…at least not tonight.

• • •

Two nights later I repeated the process with the same result. But I stayed with it, whenever I had time. Warren thought it was a waste of effort but he didn't say so directly. He *did* mention that real estate was booming, and that he could use another agent. He guaranteed I'd earn a lot more than I was making as a college professor. He mentioned an article about how people who keep irregular hours damage their brains. And he left a magazine open on the table with a story about how marriages work better when the partners spend time together.

Then, one night about six months after I'd started, the numbers coalesced and I realized I'd found what I was looking for. An object on the inner edge of the Kuiper Belt had dropped out of its orbit, probably influenced by the passage of Neptune, and was moving toward the sun. The spectroscopic analysis indicated it was 3.1 billion miles away.

Beautiful.

Warren was watching a hockey game and Liz was in the kitchen when I came out of my office. "Are you quitting for the night?" he asked. "It's early."

I looked casually at my watch. "I guess it *is* a bit early."

He froze the picture. "Why the smug smile? Did you find something?" I didn't have to say a word. "Congratulations. How big is it?"

"The diameter's about twenty-five kilometers."

"That sounds good. When will we see it?"

"Warren, I don't know how much visibility it will have. And I haven't really run the numbers yet, but I'd guess it'll be in the vicinity of Earth in about twenty years."

"So we'll be in our fifties."

"Hard to believe, isn't it?"

He broke into a grin. "I certainly married a woman with vision."

• • •

When the news broke about the comet, I became a local celebrity and the university got a nice PR boost as a result. Reporters descended, and I appeared on several TV shows and on The Science Channel. It was a gloriously happy time.

The data were made available to the world, and confirmed by everyone. Tom called me into his office. "I was surprised that you've gotten involved with comets."

"It became something of a hobby."

"I hope it hasn't been affecting your research?"

"No, Tom. I wouldn't let that happen. I was just taking an occasional break."

"Okay. Nothing wrong with that." He glanced up at the dictum that, he claimed, ruled his life: *Enjoy the moment. We don't have forever.* It was framed and hung on the wall beside a picture of him and the governor. The reality was that I'd never known anyone more committed to the task at hand, and less likely to take time off. "You know you have naming rights?"

"I had no idea." I tried not to smile.

"Well, you might want to give it some thought."

I knew what I wanted to call it, of course. But I had no wish to sound like an egomaniac. I'd gotten to know him pretty well over the years, so I decided to give him a chance to open a door for me. "Tom," I said, "if you'd discovered one of these things, what would you call it?"

"The tradition is that it should become Gibson's Comet."

"I could live with that."

• • •

I don't know that anyone became prouder of Gibson's Comet than Liz. But she was disappointed that the image on her computer screen was barely visible. "I thought comets were bright," she said. "Where's its tail?"

"It won't have one until it gets closer to the sun."

"When will that happen?" she asked.

"It'll be a while," I said.

Warren was happy for me, and gradually over the next few weeks, everything went back to normal. One evening while we were watching a *Seinfeld* rerun, I got a call from a woman who identified herself as an astronomer working at the Mauna Kea observatory in Hawaii. "*Maryam,*" she said, "*something odd's happening.*"

I couldn't imagine why she would be calling me. "What's that?" I asked.

"*We have two more comets coming in. From the same general location as yours. I'll forward the data if you like.*"

That was not good news. I wasn't excited at getting competition. But when I saw Tom at the university next morning and mentioned it, he'd already heard.

"Something's happening out there," he said.

• • •

Our local TV station, WKLS, hit a slow news period and asked me to answer some on-camera questions. The show's moderator was Judy Black, who specialized in doing inspirational, uplifting pieces. "Dr. Gibson," she said, "have we ever had three comets in the sky at the same time before?"

"Well," I said, "they're all a long way off, so I wouldn't exactly characterize them as 'in the sky.' But, yes, that's certainly unusual."

"Can you explain why it's happening?"

"Judy, we think there's been a gravitational change of some sort. We're still looking for a reason."

Her eyebrows rose. "What could cause such a change?"

"A lot of things, really. It can happen, for example, if one of the big planets gets a bit close to an object in the Kuiper Belt. That's what pulls the comets out of the Belt and sends them in our direction."

"Is that what's happening now?"

"No. Nothing's really close to the area."

"Then what is it?"

"We're still working on it, Judy."

• • •

I was on my way to the university after the show when Tom called. "*Can you come by my office?*"

"Sure," I said. "When?"

"*When can you get here?*"

"I have a class in forty minutes. I can come in after that."

"*Artie Thompson will cover for you. Come here now. As soon as you get back to the campus.*"

When I arrived, he was at his desk talking with a thin white-haired man who was seated in one of the two armchairs. Tom said hello and gave me a pained smile. "Maryam," he said, "this is Paul Crenshaw. He's the director—"

"—of the Kitt Peak Observatory. Yes, of course! Hello, Professor Crenshaw. It's an honor to meet you."

"Call me 'Paul,'" he said. His eyes were tired behind thick bifocals, and he nodded without any show of welcome. "You're the young lady who discovered the first comet, I take it?"

I nodded. And managed maybe a flicker of a smile. "Yes, that's correct, Profes—Paul. But what was so urgent?"

Tom pointed to the other chair, waited for me to sit, and took a deep breath. "First off, Maryam, if you get into any more conversations with reporters, we'd like you not to mention that there's a problem."

"I didn't say anything about a problem."

"Just don't go into details about why we have three comets, okay?"

Crenshaw was nodding.

"All right," I said. "Sure."

Tom and Crenshaw exchanged glances without speaking. I was getting scared. Had I done something seriously stupid?

Tom pushed back in his chair. "Paul flew in this morning," he said. "Kitt Peak has been looking into this."

"*Kitt Peak has? Why?*"

"Along with a lot of other people." His eyes locked on mine. "This conversation does not leave this room."

"Okay."

Crenshaw took over: "We know why there were *three* comets."

"What do you mean *were*?"

"The trajectories are changing. If that continues, and we're pretty sure it will, they won't make it into the inner solar system."

"Why? What's going on?"

"There's a brown dwarf nearby." Brown dwarfs are failed stars. They lack the mass to power a fusion reaction in their cores. They're big, they're heavy, and you don't want to get too close to one of them.

"Where is it?"

"About thirty million miles from the comets. Unfortunately, it's coming in our direction."

"My God."

"We're pretty sure it won't hit us."

"I'm relieved to hear that. But—?"

Tom picked up the thread: "It's going to disrupt some orbits. Including ours."

No way that could be good. We could expect either to get pitched into the sun, or dragged away from it altogether.

His framed dictum caught my eye. *Enjoy the moment.* "How bad's it going to be?" My voice shook.

"We're working on the details."

Right. The details.

• • •

Brown dwarfs can be almost invisible. They put out very little heat, often not much more than you'd have in your kitchen. This one was about the size of Jupiter, but had about sixty times its mass.

"So how'd your day go?" asked Warren.

I'd given my word. "Okay," I said. "How about yours?"

It wasn't the first time I'd lied to him. I hadn't told him the truth about his cooking, about whether I'd loved anyone before he came along, about how good looking I thought he was. But that was all minor league stuff. This was the first time I'd deceived him about anything important.

But he told me about a deal he was closing over on Shepperton Avenue. And I began recalibrating what mattered in life.

The following day I did another TV interview, in which I tried to brush aside the issue of the trajectory change. "Nothing of any significance," I said.

Liar, liar.

Tom promised he'd let me know any further data that came in, so you can understand that every time the phone rang over the next few days, I stopped breathing.

And finally, while I was on my way to a morning class, it came. "*When you're finished with your lecture, Maryam, come down to my office.*"

"Good news or bad?" I said.

"*Just come when you're free.*"

I kept walking, trying to keep cool. I went into my classroom. The class was Principles of Physics II: Electromagnetism and Radiation.

That I got through it at all remains one of my proudest achievements.

• • •

Tom was talking with a couple of visitors when I walked in. He excused himself immediately and explained we had important business. They left and I sat down. He closed the door and remained standing by it, his hand on the knob.

"What?" I said.

"It's going to drag us out of orbit. Same as it did to the comet."

I sat, not moving, not surprised, but with my life draining. "Do we have any chance at all?"

"I don't see how."

I sat staring at him. "When?"

"Well, that's the good news, I guess. The thing's moving slowly. The process won't begin for nineteen years."

I just sat there trying to breathe. Trying to take it all in.

"The embargo is still on, Maryam. Say nothing."

That shocked me. "You can't really keep something like this to yourself. People have a right to know."

"Sure they do. And they have almost two decades left to live normal lives. Let them know what's happening and you'll take that from them."

"It's not your call."

"You're right. It's not. They're telling the president as we speak."

• • •

I broke my promise three minutes after I got home. There was no way I could keep that kind of secret. Liz was up in her room, so I sat down and told Warren everything. As well as extracting his word that he would say nothing to anyone. And hoping he was better at it than I had been.

"End of the world?" he said.

"The data aren't complete yet, but it doesn't look as if there's any way out."

We were on the sofa. He leaned over and we embraced. "You okay?" he asked.

"What do *you* think?"

He shook his head. "Real estate values along the river are gonna crash." I don't know if I ever loved him more than I did at that moment. "Nineteen years is a long time," he added. "But it'll be hard on Liz." He sat for a minute, eyes focused on a distance place. "I'm not sure where we go from here."

"Tom's worried about what will happen if the news gets out. He thinks there'll be panic in the streets."

"He's probably right. But I won't say anything."

"Good."

"How long before it's visible to the naked eye?"

"It's very dull. It'll probably be ten years, at least."

• • •

We collected Liz and went out for pizza that night. I got pepperoni on mine. Liz, as usual, ordered black olives. And Warren got his plain. I don't ever recall an evening during which the details stood out so sharply. I can close my eyes now, and recall exactly what everyone was wearing, what we talked about, which server we had, and what the weather was like. Oddly, the brown dwarf had retreated into the darkness of my mind, and I was aware mostly of how fortunate I'd been over my lifetime, and how I appreciated having that night with my family.

I remember thinking how easy it was to forget that we live day to day under a shadow. A car accident. A crazy guy with a gun. A brain tumor. You never know. Enjoy the moment. And I did. If there's an evening in my entire life that I could go back to and relive, that would be it. We were getting ready to leave the restaurant when we noticed that it had grown quiet around us. The Italian music which routinely played had been turned off. People at the other tables were whispering, shaking their heads, and looking anxiously at each other. We asked our server what was happening. "News report," she said in a low voice. "They're saying the end of the world is coming."

When we got home, it was all over the TV. Every show had been interrupted. Sources were cited around the planet. It looked as if everybody connected with the investigation had broken whatever pledge had been made. There was even an unidentified White House source. Then we learned the President was about to speak.

Ten minutes later he was talking from Air Force One. "*My fellow Americans,*" he said, "*we have reports that a giant collapsed star has entered the solar system and is expected to collide with the Earth in twenty years. The story comes from several reliable sources. Our best and brightest minds are looking into it as I speak. We should keep in mind that we are talking about an event two decades away. So we have time to consider our options. Rest assured, I will keep you informed… .*" He looked shaken. "*They're calling it the* Maryam Object."

Warren was staring past me, and I wondered if he was reliving my birthday party.

• • •

Three days later Hollywood star Jessie Wood was caught on camera suggesting the world would be a better place if women would stop trying to grab power and stay the hell in the kitchen. It was the sort of story that would ordinarily have dominated the news cycle for the better part of a week. On this occasion, hardly anyone noticed.

PRETTY SOON THE FOUR HORSEMEN ARE GOING TO COME RIDING THROUGH

Nancy Kress

The school hallway smells of chalk and Lysol and little kids. That smell don't never change. What's changed is that this time I'm called to school and missing time I can't afford from my job 'cause of Carrie, not Sophie. Which don't really make sense. What kind of trouble can a kindergartner get into?

"Ms. Drucker? I'm Olivia Steffens," Carrie's teacher says. "We met at the Parents' Open House."

We did, but we didn't talk much. She was the property of the moms with sunglasses on top of their heads and highlights in their hair. I moved to this school district so's my girls don't have to go to that rat-ridden disgrace on Pelmar Street, but that don't mean I really belong. I shake her hand, the nails manicured pink but one broken off. That helps a little bit.

We sit in tiny chairs that she fits into better than I do. Slim, pretty, she can't be any older than me—but then, I had Sophie at sixteen. I face a row of cut-out paper pumpkins on the wall. It's October.

Ms. Steffens says, "I'm so glad you could come today. There's been an incident on the playground involving Carrie."

"What kind of incident?" If it was Sophie who'd made trouble, I'd already know. Fighting, taking lunch money—kid is on my mind all the time. Last Sunday I lit a candle to St. Pancras that we didn't move here too late for Sophie to outgrow all the shit she learned at Pelmar Street.

Ms. Steffens says, "Some older girls caught Carrie and another child, Tommy Winfield, on the playground at recess. The girls taunted them, and, well, two of the girls pulled Tommy's and Carrie's underwear off. I only learned about this when Tommy's mother called me, quite upset."

And *I* didn't learn about it at all. Little bastards. I keep my face rigid—you don't never give people that sort of edge over you. "Is that all?"

"No, I'm afraid not. Carrie went through the rest of the day, apparently, with no underwear, but your older daughter is in the perpetrators' fourth-grade classroom."

So this is about Sophie after all. I might of known.

"She found them laughing about the state of the underwear and has threatened to 'get even.' Her teacher would have been at this conference, too, but she's quite ill and the class had a substitute that day, who is now out of town. Carrie—"

"Why wasn't these kids being supervised on the playground?"

"They were, of course, but apparently not adequately. The same illness that hit Sophie's teacher has kept us really short-staffed for a week."

"You still got an obligation to protect my kids!"

"I know that." Ms. Steffens's voice gets colder. "The girls responsible will be punished. But Carrie didn't fight back, which is what I want to talk to you about. She did whatever they told her to, without even a protest. And when James LeBlanc hit her two weeks ago—the principal called you about that, I know—she also didn't fight back. She just stood there and would have let him hit her again if the lunch lady hadn't intervened."

I say, "What about the state of the underwear?"

"What?"

"You said the girls were laughing about the state of the underwear. What about it?"

Ms. Steffens looks like she said too much, which she did. She don't answer.

I say, "Never mind." The panties was probably ragged. Carrie needs new underwear, but Sophie's shoes came first because you can see shoes and not underwear. Supposedly. "So what do you want me to do about it?"

"Two things." Ms. Steffens is tougher than she looks. "First, talk to Sophie—we cannot have revenge violence in this school. Second, consider having Carrie see someone about her passivity, which does not seem entirely normal. The school counselor, Dr. Parker, is—"

"No." I stand up. "Carrie don't need no therapy. I'll handle this."

"But—"

"Thanks for letting me know." I walk out, past the rows of pumpkins with crayoned-on faces, all grinning at me like demons.

• • •

When the volcano blew up, I was three months pregnant with Carrie. It was one of the worst times in my life. Jim had just disappeared, no forwarding address, no ways for the Legal Aid lawyer to get me any child support. They never did find him. Sophie's daddy was in prison—still is—so no help there.

I got lousy taste in men. Since Carrie was born, I just stay clear of all of them. Safer that way.

So I wouldn't of paid any attention to the volcano, except that nobody could *not* pay attention to it. It was everywhere, first on the news and then in the air. Even though it blew up somewhere in Indonesia, killing I don't know how many people, the ash blew all over the world. Somebody at work told me that's why the sunsets and sunrises were so gorgeous, red and orange, like the sky itself was on fire.

• • •

I pick up Sophie from school and Carrie from after-school daycare. Carrie gives me her sweet smile. Two like her and my troubles would be over. But instead I got Sophie.

"Carrie," I say in the car, which is making that clunking noise again, "did some older girls pull off your underwear on the playground?"

"Y…e…ss."

"Why didn't you *tell* me?"

"You weren't there, you were at work," she says, with five-year-old logic. Actually, she's just barely five, the youngest kid in her class. I probably should of held her back to start kindergarten next year, but it's a lot cheaper to pay for just after-school care.

"Why didn't you fight back?"

Carrie just looks at me, her little face wrinkled, and I sigh. Sophie is, weirdly, easier to talk to.

"I pounded those bitches bloody!" Sophie said, once we got home.

"Language!" I tell her. "We don't talk that way."

"*You* do." She faces me, hands on her hips, lip stuck out. Sophie's been feisty since she was born. Also, she's going to be pretty, and I know how full my hands are going to be when she's a teenager. But she's not going to mess up her life at sixteen the way I did. I'll kill her first.

She says, "I was defending my little sister!"

"I know, but—"

"You told me to take care of her at school! Well, do I or don't I?"

"I told you no more fighting! Christ, Sophie, do you want to get expelled or something? We moved here for the school, you know that, and yet you go and—"

"I didn't go and do nothing!"

"Don't talk back to me! I said that if you got into any more fights, I was going to ground you, and I am! You come home right after school for a week and stay here, no playing with Sarah or Ava—nobody in and nobody out!"

"That's not fair! I wouldn't have to fight if Carrie would ever fight back herself!"

"She's not a—"

"I know what she is! A wimp!" Sophie flounces off to her room. But then she says it, over her shoulder: "Just like all the rest of them!"

"The rest of who?" I call, but she's already gone.

• • •

The volcano blew up on February 20 and it just kept blowing up for days. The scientists knew ahead of time that something was going to happen there, but not such a big something. It was the second-biggest blow-up since before Christ was born. Huge walls of flame rose up—I seen pictures. The explosion was heard a thousand miles away. Everything got dark for a couple hundred miles, from all the ash and rocks thrown up in the atmosphere, some as high as twenty-five miles up. Aircraft had to go way around the whole area, after a few of them got caught and fell out of the sky. Whole villages disappeared in lava and hot ash.

I felt sorry for all the people who died, of course, but I had my own troubles. Money troubles, morning-sickness troubles, man troubles. The truth is, the volcano was way over on the other side of the world, and I didn't really care that much.

Then.

• • •

I remember the name of the other kid who got pantsed on the playground: Tommy Winfield. I dig out an old phone book—we don't got internet any-more, not since Sophie had to have all that dental work done—and find the Winfields' address. After supper I leave Carrie with Sophie, which I do only for quick trips, and drive over there.

It's a toney part of town, near the Bay. Big house, trees sending down bright leaves onto the lawn. The woman who opens the door is toney and bright-colored, too, a yellow sweater tossed over her shoulders like she's some ageing model for Lands' End.

"Yes?"

"I'm Carrie Drucker's mother. She's in your kid Tommy's class at school."

Her shoulders kind of hunch and her face changes. I say, "Carrie and Tommy was both pantsed by some older girls on the playground."

"Yes, well, they—please do come in."

I do. The hall is bigger than my kitchen, with a table holding a big bouquet of fresh flowers and a floor of real stone. Well, so what? I say what I come here to say.

"I want to ask you something about Tommy. He didn't fight back, no more than my Carrie did. Is he always like that?" The word that Ms. Steffens used comes back to me. "Passive?"

"He's an introvert, and very gentle, yes. May I ask why you're asking?"

I can't really say why, not yet. But I plunge on. "Are his friends like that? The other kids in his class?"

"Why, I—well, I suppose some are passive and some aren't. Naturally. Children differ so much, don't they?"

Now I feel like a fool. The only friends of Carrie's I ever see are the twins next door, who are a lot like Carrie. I say, "Did Tommy's teacher say he should get some therapy?"

Mrs. Winfield's face changes again. "I really can't discuss that with you, Ms. Drucker. But I do want to say that I—we, my husband and I—appreciate your older daughter's attempt to protect Tommy and Carrie, if not the form of it."

All at once I want to defend Sophie for fighting, which don't make sense because I'm punishing her for fighting. This woman irritates me, even though I can see she don't intend to. It's confusing. I mumble, "Thanks, then, bye," and stumble out.

Anyway, I'm wrong again. *Some are passive and some aren't.* What makes me think I'm smart enough to think this out, when nobody else has?

I go home and start the laundry.

• • •

It was the summer after the volcano blew up that the weather got strange here—all the ways away from Indonesia in upstate New York. The spring and summer had a weird reddish fog in the air, from volcanic ash high up in the atmosphere. Sunlight didn't come through right. The winter had been bad, but even the summer was cold, really cold. We had snow in June. Mornings in July, the lake had ice on it. Some crops got killed, others didn't grow, and food got expensive.

Scientists started publishing reports about all the ash and stuff thrown out of the volcano. They said that some of it was normal for volcanoes but some wasn't. Also, that the un-normal stuff was causing strange chemical reactions high up. I still wasn't paying much attention. Carrie was born in August, and managing her and Sophie, who was five, was really hard.

Ash can stay in the upper atmosphere a long time, because it don't rain much up there.

Most of the ash ended up in Africa and Europe. I don't know why. Winds.

• • •

Saturday, the twins from next door come over to play with Carrie. DeShaun and Kezia Brown, a boy and a girl. They don't look much alike. The twins don't go to school yet because they don't turn five until November. Mary Brown don't work, but she's got a husband with a decent job so they're all right. They got a two-year-old car and internet.

"Do you want to play horsies again?" Carrie says.

"Do you?" DeShaun says. He's bigger than the girls, really big for his age, but he never bullies Carrie or Kezia. He's really sweet. Sam Brown calls him "my future linebacker" but I don't think so.

Kezia says to Carrie, "Do *you* want to play horsies? Or something else?"

They go back and forth for a while with the do-you-no-do-you's until they finally settle on horsies. As they head outside, I say, "Stay in the yard where I can see you!" It's not really a yard, just an empty lot between our Section Eight building and the Browns' little house, but Sam keeps it mowed and Mary and I do regular pick-ups of all the trash people throw out of their car windows.

I finish my coffee and mop the kitchen floor. Sophie gets up and we have an argument about her room, which is supposed to also be Carrie's room, but Sophie's junk is piled on both bunks so that Carrie slept last night on a pile of clothes on the floor. The argument goes on and on, and by the time Sophie stomps off to clean Carrie's bunk, the kids are gone from the yard.

I tear outside. "Carrie! Carrie, where are you! Kezia! DeShaun!"

I find them behind our building, where there's a sort of cement alcove beside the steps that comes down from a back door. A boy has them backed up against the dumpster. Kezia holds a drippy ice cream cone. The boy has the other two cones, which Mary must of given the kids. He licks one of them and then shoves the other one in DeShaun's face.

None of them see me. I stop and wait.

DeShaun is bigger than the other boy. He could take the little turd even if Carrie and Kezia didn't help. But all three of them just stand there, DeShaun with chocolate ice cream sliding off his nose onto the front of his hoodie. None of the three of them do anything. They look upset, not really scared. But they just stand there.

"Hey!" I yell.

The boy turns, and now *he* looks scared. He's not more than six. I don't recognize him. He drops the ice cream cone and runs.

"DeShaun, why didn't you hit him?"

DeShaun looks down at his sneakers, then up at me. I can't read his expression. Finally he says, polite—he's always polite—"It's not right to hit people."

"Well, no, not usually, but when they're attacking you—" I stop. He's looking down at his feet again.

I finally say, "Come on, let's get you cleaned up."

At lunch, Sophie spills our last carton of milk and I yell at her. "I didn't mean it!" she yells back, which is true. She goes into her room and slams the door. When I calm down, I apologize. I was only yelling at her from frustration. It's not her fault. None of it is her fault—the ice cream thing or that I forgot to bring home milk last night or my crappy job or anything.

Later on, I go to the Browns' and ask to use their computer. I bring some home-made cookies that I had in the freezer. They were saved for the girls' lunches, but I don't ever go empty-handed to ask for anything. We're not charity cases. And this is research.

• • •

The summer after the volcano, when the scientific reports of weird chemicals in the ash first came out, the theories started.

Some people said the volcano was a conspiracy, that it had been deliberately set off by white nations to poison the Asians. But nobody who wasn't already dead from the explosion seemed to be dying of any poison, and anyway how can you deliberately set off a volcano?

Some people said that the volcano was the start of the End Times, and pretty soon the Four Horsemen were going to come riding through, and then Armageddon and the New Earth. But no horsemen appeared.

Some people said that the weird chemicals didn't come from Earth, so they must've been put deep inside by aliens. I wouldn't of paid no more attention to this idea than to the others, except it was on the news that some scientists agreed that the chemicals weren't like any we had on Earth. They were brand new here. They blew all over the world and got into everything. Everybody breathed them in. They were found in breast milk.

• • •

The kindergarten class is going on a field trip to Pumpkin Patch Farm, and I'm one of the room mothers going with them. I never done this before. It means taking the day off from work without pay, and riding on a school bus, and seeing the other two room mothers in their bright ski jackets and leather boots give me sideways glances, but I go. I have to look at a whole bunch of kids Carrie's age, not just her and the twins.

I know I'm not some detective like in the mysteries from the BookMobile, but I *have* to do this.

The kids are excited. They each get a sip of cider from a tiny paper cup, see horses and kittens in the barn, and pick out a pumpkin to take home. The rule is that the pumpkin is supposed to be small enough for the child to carry by himself, but that don't always work out. Two little boys want the same pumpkin, and I watch them fight over it, pushing and hitting until Ms. Steffens breaks it up. On the bus two girls get into a tussle over who gets to sit next to who. Carrie and four others, two boys and two girls, walk in a little group around the pumpkin field, discussing the choices like they was choosing diamonds, and helping each other pick up and carry their pumpkins to the bus.

My theory is shot to hell. Some of these kindergartners are passive and some aren't.

On the bus one pumpkin rolls off the seat and smashes, and we get wailing and accusations.

• • •

The volcano was supposed to blow up 10,000 years ago. That's what some scientists are saying now, from tracing all the things that go on under the Earth's crust. Only something shifted unexpectedly next to something else, and the volcano got delayed.

I found that out on the Browns' computer, along with a lot of other stuff I never knew. Big explosions like this happened before. One was in 1816, but even bigger ones happened thousands and even millions of years ago.

• • •

The weekend after Halloween is Sophie's birthday. I almost cancel her party because on Halloween, against my orders, she took off with her friends to trick-and-treat at houses without me, where anybody could of given her apples with razor blades in them or poisoned candy. They didn't, but I had to go over each one of the million pieces of candy she brought home, and then I made her give some to Carrie, who only went to three houses with me beside her.

"But it's my birthday party!" Sophie rages, and I give in because it isn't much of a party anyway, only four girls coming over for pizza and cake. I can't afford more than that, and even the pizza is a stretch.

The girls bring presents. Two are expensive—who gives a ten-year-old a cashmere sweater? Two are cheap gimcracks, and I see that these two girls are embarrassed. After that, the party feels a little strained, and soon the girls all leave. Sophie, scowling, goes to her room, where Carrie had stayed throughout the whole thing.

I clean up, sorry that Sophie is disappointed in her party. But I'm not thinking about Sophie, or about the gifts, as much as about the girls. Two of them, one with a cheap present and one with the cashmere sweater, looked like teenagers. Already. They had on bras, the straps visible, and their faces were slimmer and sharper. The other two looked like Sophie: little girls still. But Sophie told me that they're all in her fourth-grade class. Did some get held back a year? They didn't sound any dumber than the others. (Most of the party conversation was pretty dumb.) I try to remember when I was in the fourth grade. I started out nine years old and then turned ten in November, like Sophie, and some of my friends didn't get their birthdays until spring… .

Older. Two of those girls were maybe six months older than the others. So—

Through the bedroom door, Carrie calls out something.

I race to the door, but something stops me. Carrie didn't sound hurt or mad. I pick up a dirty glass from the party ("Just milk?" the cashmere-sweater girl said, making a face. "No Coke?") and hold it between my ear and the closed door.

Sophie says, "You're a baby and a wimp and nobody likes you!"

Carrie says something I don't catch.

"It is so true! Kezia told me yesterday that she only pretends to like you so she can play with your toys! She really hates you!"

Carrie starts to cry.

"Stop that! Stop it right now, you little bitch!" *Whap.*

I shove open the door just as Sophie cries, "I'm sorry, Carrie! I didn't mean to!" By the time I pick up Carrie, Sophie is crying, too. I look at her face and I know she means it—she is sorry she tormented Carrie. She don't know why she did it.

But I do.

• • •

Punctuated equilibrium. Say that ten times. It's when evolution takes a big skip forward. It's on Wikipedia. There's a long, long time when human beings don't change much, and then all at once something happens—scientists say they don't know what—and big changes happen. Ten million years ago, or twenty million depending on who you look up, there was a sudden bunch of big changes in human genes. Forty thousand years ago, all at once and mostly all over the world, cavemen started making bone tools and painted beads and drawings on cave walls. Nobody knows why. Something affected their brains.

Ten thousand years ago, when our volcano should of blown up, people invented farming and started living in cities. Then, instead of just having little skirmishes between roving bands of hunter-gatherers, they geared up for real wars. All the wars in the Bible started, and the wars never stopped, right up until where we are now. All the wars that never would of happened if human brains weren't so violent and angry.

• • •

I cuddle Carrie, who don't cry as long as Sophie does. Carrie, my baby, one of the oldest fetuses affected by whatever stuff the volcano threw into her fetus brain. Most of the others aren't even in school yet. Kids don't get studied much until they're in school.

But two days ago I was talking on my work break with Lisa Hanreddy. She told me she went to a pre-school parent-teacher conference for her son Brandon. Lisa said he's doing good except in counting, but his teacher also praised him for being nice. "She said he's the only boy in the class that doesn't take toys away from other kids or hit them," Lisa told me, "and my heart sank. He's gonna be picked on all through school."

Yes. But it isn't the bullies that Lisa should worry about. That I should worry about, for Carrie. You can find the bad guys and stop them—some of the time anyway.

I think about a whole generation like Carrie, growing up all around the world. Whether aliens are trying to shape humans and screwing up the timing, or God is doing it and making a piss-poor job, or all the theories are just so many crocks of shit—whatever, *something* is happening here. These kids will grow up alongside the rest of us, the people like Sophie and me, and we're going to be more of a danger than the bullies. We, the good people who just get frustrated and take it out, like we all do, on whoever's closest and will stand for it—on the Carries and Kezias and DeShauns, the butts of that careless kind of cruelty, who don't ever fight back because the impulse to fight just isn't in them.

"I'm sorry, Mom," Sophie sobs. And she is.

For now.

I clutch Carrie closer. What's going to happen to her and the kids like her?

And what will they turn the rest of us into?

SPORES

Seanan McGuire

June 2028

Something in the lab smelled like nectarine jam. I looked up from the industrial autoclave, frowning as I sniffed the air. Unusual smells aren't a good thing when you work in a high-security bio lab. No matter how pleasant the odor may seem, it indicates a deviance from the norm, and deviance is what gets people killed.

I straightened. "Hello?"

"Sorry, Megan." The round, smiling face of one of my co-workers—Henry, from the Eden Project—poked around the wall separating the autoclave area from the rest of the lab. His hand followed, holding a paper plate groaning under the weight of a large wedge of, yes, nectarine pie. "We were just enjoying some of Johnny's harvest."

I eyed the pie dubiously. Eating food that we had engineered always struck me as vaguely unhygienic. "Johnny baked that?"

"Johnny baked it, and Johnny grew it," Henry said, beaming. "The first orchard seeded with our Eden test subjects has been bearing good fruit. You want a slice?"

"I'll pass," I said. Realizing that I was standing on the border of outright rudeness, I plastered a smile across my face and added, "Rachel's planning something big for tonight's dinner. She told me to bring my appetite."

Henry nodded, his own smile fading. It was clear he didn't believe my excuse. It was just as clear that he would let me have it. "Well, we're sorry if our festivities disturbed you."

"Don't worry about it." I gestured to the autoclave. "I need to unpack this before I head out."

"Sure, Megan," he said. "Have a nice evening, okay?" He withdrew, vanishing around the cubicle wall and leaving me comfortably alone. I let out a slow breath, trying to recover the sense of serenity I'd had before strange smells and coworkers disrupted my task. It wasn't easy, but I'd had plenty of practice at finding my center. Less than thirty seconds later, I was unpacking hot, sterile glassware and getting my side of the lab ready for the challenges of tomorrow.

Project Eden was a side venture of the biotech firm where I, Henry, and several hundred others were employed. Only twenty-three scientists, technicians, and managers were appended to the project, including me, the internal safety monitor. It was my job to make sure the big brains didn't destroy the world in their rush toward a hardier, easier to grow peach, or an apple that didn't rot quite so quickly after it had been picked. On an official level, I was testing the air and lab surfaces for a committee-mandated parts per million of potential contaminants. On an unofficial level, I spent a lot of time sterilizing glassware, wiping down surfaces, and ordering new gloves, goggles, and lab coats.

It was work that could have been done by someone with half my education and a quarter of my training, but the pay was good, and it gave me an outlet for the compulsions that had kept me out of field biology. Besides, the hours were great. I didn't mind being a glorified monkey if it meant I got to work in a good, clean lab, doing work that would genuinely better the world while still allowing me to quit by four on Fridays.

The team was still celebrating and eating pie when I finished putting the glassware away and left for the locker room. I hadn't been kidding about Rachel telling me to save my appetite. It had been a long day, and I wanted nothing more than to spend an even longer night with my wife and daughter.

• • •

Rachel was in her studio when I got home. She had a gallery show coming up, and was hard at work on the pastels and impressionistic still lifes that were her bread and butter. I knocked on the wall to let her know I was there and kept walking toward the kitchen. It was her night to cook—that part was true—but that didn't mean I couldn't have a little snack before dinner. The Farmer's Market was held on Tuesday afternoons. I had worked late Tuesday night, but I knew Rachel and Nikki had gone shopping, and Rachel had the best eye for produce. Whatever she'd brought home would be delicious.

The fruit bowl was in its customary place on the counter. I turned toward it, and froze. A thick layer of grayish fuzz covered its contents, turning them from a classicist's ideal still life into something out of a horror movie. "Rachel!" I shouted, not moving. It was like the information my brain had was too jarring to fully process. It would take time for all of me to get the message. "There's something wrong with the fruit!"

"You don't have to shout, I'm right here." My wife stomped into the kitchen, wiping her hands on the dishtowel she'd been using to clean her paintbrushes between watercolor overlays. She had a smudge of bright pink dust on one cheek, making her look like a little girl who'd been experimenting with her mother's cosmetics. I fell in love with her all over again when I saw that perfect imperfection.

That was the best thing about being married to my best friend, as I'd been telling people for the past fifteen years: I got to fall in love with her every day, and no one ever thought I was being weird. Sometimes normalcy is the most precious gift of all.

I didn't get the chance to tell Rachel about the fruit. Her eyes followed my position to its logical trajectory. It was almost a relief when she recoiled the same way I had, her upper lip curling upward in atavistic disgust. "What did you do?" She turned toward me, scowling. "This was all fresh when we brought it home yesterday."

I blinked at her. "What do you mean, what did I do?" I asked, feeling obscurely offended. "I can't make fruit go off just by looking at it."

"Well, then, did you bring something home from the lab?" She stabbed her finger at the gray-washed contents of the bowl. "This isn't right. I examined this fruit myself. There was nothing wrong with it."

"You got this from the farmer's market, right?" She was right about the age of the fruit: I remembered her bringing it home and dumping it into the bowl, and it had looked fine then. I'd even been thinking about how nice those peaches would taste with some sharp cheddar cheese and a bottle of artisanal hard cider. I wouldn't have done that for moldy fruit. I wouldn't have made it to the office without sterilizing the entire room.

Rachel frowned. "Yes, we did."

"There you go." I picked up the whole bowl, holding it gingerly to avoid any contact with the gray scum, and walked it over to the trash can. The decay had progressed far enough that the bowl's contents made an unpleasant squishing noise when I dumped them out. I wrinkled my nose and put it in the sink, resisting the urge to toss it into the trash with the fruit instead. "Something went bad and set off a chain reaction."

Rachel wasn't listening. She wrinkled her nose at the place where the bowl had been sitting, and before I could say anything, she ran her finger through the circle of gray fluff marking its footprint. "This crap is on the table, too. We're going to need disinfectant."

"I'll disinfect the table," I said, swallowing a jolt of panic. "Go wash your hands."

Rachel frowned. "Honey, are you having an attack?"

"No." Yes. "But this stuff reduced a bowl of fruit to sludge in less than eighteen hours. That doesn't make me feel good about you getting it on your hands." I glared at the gray circle. Rachel's finger had cut a clean line through it, showing the tile beneath. "Please. For my sake."

"Megan, you're scaring me."

"Good. Then you'll use extra soap."

"You're such a worrywart," she said, a note of affectionate exasperation in her voice. She kissed my cheek and was gone, flouncing back into the hall, leaving me alone with the faint scent of rotten fruit.

I looked at the circle for a moment longer, and then turned to the sink. I was going to need a lot of hot water.

• • •

Fungus is the great equalizer.

We give bacteria a lot of credit, and to be fair, life as we know it *does* depend on the tiny building blocks of bacteria. They allow us to digest food, recover from infections, and eventually begin the process of decaying back into the environment. But the truly heavy lifting of the decaying process comes from fungus. Fungus belongs to its own kingdom, separate from animals and vegetables, all around us and yet virtually ignored, because it's not as flashy or exciting as a cat, dog, or Venus flytrap.

There are proteins in mushrooms that are almost identical to the ones found in mammalian flesh. That means that every vegetarian who eats mushrooms instead of meat is coming closer than they would ever dream to their bloody hunter's roots. With so many things we've cataloged but don't understand, how many things are there that we don't know yet? How many mysteries does the kingdom of the fungus hold?

Rachel—after washing her hands to my satisfaction—had gone to pick up our daughter from cheerleading practice. Nikki was in the middle of one of her "dealing with either one of my mothers is embarrassing enough, I cannot handle them both" phases, which would normally have aggravated me. Tonight, I took it as a blessing. Having them both out of the house made it easier for me to go through the kitchen and systematically bleach, disinfect, and scrub every surface the fruit might have touched to within an inch of its life.

Rachel's immediate "what did you do" response wasn't unjustified. I worked in a lab full of biotech and geniuses, after all; it wasn't unreasonable to blame me when something went awry. But that was why I was always so careful. Didn't she see that? Nothing from the lab ever entered our home. I threw away two pairs of shoes every month, just to cut down the risk that I would track something from a supposedly clean room into our meticulously clean home. Whatever this stuff was, it couldn't be connected to Project Eden. It just didn't make any sense.

When I was done scrubbing down the counters I threw the sponges I'd used into the trash on top of the moldy mess that had been a bowl of nectarines and apples—the mold had continued to grow, and was even clinging to the plastic sides of the bag—and hauled the whole thing outside to the garbage bin.

I was on my knees on the kitchen floor, going through my third soap cycle, when Rachel and Nikki came banging through the front door, both shouting greetings that tangled together enough to become gloriously unintelligible, like an alphabet soup made of my favorite letters. "In here!" I called, and continued scrubbing at the linoleum like I'd get a prize when I was finished. I would, in a way. I would get the ability to sleep that night.

Footsteps. I looked up to find them standing in the kitchen doorway, and smiled my best "no, really, it's all right, this isn't an episode, it's just a brief moment of irrational cleanliness" smile. It was an expression I'd had a lot of practice wearing. The elbow-length rubber gloves and hospital scrubs probably didn't help. "Hi, guys. How was practice?"

Nikki frowned, which was almost a relief. There had been a lot of eye-rolling and stomping lately, which wasn't fun for anyone except for maybe her, and I wasn't even certain about that. Having a teenager was definitely a daily exercise in patience. "Mom, why are you scrubbing the kitchen floor? It's not Thursday."

I'd been braced for the question. I still cringed when it was actually asked. There was a weight of quiet betrayal behind it—nights when I'd missed my medication without realizing it and wouldn't let her eat until I'd measured every strand of dry spaghetti and placed it in a pot of boiling, previously bottled water; days spent searching through the women's department at Target for the only bras that had no structural or cosmetic flaws. Years of living with my OCD had left her gun-shy in a way neither Rachel nor I could have predicted when we decided to have a baby.

Nikki looked so much like me at her age, too. That was part of the terror. Nikki was sixteen, and that was roughly the age I'd been when my symptoms had really begun to solidify. Had she managed to dodge the bullet of her genetics, or was she going to start washing the skin off of her hands any day now? No one knew. No one had any way of knowing.

"Remember I told you about the fruit from the farmer's market going off?" asked Rachel, coming to my rescue as she had so many times before. "That mold was nasty. It needed to be cleaned up before we'd be able to cook in here again."

Nikki glanced to the trash can, which was so clean it gleamed. "All this over a little mold?"

"It wasn't a little mold," I said. I was starting to feel like I should have taken a picture of the trash before taking it outside. That stuff had been growing at a rate that made me frankly uncomfortable, and for more reasons than just my OCD. I might be obsessed with cleanliness, but that didn't make me immune to the allure of a scientific mystery. Mold that grew at that kind of rate was mysterious to be sure.

If it were legal to burn trash in our neighborhood, I would have already been looking for the matches.

"Uck," said Nikki: her final word on the matter. She backed out of the doorway and announced, "I'll be in my room," then turned to prance away, flipping her hair theatrically. Rachel watched her go, waiting until the characteristic sound of a door being slammed confirmed Nikki's retreat to her room. Only then did Rachel turn back to me, rolling her eyes. I managed to stifle my laughter.

"You're where she gets the stomping around and slamming doors, you know," I accused, resuming my scrubbing. "My little drama queens."

"I had to contribute something," Rachel said. There was a worried note in her voice. I glanced up to see her leaning in the doorway, arms folded, frowning as she watched me. "Honey…is this really about the mold? You can tell me if you're having a bad night. I just need to know."

I shook my head and went back to work. "I'm fine, honestly. I took my medication, and I'm not having trouble breathing." Asthma-like symptoms were often my first warning of a serious attack. "I just *really* didn't like the looks of that mold, and I don't want to risk it being carried through the house on our shoes. I already scrubbed down the table and the trash can."

"Mmm-hmm." From Rachel's tone, I could tell that she was debating whether or not to believe me. "What about the fridge?"

The smell of the bleach was soothing. I kept scrubbing. "The fruit never went into the fridge. I did a basic check for mold or signs of spoilage, found none, and left it alone. You can check if you want, as soon as I'm done with the floor."

"I will, you know."

"I know." I dropped the sponge into my bowl of sudsy water and stood, stripping off my gloves. I threw them into the trash and turned to find Rachel still looking at me with concern. I offered her a tired smile. "I'm sort of counting on it. What do you want to do for dinner?"

"How do you feel about spaghetti?" The question was neutral enough, but I understood its intent. Spaghetti was one of my triggers, and had been since Nikki was a baby. If I could tolerate irregular pasta, I wasn't having an attack.

"Spaghetti sounds great," I said. "Do you want me to go get some tomatoes from the garden?"

"That would be wonderful."

"Be right back." I stepped out of the kitchen, my bare feet feeling slightly tacky from the bleach, and kissed her cheek before starting for the back door. The floor was clean. The mold was gone. It was a beautiful evening, and it was going to be an even more beautiful night.

• • •

Rachel's spaghetti was, as always, fantastic. She had a real gift with the sauce, managing to combine basic ingredients in a way that was nothing short of magic to me. I could work up complex solutions in the lab, I could synthesize impossible things, but ask me to brown some ground turkey and I was lost. Even Nikki, who had been making vague noises about watching her weight—worrisome, given how slim she was and how often OCD was connected to eating disorders—ate a serving and a half.

Dessert would have been a fruit tart, had everything gone as planned. In the absence of the fruit, we had ice cream—pear sorbet for me, Ben and Jerry's coffee with chunks for Rachel and Nikki—while we talked about our days. As always, Nikki was happy to listen to Rachel talk about painting, and began interrupting with facts about her own infinitely interesting life as soon as I started talking about what I'd been working on back at the lab. I thought about getting offended, and settled for smiling and stealing half of Nikki's ice cream while she was distracted. Rachel's job was more interesting to hear described: she created art, something that could be seen and touched and immediately understood without years of education and practical experience. All things being equal, I'd rather hear about Rachel's job, too.

All in all, it was a pretty peaceful night at home. No, that's not right. Once I shut away the dread that still lingered in the pit of my stomach over the gray mold in the kitchen, it became a *perfect* night. It was just flawed enough to be real, and so real I wanted to repeat it over and over again for the rest of my life. If I could have had that night a hundred times, I would have been able to die a happy woman.

That's the trouble with perfect nights: No matter how good they are, you only ever get to live them once.

It was a work night for me and a school night for Nikki, and both of us were in bed by ten. Rachel joined me an hour or so later. I woke up when she pressed a kiss into the hollow of my throat, her lips practically burning my skin. She snuggled close, and we both dropped down into dreamland, where everything was safe and warm and nothing could ever hurt us, or change our perfect little world.

I woke to the sound of Rachel whispering my name, over and over again. "Megan," she said, her voice tight with some arcane worry. "Megan, wake up, please, I need you to wake up now. *Please.*" It was the panic in that final plea that did me in, yanking me straight through the layers of sleep and back into our bedroom. There was a strange, dusty scent in the air, like something left in the back of an airless room for a long time without being disturbed.

"Rachel?" I sat upright, reaching for the lamp on my side of the bed. Light would make things better. Monsters didn't thrive in the light.

"No! Don't turn it on." The panic that had woken me was even stronger now. "Megan, I…I need you to take Nikki and go next door. Call the paramedics when you get there, but don't turn on the light."

"What?" I squinted into the darkness. Rachel was sitting on the far edge of the bed. I could see her silhouette in the light coming through the open bathroom door. "Honey, what's wrong? Did you hurt yourself? Let me see."

"Oh, no." She laughed, but the panic wasn't gone. It laced through her laughter, turning it jagged and toxic. My heartbeat slowed for a moment, and then sped up as my own panic bloomed. "You don't want to see, Megan, all right? You don't want to see, and I don't want you to see, so please, just go. Get Nikki and go."

"I'm not going to do that. Honey, what's wrong?" And then, God help me, I turned on the light.

Rachel was wearing her favorite nightgown, the blue satin one with the popped and faded lace flowers around the neckline. Her back was to me and her hair was loose, hanging to hide her face from view. As I watched, she sighed so deeply that her entire body seemed to sag, the delicate tracery of her spine pressing hard against her skin.

"I should have known you'd turn on the light," she said, and twisted to face me.

I didn't gasp or recoil. I wish, looking back, that I could say I'd been a better person than that, but the truth is that I was too stunned to do anything but stare silently, trying to make sense of the single gray mitten that she had pulled over her left hand, or the patch of pale gray felt that she had glued to the corner of her left eye. Then she blinked at me, and the strands of mold clinging to her eyelashes wavered in the breeze, and my denial snapped like a broken branch, leaving me holding nothing but splinters. Before I knew it, I was standing with my back against the wall, as far from her as I could get without actually fleeing the room.

Now I understood the dry, dusty smell. It wasn't old paper or a forgotten library book. It was mold, living, flourishing mold, feasting on the body of my wife.

My throat was a desert. It didn't help that Rachel—my beautiful Rachel, who should have been the one panicking, if either one of us was going to—was looking at me with perfect understanding, like she hadn't expected any other reaction, yet still couldn't blame me for following the nature she'd always known I was slave to. She blinked again, and I realized to my horror that the sclera of her left eye was slightly clouded, like something was beginning to block the vitreous humor. Something like the spreading gray mold.

"I must have had a cut on my hand," she said. "I thought I'd scrubbed hard enough, but I guess I was wrong. And then I rubbed my eye in my sleep…maybe that's a good thing. The itching woke me up. So we can go to the hospital and they can do whatever it is you do when you get a…a fungal infection, and then it'll all be okay. Right? I just have to go to the hospital. Right?" There was a fragile edge to her words, like she was standing very close to the place where reason dropped away, leaving only a yawning chasm of blackness underneath.

She looked so sad. My girl. My wife. The woman I had promised to have and to hold, in sickness and in health, amen. And I couldn't make myself go to her. I tried—no one will ever know how hard I tried—but the muscles in my legs refused to work, and the air in my lungs refused to circulate until I was stepping backward into the doorway, away from the dry, dusty smell of mold growing on human flesh.

"I'll call the hospital," I said, and fled for the hall.

• • •

Nikki woke when the ambulance pulled to a stop in front of our house, flashing lights painting everything they touched bloody red. "Mom?" She appeared on the stairs, holding her robe shut with one hand and squinting through the curtain of her hair. "What's going on?"

I forced myself to smile at her. The EMTs already had Rachel outside. They'd taken one look at her and swung into action with a speed that impressed even me, producing gloves and sterile masks and anything else they could use to keep themselves from coming into contact with her skin. Even then they'd touched her as little as possible, guiding her with words, not hands, casting anxious looks at each other and then back at me as they moved. I understood their concern, but there was nothing I could do about it. I couldn't even force myself to follow them. The dry mold smell filled our bedroom, almost solid in its presence. I wanted to bleach the whole place, *would* have bleached the whole place, except that I knew Rachel's treatment might depend on being able to examine the spot where she'd been infected.

"Rachel's not feeling so well," I said. "I'm going to follow her to the hospital as soon as they call and tell me it's all right. I was going to come up and make sure that you were awake before I went."

Nikki's eyes got very wide and round. "You're going to leave me here?"

"No, I'm going to ask Mrs. Levine from next door to keep an eye on you." I didn't want to leave her alone in the house, but even more, I didn't want to take her to the hospital. Not until we knew what the *thing* on Rachel's arm was, and whether it was contagious.

It had to be contagious. It had been on the fruit, and then it had been on the table, and Rachel had touched the residue on the table; just touched it, nothing more than that. If this stuff wasn't contagious, she had been exposed at the same time as the fruit, and Nikki—

Sudden terror seized me. "Honey," I said, fighting to keep my voice level, "are you feeling all right?"

Nikki's eyes got even wider. "Why? Is it food poisoning? My stomach feels fine."

"No, it's not food poisoning. Hold on." I flicked on the light, illuminating the hall and stairs in a harsh white glow. Nikki squinted at me, looking affronted. I would worry about her sensibilities later. "Show me your hands."

"What? Mom—"

"*Show me your hands.*" I was using the tone Rachel always called "OCD voice"—and she wasn't kidding, exactly, even if she used the label to soften my admittedly violent reactions, turning them into something that wouldn't frighten people who weren't as used to me as she was.

Nikki had grown up with my quirks and issues. She stopped arguing and held her hands out for me to inspect. They were spotlessly clean, with short, close-clipped fingernails that had been manicured with a simple clear coat. Most importantly, there was no mold on them. I swallowed the urge to tell her to disrobe, to prove that she wasn't infected. Things weren't that bad. Things weren't going to *get* that bad. I wouldn't let them. I couldn't help her if I let them. I had to hold onto control with both hands, because if I lost it—

If I lost it, I was going to lose everything. For the first time in my life, the sense of impending doom that followed me around might actually have weight.

"Mom, what's going on?" Her voice shook a little as she pulled her robe tight around herself once more. "Where are they taking Rachel?"

"I told you. To the hospital." I turned to look at the front door, and then at the open door to our bedroom. "Go upstairs. You can get online if you want, but I don't want you down here until I've cleaned up a little." Any mold that was in our bedroom could stay; I could sleep on the couch. But the kitchen? The dining room? My fingers itched, and I rubbed them together to reassure myself that it was just the urge to clean, and not a sign of contamination.

"Okay," said Nikki meekly, and turned and fled back to her room, where she could barricade the door against me and my insatiable need to scrub the world.

Rachel's hand. Rachel's beautiful, delicate hand. Completely obscured by clinging gray.

I turned and walked straight for the closet where we kept the bleach.

• • •

The hospital called a little after five a.m., four hours after they had loaded Rachel into the back of an ambulance and left me alone with a contaminated house and a teenage daughter who refused to come out of her room. The gray mold had been growing on Rachel's latest picture, almost obscured by the pastel loops and swirls. I'd stopped when I found it, standing and staring transfixed at the delicate swirls it cut through the color. There was something strangely beautiful about it. It was hardy, and alive, and finding sustenance wherever it could. Even in pastels.

It was eating the last thing my wife had touched before she came to bed and woke me up pleading for help. I had thrown the picture in the trash and was in the process of bleaching the studio walls when the phone rang. My gloves were covered in bleach. I answered anyway. I didn't trust the receiver. "Hello?"

"May I speak to Megan Riley?"

"Speaking." It felt like my insides had been bleached along with the walls. *Please don't be calling to tell me that she's gone*, I prayed. *Please, please, don't be calling to tell me that she's gone.*

"Your wife, Rachel Riley, was admitted shortly after one o'clock this morning. She's resting comfortably, but I have some questions for you about her condition."

Relief washed the bleach away. "So she's all right?"

There was an uncomfortable pause. "I don't want to mislead you, Ms. Riley. Her condition is very serious. Anything you can tell us would be a great help."

I closed my eyes. "She came into contact with a strange gray mold that was growing on some fruit in our kitchen around five o'clock yesterday afternoon. She woke me up shortly after one with the same mold growing on her hand and eye. Judging by how advanced it was, I would estimate that it had been growing since the afternoon, and had only reached a visible stage after she went to bed. She said that it itched."

"Have you, or has anyone else in your home, come into contact with this mold?"

Yes. I've been chasing it through my house, murdering as much of it as I can find. "No, although I've poured a lot of bleach on it," I said. "My teenage daughter is here with me. She hasn't touched any of the mold, and she's clean. I didn't sterilize our bedroom. I thought you might need to examine some of the stuff growing in a relatively natural way."

There was a pause before the doctor asked, "Do you have anyone who can look after your daughter for a short time, Ms. Riley? You may want to come to the hospital."

"Is Rachel all right?"

"Her condition is stable for the moment."

We exchanged pleasantries after that, but I didn't really hear or understand them. When the doctor ended the call I hung up, opening my eyes and leaning against the counter with all my weight on the heels of my hands. My gaze fell on the sink, and on the fruit bowl, which I had scrubbed until my hands were raw before going to bed the night before.

A thick layer of gray mold was growing in the bottom.

• • •

I relaxed as soon as Nikki and I stepped into the cool, disinfectant-scented lobby of the hospital. Nothing could take away from the sense of cleanliness that pervaded this place, not even the people sitting in the chairs nearest to the admission window, waiting for their turn to see the doctor.

Nikki was wearing her robe over a pair of jeans and a pilled sweatshirt that she should have thrown away at the end of the winter. It swam on her petite frame, making her look smaller and even more fragile. I resisted the urge to put an arm around her, offending her teenage pride and making her reject me. Instead, I walked to the open window, waited for the receptionist to acknowledge me, and said, "Megan and Nikki Riley. We're here to see Rachel Riley?"

Her eyes went wide with comprehension and something that looked like fear. "Please wait here," she said, before standing and vanishing behind the dividing wall. I stepped back, rubbing my chapped hands together and wishing I didn't feel quite so exposed. Something was wrong. I knew it.

"Ms. Riley?"

Nikki and I turned to the sound of our last name. A door had opened behind us, and a doctor was standing there, looking weary and worried, wearing booties and a plastic hair cap in addition to the expected lab coat and scrubs. I stepped forward.

"I'm Megan Riley," I said.

"Good. I'm Dr. Oshiro. This must be Nicole." He offered Nikki a tired, vaguely impersonal smile. "There are some snack machines at the end of the corridor, Nicole, if you'd like to go and get something to eat while your mother and I—"

"No." She grabbed my hand, holding on with surprising force. "I want to see Rachel."

The doctor looked at me, apparently expecting support. I shook my head. "I told her she could stay home if she wanted to." Although not in the house, dear God, not in the house; not when mold could grow on a ceramic bowl that had already been bleached and boiled. We'd have to burn the place to the ground before I'd be willing to go back there, and even then, I would probably have avoided contact with the ashes. "She said she wanted to see her mother, and I try to accommodate her wishes."

The doctor hesitated again, taking in the obvious physical similarities between Nikki and I, and comparing them to dark-skinned, dark-haired Rachel, who couldn't have looked less like Nikki's biological mother if she'd tried. Family is a complicated thing. Finally, he said, "I don't want to discuss Ms. Riley's condition in public. If you would please come with me...?"

We went with him. For once, I didn't feel like the people still waiting were watching with envy as I walked away: they had to know what it meant when someone arrived and was seen this quickly. Nothing good ever got you past the gatekeeper in less than half an hour.

The air on the other side of the door was even cooler, and even cleaner. The doctor walked us over to a small waiting area, guiding Nikki to a seat before pulling me a few feet away. Neither of us argued. We were both in shock, to some degree, and cooperation seemed easier than the alternative.

Voice low, he said, "Ms. Riley's condition is complicated. We have been unable to isolate the fungal infection. To be honest, we've never seen anything this virulent outside of laboratory conditions. We've managed to stabilize her, and she's not in much pain, but the fungus has devoured the majority of her left arm, and patches are beginning to appear elsewhere on her body. Barring a miracle, I am afraid that we will have no good news for you here."

I stared at him. "Say that again."

Dr. Oshiro visibly quailed. "Ms. Riley..."

"Outside of lab conditions, you said. Is this the sort of thing you've seen *inside* lab conditions?"

He hesitated before saying, "Not this, exactly, but there have been some more virulent strains of candida—the fungus responsible for yeast infections—that have been recorded as behaving in a similar manner under the right conditions. They had all been modified for specific purposes, of course. They didn't just *happen*."

"No," I said numbly. "Things like this don't just happen. Excuse me. Is there somewhere around here where I can go to make a phone call?"

"The nurse's station—"

"Thank you." And I turned and walked away, ignoring Nikki's small, confused call of "Mom?" at my receding back.

I just kept walking.

• • •

The phone at the lab rang and rang; no one answered. I hung up and dialed again: Henry's home number. He picked up on the second ring, sounding groggy and confused. "Hello?"

"What did you do?" I struggled to make the question sound mild, even conversational, like it wasn't the end of the world waiting to happen.

"Megan?" Henry was waking up rapidly. Good. I needed him awake. "What are you talking about?"

"*What* did you *do*?" All efforts at mildness were gone, abandoned as fast as I had adopted them. "How much fruit is Johnny's orchard producing? Where have you been sending it?"

And then, to my dismay and rage, Henry laughed. "Oh my God, is that what this is about? You figured it out, and now you want to yell at me for breaking some lab protocol? It can wait until morning."

"*No it can't.*"

Henry wasn't my teenage daughter: he'd never heard me use that tone before. He went silent, although I could still hear him breathing.

"What did you do? How did you slip her the fruit?" I was a fool. I should have realized as soon as I saw the mold...but maybe I hadn't wanted to, on some level. I'd already known that it was too late.

God help me, I'd wanted my last perfect night.

"Maria from reception. We had her meet your wife in the parking lot and say she'd bought too many peaches. It was going to get you to come around to our way of thinking, but Megan, the fruit is safe, I promise you—"

"Have there been any issues with contamination of the samples? Mold or fungus or anything like that?"

There was a long pause before Henry said, "That's classified."

"What kind of mold, Henry?"

"That's classified."

"How fast does it grow?"

"Megan—"

"Does it grow on living flesh?"

Silence. Then, in a small, strained voice, Henry said, "Oh, God."

"Did it get out? Did something get loose in the orchard? Who decided testing genetically engineered food on human subjects was a good idea? No, wait, don't tell me, because I don't care. How do I kill it, Henry? You made it. How do I kill it?"

"It's a strain of *Rhizopus nigricans*—bread mold," said Henry. "We've been trying to eliminate it for weeks. I…we thought we had it under control. We didn't tell you because we thought we had it under control. We didn't want to trigger one of your episodes."

"How kind of you," I said flatly. "How do I kill it?"

His voice was even smaller when he replied, "Fire. Nothing else we've found does any good."

"No anti-fungals? No poisons? Nothing?"

He was silent. I closed my eyes.

"Who decided to give it to my wife?"

"I did." His voice was so small I could barely hear it. "Megan, I—"

"You've killed her. You've killed my wife. She's melting off her own bones. You may have killed us all. Enjoy your pie." I hung up the phone and opened my eyes, staring bleakly at the wall for a long moment before realizing that the nurses whose station I'd borrowed were staring at *me*, mingled expressions of horror and confusion on their faces.

"I'm sorry about that," I said. "Maybe you should go home now. Be with your families." There wasn't much else left for them to do. For any of us to do.

• • •

Rachel was in a private room, with a plastic airlock between her and the outside world. "The CDC is on their way," said Dr. Oshiro, watching me and

Nikki. Anything to avoid looking at Rachel. "They should be here within the day."

"Good," I said. It wasn't going to help. Not unless they were ready to burn this city to the ground. But it would make the doctors feel like they were doing something, and it was best to die feeling like you might still have a chance.

The bed in Rachel's room was occupied, but where my wife should have been there was a softly mounded gray *thing*, devoid of hard lines or distinguishing features. Worst of all, it moved from time to time, shifting just enough that a lock of glossy black hair or a single large brown eye—the right eye, all she had left—would come into view, rising out of the gray like a rumor of the promised land. Nikki's hand tightened on mine every time that happened, small whimpers that belonged to a much younger child escaping her throat. I couldn't offer her any real comfort, but I could at least not pull away. It was the only thing I had to give her. I could at least not pull away.

The doctors moved around the thing that had been Rachel, taking samples, checking displays. They were all wearing protective gear—gloves, booties, breathing masks—but it wasn't going to be enough. This stuff was manmade and meant to survive under any conditions imaginable. They were dancing in the fire, and they were going to get burnt.

All the steps I'd taken to keep my family safe. All the food I'd thrown away, the laundry I'd done twice, the midnight trips to the doctor and the visits from the exterminator and the vaccinations and the pleas…it had all been for nothing. The agent of our destruction had grown in the lab where I worked, the lab I'd chosen because it let me channel my impulses into something that felt useful. I hadn't even known it was coming, because people had been protecting me from it in order to protect themselves from me. This was all my fault.

Dr. Oshiro was saying something. I wasn't listening anymore. One of the nurses in Rachel's room had just turned around, revealing the small patch of gray fuzz growing on the back of his knee. The others would spot it soon. That didn't matter. The edges told me that it had grown outward, eating through his scrubs, rather than inward, seeking flesh. The flesh was already infected. The burning had begun.

"Mom?" Nikki pulled against my hand, and I realized I was walking away, pulling her with me, away from this house of horrors, toward the outside world, where maybe—if we were quick, if we were careful—we still stood a chance of getting out alive. Nikki was all I had left to worry about.

Rachel, I'm sorry, I thought, and broke into a run.

SHE'S GOT A TICKET TO RIDE

Jonathan Maberry

-1-

Kids, you know?

Tough to raise a kid in almost any household.

Tough to raise a kid with all the shit going on in the world.

You can't lie to them and say it's all going to be okay, because pretty much it's not all going to be okay. There's stuff that's never going to be okay. Neither well-intentioned rationalization, protective lies, or outright bullshit is going to make it all right.

Bad stuff happens to good people.

That's one of those immutable laws, like saying "everybody dies." They do. Some things are going to happen no matter how much we don't want them to. Even despite a lot of serious effort to prevent them from happening.

Rape happens.

Murder happens.

Abuse happens.

Go bigger: Wars happen. Poverty happens. Famine happens.

Take it from an arbitrary perspective: Tsunamis happen. Earthquakes and tornados happen.

Shit happens.

And it happens, a lot of the damn time, to good people. To the innocent. To the unprotected. To the undeserving.

Try to tell a kid otherwise and they know you're lying.

Lie too much about it and they stop believing anything you tell them.

They stop believing you.

They stop believing *in* you, which is worse.

They stop believing in themselves, which is worst of all.

I see what happens when parents cross that line.

When they call me in, the kid has crossed some lines of his own. We're not talking about "acting out." It's not selling dope to earn fun money or selling yourself as the fun guy. It's not fucking everyone who comes within grabbing distance as a way of making a statement. It's not getting a tattoo or fifteen piercings or going Goth.

We're talking a different set of lines.

When they call me in, the kids have crossed a line that maybe they can't cross the other way. Either they're so lost they can't find it, or they're so lost they don't think there ever *was* a line. All they can see is the narrow piece of ground on which they're standing in that moment. Everything else is chaos. They don't want to move because who would step off of solid ground into chaos? So they stay there.

That's when they call me in.

Sometimes that narrow strip of ground is called a "crack house," and they're giving five dollar blow jobs so they can buy some rock.

Sometimes it's some little group of nutbags who want to build bombs and blow shit up.

And sometimes it's a cult.

A lot of what I do is with kids in cults.

They go in.

I go in and get them out.

When I can.

If I can.

Sometimes I bring back something that spits poison and is going to need to be in a safe place with meds and nurses and lots of close observation. Sometimes I bring back someone who will always be on some version of suicide watch. Sometimes I bring back a kid who is never—*ever*—going to be "right" again, because they were never right to begin with. Or kids who have traveled so far into alien territory that they don't even know what language you're speaking.

They spook the shit out of me, the kids who are so lost they're empty. Like their bodies are vacant houses haunted by shadows of who they used to be, who people *thought* they were.

That's sad.

That's why a lot of guys who do what I do drink like motherfuckers.

A *lot* of us.

Sometimes you get lucky and you find a kid who's maybe thinking that they crossed the wrong line. A kid who wants to be found, who wants to be rescued. A kid who is maybe drifting on a time of expectations because they hope, way down deep, that mommy or daddy gives enough of a genuine shit to come looking. Or at least to *send* someone looking.

Those are great. Do a couple like that in a year and maybe you dial down the sauce. Go a couple of years without one of those jobs and maybe you retire to sell TVs at Best Buy or you eat your gun.

I've had enough bad years that I've considered both options.

And then there are those cases where you find a kid who isn't lost on the other side of that line. I'm talking about a runaway who found what he or she has been looking for. Even if it's a cult. Even if it's a group whose nature or goals or tenets you object to with every fiber of your being. When you find a kid who ran away and found himself…what the fuck are you supposed to do then?

It's a question that's always lurking there in the back of your mind, but it's one you seldom truly have to ask yourself.

It wasn't even whispering to me when I went over the wall at the Church of the Nomad World.

-2-

My target was an eighteen year old girl.

Birth certificate has her name as Annabeth Fiona Van Der Kamp, of the Orange County Van Der Kamps. Only heir to a real estate fortune. My intel on her gives her name as Sister Light.

Yeah, I know.

Anyway, Sister Light was a few days away from her nineteenth birthday, at which point the first chunk of her inheritance would shift from a trust to her control. It was feared—and not unreasonably so—that the girl would sign away that money to the Church of the Nomad World.

That chunk was just shy of three-point-eight million.

She'd get another chunk the same size at twenty. At twenty-one, little Sister Light would get the remainder out of trust. Thirty-four million in liquid cash and prime waterfront properties, including two in Malibu.

Mommy and Daddy's lawyers hired me to make sure none of that happened.

I would like to think that they also had their daughter's emotional, physical and—dare I say it with a straight face?—spiritual wellbeing in mind.

Nope, can't really keep a straight face on that one.

But, fuck it. It's a cult, so maybe the Van Der Kamps are the lesser of two evils. I'm not paid to judge.

So over the wall I go.

-3-

The Church of the Nomad World is located on the walled grounds of an estate. The estate was sold at auction after the previous owners went to jail for selling lots and lots of cocaine. The church officials, according to my background checks, were very businesslike during the purchase and all through the legal stages. They wore suits. They spoke like ordinary folks. Their CFO wore a Rolex and drove a Beamer.

It wasn't until after the title and licenses were squared away, the walls and gates repaired, and the 501(c)(3) papers were in place that the church changed its name. Until that point it was the Church of the World, which sounds like every other vanilla flavored post-Tea Party fundamentalist group. Not that they put a sign up. They *became* the Church of the Nomad World in name only. That label appears on no forms, no licenses, no tax documents.

Everybody knows about it, though.

At least everyone who follows this sort of thing.

As I wandered the grounds, I saw signs of the things they taught in this church. Lots of sculptures of the solar system. The current thinking is that we have eight planets—Pluto having been demoted—and then there are five dwarf planets: Ceres, Haumea, Makemake, Eris, and our old friend Pluto. Plus four hundred and twenty-odd moons of various sizes, plus a shitload of asteroids. Millions of them. I noticed that many of the more elaborate sculptures included Phaëton, the hypothetical planet whose long-ago destruction may account for the asteroid belt between Mars and Jupiter. Those same sculptures had a second moon orbiting the Earth: Lilith, a dark moon that was supposed to be invisible to the naked eye. So, whoever made the sculpture naturally painted it black.

Had to get the details right.

One sculpture of Earth not only had Phaëton, but Petit's moon, the tiny Waltemath's moons, and some other apocryphal celestial bodies I couldn't name.

However here on the grounds, there is an additional globe in all of the solar system sculptures and mobiles. It's big—roughly four times the size of any representation of the Earth. It's brown. And it has a name.

Nibiru.

For a lot of conspiracy nuts, Nibiru is the Big Bad. They variously describe it as a rogue planet, a rogue moon, a brown dwarf star, a counter-Earth, blah blah blah. They say it's been hiding behind the sun, hence the reason we haven't seen it. They say that it has an elliptical orbit that—just by chance—swings it at angles that don't allow any of our telescopes to see it.

But they say it's coming.

And, of course, that it will destroy us.

End of Days shit.

Bunch of Doomsday preppers are building bunkers in the Virginia hills so they can survive the impact.

Take a moment on that.

Worst case scenario is a brown dwarf star—best case scenario is a rogue moon. Hitting the Earth. And they think reinforced concrete walls and a couple of cases of Spam are going to see them through it?

Their websites talk about the Extinction Event, but they're building bunkers and stockpiling ammunition so they can Mad Max their way through... what, exactly? Even if they didn't die during a collision, that would likely crack the planet and send a trillion trillion cubic tons of ash and dust into the atmosphere. Even if they didn't immediately choke to death or freeze during the ensuing ice age. Even if the atmosphere wasn't ripped away and the tectonic plates knocked all to hell and gone. Even if they lived through a computationally impossible event, what exactly would they be surviving for?

That's the question.

It's also the question the Church of the Nomad World claimed to have an answer for. For them, the arrival of Nibiru was, without doubt, a game-ending injury for old Mother Earth. No going to the sidelines for stretches and an ice pack and then back in for the next quarter. Nibiru was the ultimate deal closer for the planet. Everyone and everything dies. All gone. Kaput. Sorry folks, it's been fun.

But here's the fun part: Nibiru isn't going to be destroyed in the same collision. Nibiru is going to survive. It's barely going to be dented. And the vast, ancient, high-minded and noble society of enlightened beings on Nibiru are going to reach out with "sensitivity machines"—I'm not making this up—and harvest those people who are of pure intent and aligned with the celestial godforce.

Don't look at any of that too closely or you'll sprain something.

I got all this from two of my sources. I did my homework before coming here. One source is Lee Kang, a doctor of theology at Duke Divinity School. You've probably seen him on TV. Did that book couple of years back about how science and religion don't need to stand around kicking each other in the dicks. About how a rational mind can have both flavors. He was hilarious on *The Daily Show*. Killed it on *Jimmy Fallon*.

The other source is my science girl, Rose Blum. Rosie the Rocketeer. An actual rocket scientist. Well, her business card says "Observational Physicist," which is too much of a mouthful. Smartest carbon-based life-form I have ever gotten hammered with. There are some nights I can barely recall knocking back Irish car bombs in a dive bar near the Jet Propulsion Lab La Cañada Flintridge near L.A. Her job is looking at the solar system using radio astronomy, infrared astronomy, optical astronomy, ultraviolet, X-ray, and gamma ray astronomy and every other kind of astronomy there is. She also works closely with some of the world's top theoretical astrophysicists. Believe me, if there was something coming toward Earth that was big enough to destroy the planet, she'd know.

She would absolutely know.

I'd had some long talks with her when I first started looking for Sister Light. Rosie was always a high-strung woman. Prone to nervous laughs, mostly at the wrong times. She was also one of the few hardcore scientists I'd met who hadn't lost her faith. She went to synagogue every week and took frequent trips to Israel.

The last time I spoke with her was ten days ago. I'd wanted to bone up on the Nibiru stuff so I would have the ammunition to counter whatever programming they'd force-fed to the girl. Rosie was in a hotel room in Toronto, about to begin a big three-day international symposium on NEOs (near-Earth objects). Nibiru was on the agenda because NASA and other groups wanted to have a clear and cohesive rebuttal to the growing number of crackpot conspiracy theories. Now that the Mayan calendar thing was well behind us, the apocalypse junkies had really gotten behind the imaginary, invisible, rogue dwarf star.

Can you imagine what those conversations must be like? All those scientists, with all that scientific data, trying to combat something with zero supporting evidence—and having a hard time doing it. Emails and phone calls were choking NASA's Spaceguard program, Near-Earth Asteroid Tracking, Lowell Observatory Near-Earth-Object Search, Catalina Sky Survey, Campo Imperatore Near-Earth Object Survey, the Japanese Spaceguard Association, and Asiago-DLR Asteroid Survey, the Minor Planet Center, and other organizations whose job it was to look for things in space that could endanger the Earth.

And some pinhead from Fox News even snuck in a question about it at a White House press conference, which made it blow up even bigger.

Rosie must have been feeling it, too. She was even more jumpy than usual when we spoke on the phone.

"How's it going over there?" I asked.

"It's complicated."

"I bet."

"There are protestors outside the convention center. Hundreds of them, from all over."

"Seriously? Why? What are they protesting?"

"They…um…think we're here to decide on how best to hide the truth from the world."

I laughed. "Ri-i-i-ight. That's why they brought the top astrophysicists from around the world together. That's why they advertised the conference. That's why they're doing it all in plain sight, because you're all trying to hide something."

"This is serious, John. The crowds are really scary. We have a lot of security, and they don't want us to leave the convention center without an escort. They even have police patrolling our hotels."

"That's nuts. What do they think is going to happen?"

"I don't know. We have a conference in a few minutes. Someone from Homeland is coming in to talk to us about it."

"Homeland? Why them? Most of the apocalypse cults aren't dangerous. At least not in that way. I mean, sure the Heaven's Gate people killed themselves, but that was mass suicide, not terrorism. It wasn't a terrorist thing. They weren't looking to hurt anyone else."

"I don't know, John. I'll call you in a couple of days. When I get back to California."

"Okay."

"But…with that girl you're looking for…?"

"Yeah?"

"Be gentle with her. She's eighteen. She waited until she was of legal age before she joined that church."

"I know, but—"

"Maybe she really believes in this."

"If she does, that's an arguable case for irrational behavior."

Rosie took a few seconds with that. "Every religion looks irrational from the outside. It all looks crazy, from a distance. If you're not a believer. We Jews believe in plagues of locusts, giant bodies of water parting, burning bushes, people being turned into pillars of salt. You Christians worship someone who cast out demons and raised the dead. Why should we be allowed to believe in that stuff and this girl not be allowed to believe in something like Nibiru?"

"Hey, you're the one who told me that the laws of physics and gravitational dynamics can't support the presence of a celestial body that big without us seeing its effect on pretty much everything. You went on and on about that, sweetie. You're the rational got-to-measure-it-to-believe it science nerd. I'm just a hired thug."

She usually laughed at stuff like that. She didn't this time.

She told me again that she'd call me, and that was the last time I talked to her.

I've been trying to get through to her office since the conference ended, but her voicemail's jammed. Probably crank callers asking about Nibiru. Rosie was pretty high profile in the news stories about the gig in Toronto. She's been very vocal about the scientific impossibility of it all.

Wish I could get her on the phone. Any new info she could give me might help with breaking Sister Light away from the Church of the Nomad World.

I'd need it, too, because my read on Sister Light was that she was more a true believer than a lost soul. That's important to know because you have to have an approach. The lost ones are beyond conversations. They are terrified of finding out that they're wrong. So much so that they'll hurt themselves rather than face the truth. Buddy of mine had to call parents once to tell them their daughter slashed her own throat when she spotted the pick-up team coming to take her home.

Imagine that.

Fifteen-year-old girl who'd rather take a pair of fabric scissors to her throat instead of going back to whatever hell she'd fled. Whether their problems are real or imagined, kids like that are sometimes too far gone.

Not everyone can be saved. The people here at the Church should understand that. They believe only their initiates are going to hitch a ride on Nibiru. The rest of the unworthy or unrepentant will become stardust.

Stardust.

Sounds better than saying we'll all burn in hellfire, which is what most of these nutbags say.

Stardust doesn't actually sound that bad.

Stardust.

Star stuff.

I spotted her five minutes after I climbed the wall. Sitting on a bench by herself. No watchdogs.

Sister Light.

She was five foot nothing. A slip of a thing, with pale hair and paler skin, and eyes the color of summer grass. Not especially pretty. Not ugly. No curves, but a good face and kind eyes.

Intelligent eyes.

She was sitting on a stone bench in a little grove of foxtail palms and oversized succulents. A small water feature burbled quietly and I think there was even a butterfly. You could have sold a photo of that moment to any calendar company.

All around the grove was a geometric pattern of white rectangular four-by-seven foot stones. They fanned out from where she sat like playing cards. Four or five of them, covering several acres of cool green grass

The girl was wearing a white dress with a pale blue gardening apron. White gloves tucked into the apron tie. Her head was covered with the requisite blue scarf that every woman in the Church wore. The men all wore blue baseball caps with circles embroidered on them. Symbolic of the nomad world, I supposed.

I'd come dressed for the part. White painter's pants, white shirt, blue cap.

Stun gun tucked into the waistband of my pants, hidden by the shirt. Syringe with a strong but safe tranquilizer. A lead-weighted sap if things got weird. A cell phone with booster chip so I could talk to Rosie, Lee or, at need, my backup. Three guys in a van parked around the corner. Three very tough guys who have done this before. Guys who are not as nice as I am, and I'm not that nice.

As I approached she set down the water bottle she'd been drinking from and watched with quiet grace as I approached.

She smiled at me. "You're here to take me back, aren't you?"

-4-

I slowed my approach and stopped at the edge of the little grove.

"What do you mean, sister?" I asked, pitching my voice so it was soft. The smile I wore was full of lots of white teeth. Very wholesome.

She shook her head.

"You're not one of us," she said.

"I'm new."

"No, you're not."

"How do you know?"

"I know."

"*How* do you know?"

The girl looked at me with eyes that were a lot older than eighteen. Very bright lights in those eyes. It made me want to smile for real.

"Mind if I sit down?"

"Who are you?"

"A friend."

"No, I mean…what's your name?"

"Oh. John Poe."

"Poe? Like the writer."

"Like that."

"Nice. I read some of his stuff in school. The one about the cat, and the one about the guy's heart under the floorboards."

"Scary stuff."

"I thought they were sad. Those poor people were so lost."

I said nothing.

She nodded to the empty end of the bench. "It's okay for you to sit down."

I sat, making sure that I didn't sit too close. Invading her little envelope of subjective distance was not a good opening move. But I also didn't sit too far away. I didn't want to give her a wall of distance either. You have to know how to play it.

We watched a couple of mourning doves waddle around poking at the grass.

"My parents sent you," she said, making it a statement rather than a question.

"They care about you."

Her reply to that was a small, thin smile.

"They want to know you're okay," I said.

"Do you really believe that?"

"Of course. They're your parents."

She studied my face. "You don't look that naïve, Mr. Poe."

And you don't sound like an eighteen-year-old, I thought.

Aloud I said, "If that's something you'd like to talk about, we can. But is here the best place?"

"It's safer."

"Safer for whom?"

"For me," she said. "Look, I understand how this is supposed to work. You come on very passive and friendly and helpful and you find a way to talk me into leaving the grounds with you. To have a chat at a diner or something like that. Then once we're off the church grounds, you grab me and take me to my parents."

"You make it sound like an abduction. All I want to do is bring you home."

"No. You want to *take* me to where my parents live." She patted the bench. "*This* is home, Mr. Poe." She gestured to the lush foliage around us. "And this." And finally she touched her chest over her heart. "And this."

"Okay, I get that. Our home is where we are. Our home is our skin and our perceptions. That's nice in the abstract, but it isn't where your family is. They're at your *family* home, and they're waiting for you."

Her smile was constant and patient. I wanted to break through that level of calm control because that's where the levers are. Fear is one level. Insecurity, which is a specific kind of fear, is another. There are a lot of them.

"Mr. Poe," she said before I could reach for one of those levers, "do we have to do this? I mean, I understand that you're being paid to be here, and maybe there's a bonus for you to bring me back. I know how Daddy works, and he likes his incentives. I think it's easier if we can just be honest. You want to earn your paycheck. Daddy and Mommy want me back so they can put me in a hospital, which would make them legal guardians of me *and* my money. They think I'm nuts and you think I've been brainwashed. Is that it? Did I cover all the bases?"

I had to smile. "You're a sharp kid."

"I'm almost nineteen, Mr. Poe. I stopped being a kid a while ago."

"Nineteen is pretty young."

She shook her head. "Nineteen is as old as I'm ever going to get."

We sat with that for a moment.

"Go on," she encouraged, "say it."

"Say what?"

"Say anything. I just said that I wasn't going to get any older. That probably sounds suicidal to you. Or fatalistic. Maybe it's a sign of deep-seated depression. Go on. Make a comment."

What I said was, "You're an interesting girl."

"Person. If you don't want to call me a 'woman,' then call me a person. I'm not a girl."

"Sorry. But, yes, you're a very interesting person."

"Which goes against the 'type,' doesn't it?"

"Which type?"

"Well, if I was political, or if this was some kind of radical militant group, then you'd expect me to be more educated. You'd expect me to rattle off a lot of Marxist or pseudo-Marxist tripe. But the Church isn't radical. Not in that way. We don't care at all about politics. I know I don't. We're what people like you would call a 'doomsday cult.'"

"If that's the wrong phrase, tell me which one to use."

She laughed. "No, it's fine. It's pretty much true."

"What's true?"

"The world's going to end."

"Because of Nibiru?"

"Sure."

"And—what is it, exactly? People can't seem to agree."

"Well," she said with a laugh, "it's not a dwarf brown star."

"It's not?"

"You think I don't know about this. You think I'm a confused little girl in a weirdo cult thinking we're all going to hitch a ride on a passing planet. You think this is Heaven's Gate and Nibiru is another Hale-Bopp. That's what you think."

Again, she wasn't framing it as a question.

"Well, let me tell you," she continued, "what they tell us here in the church. One of the first things they did was to explain how it couldn't possibly be a brown dwarf because that would mean it was an object bigger than Jupiter. Even in the most extreme orbit, it would have been spotted, and its gravitational pull would have affected every other planet in our solar system."

I said, "Okay."

"And if it was a giant planet four times larger than the Earth, which is what a lot of people are saying on the news and on the Net, then if it was coming toward the Earth it would be visible to the naked eye. And that would also warp the orbits of the outer planets. And it can't have been a planet concealed behind the sun all this time because that would be geometrically impossible."

"You know your science."

"They *teach* us the science here."

"Oh."

"That surprises you, doesn't it."

"I suppose it does. Why do you think they do that?"

"No," she said, "why do *you* think they do it? Why teach us about the science?"

"If you want me to be straight with you, then it's because using the truth is the easiest way to sell a lie. It's a conman's trick. It's no different than a magician letting you look in his hat and up his sleeve before he pulls a rabbit out. They don't let you look at where he's keeping the rabbit."

"That might be true if the church was trying to sell us something. Or sell us on something."

"You're saying they're not?"

"They're not."

"So, they have no interest at all in your trust fund?"

"A year ago, maybe," she said offhand. "Two years ago, definitely. Not anymore."

"What makes you believe that?"

"Because Nibiru is coming."

"You said that it wasn't."

"No," she said, "I said that it wasn't a brown dwarf or a rogue planet."

"You're group's called the Church of the Nomad World. Emphasis on 'world.'"

"I know. When they started, they were using the rogue world thing in exactly the way you think they still are."

"Uh huh. And there are YouTube videos of your deacons talking about how the gravity of Nibiru is going to cause the Earth to stop spinning, and that after it leaves the Earth's rotation will somehow restart."

"Those videos are old."

"Six years isn't that old."

"Old enough," she said. "Nobody says that anymore. Not here. Besides, if the world were to somehow stop rotating the core heat would make the oceans boil. And you couldn't restart rotation again at the same rate of spin. The law of the conservation of angular momentum says it's impossible."

"You understand the physics?"

"We all do," she said, indicating the others who walked or sat in the garden. "We study it."

Her tone was conversational and calm, her demeanor serene.

"Then what do your people believe?" I asked.

"Nibiru is coming."

"But—"

"You look confused," she said.

"I am confused. If it's not a brown dwarf and it's not a rogue planet, then what *is* Nibiru?"

"Ah," she said, nodding. "That's the right question."

"What?"

"That's the question you should have been asking."

"Okay, fine, I'm asking it now. What is—?"

"It's an asteroid," she said.

"An asteroid."

"Yes."

"That you think is going to hit the Earth?"

"No."

"Then—"

"It's going to hit the Moon," she said. "And the Moon will hit the Earth."

"An asteroid that big and no one's seen it?"

"Sure they have, Mr. Poe. A lot of people have seen it. Why do you think everyone's so upset? It's all over the news, and it's getting worse. There are all those books about it. Everyone's talking about it."

"Talking, sure, but there's no evidence."

"There are lots of pictures," she said, her manner still calm. "But I guess you think they're all doctored. Solar flares causing images on cameras, that sort of thing."

"And they disprove those things as fast as they go up."

"I know. Some of them. Like the one of Nibiru that was on YouTube a few years ago that they said was a Hubble image of the expanding light echo around the star V838 Mon. Yes, most of the images have been discredited. Most, not all. There are a bunch that still get out there, and NASA and the other groups say they're faked."

"They *are* fakes."

"You say that, but you don't actually know that, do you?"

I dug my cell phone out of my pocket. "I pretty much do. I have one of the top observational astrophysicists on speed dial. She's been my information source for this ever since I began looking for you."

Sister Light nodded. "Okay. Was she at the conference in Toronto?"

I grinned. "You keep up with the news. Yes, she was there."

"What's her name?"

"Rose Blum."

She nodded. "She's good. I read a couple of her books."

"You *understood* her books?"

"Some of it. Not all the math, but enough. She's right about almost everything."

"Except Nibiru, is that right?"

"If she says it doesn't exist, then no. If she told you that there was no dwarf sun or giant planet about to hit the Earth, then she was telling you at least some of the truth. But have you actually asked her if she knows anything about the asteroid heading toward the dark side of the moon?"

"I'm pretty sure she'd have said something," I said, chuckling.

Sister Light shook her head. "I'm pretty sure she wouldn't."

"I could call her."

She stood up and walked over to one of the stone rectangles set into the grass. I joined her, standing a polite distance to one side. There was writing on the stones which I hadn't taken note of before. I stepped onto the grass and read what was carved into the closest one.

Myron Alan Freeman.

It took me a moment, but I found the name amid the jumble of information I'd studied about the Church.

Freeman was a deacon, one of forty men and women who helped run the organization.

Below his name was the word: Peace.

I stiffened and cut a look at Sister Light. She nodded to the other stones, and I walked out into the field. Each of them had a name. Some I recognized, others I didn't. All of them had the word 'peace' on them.

My throat went totally dry and I wheeled to face her. My heart was racing. I raised my shirt and gripped the butt of the stun gun.

"What the fuck is this?" I demanded.

"What does it look like?"

"It looks like a fucking cemetery."

She nodded. "That's what it is."

I drew my weapon but held it down at my side. "All of them?"

"Yes."

"Every stone here?"

"Yes."

"Dead?"

"Yes?"

"Who killed them?"

Her face was sad. "Not everyone wants to wait for it to happen, Mr. Poe."

"You're saying they killed *themselves*?"

"Nobody here commits murder. It's against our beliefs. Only God has the right to take a human life."

"God…?"

"The one true God, Mr. Poe. The one who has sent his angel, Nibiru, to end the suffering of all mankind."

I looked for the crazy. I looked for that spark of madness in her eyes. The religious zeal. The disconnect.

I looked.

And looked.

"We believe," she said. "We don't require anyone else to. We don't proselytize. We're not looking for new members. We get a lot of them, though. People see the truth, they read through the lies in the media, the lies told by NASA and Homeland and everyone else. They see what's coming and they know what it means. And they come to us."

"For *what*?"

"Some of them want to be loved before it all ends. That's why I'm here. My parents are so cold, so dismissive. I didn't leave because I was acting out. I wasn't going through teenage angst. I came looking for a place to belong so I could wait out the time that we have left among those who don't judge, don't hate, don't want anything from me except whatever love I want to share. I'm only eighteen, Mr. Poe. I'll be dead within a few months of my nineteenth birthday. I won't have a future. I won't have a husband or kids or any of that. I have this. This is the only chance I'll ever have to *give* love. Here in the Church…I have love. I have peace. I have prayer."

She turned away from the stone markers.

The grave markers.

"I want to live all the way to the end. I don't want to commit suicide."

"Why? What do you think is going to happen if this asteroid is real? Will you be transported off to a new world? Will you be elevated to a higher consciousness?"

I couldn't keep the bitterness out of my voice.

"No," she said simply. "When Nibiru hits the moon and the moon hits the Earth, I'll die. It'll probably hurt. I'll be scared. Of course I will. But I'll die here, among my friends, content with the will of God."

I wanted to slap her.

I really did.

I wanted to hit her until she didn't believe this bullshit anymore. We stood there in a churchyard surrounded by the graves of five hundred suicides.

"You need help," I said. "Everyone here does."

"No we don't. We've found what we need. We don't require anything else but to be left alone to pray, to love each other, and to die."

She nodded to the stun gun I held.

"You can use that on me. You can take me by force. No one here is going to try and stop you, and you probably have help somewhere close. So…sure, you can take me against my will. If you do, and if they manage to lock me away somewhere where I can't escape or can't take my life, it won't change anything. I'll still die. We all will. However you'll die knowing that you robbed me of being happy before I died." She stepped close to me and looked up into my eyes. "Is that what you want, Mr. Poe? Is that what you really think is best for me? Will taking me out of here actually keep me 'safe'?"

-5-

I got home around eight that night.

Last night.

I let the other guys go. Told him that we'd drawn a blank. Told them I'd call when I had a fresh lead. It was all the same to them. They were day players.

At my apartment, I cracked a fresh beer and took it out to the deck to watch the sky.

The moon was up. Three-quarter moon.

I drank the beer. Got another. Drank that.

Sat with the moon until it was down.

I tried fifteen times to get Rosie Blum on the phone.

Fifteen.

Cell. Office. Home answering machine.

Finally someone picked up.

Not Rosie, though.

It was her roommate. Rachael Somethingorother. A junior astrophysicist.

"Hello—?"

There was something about the way she said it. Tentative and a little weary. Like she was afraid of a call. Or of another call.

"Rachael? It's John Poe," I said. "Is Rosie there? I've been trying to get her for days and she's not picking up. I really need to talk to her. Is she there?"

She took too long to reply.

Too long.

"John…I'm so sorry," she said.

So sorry.

"What happened?" I asked.

"It…it's going to be in the papers. God, I'm sorry. I thought someone would have called you."

"What's going to be in the papers? What's wrong? Where's Rosie?"

"She's gone…," she said. "I didn't even know she *had* a gun. Oh god, there was so much blood…oh god, John…"

I stared at the night. Listened to the voice on the phone.

"When…?" I asked softly.

"Last night," said Rachael. "When she and Dr. Marcus got back from Toronto. They came back from the airport and they went straight into her room without saying anything. I thought…well, I thought that maybe they were together now. That they'd hooked up in Toronto and, well, you know…"

"What happened?"

"Like I said, I didn't even know she had a gun until I heard the shots."

"Shots?"

"Yes. Oh god, John…she shot him in the head and then put the gun in her…in her…"

She may have said more. There must have been more to the story, but I didn't hear it.

I dropped my hand into my lap, then let it fall down beside my deck chair. The phone landed hard and bounced away. Maybe it went over the rail. I don't know. I haven't looked for it.

I'm sitting here now, and I don't know why I'm recording this. I mean… who the fuck am I leaving a record for?

I watched the news this morning.

Sixteen suicides. Eight of the speakers at the Toronto conference.

Eight others who were there.

Not counting Rosie and Dr. Marcus.

Eighteen.

All of them there to talk about Nibiru. To work out what kind of message to tell the world.

Eighteen.

I guess the message is pretty clear.

I'm going to leave this recorder here on the dashboard. Not sure what good it would do for someone else to find it.

Across the street I can see the wrought iron gates and the granite pillars. And beyond that the white stones in the green grass.

I can see Sister Light standing there, watching my car.

Watching me.

Waiting for me.

Smiling at me.

She lifts her hand.

A welcome gesture.

Okay, I tell myself.

Okay.

AGENT UNKNOWN

David Wellington

Wilmington, DE

"Fucking animals," Whitman hissed, as a gray hand reached for the cuff of his pant leg. He kicked it away. For a second he looked down into the man's slack face. Nothing there. He looked lower and saw the hypodermic still plunged into the man's arm. He tried to tell himself the junkie was just sick, a victim of a disease, but that metaphor had never really held water for him.

A field agent for the CDC, Whitman knew what diseases really were and knew that addiction was a very different kind of disorder.

He waved his flashlight around the room, looking for anyone conscious enough to tell him why he'd come here. He saw three people lounging on pieces of broken furniture or just slumped on the floor, all of them as wasted as the one who'd tried to grab him. Someone in this house had called the police to report violent behavior. The caller had reported that the violent individual was non-communicative and had bloodshot eyes. That had been enough of a red flag for the local cops to send for Whitman.

He'd been in Philadelphia two hours ago. The latest situation report said the cops had contained the suspect and would wait until he arrived before making an arrest. So far, so good—there might be a chance to get a live subject here, and that might make all the difference.

Whitman hadn't known what he was getting into, though, when he hit the ground with his sampling gear. He'd had no idea he was walking into a shooting gallery.

He heard the crackle of a police radio and looked up. A uniformed cop waved him over, a big guy with a bristly mustache and dead eyes. "Sergeant Crispen," he said, and shook Whitman's hand.

"How many people are in this house?" Whitman asked.

Crispen shrugged. "Maybe a dozen. Normally we would've moved 'em out of here but your people said to sit on 'em instead, keep 'em here."

Whitman nodded. "They'll need to be quarantined, just in case. Where's the subject?"

"Through here," Crispen said. He flicked on his own flashlight—the house had no working lights—and gestured down a short hallway. Two more cops stood at its end, flanking a closed door.

"Do you know who called this in?" Whitman asked.

"One of the other junkies—he's pretty messed up. We have him in the kitchen. Bites and scrapes all over him; though with this sort… who knows—could be completely unrelated. We, uh, haven't been able to get a statement yet."

Whitman could well imagine. If the symptoms were bloodshot eyes and aphasia, probably everyone in the house was a potential subject. "Alright," he said. "I'd better go in and take a look."

"The one in there's pretty psycho. I'm not sure it's safe—"

Whitman cut him off by pulling the Taser out of his jacket. "I'll be okay."

The cop looked at the weapon in Whitman's hand and just shrugged.

The door wasn't locked. It looked like someone had kicked it open at one point and it had never been repaired. Whitman stepped inside the dark room and moved his flashlight carefully across the furniture. He saw a dresser with no drawers, a broken television set. On the far side of the room a pile of blankets had been heaped on the floor. It was moving. Just rising and falling slowly, as if someone was under there, breathing.

"What's your name?" Whitman called out, in case this was a false lead. "I'm Whitman. I'm here to help. Can you speak to me? Can you tell me your name?"

There was no response. The pile of blankets kept breathing. Whitman took a step closer. "I need you to say something," Whitman announced. "Can you come out of there? Are you sick?"

The idea of reaching into those blankets with his hands made Whitman's blood run cold. Somebody had to make an assessment, though, and he'd drawn the short stick. He looked around for a piece of wood, for anything he could use to push the blankets back. For a second or two he moved the flashlight away from the blanket pile.

When he looked back the subject was up and running across the room, straight at him. In the flashlight beam the subject's eyes were so red they glowed.

Whitman had a moment to register what was happening. Most of that time he spent thinking to himself, *teeth, nails, open sores*—the things you had to stay away from, the things that could get you contaminated.

He saw the teeth all right. They were yellow and broken and they snapped at the air and they were coming right for his throat.

He brought the Taser up but never had a chance to fire it. The subject lashed out with both arms, knocking Whitman's hands away. His flashlight spun free of his grip and Whitman felt a hundred and twenty pounds of stinking flesh collide with his chest, knocking him down, spinning him sideways.

He felt those teeth meet around his gloved hand. Felt them press down.

There was a gunshot, incredibly loud and bright in the dark room, and then people were running and shouting and Whitman's heart beat so loud in his ears he was sure it would burst. He recovered himself and scrambled to his feet, raced out the door, down the hall, following the back of one cop who was running away from him, running toward the front door of the house, and then they were outside in the blinding sunlight. He threw one arm over his eyes but kept running. Ahead of him the street sloped down a hill, cheap houses and check cashing stores on either side, high tension wires strung overhead. He saw the cops, all three of them, and then he saw the subject, for the first time getting a clear look.

It was a woman, no, a girl of no more than twenty, dressed in nothing but an open flannel shirt and a stained pair of panties. In the sunlight her eyes just looked bloodshot. She staggered down the hill, her legs not quite working properly, her face turning in one direction, then the other. Her hair was a dark thicket of tangles that barely moved as it swung around.

Crispen and his men had drawn their guns and were shouting for her to stop. Whitman cursed as he dashed past them. If she got away—if she ducked into an alley—they might never find her again. He didn't waste his breath shouting at her. What was left of her brain wouldn't be able to make sense of words. He got as close as he dared and lifted the Taser, pointed it at her back.

She started to turn, to look at him, and she was hissing. Ready to fight.

He pulled the trigger. The two tiny barbs went right through her shirt, and the Taser made its horrible clacking sound. She dropped to the pavement, twitching and kicking, but she didn't scream. She didn't make any sound at all.

Behind Whitman, Crispen came running up, his weapon held in both hands. "You got her," he said, over and over again, "you got her," and Whitman could hear the relief in the cop's voice.

"This time," Whitman said. "Yeah."

• • •

Atlanta, GA

Dan Philips watched from an observation suite as they brought Subject 13 in. She was alive—that was good. It was crucial.

Twelve bodies lay in a morgue deep inside the CDC complex that was Philips' headquarters. Twelve bodies, or what was left of them. Bit by bit, organ by organ, they were being dismantled, their cells broken down in centrifuges, their bacterial and viral load analyzed by legions of technicians with scanning electron microscopes. But dead bodies could only tell you so much.

On his television screens Philips watched his field agent sign the new subject in. Nobody bothered to read her any rights or even give her any comforting words as she was shoved into a negative pressure room. Nobody touched her if they could help it. They'd bound her hands behind her back and put a plastic mask over her mouth. She was a known biter and the CDC didn't mess around with those.

The room was kept at a slightly lower atmospheric pressure than the corridor outside, so that when the door was opened air flowed in rather than out—hopefully making sure any pathogens she carried stayed inside with her. No one was allowed into the room without wearing a level two biohazard suit. Cameras on the walls tracked her at all times, and other instruments monitored her body temperature, her heart rate, and her blood oxygen levels.

Director Philips had been a neurosurgeon, once, a long time ago. Now he had the perfect hair and twinkling eyes of a politician. He didn't smile as Whitman stepped into the observation suite. For a long while they just watched the subject together.

Not that there was much to see. Once the suited technicians left the room, she seemed to simply collapse. With no one to bite or attack, she just crouched on the floor—ignoring the bed they'd provided for her—and rocked back and forth in what was obviously a self-comforting gesture.

Eventually, Philips cleared his throat. "You must have made record time."

Whitman nodded. Of the twelve bodies in the morgue, not a single one had died of natural causes. Ever since they'd alerted the police networks to the new disease, Whitman was called in every time the cops found a potential subject. But it could take him hours, even days, to arrive after he got the call. The subjects were so violent the police usually had to shoot them to keep them from hurting anybody. Cops didn't mess around with biters, either. "I was close by, and we had a helicopter ready to lift off. Everything kind of came together."

"This is what we need," Philips said, sighing in relief. "This is what we need to beat this thing, I know it."

The disease that afflicted Subject 13 was definitely some kind of brain fever, they were sure of that. But that was almost the only thing they knew. When the cops had killed the previous twelve they'd ruined the best chance the CDC had to study this thing as it progressed. Subject 13 could be a very important catch.

Bringing her in alive also meant they could get some epidemiological data, too. They couldn't question her—like all of the subjects, she was completely incapable of speech—but they could study her clothing for any trace of environmental toxins, look at her teeth to get an idea of her diet. The clue to identifying the pathogen could come from anywhere.

They definitely needed some kind of clue. 13, and the twelve bodies in the morgue, were just the tip of the iceberg, they were sure. There was no way to know how many other people had been infected with the pathogen, how many people they'd missed. Early cases might have been dismissed as PCP overdoses or just psychotic breaks. Subjects might have wandered out into traffic and gotten themselves killed before they were diagnosed.

If they were going to figure this thing out—isolate the pathogen and come up with a vaccine or at least some kind of treatment—they needed information, and that meant finding a live subject. Whitman had been given that duty because he was a senior field agent.

"What's her name?" Philips asked.

Whitman blinked in surprise. "Sorry?"

"Her name," the Director repeated. "She must have one."

Whitman thought for a second but nothing came to him. "They told me but…I forgot. It's in my report." He rubbed his temples with his fingertips as if that would jog his memory. "It's been a long day, Director, and if—"

Philips reached over and grabbed Whitman's right hand.

Both of them looked at the two red dots on Whitman's index finger, tiny bruises that were clearly the imprints of teeth.

Philips raised an eyebrow.

He didn't need to ask aloud. Whitman knew what the question was. "She bit through my glove. Yeah. But she didn't break the skin."

"You're absolutely certain?"

Whitman looked away. "Absolutely."

Philips wondered if his agent was telling the truth. He had a strong enough incentive to lie. If he had been infected, if there was any chance, well—Whitman would very quickly find himself in a negative pressure room of his own. But Philips knew he needed Whitman, still. He nodded and turned back to the monitors, back to watching 13 rock back and forth.

• • •

Atlanta, GA

This was a bad one.

Whitman had been through some bad ones before. After washing out of med school with a biology degree, he'd joined the CDC just in time to get in on the circus that was SARS. He'd see outbreaks of cholera and TB in cities up and down the eastern seaboard, and of course the *e. coli* flare-ups that hit every time a restaurant tried to save some money by buying second-grade meat. As a field agent, he didn't even have the luxury of looking at it through a microscope or the plastic viewport of a containment suit. He'd been down in the streets with the panicking victims, often wearing no more than a surgical mask and a pair of latex gloves, covered in blood and much worse day after day. The bad ones left him with nightmares and a need to wash his hands every time he passed a sink.

This one… it was worse, maybe. Nobody had coughed in his face on this case, nor had he had to watch anybody die. But he knew those bloodshot eyes were going to haunt him.

There was nothing there. Nobody home.

The nice thing about the bad ones, of course, was that they didn't last. Killer pathogens had a way of burning themselves out, wiping out their host populations before they could pass on their genes, or simply mutating out of the killer phase. In the worst cases it just meant somebody had to isolate the pathogen and find a counteragent in a hurry. And he wouldn't be the one pulling all-nighters for a week to make that happen.

The very best thing about the bad ones was that he got to go home. He wasn't the one who had to make the decisions about who to quarantine, or who got the actual vaccine and who got the very convincing placebo.

That night, he managed to sleep for nearly seven hours in a row with no one bothering him. When the phone rang, he answered it. Because he knew if he didn't they would start texting him. And if he ignored the texts they would send someone to knock on his door. He had signed the contract and he knew it said he was *always* on call.

"I'm on vacation," he told the phone. "Call me in three days."

It was Philips. Not a good sign, if the Director was making the call himself. "All vacation time is rescinded, as of now."

"You're taking away my days off for—"

Philips' voice got very, very serious. "Vacation time is rescinded for *all* CDC personnel until further notice."

Whitman got out of bed, the cell phone cradled between his ear and his shoulder as he grabbed his pants. The CDC employed 15,000 people. If they were all being called in, that meant one thing.

Epidemic.

"Where am I going?" Whitman asked.

"Flagstaff."

"Arizona? Seriously?"

All thirteen known cases of the mystery brain disorder had come from the northeast corridor, from Vermont down to Washington, DC. What the hell was it doing out west?

Whitman buttoned his shirt one-handed. "Did 13 tell us something?" he asked.

"Nothing we wanted to hear."

• • •

Flagstaff, AZ

Whitman had a welcoming party waiting for him when his plane landed: the local sheriff, a guy in a short-sleeve, button-down shirt from Public Health, and a couple of ranchers in cowboy hats and permanent tans. Whitman might have sent the ranchers away until the sheriff explained the situation.

Subject 14 was alive, and he wasn't going anywhere. It looked like he might have been some kid, some teenager just out for a long drive in the desert. Now he was stuck in a barbed wire fence. He kept trying to drag himself free, pulling at his clothes and his leg where it was tangled in the wire. The fence marked the divide between two pastures—hence the ranchers, who argued the whole time about who was liable if the kid died on the fence.

"I figure if he just calmed down a second, thought it through, he could get himself free," the sheriff said. They had parked about two hundred yards from where 14 was stuck. He hadn't shown any sign of noticing them yet. Whitman was happy to keep his distance. "He's not firing on all cylinders, is he?" He handed a pair of binoculars to Whitman.

Bloodshot eyes. A lot of open wounds on that leg. This was going to be dicey.

Whitman frowned. "What's that stuff by his feet? Looks like a torn-up paper bag. Was he carrying that when you found him?"

"We had orders not to approach, but it took you twelve hours to get out here after we called it in," the guy from Public Health said. "I had a sandwich in my car—it was going to be my lunch. I got as close as I dared and then I tossed it to him."

"Did he eat it?" Whitman asked.

"The sandwich and part of the wrapper it came in. I was worried he might choke."

Through the binoculars Whitman watched as 14 pulled and pulled at the wire. A piece of his pantleg tore free, curling down over his knee cap.

No, Whitman thought. That wasn't his pant leg. It was the skin of his thigh.

Limited pain response, he thought, adding to the catalog of symptoms for this new disease. Maybe some kind of neuropathy?

The immediate problem was that 14 was now one third of the way free of the fence. A couple more tugs and he would be out and running right toward them, looking for someone to bite or scratch.

Whitman made a call to bring in a helicopter that could take 14 away from all this. Then he waded across the pasture, looking out for cow pats, and pulled his Taser from his jacket. 14 went down, slumping across the fence.

"You have any wire cutters?" Whitman asked the sheriff. "I'm going to have to cut him free."

One of the ranchers took off his cowboy hat and slapped it against his leg. "Who's gonna pay to fix the damage to my fence?"

• • •

The helicopter lifted away from the field and carried subject 14 off, and the ranchers dispersed. The sheriff waited in his truck while Whitman made some calls. As he was finishing up, the weedy guy from Public Health came trotting up, a serious look in his eye.

"This, uh… well, anything I should know about this?" he asked.

Whitman switched off his phone and looked up. "What do you mean?"

"Just. You know. Should I tell the local doctors to be on the lookout for anything? Any precautions they should take?"

Whitman frowned.

He could tell the man what they'd discovered from studying subject 13. He could say that it was fluid-borne. They'd traced 13's history enough to know she once shared needles with subject 8. They'd also found a link between subject 5 and subject 2: 5 had donated blood once, and 2 had received some of it in a transfusion following an appendectomy.

But—why didn't the Public Health guy know that already? It was the first break in the case, and it should have gone out to every doctor in the country, every police department, every public health official. So far the

CDC had kept the media from finding out about the mystery illness—no need to cause a panic—but the caregivers should already have been notified.

If this guy didn't know what was going on, that meant Director Philips didn't want him to know. For reasons Whitman couldn't imagine.

Still.

"Nope," Whitman said. "Nothing to worry about. If something comes up, we'll be sure to let you know."

• • •

Atlanta, GA

Back in the observation suite again. A new living subject. Philips sipped at his coffee. He felt like he hadn't slept in days.

"What's going on?" Whitman demanded. "Damn it, I have a right to know, at least. You've got me out in the field, putting myself at risk. If it wasn't for me, you wouldn't have your two live subjects—"

"Six," Philips interrupted.

"What?"

The director sat back in his chair. Whitman was right, he decided. He should know what was going on. "Did you think you were the only field agent I had working on this? We've got six live subjects in the negative pressure rooms."

He watched Whitman's jaw fall open. "How many? How many reported cases?"

Philips took a long, deep breath before answering. "Eighty-nine. Confirmed."

"How long has this been going on?" Whitman asked.

"The first case we're sure about showed up seven years ago. For a long time then there was nothing. We thought it was just some fluke. But then more of them came to light," Philips said.

Whitman shook his head. He walked across the room to where a monitor showed the feed from Subject 13's room. She was still sitting there, rocking back and forth. She'd moved to a different corner of the room but that was the only change.

"What's going on?" Whitman asked.

"Tell me something, first," Philips said. "Tell me why you didn't finish medical school."

Whitman grimaced. "I wasn't empathetic enough, they said. My bedside manner was lousy."

"When you didn't know 13's name, I thought as much," Philips told him. "Most doctors—we aren't equipped for this. We take an oath, you see. 'First, do no harm.' Even when it could save other lives."

"What are you getting at?" Whitman demanded.

Philips nodded at the screen. At subject 13.

"The President called me this morning."

"The President of the United States?" Whitman asked. "He's been briefed about this case?"

"He's being updated every twelve hours."

Philips closed his eyes and took a deep breath.

"He called…to give me the authorization to find this thing no matter what it takes. You see, we can't detect anything in her system. No virus. No bacterium, no fungal infection, no parasites. This thing's invisible."

"For now," Whitman pointed out. "We couldn't find HIV for a long time, either, but we did."

Philips shook his head. "It isn't like that. And anyway, we don't have time to find out. This thing is spreading, and it's moving fast. We have eighty-nine confirmed cases today. We could have a thousand tomorrow. The President gave me authorization to euthanize her and do an autopsy."

Whitman was stunned. "But she's a…a living person. A human being. She may be brain dead, but she still has basic rights."

"Not, apparently, in the face of an epidemic. I was supposed to do it this morning, but I couldn't. I couldn't bring myself to kill her, even in the name of public good. Though maybe it's not just squeamishness. I have a suspicion I know what it actually is. But oh, Lord, do I want to be wrong this time."

He looked up at Whitman with pleading eyes. The question went unasked but they both knew it. Philips desperately wanted Whitman to say he would do it. Go down to the negative pressure room and kill Subject 13 so they could cut her open.

But Philips knew it couldn't be that easy.

• • •

First thing in the morning, they came for subject 13.

She was in a straitjacket and her facial mask, but they didn't take any chances. A technician in a bite-proof containment suit stood outside the room and shot her with a massive dose of sedative. Once she was unconscious they strapped her to a gurney and wheeled her into an operating room where three doctors waited. One of them was Philips.

Each of the doctors had a hypodermic needle. Two of them were filled with harmless saline solution. The other had the same chemical cocktail used for lethal injections in prisons. None of the doctors knew which of them had the bad needle.

That was intentional.

One by one they made their injections.

• • •

Chicago, IL

Whitman wasn't asleep when the next call came in. Somehow he'd known it was coming. Another mission.

"This one's a little different," Philips told him.

He was on a plane an hour later. Fully briefed by the time he set down.

The church had been Catholic once, but it had been sold to some other denomination. Whitman didn't bother finding out which one. Outside, a dozen policemen stood around looking bored—nobody had told them what was going on. Inside the church was all frothy stonework and stained glass and lanterns hanging from chains. Holy men in severe suits stood around wringing their hands and clutching bibles, unwilling to meet Whitman's gaze.

A middle-aged woman called his name and told him to come with her. She led him down a flight of stairs into a basement with tan-painted walls that glared in the overhead fluorescents.

"How long has this been going on?" Whitman asked.

The woman wouldn't make eye contact, either. The church had fought with the CDC, even threatened legal action. A federal judge had slapped that down—the church had no choice but to turn over its parishioners now. "About thirty-nine months," the woman said. She was in charge of the church's community outreach. Running homeless shelters and literacy programs. And their hospice.

"The doctors said there was nothing they could do," she explained. "We kept them fed, gave them clothing, and kept them clean. Was that so wrong?"

Whitman ignored her and went to the door she indicated. A small glass panel reinforced with chicken wire looked into what might have been a classroom once. There were cots lined up inside, though nobody was using them. Instead, the room's inhabitants sat on the floor, rocking back and forth, hugging themselves. They were mostly naked and they looked filthy.

"We did what we could," the woman said in a quiet voice.

There were twenty-five people in that room, at least. Every one of them a living subject. A sufferer of the new pathogen.

"Jesus," Whitman said.

"Please, in this place, don't take His name in vain," the woman said.

Whitman stared at her. "You just herded them in there, together, and... and warehoused them? These people need medical care."

"Their families couldn't afford to look after them. Neither can we. When it was just one or two of them at a time, maybe... but there are more every day."

Whitman shook his head. He didn't even know how to proceed.

• • •

Atlanta, GA

Subject 13 died with a long, sustained breath that just...stopped. In the observation suite, Philips covered his eyes and wept for a moment. Then he pulled on a level four containment suit and headed down to the surgery. He plugged in the various hoses for his air supply. Checked the seals on his gloves. Picked up a bone saw and got to work.

The top of subject 13's skull came away in one neat, clean piece. Philips had been a very good surgeon, once.

With a scalpel he cut away her brain and lifted it into a waiting pan. A nurse took it away to the microtome room, where it would be cut down into exceedingly thin slices. The slices would then be prepared on microscope slides.

Philips closed his eyes. He didn't want to see what came next.

But it was his job. And nobody else was volunteering to do it for him.

• • •

Chicago, IL

"Keep it moving, don't let them get up if you can," Whitman called through the door. Inside the room, a dozen cops were squeezed in with the subjects, outnumbered but at least they had all the advantages he could give them. They'd waited for proper gear to come in—riot armor, face shields, heavy bite-proof gloves. One by one they got the subjects ready for transport. In contrast with the cops' high-tech gear, they'd gone primitive for the restraints—plastic self-locking loops for handcuffs and thick canvas bags to put over the subjects' heads. A fleet of ambulances stood outside, waiting to take the subjects away.

Whitman turned to the woman who had been caring for the subjects all this time. She was weeping openly, now. "You said you cleaned them—I assume that means you hosed them off once a week. Did you or your staff have any direct contact with them?"

The woman stared at him through her tears. "Of course," she said. "We didn't treat them like animals."

Whitman lifted one hand in perfunctory apology. It didn't give him pleasure to be mean to people. He just didn't have time for bullshit. "Were any of you bitten?"

"It…happens," the woman said, with a shrug.

Crap. Whitman had a feeling he was going to have to bring the church staff in as well, if just for observation.

"No one ever got sick from a bite, so we assumed it wasn't contagious," the woman explained.

Inside the room someone shouted. Whitman couldn't make out the words. He stepped toward the doorway, just in time to see a cop smash a subject's teeth out with his baton. Another cop waded through the subjects to try to help, but three of the infected grabbed him and pulled him off his feet.

One of them started tearing the cop's face shield off.

"Out now!" Whitman shouted, but it was too late. The cops all drew their batons and started laying into the subjects around them. But there was no order to it, no discipline. They were just scared.

Whitman reached for the nearest cop and grabbed his shoulder. The man whirled around and smacked Whitman right in the gut with his baton. Whitman fell backwards, out of the doorway, clutching his stomach.

That was when everything went to shit.

• • •

Atlanta, GA

Philips adjusted the focus on the microscope. It didn't help. The tiny holes were there and couldn't be ignored. It was exactly what he'd expected to see.

"Give me sample 39a," he said, and a technician changed the slide. Philips didn't even lift his head from the eyepieces. Pink and white ovals filled the view, looking a great deal like a close-up of a slice of salami. That was normal, it was what healthy brain tissue looked like. But subject 13 hadn't been healthy. This slice of her brain, like all the others, was riddled with thousands of microscopic holes. Like it had been eaten away by tiny mice working at random.

"Sample 40a," Philips said.

• • •

Chicago, IL

A man in a black suit ran screaming from the church, his face torn open and blood soaking into his collar. The stained glass windows lit up from inside with the bright flashes of gunshots. Whitman stumbled out of the church, one arm wrapped around the screaming woman who had run the hospice program. She was unhurt but inconsolable. He pushed her away from him and turned around to look back inside. A subject in a torn sweatshirt was stomping up the pews, blood slicking the front of his jaw. A cop was down by the pulpit, not moving.

Whitman grabbed his Taser from inside his jacket. He fired it into the subject's chest and the subject went down, at least momentarily. Whitman ran over to the cop and checked his pulse. The cop was alive and breathing but he wasn't getting up. Shock, Whitman thought. The man had succumbed to shock after getting three of his fingers bitten off.

Whitman had enough medical training to know what to do. He took off his belt and wrapped it around the cop's wrist, pulling it as tight as he could to make a tourniquet.

Behind him the subject pulled himself back onto his feet, using the side of a pew for leverage. He didn't make a sound.

Whitman grabbed for his Taser again, but that was useless—it was a one-shot weapon. He'd never needed more than one shot before.

The subject took a halting step toward him. It was still shrugging off the effects of the Taser.

Another step.

Behind Whitman, more subjects were coming up the stairs.

• • •

Washington, DC

There were other people in the room, but Philips barely noticed them. He forced himself to make eye contact with the President. He forced himself to speak.

"Our finding is that this is a prion disease," he said.

The President must have been given a pre-briefing, because he said, "Like Creutzfeldt-Jakob, or Kuru? I'm not entirely sure what a prion is."

Philips nodded. "Those two diseases are prion diseases, yes. A prion is a kind of pathogen that is not technically alive. A protein that has gotten folded the wrong way. Prions are normally only spread by exposure to brain tissue from an infected individual. But this one is different. It has…well, mutated is the wrong word. But it has changed. This one is spread by fluid contact."

"Like a virus."

"Yes. But unlike viruses even the slightest exposure is enough to infect someone. The prion enters the brain and once there it cannot be ejected. Our bodies' immune systems do not react to its presence at all. Safe inside its host, it begins to replicate. It makes more copies of itself. Over time these copies have a destructive effect on the brain tissue."

"How destructive?"

Philips cleared his throat. "Over time they lead to complete failure of the cerebrum. This particular prion leaves a victim essentially brain dead. The subjects we observed have no higher brain function at all—no thoughts. Their inner lives are replaced completely with animal drives. Hunger. The need for sleep. Fight or flight reflexes."

"That's why they attack anyone they see?"

"Yes," Philips answered. "Yes, that's…that's why."

"How do we cure this? Or even treat it?"

"We can't," Philips said. "There's nothing we can do for them. Once the prion has replicated enough, the brain shuts down and we can't stop it."

The president shook his head. "What about detection? If we catch it early enough, can we help these poor people?"

"There's no way to detect it."

"I'm sorry?"

"There's no test for prion infection. Nor are there any symptoms, until it's far too late. The only way to tell if someone has this disease is to dissect their brain." Philips tried a weak smile. "Post-mortem, of course."

The President whispered something to one of his advisers. Then he turned to face Philips again. "How long does it take, from exposure to mental breakdown?"

"That…may be the worst part. Assuming this pathogen is similar to known prions, it could have an incubation phase of as long as twenty years."

The President leaned forward. "You're saying these…these subjects of yours might have gotten infected twenty years ago? That they could have been infecting other people the whole time? And we didn't know about it until now?"

"I'm afraid so."

• • •

Chicago, IL

Whitman fumbled with the leather strap on the cop's belt. He was so scared his fingers barely worked.

The subject took another step closer. Its eyes glowed like red lamps.

It bent over, its jaws snapping at Whitman's face. Fell to its knees and crawled toward him.

The catch came loose. Whitman pulled the cop's gun free and lifted it, surprised at how heavy it was. He'd never fired a gun before. He pointed it at the subject's face and pulled the trigger.

Nothing happened. The subject crawled closer. In another second it was going to bite him. Whitman kicked at it but the subject just grabbed his ankle and leaned in to bite his leg.

Safety. The safety must be on. Whitman found a little lever on the side of the gun. Flipped it down.

The subject's teeth were inches from Whitman's flesh.

He blew its head off. Blood and brain tissue went everywhere, some of it flecking Whitman's face. He clamped his mouth shut to keep any of it from getting inside.

Then he turned and faced the entrance to the stairway. More subjects were coming up.

He hoped he had enough bullets.

• • •

Washington, DC

"Let's, uh, let's move on to recommendations," the President said, flipping through the thin dossier Philips had brought. "You say we can't treat these infected people. We can't even make them comfortable."

Philips inhaled sharply. "No. The best course there is…euthanasia. I don't say this lightly."

"I'm sure you don't. But what about the healthy population? How do we keep them safe?"

"The only measure available to us is quarantine. We need to look at everyone who has reached the brain death phase very carefully. We need to look into their lives and find everyone they've had contact with, everyone they've exchanged fluids with, over the last two decades. And we need to separate those people from the healthy population. This needs to be done immediately. We won't be able to stop the prion from spreading, not altogether. But we need to minimize that spread."

The President studied the documents in front of him for a long while without speaking. Finally he looked up. "Anybody they've exchanged fluids with. You're talking about blood transfusions, shared needles, sexual contact—"

"Sir," Philips interrupted, "This isn't an STD. Even the slightest contact can lead to exposure. Even so little as an open mouth kiss."

"Every single person these infected subjects have kissed."

"And everyone who has kissed someone they have kissed."

"Rounded up and put in quarantine. That's got to be a lot people."

Philips lowered his gaze. "We've done the math. The spread is exponential—if one person infects ten in those twenty years, and those ten go on to infect ten others, and so on—"

"Give me a number," the President demanded.

"Perhaps twenty percent of the entire population of the country is at risk for testing positive for the prion disease," Philips replied.

The president's hands trembled as he set the dossier down on the table. "One in five people, rounded up and put in camps for… for what, for twenty years until we're sure they're safe? That's logistically impossible. Not to mention unconscionable."

"It's necessary," Philips told him. "If we don't do it, this will be the end of the human race."

ENLIGHTENMENT

Matthew Mather

The ancient subway car rattled toward me, its wheels squealing. An encircled "Q" glowed on the front of the driverless lead car. It was the express train, rolling without stopping on its way past the 29th Street station. I was standing near the end of the platform, next to the far wall. The squealing stopped as the train began to clear the station and accelerate back up to speed.

The lead car was almost at me, and I stepped onto the edge of the platform, staring at the empty driver's seat of the subway car as it rushed closer.

"Hey, lady!" someone called out.

The train was now just feet away from me. I stepped toward the ledge and the empty space beyond.

"Lady, watch—"

The squealing began again, this time ear-shattering, but it was too late. I leaned in, feeling the train crash into me. There was no pain, just a flash of white before blackness descended.

• • •

One Year Earlier

I first met Michael at a "How Can I Believe?" church meeting on the Upper East Side, at the third in a series of presentations about coming to intellectual grips with the divine, of how to believe in miracles. The real miracle was that I managed to get out of the house. A gaping hole had opened in the fabric of my life, so there I was, hoping to find...

Something.

The scene that evening wasn't inspiring, however: a collection of ill-fitting people clinging to jackets and mittens, asking if this seat or that was taken and sharing blank smiles. The woman beside me glanced my way, as if to start small talk, but I looked away. *This was a mistake.* Checking my phone, it was two minutes past eight. Yawning, I reminded myself that even Einstein believed in God.

It was hot in the church basement, and coming in from the cold outside I squirmed. Sweat pooled in the small of my back. *Should I remove a layer?* I'd taken off my winter coat, but still had on a shirt and sweater with a scarf wrapped around my neck. Watching bulges of fat spring free as the people around me stripped down, I decided against it.

A cup of translucent coffee hung between my hands—I'd brought my own calorie-free sweetener—and despite the heat I took tasteless sips that burnt my tongue. *Did I lock the door when I left home?* I resisted the urge to leave, to go home and check. I'd already checked twice. Looking at my phone again, they were already five minutes late in starting. I was about to leave when a voice behind me said: "So, what do you think of these meetings so far?"

I strained to look around and found a man smiling at me.

A very attractive man.

I smiled back. "Um, well, I'm getting something out of it." Swivelling sideways on my chair to face him, I noticed his hair was graying at the temples, just like my dad's had. I hadn't noticed this man at any of the other meetings, but then I usually had my social blinders on.

The man's smile curled up at its edges. "Is that what you came for, to *get* something?"

Why else would I be here? But he was right. *I shouldn't just be here just to* get *something.* "I mean, I'm here to try to make myself a more whole person."

He nodded. "I know exactly what you mean." Shifting in his chair, his coat fell to one side to reveal his right arm below a short sleeve shirt. The arm shone dully in the fluorescent light: smooth metal and wires. He saw me staring and pulled his coat back up.

My cheeks burned. *Why did I have to say 'whole person'?*

His smile wavered, but only for a moment. "I was in the wars."

I forced a grin. "Of course." I'd heard the stories of veterans returning with mangled bodies mechanically reconstructed. *If only my brother had been so lucky.* I shook off the thought.

He extended his robotic arm. "Don't be embarrassed. My name is Michael."

I took his hand. It was cool and hard. "Effie," I mumbled, wondering what his eyes saw when they looked at me. *Fat and frump*, answered a voice in my head. My body tingled as I touched his prosthetic.

"Very nice to meet you, Effie," Michael whispered, still holding my hand.

The speaker at the head of the room announced the start to the session. "Today we will be discussing the role of original sin," he said, and the murmur of conversation stopped.

I let go of Michael's mechanical hand and turned to listen.

• • •

After what seemed an eternity, the meeting came to an end. People were standing and gathering their belongings, checking that they hadn't left anything behind.

Even struggling to keep my eyes open, I'd been thinking about Michael the whole time.

Was I rude? I knew I should've worn something more flattering. I frowned. *Did I lock the door?* Resisting the urge to bolt, I pretended to check my pockets for something while I listened to Michael chatting behind me. I waited until he fell silent, and then turned as casually as possible.

"So what did you think?" I asked. I winced. *I should've come up with something more intelligent.* It never ceased to frustrate me how I could be so brilliant in the lab, yet so useless in a room of people I didn't know.

Michael flashed his warm smile again. "It was" —he shrugged— "interesting." In a hushed voice he added, "But I do have a hard time with the way evangelicals make such literal interpretations."

"I know what you mean." If he'd noticed me nodding off he didn't say anything. I glanced around. "I mean, do they think Moses literally split the seas and walked along the seabed to freedom?" I felt guilty as the words came out, wondering if anyone else heard me. But then I realized this was why I'd come here, to find ways to talk about my over-intellectualized feelings about the Bible.

We began to walk toward the door of the now empty room.

"I love the Church," Michael said, "but I have a bit of a problem with the way they're selectively metaphoric."

"How do you mean?"

Michael opened the door for me. "Like insisting on a literal interpretation of Moses splitting the seas, yet on Sunday mornings drinking wine and claiming it's the blood of Christ."

I hadn't thought of it like that. I took another look at him as he held the door open. *Good-looking* and *smart. There's no way he would be interested in me*, the voice in my head told me, but we continued chatting as we wound our way out of the building, my rubber boots squeaking across the linoleum floors while our voices echoed through the empty hallways.

It was dark outside. Snowflakes appeared in the conical pools of bioluminescent street lighting that glowed bright as we approached. I looked down at my footprints in the newly fallen snow. I used to love snow as a child, but now winter was just cold. I shivered. We stood and faced each other.

"Goodnight, Effie."

A moment of silence was filled with the hum of automated car-pods sweeping down Second Avenue.

"Goodnight."

Michael glanced away and then back at me. "See you next time?"

Warmth blossomed in the pit of my stomach. "Yes, next time."

With a nod, Michael walked off into the thickening snowfall. I walked the opposite way to make for the subway home, and for the first time in a long time I watched the falling snowflakes and marvelled at their quiet beauty.

Then I did something I never did. Turning, I called out, "Michael, do you want to get a coffee or something?" Even in the cold my face flushed hot.

In the distance, Michael turned around. He didn't hesitate. "Sure."

We found a coffee shop on Second. There was a line at the counter.

"Even a slime mold," Michael said as I stomped the cold and nerves out of my feet, "even a single-celled organism can solve a maze to find food." He pointed at some icing-laden muffins. "Speaking of rewards, want one?"

I shook my head. "I'm—"

"Vegan?" Michael finished my sentence for me.

I nodded. *How did he guess?* But more than that, the label under the muffins said four hundred calories. *Four hundred.*

"Don't worry, they're vegan muffins." Michael was already holding up two fingers.

I hadn't noticed the small print under the caloric label.

"Come on, it's the holidays," he added cheerfully.

The server had already pulled the muffins onto a plate. I shrugged okay, then peered through the window of the café as a heavy transport roared down Second Avenue. Not for the first time, I imagined how easy it would be to trip in front of one.

"You okay?"

On a video panel above and behind the counter, a news anchor was in the middle of a story, ". . . *unexplained disappearances continue throughout the five boroughs, police are now investigating what they describe as a cult*. . ."

I blinked, pulling my attention away from the video to look into Michael's eyes. He glanced at the news report as well. "Yes, I'm fine," I replied.

"You sure?"

Nodding yes, I smiled and took the coffees while Michael took the plate of muffins. We wound our way to a quiet spot in the corner, away from the noise and the holographic Santa sleigh weaving its way through the bustling crowd of shoppers. I disliked crowds of people, but then I also hated being alone—my life was a slow bleed on the knife edge between the two.

A simulated fire crackled in our corner, and we sank into armchairs. Pushing the plate toward me, he picked up his muffin. I leaned forward and began crumbling mine into pieces, taking a morsel to eat while grabbing my coffee for a sip.

My chest tightened. *What should I say?*

"So what do you do for work?" Michael asked.

I smiled with relief. Something I knew. "I'm a lab monkey. I work in research."

"Oh? What kind?"

"I'm sure you'd find it boring."

Michael smiled and waved me on, his mouth full of muffin.

"Right now, I'm researching airborne transmission methods of viral gene therapy in conspecific populations, it's a way…" *Wait, what am I doing? There's no way he could—*

"To introduce gametes that take precedence over heterospecific ones?" Michael said around his muffin. He swallowed and sipped his coffee. "Targeted auto-distribution of vaccines, huh? Very interesting, would save billions of dollars."

I stared at him, dumbfounded. "How do you…I mean… ?" My voice trailed off.

"I apologize, I'm just excited to meet a woman of your intelligence. I have many interests, but I am merely an amateur." Michael smiled and took another bite of his muffin. "Please, continue."

Taking a deep breath, I sat upright, parting my legs to slide closer toward him. "You're right, but it's not about the money."

"Saving millions of lives, then?"

I crumbled more of my muffin. "I'm more interested in animal life. What's happening to frogs, to thousands of other species, whether there might be a way to save them."

Michael moved closer to me. "Amazing. And you have funding?"

I looked at the floor. "For human research, but I'm hoping…"

Again I paused. He'd already finished his muffin. I leaned forward to pull the last of mine apart, sweeping some crumbs into my hand that I dropped onto the floor when Michael looked away.

He looked back at me and slid forward in his chair. "All living creatures share intelligence and emotion, with differences being in degree, not in kind."

I nodded. "Exactly. I mean, a human baby isn't any smarter than an octopus, yet people are okay with killing and eating them. But killing a baby, oh, no, that's not allowed." I tensed. *Was that too much?* "I mean like when Jonathan Swift said—"

"That a young healthy child, well nursed, is a most delicious and wholesome food, whether stewed, roasted, baked, or boiled… ?"

I laughed out loud before I could contain myself, earning the stares of people looking to see what was so funny. Nobody I knew would have even understood that reference, never mind being able to come up with the quote.

Michael smiled at our shared secret. "I realize you're being dramatic to make a point." He shook his head and his smile disappeared. "Original sin. If anything, we should be atoning for the sins we've committed against all the living creatures we've murdered to satiate our own appetites. Speciesism is a terrible thing…"

A warm tickling began in my toes, rising up through my groin and into my cheeks. *Did he really just say that?*

We chatted about our feelings toward food and what food had feelings until Michael had to go. I bid him farewell, then rushed to the ladies' room. I waited until it was empty, leaned over a pee-spotted toilet, and stuck a finger down my throat.

• • •

A few weeks later, the meetings and coffees had become a regular thing; Michael and I even joined the next church session together. He shared some of his war stories, and I shared how I'd lost my brother over there, even opening up about my parents and the recent accident that had stolen them from me. I was busy demolishing another muffin, pecking crumbs from it, when Michael finally asked.

"Do you want to join me for dinner at my place next week?"

"I'd love to," I answered. I felt a flush. I tried to remember if I'd turned down the heating when I left the house. *Had I locked the door?*

"Wonderful. I'm having some friends over for a special meal."

I looked down, knocked a few crumbs into my lap. "Of course." I'd thought he was inviting me there alone.

"On one condition." Michael glanced at my muffin. "You must eat absolutely everything that I serve."

I couldn't tell if he was trying to be funny or serious. Nodding, I pulled my hands back and burrowed them into the pockets of my coat.

Michael raised one hand like an oath. "*Promise.*"

Forcing a smile, I pulled out one hand and raised it. "I promise."

Excusing myself, I headed for the bathroom.

• • •

I stopped at the top of the subway stairs, my teeth aching from sucking the cold winter air. My stomach hurt, but not like usual. I wasn't good with new people. At the lab, this worked in my favor. Just me and my slides and whirring centrifuges. No idle chitchat needed, and most of my colleagues fell into this same spectrum of awkwardness.

A fresh coating of snow squeaked underfoot on the sidewalk outside. At his address, I looked up and saw lights on, people framed in the window, talking, holding drinks. *Maybe I should go home, tell him I wasn't feeling well.* I looked at his door. *Did I lock my door?* Stop it. *Even if you didn't, you can't go back now.* And then his door opened, spilling bubbling conversation onto the street.

"Effie! Come in. Come in!" It was Michael.

Smiling, my internal debate settled for me, I trotted up the stairs.

Michael took my coat and hung it in an entrance closet, then ushered me inside. The entranceway led into a large main room with high ceilings and ornate moldings. He led me to a side table where a cauldron was steaming on a hot plate. Dipping a ladle into it, he filled a small china cup.

"Mulled wine," Michael explained, offering it to me.

I nodded and accepted the cup from him.

"I thought it would be a nice antidote to the cold," Michael added. "*Glogg* you Scandinavians call it, yes?"

I didn't usually drink much, but I could use one now.

Michael turned to a small man standing next to us. "Ah, Martin, I'd like to introduce you to someone. Effie is a synthetic biologist…"

Blushing, I glanced at the floor and took a sip from my wine.

Michael grimaced. "I meant *Dr. Hedegaard* is a synthetic biologist, please excuse my familiarity, I didn't mean—"

"Don't be silly," I whispered, leaning in and grabbing his arm. "I'm just embarrassed at the attention."

"Synthetic biologist. Very interesting," said the small man, smiling and ignoring our exchange. He was short—stooped—with gray stubble atop his head and photoreceptors shining in his empty eye sockets: artificial eyes. He looked familiar. "Do you view your work as a continuation of natural evolution?"

I nodded and tried not to stare at his synthetic eyes. "Depending how you think of it. If you think a termite mound is natural, then so is a machine gun. Everything is natural."

"And what do you think of the *natural* state of human evolution?"

"A dead end," I said without hesitation.

The man's artificial eyes glittered.

"Dr. Hedegaard is a very passionate," Michael laughed. "And on that note, I must attend to dinner." He disappeared into the kitchen.

Left alone in a room of strangers, I'd usually melt into a corner, but here I became the center of the party, dragged into one fascinating conversation after another. It was a breath of fresh air to be in a room of intellectual equals, somehow feeling like I was back in my lab, safe and in control.

While we chatted, I inspected the guests. Many had a prosthetic limb, and not hidden, but exposed. Proud, even. One of them ventured that he was in the wars with Michael. *Makes sense.* I didn't mention that I'd lost my brother there. Wrapped in my layers of clothing, I began admiring their sleek metal prosthetics.

Michael swept back into the room.

"Dinner is served!" he announced.

Smiling, the small man with artificial eyes bowed to allow me to walk ahead of him. The guests moved into the dining room, and aside from the chair at the head of the table, only one other seat was left empty. I sat and arranged myself, smoothing the napkin in my lap. The first course was served, and I nodded thank you as a waiter placed a plate before me.

I recoiled.

It appeared to be some kind of meat, but perhaps it was imitation? Michael appeared from the kitchen and sat beside me, hoisting his champagne flute into the air. "A toast!"

Everyone else raised their glasses. I fumbled for mine.

Michael looked around the table. "A toast to old friends." He made eye contact with each person in turn, nodding and smiling, and finished by looking at me. "And to new." He clinked my glass. "A toast to the truth, to sacrifice, and to the brotherhood of all things living!"

"To sacrifice!" erupted a chorus around the table.

I raised my glass and took a sip before inspecting my appetizer again. Everyone else began eating.

Michael was watching me. "Trust me, Effie."

The way he looked at me made me think of my father when he'd taught me to swim, late in my childhood. I'd been terrified. *Let go, Effie*, my dad had whispered, holding me close, *trust me.* Swimming was now one of my greatest pleasures.

Picking up my knife and fork, I sectioned off a piece of the thing on my plate and placed it in my mouth. I chewed. The texture was soft and salty, recalling a distant memory of pork. I hadn't eaten meat since I was a pre-teen and had declared my parents murderers. The memory made me ill.

Michael's prosthetic hand, now oddly warm, was on my forearm.

"Trust me," he repeated.

I made a promise, I reminded myself, and so I smiled and swallowed and began carving off another piece. I fought down each bite, resisting the urge to escape to the bathroom. Just when I'd finished it, the main course was served.

My heart sank.

In a large serving dish in the middle of the table, a bone protruded rudely from flesh that fell away into caramelized onions and roasted potatoes. The circling waiters began serving thick slabs of what must be meat.

Is Michael making fun, taking advantage? I panicked, with only Michael's steady gaze keeping me from flying into space. Poking at my potatoes and carrots, I ventured to try a scrap of the meat.

Popping it into my mouth, I chewed, tears in my eyes, but I couldn't stand it anymore. Pulling Michael to me I whispered, "What is that?"

He smiled. "The more relevant question is: Who is that?"

"What do you mean, *who*?" I hissed.

"Effie, I think you have just tasted human flesh for the first time."

The conversation around the table stopped.

I gagged. "Is this some kind of joke?"

Michael remained still. "In fact, tonight you are part of a very special evening. Tonight I am sharing my flesh, my body with all of you."

I looked around the table. Nobody else was even surprised. They looked pleased.

The joke was on me.

I fought back the simultaneous urge to throw my plate against the wall and to empty the contents of my stomach all over the table. The cloying smell of decay rose up from my plate. Without realizing it, I was already standing.

"This is sick," I cried, staring into Michael's blue eyes, "I thought—"

"You thought you were eating an animal? Some poor creature who could not choose this fate? No, Effie, I choose this. I give freely—"

I convulsed. "No. Nobody would—it's too disgusting." Now I was sure I was going to throw up.

But Michael held me. "Since time began, we've been consuming the Earth, consuming our fellow living creatures. Now we have the ability to sate our hunger by consuming *ourselves*. It's the only way."

I tasted bile in the back of my throat. "Why would you do this?"

"Because I'm a Christian. Are you not?"

I nodded.

"Is Christianity not a cult of cannibalism? Do we not make a weekly pilgrimage to eat the body and blood of our savior? We..." He extended his arms, palms up, toward his guests. ". . . have made our religion even more personal. Every one of us is our own savior containing that same spark of the divine. Just as consuming Christ is sacred, so consuming ourselves is a symbolic act that brings us closer to the god living in all of us—sacrificing a part of ourselves to atone for our sins, eating a small part of ourselves to atone for our share in mankind's sins."

The blood drained from my face. "This is crazy." But everyone was staring at me like *I* was the crazy one. "This is—"

But I didn't finish my sentence. Tears streaming down my face, I ran for the door and out into the cold, ripping my coat from its hanger on the way out. Pounding down the stairs, I skidded onto the sidewalk and sprinted away. Catching the cold metal of a railing at the subway entrance, I leaned over and began retching and crying in heaving sobs. An automated transport growled past, and I imagined myself falling in front of it. The stars were bright diamonds overhead, out of reach in a dead black sky.

• • •

I stared at my reflection in the bedroom mirror. Flaccid skin hung in bunches from my knobby bones. *That's not me, that can't be me.* In disgust, I covered myself with my gown and shuffled to the closet to begin layering up. It was past noon already. I hadn't been out of my apartment in days, had been forcing my dog Buster to do his business on my tiny fifth floor balcony. Everything was an effort. During the day, I could barely keep my eyes open. At night, I'd lay awake, my thoughts swirling and frustrations mounting.

My phone chimed. I groaned but accepted the call. My boss's face appeared.

"Dr. Hedegaard, will we be seeing you in the lab today?" He wasn't buying my excuses anymore. "I don't need to remind you that you're the leader of this project team. A *physical* presence is still required from time to time."

"Yes, yes," I scowled. Even working from home, exhausted, I was keeping up with my workload, probably putting in twice the number of hours as anyone else. While not everyone had God-given intelligence, everyone could at least work hard, and my boss failed in both categories. For the hundredth time I asked myself why I submitted to working for him, for *them.*

Weeks had passed since the dinner. I was ignoring calls from friends. When isolation overcame exhaustion, I'd take Buster out for short walks. The people passing me on the streets, the cars, the looming lampposts, the newspaper boxes with their horrific headlines—I saw everything as though from the bottom of a well. *How can these people just chit-chat with each other? How does the world make any sense to them?*

I finally decided to attend another church meeting. I needed to find strength and salvation, to find some way out. Before arriving, I'd built up scenarios of how I would ignore Michael if I saw him, how I would give him a perfunctory hello and behave as if nothing had happened. As it turned out, he wasn't there, and after the meeting, a desperation seeped in. *Did something happen to him?* Now I needed to know he was okay, even if I thought what he was doing wasn't.

Or was it?

Who was he hurting? *Nobody*. I'd played back his phone messages over and over, his apologies, his clarifications for where the meat came from, that it was lab-grown replacement organs, that they weren't butchers. Perhaps it was my own failure, my own closed mind that was the real problem. He might have explained it all to me first, but then I'd never have gone to his home. I thought about his friends that I'd spoken to there, how intelligent they were. Eating lab meat didn't harm any animals, and it was genetically pure. The idea did make a certain…sense, I had to admit.

After church, I rushed home and called him to accept his apology, to offer one of my own, but Michael didn't answer.

And he didn't return my calls.

• • •

"Five thousand dollars for peace of mind," the med-world avatar said. I scrolled through the list of options: five grand for a liver patch, ten for whole one, twenty-five for a kidney and two hundred for a heart.

Organ replacement was a big business.

I'd done some research. Almost every time a human population faced an environmental collapse, it resorted to cannibalism as a way to rebalance: central Europe in the fifth millennium BC; the Anasazi in the 12th century; Papua New Guinea and Ukraine in the 20th century. The list went on and on as if it was a hardwired response to human-induced local ecosystem collapse. Now that local system spanned the entire planet. Human biomass would soon exceed 500 billion tons, more than any other single species, even Antarctic krill.

What am I doing? I sighed and closed my tablet. Without missing a beat, the voice in my head answered, *Why not, though?* It's not like I'd hurt anyone, and nobody needed to know.

I made my decision.

I logged back on and the med-world avatar said that I needed a medical center if I wanted a delivery made. One phone call later and I'd set-up a drop-off at a local clinic with my friend Mary. I finished our call with a promise to plan an evening together soon.

Next thing, I was heading into the bathroom, wiping the inside of my mouth with a cotton swab and placing it into a double-sealed plastic bag. Moments later, I'd filled in the med-world forms and left the bag out on my balcony for a delivery drone to pick up.

It was done.

My phone rang. Michael's number popped up. "Michael, hello! How are you?" I answered before the first ring had finished.

His face appeared on my screen. "Very good. Sorry about not calling back right away—"

"Don't worry, I was just making sure you were okay." I paused. "I didn't see you at the church meetings" —another pause— "and I'm sorry about your dinner. About the way I acted."

He took a deep breath. "That's not why I didn't return your calls."

My heart was in my throat. "No?"

"No." He wiped his face with his biological hand. "You have your own path to follow. Self-discovery is an important part of my faith."

"That's…well…I understand." I wanted to tell him how much I missed our chats—how much I missed *him*.

"I've been thinking about you, Freyja. I wish you luck in finding what you're looking for."

It was the first time he'd ever used my full name. The tingling warmth I'd felt when I first met Michael returned. "Thank you."

"You take care."

With a smile, he severed the connection.

• • •

Fat snowflakes fell outside my kitchen window while jazz played inside. A real fire crackled in my old fireplace, the first time I'd used it in years. Buster was laid out at my feet as I prepared dinner. I dropped down scraps of veggies from time to time that he snapped up.

An entertainment show was playing on the wall of my living room. "…*billionaire Martin Ludwig is continuing his buying spree…*" said the reporter. I glanced at the display, into glittering photoreceptors. It was the same face of the small man I'd met at Michael's party.

I knew he'd looked familiar. Returning to preparing my dinner, the voice inside my head said, *You see? Those are the kinds of people you need to surround yourself with.*

Delivery of my liver patch had taken two weeks. During the wait, I'd started taking Buster for long walks, waking up early to get back on track with my gene therapy research work. I even attended a rally for ending animal farming.

Slitting open the thermal bio-containment packaging that my liver had arrived in, I removed the organ. It was cold and wet, tinged purple and reddish brown. Closing my eyes, I squeezed it, trying to see if my proprioperceptive sense would magically expand to contain this new chunk of my flesh. I waited, eyes closed. Somehow it did feel like a part of me; somehow my skin sensed this wasn't alien flesh.

This thing was a part of me.

I dropped it into the frying pan.

An intense hunger gripped me. I was used to being hungry, but this was different. Watching my liver sizzle, I began salivating painfully. My nostrils flared. Picking up a fork, I turned it, trying to brown it evenly, but then, unable to wait, I used the side of the fork to nip off a piece and popped it into my mouth.

At first I rolled it around my tongue. Then I chewed, sucking the juices from it; I moaned as I swallowed, remembering guilt-free days of eating meat as a youth, eating and *enjoying*. Stabbing and ripping with the fork, I ground off another piece against the bottom of the frying pan. It was still raw. Pinpricks of blood popped from the edges of the ragged meat, but I gobbled it down.

The pan was empty before I realized what I was doing. Using the back of my hand, I wiped a streak of spittle from the side of my mouth.

Buster whined at my feet, sensing something was going on. I looked down at him.

"Not for you, little Buster, this is all for mummy."

He always preferred human food to his own food. *Human food.* And for the first time in longer than I could remember, I laughed, and then another thought: *You are what you eat.* I laughed again.

• • •

Personal organ stockpiling was something everyone with money was doing, I'd found out. I talked about it with anyone who would listen. I was finally sleeping at night. Michael got back in touch with me, and our coffee dates became regular again.

"Sharks kill eleven humans a year on average!" I exclaimed to him one evening, startling some other customers. "Do you know how many sharks humans kill?"

He shook his head.

"Eleven thousand *an hour*!" I slammed my coffee down. "What are we going to do about this?"

Michael shrugged and took a sip from his coffee. "What can we do?"

"Stop being hypocrites," I said, sipping my coffee and looking back to my tablet. I had an order page up. A liver and a pound of thigh muscle. I chose two-day delivery to the clinic to make sure I would get them in time for my next private Sunday evening dinner party.

• • •

"What do you mean, you won't let me send them there anymore?"

"Effie, I can't imagine what you must be going through…" My friend Mary's face grimaced in my phone's display. "…but this is getting weird. My boss is wondering who all these packages are for. I thought this was just a once or twice thing? Why don't you get them delivered to your own lab?"

I couldn't tell her that half my deliveries were already going to my lab, and that my boss was growing suspicious as well.

"This project is just taking longer than we thought." I used the royal "we" without explanation. My little white lie was becoming a big one, even with my credentials to back me up. "You're right. Sorry. Listen, we should go out like we said."

"Uh-huh." She arched her eyebrows and disconnected.

Sighing again, I looked down at Buster. "Do *you* want to go out?"

Buster barked yes, and I went to fetch his leash. Spring was here, but outside it was still chilly, and we made our way into the small wooded park near my apartment. Walking through the bare trees, I remembered stories my mother had told me about the *myling*, the ghosts of babies who were abandoned in the forests at birth, left to die in the frozen wilderness, their souls forever doomed to wander alone.

I began scheming for ways to keep my packages coming.

• • •

It wasn't fair. Any idiot could feed themselves like a pig and get millions from medical insurance to fix their diabetes. But ask them to cover the cost of artificial organs, and there were forms and questions. I made a stab at requiring the deliveries for religious reasons, but this just elicited "You're kidding, right?" from my insurance adjuster.

After engineering an intricate web of delivery routes, they were all getting closed down, one by one. Even if I could find a way to keep the packages coming, money was becoming a serious issue. Custom-grown organs weren't cheap. I'd used up my savings, maxed out my credit lines, and I was dipping into my retirement savings, eating away at my future.

Desperate, I tried Michael.

"Effie, you've come a long way since I met you," Michael replied after I asked him for a loan. "I'm sensing a real transformation."

"I don't know what to do." I hated myself for asking for money, for appearing weak.

We were back in our coffee shop. The heat of summer was gone, replaced with the chill of coming winter. Red leaves were falling from the skeletons of trees outside.

"Money," said Michael, "is not the solution to any of life's problems." He held my hands in his. Both of his arms were prosthetic now. "I applaud the enthusiasm that you've taken to our holy sacrament, but you need to find your own way through this."

There was only one way—had *always* only been one way—I realized now.

Michael squeezed my hands. "The only constant in life is change. Life is ever evolving. It's not about *being* something; it's about *becoming* something."

I nodded. "Can I come for dinner with the Church again?"

His eyes seemed to stare through mine, seeing through me into my soul.

"Only you can answer that," he replied.

• • •

The ancient subway car rattled toward me, its wheels squealing. An encircled "Q" glowed on the front of the driverless lead car. It was the express train, rolling without stopping on its way past the 29th Street station. I was standing near the end of the platform, next to the far wall. The squealing stopped as the train began to clear the station and accelerate back up to speed.

The lead car was almost at me, and I stepped onto the edge of the platform, staring at the empty driver's seat of the subway car as it rushed closer.

"Hey, lady!" someone called out.

The train was now just feet away from me. I stepped toward the ledge and the empty space beyond.

"Lady, watch—"

The squealing began again, this time ear-shattering, but it was too late. I leaned in, feeling the train crash into me. There was no pain, just a flash of white before blackness descended.

• • •

A keening whine woke me. Opening my eyes, I could see snow falling outside my window, but it wasn't enough to stop emergency services. I hadn't been at my office in months—on sick leave, or, more accurately, rehabilitation leave—so I brought my work home. Glancing at my side table, the cover sheets of the latest data downloads glowed on my tablet: Structural basis of lentiviral subversion in cellular degradation, genomic sequencing of flesh-eating bacteria, and new trial results of viral gene-therapy.

It was nearly 9 a.m.

I sat up in bed and arched my back. My whole body ached. Swinging my legs off the bed, I stood and wobbled, still not quite used to it. I pulled down the blinds to cocoon myself.

Again the whining. "Buster, baby, please stop, someone will be here in a few minutes."

Walking into the bathroom, the lights glowed on by themselves. I reached my arms above my head in another stiff-morning-stretch and stopped to inspect myself.

In the mirror I gleamed like a silvery spider, my slender arms glittering in the light reflecting from overhead. I'd chosen to keep my prostheses with exposed metal, wiring junctions and all, to keep the weight down.

My legs were now lithe titanium-alloy slivers that supported the stump of my body between them. The meat of my midsection was criss-crossed with angry red scars where organs had been removed and replaced.

The first steps had been easy.

After some haggling, I'd convinced a doctor to amputate both of my arms, even gaining possession of them after the fact. I hosted my first Church dinner with my bicep as the main course. It was my coming out party. Eating my own flesh—my own true flesh—made my spirit soar, the cracks in my soul closing with each piece of my body that I consumed. As I devoured myself, I filled myself, making myself both more and less at the same time.

When it came to my legs the doctors had balked. They'd refused more amputations, and I couldn't afford a trip to one of the far-off places medical tourists could go to have this sort of work done.

But…

Just one misplaced step on the subway, and a leg was severed. Slip in the shower at the wrong angle and you could rupture a kidney. I always refused the insurance payments, only asking for the prostheses and organ replacements. I arranged for a round-the-clock medical monitor so that every accident brought near-instantaneous responses by emergency teams.

The pain was excruciating but cleansing.

I admired myself in the mirror, my misshapen torso laced with the cuts and lashes of my salvation. Taking a deep breath, I prepared for perfection, taking one final look into my eyes before closing them tight. Slowing my breathing, my mind filled until it was a cool, calm lake.

"If thine eyes offend thee..." I intoned over the yelps of Buster. Reaching toward my face with my hands, I paused, and then dug my spiny metal fingers into my eyes.

The world exploded in a rapture of pain. Black circles danced in my vision as my eyesight faded. I screamed. Tightening my grip, I pulled harder, feeling the optic nerves resisting my efforts. Finally, with a wet pop, one and then the other snapped elastically. Blood coursed down my face. Dropping to my knees, I stuffed my eyeballs into my mouth and began chewing. Gagging, crying, I tried to swallow, and with a final effort managed to get them down.

"Don't worry, Buster," I choked out between sobs, "someone will be here soon, baby!"

Already the paramedics had been alerted by my health monitoring service. They'd arrive in five minutes, and by tomorrow I would be seeing through new eyes.

A chime signalled an incoming call.

"We are so proud of you," announced a familiar voice.

My heart filled with a bliss that blotted out the pain. I wanted to cry, and maybe I did—it was hard to tell. With the back of one mechanical hand, I wiped away my bloody tears of joy. "Thank you, Father Michael."

I felt as light as a feather.

"I have spoken to God this day," Father Michael continued. "Mankind's depravity has once again permeated every part of his being, every man's heart so sin-stained that nothing they touch is not evil. A new Flood is coming to cleanse God's Earth, but not one of water, this deluge will be one of flesh and blood..."

He wasn't just speaking to me—he was addressing the whole rapidly growing body of the Church, assembled virtually around the world to observe my ceremony. He took control of my robotic prostheses, and I could feel myself standing.

"Freyja, you are accepted into the Church of Sacrificial Atonement. You will be the knife that cuts the rotting flesh from our God's Earth. In your own blood I baptize you reborn, from now on to be known as Saint Freyja."

"Freyja," he repeated, "archangel of love…"

He paused, holding me high for all to see in my glory.

"…and of death."

SHOOTING THE APOCALYPSE

Paolo Bacigalupi

If it were for anyone else, he would have just laughed in their faces and told them they were on their own.

The thought nagged at Timo as he drove his beat-up FlexFusion down the rutted service road that ran parallel to the concrete-lined canal of the Central Arizona Project. For any other journo who came down to Phoenix looking for a story, he wouldn't even think of doing them a favor.

All those big names looking to swoop in like magpies and grab some meaty exclusive and then fly away just as fast, keeping all their page views and hits to themselves...he wouldn't do it.

Didn't matter if they were *Google/NY Times*, Cherry Xu, *Facebook Social Now*, Deborah Williams, *Kindle Post*, or *Xinhua*.

But Lucy? Well, sure. For Lucy, he'd climb into his sweatbox of a car with all his camera gear and drive his skinny brown ass out to North Phoenix and into the hills on a crap tip. He'd drive this way and that, burning gas trying to find a service road, and then bump his way through dirt and ruts, scraping the belly of the Ford the whole way, and he still wouldn't complain.

Just goes to show you're a sucker for a girl who wears her jeans tight.

But it wasn't just that. Lucy was fine, if you liked a girl with white skin and little tits and wide hips, and sometimes Timo would catch himself fantasizing about what it would be like to get with her. But in the end, that wasn't why he did favors for Lucy. He did it because she was scrappy and wet and she was in over her head—and too hard-assed and proud to admit it.

Girl had grit; Timo could respect that. Even if she came from up north and was so wet that sometimes he laughed out loud at the things she said. The girl didn't know much about dry desert life, but she had grit.

So when she muttered over her Dos Equis that all the stories had already been done, Timo, in a moment of beery romantic fervor, had sworn to her that it just wasn't so. He had the eye. He saw things other people didn't. He could name twenty stories she could still do and make a name for herself.

But when he'd started listing possibilities, Lucy shot them down as fast as he brought them up.

Coyotes running Texans across the border into California?

Sohu already had a nine part series running.

Californians buying Texas hookers for nothing, like Phoenix was goddamn Tijuana?

Google/NY Times and *Fox* both had big spreads.

Water restrictions from the Roosevelt Dam closure and the drying up of Phoenix's swimming pools?

Kindle Post ran that.

The narco murders that kept getting dumped in the empty pools that had become so common that people had started calling them "swimmers"?

AP. Fox. Xinhua. LA Times. The Talisha Brannon Show. Plus the reality narco show *Hard Bangin'*.

He kept suggesting new angles, new stories, and all Lucy said, over and over was, "It's been done." And then she'd rattle off the news organizations, the journos who'd covered the stories, the page hits, the viewerships, and the click-thrus they'd drawn.

"I'm not looking for some dead hooker for the sex and murder crowd," Lucy said as she drained her beer. "I want something that'll go big. I want a scoop, you know?"

"And I want a woman to hand me a ice-cold beer when I walk in the door," Timo grumped. "Don't mean I'm going to get it."

But still, he understood her point. He knew how to shoot pictures that would make a vulture sob its beady eyes out, but the news environment that Lucy fought to distinguish herself in was like gladiatorial sport—some winners, a lot of losers, and a whole shit-ton of blood on the ground.

Journo money wasn't steady money. Wasn't good money. Sometimes, you got lucky. Hell, he'd got lucky himself when he'd gone over Texas way and shot Hurricane Violet in all her glory. He'd photographed a whole damn fishing boat flying through the air and landing on a Days Inn, and in that one shot he knew he'd hit the big time. Violet razed Galveston and blasted into Houston, and Timo got page views so high that he sometimes imagined that the Cat 6 had actually killed him and sent him straight to Heaven.

He'd kept hitting reload on his PayPal account and watched the cash pouring in. He'd had the big clanking *cojones* to get into the heart of that clusterfuck, and he'd come out of it with more than a million hits a photo. Got him all excited.

But disaster was easy to cover, and he'd learned the hard way that when the big dogs muscled in, little dogs got muscled out. Which left him back in sad-sack Phoenix, scraping for glamour shots of brains on windshields and trussed-up drug bunnies in the bottoms of swimming pools. It made him sympathetic to Lucy's plight, if not her perspective.

It's all been done, Timo thought as he maneuvered his Ford around the burned carcass of an abandoned Tesla. *So what if it's been motherfucking done?*

"There ain't no virgins, and there ain't no clean stories," he'd tried to explain to Lucy. "There's just angles on the same-ass stories. Scoops come from being in the right place at the right time, and that's all just dumb luck. Why don't you just come up with a good angle on Phoenix and be happy?"

But Lucy Monroe wanted a nice clean virgin story that didn't have no grubby fingerprints on it from other journos. Something she could put her name on. Some way to make her mark, make those big news companies notice her. Something to grow her brand and all that. Not just the day-to-day grind of narco kills and starving immigrants from Texas, something special. Something new.

So when the tip came in, Timo thought what the hell, maybe this was something she'd like. Maybe even a chance to blow up together. Lucy could do the words, he'd bring the pics, and they'd scoop all the big name journos who drank martinis at the Hilton 6 and complained about what a refugee shit hole Phoenix had become.

The Ford scraped over more ruts. Dust already coated the rear window of Timo's car, a thick beige paste. Parallel to the service road, the waters of the Central Arizona Project flowed, serene and blue and steady. A man-made canal that stretched three hundred miles across the desert to bring water to Phoenix from the Colorado River. A feat of engineering, and cruelly tempting, given the ten-foot chain-link and barbed wire fences that escorted it on either side.

In this part of Phoenix, the Central Arizona Project formed the city's northern border. On one side of the CAP canal, it was all modest stucco tract houses packed together like sardines stretching south. But on Timo's side, it was desert, rising into tan and rust hill folds, dotted with mesquite and saguaro.

A few hardy subdivisions had built outposts north of the CAP's moat-like boundary, but the canal seemed to form a barrier of some psychological significance, because for the most part, Phoenix stayed to the south of the concrete-lined canal, choosing to finally build itself into something denser than lazy sprawl. Phoenix on one side, the desert on the other, and the CAP flowing between them like a thin blue DMZ.

Just driving on the desert side of the CAP made Timo thirsty. Dry mouth, plain-ass desert, quartz rocks and sandstone nubs with a few creosote bushes holding onto the dust and waving in the blast furnace wind. Normally, Timo didn't even bother to look at the desert. It barely changed. But here he was, looking for something new—

He rounded a curve and slowed, peering through his grimy windshield. "Well I'll be goddamned…"

Up ahead, something was hanging from the CAP's barrier fence. Dogs were jumping up to tug at it, milling and barking.

Timo squinted, trying to understand what he was seeing.

"Oh yeah. Hell yes!"

He hit the brakes. The car came grinding to a halt in a cloud of dust, but Timo was already climbing out and fumbling for his phone, pressing it to his ear, listening to it ring.

Come on, come on, come on.

Lucy picked up.

Timo couldn't help grinning. "I got your story, girl. You'll love it. It's *new*."

• • •

The dogs bared their teeth at Timo's approach, but Timo just laughed. He dug into his camera bag for his pistol.

"You want a piece of me?" he asked. "You want some of Timo, bitches?"

Turned out they didn't. As soon he held up the pistol, the dogs scattered. Animals were smarter than people, that way. Pull a gun on some drunk California frat boy and you never knew if the sucker was still going to try and throw down. Dogs were way smarter than Californians. Timo could respect that, so he didn't shoot them as they fled the scene.

One of the dogs, braver or more arrogant than the rest, paused to yank off a final trophy before loping away; the rest of the pack zeroed in on it, yipping and leaping, trying to steal its prize. Timo watched, wishing he'd pulled his camera instead of his gun. The shot was perfect. He sighed and stuffed the pistol into the back of his pants, dug out his camera, and turned to the subject at hand.

"Well hello, good-looking," he murmured. "Ain't you a sight?"

The man hung upside down from the chain link fence, bloated from the Phoenix heat. A bunch of empty milk jugs dangled off his body, swinging from a harness of shoelace ties. From the look of him, he'd been cooking out in the sun for at least a day or so.

The meat of one arm was completely desleeved, and the other arm… well, Timo had watched the dogs make off with the poor bastard's hand.

His face and neck and chest didn't look much better. The dogs had been doing some jumping.

"Come on, *vato*. Gimme the story." Timo stalked back and forth in front of the body, checking the angles, considering the shadows and light. "You want to get your hits up don't you? Show Timo your good side, I make you famous. So help me out, why don't you?"

He stepped back, thinking wide-frame: the strung-up body, the black nylon flowers woven into the chain link around it. The black guttered candles and cigarettes and mini liquor bottles scattered by the dogs' frenzied feeding. The CAP flowing behind it all. Phoenix beyond that, sprawling all the way to the horizon.

"What's your best side?" Timo asked. "Don't be shy. I'll do you right. Make you famous. Just let me get your angle."

There.

Timo squatted and started shooting. *Click-click-click-click*—the artificial sound of digital photography and the Pavlovian rush of sweaty excitement as Timo got the feel.

Dead man.

Flowers.

Candles.

Water.

Timo kept snapping. He had it now. The flowers and the empty milk-jugs dangling off the dude. Timo was in the flow, bracketing exposures, shooting steady, recognizing the moment when his inner eye told him that he'd nailed the story. It was good. *Really* good.

As good as a Cat 6 plowing into Houston.

Click-click-click. Money-money-money-money.

"That's right, buddy. Talk to your friend Timo."

The man had a story to tell, and Timo had the eye to see it. Most people missed the story. But Timo always saw. He had the eye.

Maybe he'd buy a top-shelf tequila to celebrate his page view money. Some diapers for his sister Amparo's baby. If the photos were good, maybe he'd grab a couple syndication licenses, too. Swap the shit-ass battery in the Ford. Get something with a bigger range dropped into it. Let him get around without always wondering if he was going to lose a charge.

Some of these could go to *Xinhua*, for sure. The Chinese news agencies loved seeing America ripping itself to shit. BBC might bite, too. Foreigners loved that story. Only thing that would sell better is if it had a couple guns: *America, the Savage Land* or some shit. That was money, there. Might be rent for a bigger place. A place where Amparo could bail when her boyfriend got his ass drunk and angry.

Timo kept snapping photos, changing angles, framing and exposure. Diving deeper into the dead man's world. Capturing scuffed-up boots and plastic prayer beads. He hummed to himself as he worked, talking to his subject, coaxing the best out of the corpse.

"You don't know it, but you're damn lucky I came along," Timo said. "If one of those citizen journalist *pendejo* lice got you first, they wouldn't have treated you right. They'd shoot a couple shitty frames and upload them social. Maybe sell a Instagram pic to the blood rags...but they ain't quality. Me? When I'm done, people won't be able to *dream* without seeing you."

It was true, too. Any asshole could snap a pic of some girl blasted to pieces in an electric Mercedes, but Timo knew how to make you cry when you saw her splattered all over the front pages of the blood rags. Some piece of narco ass, and you'd still be bawling your eyes out over her tragic death. He'd catch the girl's little fuzzy dice mirror ornament spattered with blood, and your heart would just break.

Amparo said Timo had the eye. Little bro could see what other people didn't, even when it was right in front of their faces.

Every asshole had a camera these days; the difference was that Timo could *see*.

Timo backed off and got some quick video. He ran the recording back, listening to the audio, satisfying himself that he had the sound of it: the wind rattling the chain link under the high hot Arizona sky; meadowlark call from somewhere next to the CAP waters; but most of all, the empty dangling jugs, the three of them plunking hollowly against each other—a dead man turned into an offering and a wind chime.

Timo listened to the deep *thunk-thunk-thunk* tones.

Good sounds.

Good empty desert sounds.

He crouched and framed the man's gnawed arm and the milk jugs. From this angle, he could just capture the blue line of the CAP canal and the leading edge of Phoenix beyond: cookie-cutter low-stories with lava-rock front yards and broke-down cars on blocks. And somewhere in there, some upstanding example of Arizona Minute-Man militia pride had spied this sucker scrambling down the dusty hillside with his water jugs and decided to put a cap in his ass.

CAP in his ass, Timo chuckled to himself.

The crunch of tires and the grind of an old bio-diesel engine announced Lucy's pickup coming up the dirt road. A trail of dust followed. Rusty beast of flex-fuel, older than the girl who drove it and twice as beat up, but damn was it a beast. It had been one of the things Timo liked about Lucy, soon as he met her. Girl drove a machine that didn't give a damn about anything except driving over shit.

The truck came to a halt. The driver's side door squealed aside as Lucy climbed out. Army green tank top and washed out jeans. White skin, scorched and bronzed by Arizona sun, her reddish brown hair jammed up under an ASU Geology Department ball cap.

Every time he saw her, Timo liked what he saw. Phoenix hadn't dried her right, yet, but still, she had some kind of tenacious-ass demon in her. Something about the way her pale blue skeptical eyes burned for a story told you that once she bit in, she wouldn't let go. Crazy-ass pitbull. The girl and the truck were a pair. Unstoppable.

"Please tell me I didn't drive out here for a swimmer," Lucy said as she approached.

"What do you think?"

"I think I was on the other side of town when you called, and I had to burn diesel to get here."

She was trying to look jaded, but her eyes were already flicking from detail to detail, gathering the story before Timo even had to open his mouth. She might be new in Phoenix, but the girl had the eye. Just like Timo, Lucy saw things.

"Texan?" she asked.

Timo grinned. "You think?"

"Well, he's a Merry Perry, anyway. I don't know many other people who would join that cult." She crouched down in front of the corpse and peered into the man's torn face. Reaching out, she caressed the prayer beads embedded in the man's neck. "I did a story on Merry Perrys. Roadside spiritual aid for the refugees." She sighed. "They were all buying the beads and making the prayers."

"Crying and shaking and repentance."

"You've been to their services, too?"

"Everybody's done that story at least once," Timo said. "I shot a big old revival tent over in New Mexico, outside of Carlsbad. The preacher had a nasty ass thorn bush, wanted volunteers."

Timo didn't think he'd ever forget the scene. The tent walls sucking and flapping as blast-furnace winds gusted over them. The dust-coated refugees all shaking, moaning, and working their beads for God. All of them asking what they needed to give up in order to get back to the good old days of big oil money and fancy cities like Houston and Austin. To get back to a life before hurricanes went Cat 6 and Big Daddy Drought sucked whole states dry.

Lucy ran her fingers along the beads that had sunk deep into the dead man's neck. "They strangled him."

"Sure looks that way."

Timo could imagine this guy earning the prayer beads one at time. Little promises of God's love that he could carry with him. He imagined the man down in the dirt, all crying and spitty and grateful for his bloody back and for the prayer beads that had ended up embedded in his swollen, blackening neck, like some kind of Marti Gras party gone wrong. The man had done his prayers and repentance, and this was where he'd ended up.

"What happened to his hand?" Lucy asked.

"Dog got it."

"Christ."

"If you want some better art, we can back off for a little while, and the dogs'll come back. I can get a good tearaway shot if we let them go after him again—"

Lucy gave Timo a dirty look, so he hastily changed tacks. "Anyway, I thought you should see him. Good art, and it's a great story. Nobody's got something like this."

Lucy straightened. "I can't pitch this, Timo. It's sad as hell, but it isn't new. Nobody cares if Old Tex here hiked across a thousand miles of desert just to get strung up as some warning. It's sad, but everyone knows how much people hate Texans. *Kindle Post* did a huge story on Texas lynchings."

"Shit." Timo sighed. "Every time I think you're wise, I find out you're still wet."

"Oh fuck off, Timo."

"No, I'm serious girl. Come here. Look with your eye. I know you got the eye. Don't make me think I'm wasting my time on you."

Timo crouched down beside the dead man, framing him with this hands. "Old Tex here hikes his ass across a million miles of burning desert, and he winds up here. Maybe he's thinking he's heading for California and gets caught with the State Sovereignty Act, can't cross no state borders now. Maybe he just don't have the cash to pay coyotes. Maybe he thinks he's special and he's going to swim the Colorado and make it up north across Nevada. Anyways, Tex is stuck squatting out in the hills, watching us live the good life. But then the poor sucker sees the CAP, and he's sick of paying to go to some public pump for water, so he grabs his bottles and goes in for a little sip—"

"—and someone puts a bullet in him," Lucy finished. "I get it. I'm trying to tell you nobody cares about dead Texans. People string them up all the time. I saw it New Mexico, too. Merry Perry prayer tents and Texans strung up on fences. Same in Oklahoma. All the roads out of Texas have them. Nobody cares."

Wet.

Timo sighed. "You're lucky you got me for your tour guide. You know that, right? You see the cigarettes? See them little bitty Beam and Cuervo bottles? The black candles? The flowers?"

Timo waited for her take in the scene again. To see the way he saw. "Old Tex here isn't a *warning*. This motherfucker's an *offering*. People turned Old Tex into an offering for Santa Muerte. They're using Tex here to get in good with the Skinny Lady."

"Lady Death," Lucy said. "Isn't that a cult for narcos?"

"Nah. She's no cult. She's a saint. Takes care of people who don't got pull with the Church. When you need help on something the Church don't like, you go to Santa Muerte. The Skinny Lady takes care of you. She knows we all need a little help. Maybe she helps narcos, sure, but she helps poor people, too. She helps desperate people. When Mother Mary's too uptight, you call the Skinny Lady to do the job."

"Sounds like you know a lot about her."

"Oh hell yes. Got an app on my phone. Dial her any time I want and get a blessing."

"You're kidding."

"True story. There's a lady down in Mexico runs a big shrine. You send her a dollar, she puts up an offering for you. Makes miracles happen. There's a whole list of miracles that Santa Muerte does. Got her own hashtag."

"So what kind of miracles do you look for?"

"Tips, girl! What you think?" Timo sighed. "Narcos call on Santa Muerte all the time when they want to put a bullet in their enemies. And I come in after and take the pictures. Skinny Lady gets me there before the competition is even close."

Lucy was looking at him like he was crazy, and it annoyed him. "You know, Lucy, it's not like you're the only person who needs an edge out here." He waved at the dead Texan. "So? You want the story, or not?"

She still looked skeptical. "If anyone can make an offering to Santa Muerte online, what's this Texan doing upside down on a fence?"

"DIY, baby."

"I'm serious, Timo. What makes you think Tex here is an offering?"

Because Amparo's boyfriend just lost his job to some loser Longhorn who will work for nothing. Because my water bill just went up again, and my rationing just went down. Because Roosevelt Lake is gone dry, and I got Merry Perrys doing revivals right on the corner of 7th and Monte Vista, and they're trying to get my cousin Marco to join them.

"People keep coming," Timo said, and he was surprised at the tightness of his throat as he said it. "They smell that we got water, and they just keep coming. It's like Texas is a million, million ants, and they just keep coming."

"There are definitely a lot of people in Texas."

"More like a tsunami. And we keep getting hit by wave after wave of them, and we can't hold 'em all back." He pointed at the body. "This is Last Stand shit, here. People are calling in the big guns. Maybe they're praying for Santa Muerte to hit the Texans with a dust storm and strip their bones before they get here. For sure they're asking for something big."

"So they call on Lady Death." But Lucy was shaking her head. "It's just that I need more than a body to do a story."

"But I got amazing pics!"

"I need more. I need quotes. I need a trend. I need a story. I need an example…"

Lucy was looking across the CAP canal toward the subdivision as she spoke. Timo could almost see the gears turning in her head…

"Oh no. Don't do it, girl."

"Do what?" But she was smiling, already.

"Don't go over there and start asking who did the deed."

"It would be a great story."

"You think some motherfucker's just gonna say they out and wasted Old Tex?"

"People love to talk, if you ask them the right questions."

"Seriously, Lucy. Let the cops take care of it. Let them go over there and ask the questions."

Lucy gave him a pissed-off look.

"What?" Timo asked.

"You really think I'm that wet?"

"Well…"

"Seriously? How long have we known each other? Do you really think you can fool me into thinking the cops are gonna give a shit about another dead Merry Perry? How wet do you think I am?"

Lucy spun and headed for her truck.

"This ain't some amusement park!" Timo called after her. "You can't just go poke the Indians and think they're gonna native dance for you. People here are for *real!*" He had to shout the last because the truck's door was already screeching open.

"Don't worry about me!" Lucy called as she climbed into the beast. "Just get me good art! I'll get our story!"

• • •

"So let me get this straight," Timo asked, for the fourth or fifth time. "They just let you into their house?"

They were kicked back on the roof at Sid's Cafe with the rest of the regulars, taking potshots at the prairie dogs who had invaded the half-finished subdivision ruins around the bar, trading an old .22 down a long line as patrons took bets.

The subdivision was called Sonora Bloom Estates, one of those crap-ass investments that had gone belly up when Phoenix finally stopped bailing out over-pumped subdivisions. Desert Bloom Estates had died because some bald-ass pencil-pusher in City Planning had got a stick up his ass and said the water district wasn't going to support them. Now, unless some company like IBIS or Halliburton could frack their way to some magical new water supply, Desert Bloom was only ever going to be a town for prairie dogs.

"They just let you in?" Timo asked. "Seriously?"

Lucy nodded smugly. "They let me into their house, and then into their neighbor's houses. And then they took me down into their basements and showed me their machine guns." Lucy took a swig of Negro Modelo. "I make friends, Timo." She grinned. "I make a *lot* of friends. It's what I do."

"Bullshit."

"Believe it, or don't." Lucy shrugged. "Anyway, I've got our story. 'Phoenix's Last Stand.' You wouldn't believe how they've got themselves set up. They've got war rooms. They've got ammo dumps. This isn't some cult militia, it's more like the army of the apocalypse. Way beyond preppers. These people are getting ready for the end of the world, and they want to talk about it."

"They want to talk."

"They're *desperate* to talk. They *like* talking. All they talk about is how to shove Texas back where it came from. I mean, you see the inside of their houses, and it's all Arizona for the People, and God and Santa Muerte to back them up."

"They willing to let me take pictures?"

Lucy gave him another smug look. "No faces. That's the only condition."

Timo grinned. "I can work with that."

Lucy set her beer down. "So what've you shot so far?"

"Good stuff." Timo pulled out his camera and flicked through images. "How about this one?" He held up the camera for her to see. "Poetry, right?"

Lucy eyed the image with distaste. "We need something PG, Timo."

"PG? Come on. PG don't get the hits. People love the bodies and the blood. *Sangre* this, *sangre* that. They want the blood, and they want the sex. Those are the only two things that get hits."

"This isn't for the local blood rags," Lucy said. "We need something PG from the dead guy."

She accepted the rifle from a hairy biker dude sitting next to her and sighted out at the dimming landscape beyond. The sun was sinking over the sprawl of the Phoenix basin, a brown blanket of pollution and smoke from California wild fires turning orange and gaudy.

Timo lifted his camera and snapped a couple quick shots of Lucy as she sighted down the rifle barrel. Wet girl trying to act dry. Not knowing that everyone who rolled down to Phoenix tried to show how tough they were by picking up a nice rifle and blasting away at the furry critters out in the subdivisions.

The thought reminded Timo that he needed to get some shots of Sumo Hernandez and his hunting operation. Sucker had a sweet gig bringing Chinese tourists in to blast at coyotes and then feed them rattlesnake dinners.

He snapped a couple more pictures and checked the results. Lucy looked damn good on the camera's LCD. He'd got her backlit, the line of her rifle barrel across the blaze of the red ball sun. Money shot for sure.

He flicked back into the dead Texan pictures.

"PG, PG… ," Timo muttered. "What the fuck is PG? It's not like the dude's dick is out. Just his eaten-off face."

Lucy squeezed off another shot and handed the rifle on.

"This is going to go big, Timo. We don't want it to look like it's just another murder story. That's been done. This has to look smart and scary and real. We're going to do a series."

"We are?"

"Hell yes, we are. I mean, this could be Pulitzer type stuff. 'Phoenix's Last Stand.'"

"I don't give a shit about Pulitzers. I just want good hits. I need money."

"It will get us hits. Trust me. We're onto something good."

Timo flicked through more of his pictures. "How about just the beads in the guy's neck?" He showed her a picture. "This one's sweet."

"No." Lucy shook her head. "I want the CAP in it."

Timo gave up on stifling his exasperation. "PG, CAP. Anything else, ma'am?"

Lucy shot him a look. "Will you trust me on this? I know what I'm doing."

"Wet-ass newcomer says she knows what she's doing."

"Look, you're the expert when it comes to Phoenix. But you've got to trust me. I know what I'm doing. I know how people think back East. I know what people want on the big traffic sites. You know Phoenix, and I trust you. Now you've got to trust *me*. We're onto something. If we do it right, we're going to blow up. We're going to be a phenomenon."

The hairy biker guy handed the rifle back to Lucy for another shot.

"So you want PG, and you want the CAP," Timo said.

"Yeah. The CAP is why he died," she said absently as she sighted again with the rifle. "It's what he wanted. And it's what the Defending Angels need to protect. It's what Phoenix has that Texas doesn't. Phoenix is alive in the middle of a desert because you've got one of the most expensive water transport systems in the world. If Texas had a straw like the CAP running to some place like the Mississippi River, they'd still be fine."

Timo scoffed. "That would be like a thousand miles."

"Rivers go farther than that." Lucy squeezed off a shot and dust puffed beside a prairie dog. The critter dove back into its hole, and Lucy passed the rifle on. "I mean, your CAP water is coming from the Rockies. You've got the Colorado River running all the way down from Wyoming and Colorado, through Utah, all the way across the top of Arizona, and then you and California and Las Vegas all share it out."

"California doesn't share shit."

"You know what I mean. You all stick your straws in the river, you pump water to a bunch of cities that shouldn't even exist. CAP water comes way more than a thousand miles." She laughed and reached for her beer. "The irony is that at least Texans built where they *had* water. Without the CAP, you'd be just like the Texans. A bunch of sad-ass people all trying to move north."

"Thank God we're smarter than those assholes."

"Well, you've got better bureaucrats and pork barrels, anyway."

Timo made a face at Lucy's dig, but didn't bother arguing. He was still hunting through his photos for something that Lucy would approve of.

Nothing PG about dying, he thought. Nothing PG about clawing your way all the way across a thousand miles of desert just to smash up against chain link. Nothing PG about selling off your daughter so you can make a run at going North, or jumping the border into California.

He was surprised to find that he almost felt empathy for the Texan. Who knew? Maybe this guy had seen the apocalypse coming, but he'd just been too rooted in place to accept that he couldn't ride it out. Or maybe he'd had too much faith that God would take care of him.

The rifle was making the rounds again. More sharp cracks of the little .22 caliber bullets.

Faith. Maybe Old Tex's faith had made him blind. Made it impossible for him to see what was coming. Like a prairie dog who'd stuck his head out of his burrow, and couldn't quite believe that God had put a bead on his furry little skull. Couldn't see the bullet screaming in on him.

In the far distance, a flight of helicopters was moving across the burning horizon. The thud-thwap of their rotors carried easily across the hum of the city. Timo counted fifteen or twenty in the formation. Heading off to fight forest fires maybe. Or else getting shipped up to the arctic by the Feds.

Going someplace, anyway.

"Everybody's got some place to go," Lucy murmured, as if reading his mind.

The rifle cracked again, and a prairie dog went down. Everyone cheered. "I think that one was from Texas," someone said.

Everyone laughed. Selena came up from below with a new tray of bottles and handed them out. Lucy was smirking to herself, looking superior.

"You got something to say?" Timo asked.

"Nothing. It's just funny how you all treat the Texans."

"Shit." Timo took a slug from his beer. "They deserve it. I was down there, remember? I saw them all running around like ants after Hurricane Violet fucked them up. Saw their towns drying up. Hell, everybody who wasn't Texas Forever saw that shit coming down. And there they all were, praying to God to save their righteous Texan asses." He took another slug of beer. "No pity for those fools. They brought their apocalypse down on their own damn selves. And now they want to come around here and take away what we got? No way."

"No room for charity?" Lucy prodded.

"Don't interview me," Timo shot back.

Lucy held up her hands in apology. "My bad."

Timo snorted. "Hey everybody! My wet-ass friend here thinks we ought to show some charity to the Texans."

"I'll give 'em a bullet, free," Brixer Gonzalez said.

"I'll give 'em two!" Molly Abrams said. She took the rifle and shot out a distant window in the subdivision.

"And yet they keep coming," Lucy murmured, looking thoughtful. "They just keep on coming, and you can't stop them."

Timo didn't like how she mirrored his own worries.

"We're going to be fine."

"Because you've got Santa Muerte and a whole hell of a lot of armed lunatics on your side," Lucy said with satisfaction. "This story is going to make us. 'The Defending Angels of Phoenix.' What a beautiful scoop."

"And they're just going to let us cover them?" Timo still couldn't hide his skepticism.

"All anyone wants to do is tell their story, Timo. They need to know they matter." She favored him with a side-long smile. "So when a nice journo from up north comes knocking? Some girl who's so wet they can see it on her face? They love it. They love telling her how it is." Lucy took a sip of her beer, seeming to remember the encounter. "If people think you're wet enough, you wouldn't believe what they'll tell you. They've got to show how smart and wise they are, you know? All you need to do is look interested, pretend you're wet, and people roll right over."

Lucy kept talking, describing the world she'd uncovered, the details that had jumped out at her. How there was so much more to get. How he needed to come along and get the art.

She kept talking, but Timo couldn't hear her words anymore because one phrase kept pinging around inside his head like a pinball.

Pretend you're wet, and people roll right over.

• • •

"I don't know why you're acting like this," Lucy said for the third time as they drove out to the see the Defending Angels.

She was driving the beast, and Timo was riding shotgun. He'd loaded his gear into her truck, determined that any further expenses from the reporting trip should be on her.

At first, he'd wanted to just cut her off and walk away from the whole thing, but he realized that was childish. If she could get the hits, then fine. He'd tag along on her score. He'd take her page views, and then he'd be done with her.

Cutting her off too soon would get him nothing. She'd just go get some other *pendejo* to do the art, or else she might even shoot the pictures herself and get her ass paid twice, a prospect that galled him even more than the fact that he'd been manipulated.

They wound their way into the subdivision, driving past ancient Prius sedans and electric bikes. At the end of the cul-de-sac, Lucy pulled to a halt. The place didn't look any different from any other Phoenix suburb. Except apparently, inside all the quiet houses, a last-battle resistance was brewing.

Ahead, the chain link and barbwire of the CAP boundary came into view. Beyond, there was nothing but cactus-studded hills. Timo could just make out the Texan on the far side of the CAP fences, still dangling. It looked like the dogs were at him again, tearing at the scraps.

"Will you at least talk to me?" Lucy asked. "Tell me what I did."

Timo shrugged. "Let's just get your shoot done. Show me these Angels of Arizona you're so hot for."

"No." Lucy shook her head. "I'm not taking you to see them until you tell me why you keep acting this way."

Timo glared at her, then looked out the dusty front window.

"Guess we're not going to see them then."

With the truck turned off, it was already starting to broil inside. The kind of heat that cooked pets and babies to death in a couple hours. Timo could feel sweat starting to trickle off him, but he was damned if he was going to show that he was uncomfortable. He sat and stared at the CAP fence ahead of them. They could both sweat to death for all he cared.

Lucy was staring at him, hard. "If you've got something you want to say, you should be man enough to say it."

Man enough? Oh, hell no.

"Okay," Timo said. "I think you played me."

"Played you how?"

"Seriously? You going to keep at it? I'm on to you, girl. You act all wet, and you get people to help you out. You get people to do shit they wouldn't normally do. You act all nice, like you're all new and like you're just getting your feet under you, but that's just an act."

"So what?" Lucy said. "Why do you care if I fool some militia nutjobs?"

"I'm not talking about them! I'm talking about me! That's how you played me! You act like you don't know things, get me to show you around. Show you the ropes. Get you on the inside. You act all wet and sorry, and dumbass Timo steps in to help you out. And you get a nice juicy exclusive."

"Timo…how long have we known each other?"

"I don't know if we ever did."

"Timo—"

"Don't bother apologizing." He shouldered the truck's door open.

As he climbed out, he knew he was making a mistake. She'd pick up some other photographer. Or else she'd shoot the story herself and get paid twice for the work.

Should have just kept my mouth shut.

Amparo would have told him he was both dumb and a sucker. Should have at least worked Lucy to get the story done before he left her ass. Instead he'd dumped her, and the story.

Lucy climbed out of the truck, too.

"Fine," she said. "I won't do it."

"Won't do what?"

"I won't do the story. If you think I played you, I won't do the story."

"Oh come on. That's bullshit. You know you came down here for your scoop. You ain't giving that up."

Lucy's stared at him, looking pissed. "You know what your problem is?"

"Got a feeling you're going to tell me."

"You're so busy doing your poor-me, I'm from Phoenix, everyone's-out-to-get-me, we're-getting-overrun wah-wah-wah routine that you can't even tell when someone's on your side!"

"That's not—"

"You can't even tell someone's standing right in front of you who actually gives a shit about you!" Lucy was almost spitting she was so mad. Her face had turned red. Timo tried to interject, but she kept talking.

"I'm not some damn Texan here to take your water, and I'm not some big time journo here to steal your fucking stories! That's not who I am! You know how many photographers I could work with? You know how many would bite on this story that I went out and got? I put my ass on the line out here! You think that was easy?"

"Lucy. Come on…"

She waved a hand of disgust at him and stalked off, heading for the end of the cul-de-sac and the CAP fence beyond.

"Go find someone else to do this story," she called back. "Pick whoever you want. I wouldn't touch this story with a ten-foot-pole. If that's what you want, it's all yours."

"Come on, Lucy." Timo felt like shit. He started to chase after her. "It's not like that!"

She glanced back. "Don't even try, Timo."

Her expression was so scornful and disgusted that Timo faltered.

He could almost hear his sister Amparo laughing at him. *You got the eye for some things, little bro, but you are blind blind blind.*

She'll cool off, he thought as he let her go.

Except maybe she wouldn't. Maybe he'd said some things that sounded a little too true. Said what he'd really thought of Lucy the Northerner in a way that couldn't get smoothed over. Sometimes, things just broke. One second, you thought you had a connection with a person. Next second, you saw them too clear, and you just knew you were never going to drink a beer together, ever again.

So go fix it, pendejo.

With a groan, Timo went after her again.

"Lucy!" he called. "Come on, girl. I'm sorry, okay? I'm sorry…"

At first, he thought she was going to ignore him, but then she turned.

Timo felt a rush of relief. She was looking at him again. She was looking right at him, like before, when they'd still been getting along. She was going to forgive him. They were going to work it out. They were friends.

But then he realized her expression was wrong. She looked dazed. Her sunburned skin had paled. And she was waving at him, waving furiously for him to join her.

Another Texan? Already?

Timo broke into a run, fumbling for his camera.

He stopped short as he made it to the fence.

"Timo?" Lucy whispered.

"I see it."

He was already snapping pictures through the chainlink, getting the story. He had the eye, and the story was right there in front of them. The biggest luckiest break he'd ever get. Right place, right time, right team to cover the story. He was kneeling now, shooting as fast as he could, listening to the digital report of the electronic shutter, hearing money with every click.

I got it, I got it, I got it, thinking that he was saying it to himself and then realizing he was speaking out loud. "I got it," he said. "Don't worry, I got it!"

Lucy was turning in circles, looking dazed, staring back at the city. "We need to get ourselves assigned. We need to get supplies…We need to trace this back…We need to figure out who did it…We need to get ourselves assigned!" She yanked out her phone and started dialing madly as Timo kept snapping pictures.

Lucy's voice was an urgent hum in the background as he changed angles and exposures.

Lucy clicked off the cell. "We're exclusive with *Xinhua*!"

"Both of us?"

She held up a warning finger. "Don't even start up on me again."

Timo couldn't help grinning. "Wouldn't dream of it, partner."

Lucy began dictating the beginnings of her story into her phone, then broke off. "They want our first update in ten minutes, you think you're up for that?"

"In ten minutes, updates are going to be the least of our problems."

He was in the flow now, capturing the concrete canal and the dead Texan on the other side.

The dogs leaped and jumped, tearing apart the man who had come looking for water.

It was all there. The whole story, laid out.

The man.

The dogs.

The fences.

The Central Arizona Project.

A whole big canal, drained of water. Nothing but a thin crust of rapidly drying mud at its bottom.

Lucy had started dictating again. She'd turned to face the Phoenix sprawl, but Timo didn't need to listen to her talk. He knew the story already—a whole city full of people going about their daily lives, none of them knowing that everything had changed.

Timo kept shooting.

LOVE PERVERTS

Sarah Langan

On Display at the Amerasian Museum of Ancient Humanity, 14,201 C.E.

I'm checking my Red Cross crank phone when Jules walks up. We're the last American colony not to get implants, which places us pretty firmly in the technological third world. My pipeline town in Pigment, Michigan might as well be a flood plain in Bangladesh.

"Ringing mommy dearest?" Jules asks.

"The Crawfords remain indisposed," I tell her.

"Sucker-boy," Jules says, not in a mean way, though she's capable of that. She's got Schlitz-sticky hair down to her hips and her cheeks are covered in glitter from last night's rave. Colony Fourteen's heat and electricity got shut off last week, so her nips push through the spandex cat-suit she's wearing, hard as million year-old fossils. We're all about energy conservation here at the dawn of apocalypse.

"I'm just curious," I say. "I mean, I don't even know if they made it to Nebraska."

Jules hip-checks my locker so it rattles. She's got this rage she doesn't know she's carrying—it's made her heavy-footed and graceless. "Here's what you do…" She pretend-cranks a gear at her temple. "You just delete. Done! They're dead."

"Yeah. Okay," I say. Like that's possible. They've been my parents for seventeen years. Not to mention my baby sister Cathy, who they totally don't deserve. And by the way, I know it's whom. I'm just not an asshole, like you.

"Chillax! You think too much. I did the same thing with my ex until I figured it out. Then I just pretended he died and it was his robot clone I had to sit next to in Mrs. Viotes' art. Delete!"

"Colby Mudd?" I ask.

"Don't even say his name. Can you believe he's still here? I mean, half the town is dead, but he's still noshing turkey jerky? Jeez! My God! What does he see in that spoiled princess? You're bringing me down. Point is, fuck your family! I'm your family!"

"Sure. I'll just change my last name or some nonsense. How was the rest of last night?"

Jules blushes, giggles. Glitter abraids the whites of her eyes, making them red.

"That good?"

I left around midnight. Home brew drugs are for hicks, case in point: As soon as Avery Ryan from the bowling team broke out the meth, everybody went native. They dragged this black-light-painted hunk of granite to the middle of the factory floor and prayed to it like it was weeping Jesus on the cross. For the big finale, a mirror-clad priestess offered herself up. She shattered her mirrors against it, cutting herself bloody. Then everybody started screwing. Clothes off in negative-ten degree weather, spilled corn whisky turned black ice on the floor. Kids, grown-ups, pipeline scabs and militia, all partying together like some prediction straight out of Revelation.

I mean, what the hell?

Growing up, my dad's job in resource excavation took us all over, and every place was the same: falling apart. It got a lot worse two years ago, when an astronomer played with some numbers and reconfigured Aporia's trajectory. He predicted a direct hit somewhere near Chicago. We'd all known a big one was due, give or take a billion years. But nobody could agree on what to do about it. Since the Great Resources Grab of the '20s, the colonies weren't talking to each other. Asia was all messed up. And you know the French. I mean, they see a problem and they step over it and blame the dog.

Anyway, some private multinationals got together, which goes to show you they're not all bad. They tried redirecting Aporia by attaching rockets. They tried spattering its far-side with black paint, so the sun's rays altered its trajectory. They tried opening a black hole, which wound up swallowing most of Long Island before it collapsed.

Then President Brett Brickerson, the former child actor from *Nobody Loves an Albatross*, got on the Freenet last month and announced that we had one last hope: shooting a nuke rocket at it, head on. He laid down Martial Law in all of America's sixteen colonies. Pipeline towns like Pigment saw the heaviest military occupation. It's supposed to be our job to siphon every last drop for the rocket.

Pretty soon after that, the refinery guys striked. They said the government wasn't playing fair. President Brickerson accused them of holding the entire planet hostage. Next thing, they were all dead and buried in mass graves. The scabs took their place—guys from all over, paid in gold bars. Like the hired guns, they did whatever they wanted, to anybody they wanted, for the simple reason that nobody was around to stop them.

The locals started leaving for Antarctica and Australia. The ones stuck here once the law clamped down got hysterical, suicidal, and shot, not necessarily in that order. "What's the point of going on like this?" I overheard my mom asking my dad, which I found pretty insulting. I mean, I'm the point, right? Me and Cathy. We're the whole goddamned point.

The stores sold out of supplies and the school's cafeteria just served jerky and canned corn, a donation from the heartland. You can't be seen on the streets without the militia messing with you for vagrancy. Non-compliants hide in their shelters at the old Chevy Factory. It's quiet during the day, while everybody sleeps off their rave.

Last night's theme was cosmic mirrors, hence the shattered priestess. I didn't bother with that nonsense. I just wore my uniform: jeans and an ironic Dead Man's Plaid t-shirt, plus two denim jackets since some burnout stole the winter coat out of my locker. Jules wrapped herself in tin foil and glitter, teeth chattering the whole walk there. Some of the really popular kids showed up in fancy stolen cars they'd made the underclassmen push. Total *Mad Max* shit.

Used to be, only the locals knew about the raves. But then the militia and scabs started showing up. They're bad people. I read my Faulkner and I know what you're thinking: nobody's absolutely good or absolutely bad. But ask yourself this: what kind of sociopaths occupy America's fourteenth colony, imprisoning its citizens inside ground zero, under the pretense of "maintaining order for urgent oil extraction?"

Let me explain something to you, because I'm taking basic physics this year, so I know. Aporia is one mile-wide and more dense than iron. Nukes will crack her, but at this point, she'll hit Earth no matter what. Only, if she breaks into pieces, she'll be more democratic about impact. She'll slide into the President's bunker in Omaha, or the shelters in Rio, or the Sino-Canadian stockpiles under the glaciers. So what do you think? Do you think that's the plan?

Or do you think President Brickerson and all the other world leaders are lying, and there is no nuke rocket? Do you think the governments and corporations joined forces, and built escape shelters? Do you think the pipelines are heading straight for those shelters, for use after the apocalypse, for the lucky survivors with tickets to the show?

Thanks, Mr. President.

Thank you, too, dear reader.

No, wait. Scratch that. Fuck you, dear reader. Seriously, Fuck you.

So, yeah, back to the militia and pipeline scabs. What kind of morons suck the oil from a dying civilization's veins for a few worthless pounds of gold? They show up at high school parties and screw girls thirty years younger. Screw guys like me, too, when they can get me loaded enough.

How many prisons did they crack open to staff this operation? How many pedophile dormitories did they raid? You think I'm kidding, but seriously, who else do you think they could get?

So yeah, I read my Faulkner. But did that dude ever live in Pigment three days before human annihilation?

I used to be so into the zombie apocalypse. I figured I'd be this hero in a society risen from ashes. Me, the phoenix of the new world order. But the real thing sucks. Because I'm going to die, and I can't figure out which is more cowardly; resigning myself to that fate or fighting against it.

At my locker, glittering Jules grins. It's eerie. Why's she happy? "Last night. After you left. Here's what happened," she says, then lifts her fuck finger at me, holds it. Then her index and thumb rise as she mouths: *one, two, three.*

"What?" I ask, but I already know. Jules is such a wreck.

"A three-way," she says. "One of 'em stuck a rifle up my cooter!"

"I guess you can scratch that off your bucket list."

"Right on the dance floor. Everybody was clapping. Don't give me that *concerned dad* look, Crawford, he shot it empty first…"

"Discharge."

"Vocab king!" She winces, lowers her voice. "I think Colby was there… Like, clapping."

"He's not worth you."

"Jeaaa—lous?" Jules grinds me in her gauze-thin cat-suit.

"Don't," I say. She grinds even freakier, which means she's pissed off. Because a machine gun up your hole probably sounds okay when you're high, but not the next morning when your female parts and what-have-you probably hurt. But there's no point talking about it. Aporia's hitting in less than three days, so who wants to spend the time crying over sexual violation by blunt object?

I realize I'm mad, too. At myself, for leaving her alone with those scabs. At her, for being so stupid. At colony fourteen, for buckling so easily. At everybody. Especially the people on the other side of my crank-phone, who won't tell me where they are, or how I can find them, or even if my baby sister—whose stuffed bunny they forgot—survived the trip.

"Faggot," Jules sneers. She's gone completely radioactive. It's about the machine gun. It's about the asteroid. It's about her denial-blind mom and sister who think Aporia's a hoax. Mostly, it's about me. Because I love her in every way but the way she wants.

"Don't be mean to me," I tell her. "You're my only friend."

"I'm not mean; I'm honest! You're a faggot orphan and once your family got their tickets, they threw you away," she shouts with veiny-necked rage.

"You're trash. Your sister's a stripper. You're dumb as…toast?" I shout back. This last part isn't true. She's one of the sharpest people I know.

Nobody's listening, not even the militia or my old gym teacher or Colby Mudd, who trifled with Jules to make another girl jealous, and she'll never see that, because she uses men like spikes to stab herself against.

"They're *not* trash. One of 'em said he'd marry me!" Jules flashes her hand. She's wearing a small, yellow-gold engagement ring. It had to have come from a dead body. Some salt-of-the-earth old lady, a suicide pact with her true love after fifty good years.

"God, Jules."

The homeroom bell rings. The halls clear like mopped-up jimmy sprinkles. Front and back door militia in desert fatigues bang the butts of their guns against cinderblock. They're like orangutans at mealtime.

"It's jewelry from a man," Jules says, and I can tell she hates it, and the hand that wears it, and herself.

"Throw it away, Jules. It's garbage!" I tell her.I'm so upset about all this that I go a little crazy. I imagine cutting her up. Peeling her skin off and poking out her eyes.

Jules squeezes out a pair of tears. "You're just mad because someone loves me, and nobody loves you."

And the guns are banging, and my homeroom teacher is waving for me to come in. Only it's my gym teacher, because my real homeroom teacher is gone. Faces keep dropping away. No one knows what happened to them. It's like a visual representation of Alzheimers. "That's an awful thing to say," I tell her.

Jules starts laughing.

I'm walking away. The sound of her gets louder as it echoes.

"Hospital tonight?" she calls.

I hate her.

"Sorry, Tom Crawford," she calls. "I suck, literally. I'm a spooge-whore-bitch."

I keep walking with these iron-heavy feet, imagining the whole world on fire. I am the asteroid. Dense and without feeling. I am the destroyer of all in my path.

She flings the ring so it skates past me down the hall. I turn back and there's Jules. She fluffs her hand out in pretend-pompousness as she bows, then blows me a kiss. "I'm your dumb-as-toast best friend."

I pretend-twist a gear along my temple. "Forgotten. Forgiven. Everybody but you is dead, you big skank."

• • •

Mr. Nguyen is the only real teacher left, and he's taking it seriously. He passes out a physics quiz, which he's written by hand because there aren't any crank printers. We're supposed to convert joules and calculate work. There's only four other students here, and none of us have pens.

I crank, then send a text on my phone: **Where are you? Is Cathy OK? If you only have two tickets and she's not allowed in, I'll come get her. Does she need Baby Bunny?**

Nguyen hands me five ball point Bics and gestures for me to pass the rest around. The guy's relentless. He wears dirty polyester button-downs and his parents were refugees from Vietnam. Last plane out and all that. He probably wishes he was still there.

"Focus," he says. But I can't. My paper's black letters on white. They could scramble and rearrange, and then what would they be?

Nguyen perches on the edge of his desk. He's got three small kids at home. His wife is fat. Not like Orca. Happy, well-fed Hobbit fat. "Young ladies and gentlemen," he says. "What if it's not the end of the world, and you're still accountable for your actions? Did you think of that? Take your test."

In my mind, everybody in this room goes bloody. They're just meat, and I'm wondering: Where's the stunt camera? I mean, really. Death by asteroid? I thought I was more important than this.

The loudspeaker clicks on. Everybody twitches. Maybe it's a militia-led public execution. They happen often enough that I'm starting to look forward to them. The routine comforts me. Which is fucked up, obviously. I know that, so don't take notes or underline this or whatever.

The assistant principal or vice-secretary or some jackass's voice pipes through. "This can't be right," she says.

"*Just read it!*" some guy demands.

"Darlins, I got some bad news," she says. I realize it's Miss Ross, a native Colony Eight who teaches auto shop. She gave me a C-, which I hated her for but deserved. "Aporia's gonna interrupt satellite communication pretty soon, so don't be surprised if your phones stop working. Also, new research tells us that impact is thirty-six hours away; not three days. Angle's closer to 70 percent. They're saying Detroit—what's that, about a hundred and fifty from here?—can that be right?"

"*Keep reading*," the other voice tells her through a muffle of static.

"Dang it! I heard you the first time!" she says. "About ten minutes ago, President Brickerson sent out a last communication. Since most of your crank phones don't have Freenet, the militia wants me to pass it along… Brickerson says not to worry. The rocket will…eviscerate? Sure, okay, that's a word. It'll eviscerate Aporia before impact. Until then, we gotta stay put. So there's no looting, transgressors between colonies'll be shot. Anyone caught stealing fuel'll be shot ....Anyone messing ....Ah, forget it. Run, darlins'. Just run. Get as far away as—"

Nguyen clicks off the loudspeaker. It doesn't spare us. We still hear the gunshot. I go hard in a place that ought to be soft over something like this, which doesn't mean I enjoy it. I've also been known to fantasize about drowning puppies, and I kind of like puppies.

Nguyen lets the reverb settle, then takes the quiz from my desk and crinkles it into a ball. Tosses it like a hoop-shot but misses the garbage. "Who wants a lesson in falling bodies?"

Twenty minutes later, he's got it all written out. Seventy degrees, density = 8000kn/m3, speed at impact: 30km/s. Force = a trillion megatons. He's not smiling or pretending to be brave. He touches the word *megatons* on the blackboard, totally freaked out.

"Meg-A-Tons..." he says. The guy's a Tesla nerd—he figured out how to turn garbage into gasoline and there's rumors he siphoned the refinery's generators to power his house. "Would you ladies and gentlemen find it comforting to have me describe impact to you?"

I'm not ready to be comforted. There's still tricks in this pony. But everybody else seems relieved, like, Thank God. They can finally all surrender to the awful truth.

Nguyen squints, picturing the whole thing. "If it collides with Detroit, we'll see the blaze in under a minute. Brighter than the sun. The whole sky will be red. Don't worry. It won't hurt. Our nerves will go before our minds ....It's like the distance between thunder and lightning during a storm. It should be quite beautiful."

I'm thinking about how if you cut somebody's head off fast enough, then turn it around, they can see their own detached body. This does not sound especially beautiful to me. "What about people in Omaha? Offutt? My family's there," I say.

He slaps his khakis with his wooden pointer, then winces in pain. It's a weird thing to do, all things considered. "All three of them left without you?"

I nod. "Yeah. I know it's supposed to be whole families, but I guess the president cut down on tickets. So I told them to go ahead without me." I'm lying, obviously. If I had my way, my parents would have stayed behind like grown-ups, and it would be me and Cathy in that shelter.

"You didn't get a ticket?" Nguyen asks.

I nod. Nguyen looks at me for an uncomfortably long time. Slaps his leg with the pointer again. It's weird. I can't be the only loser he knows who got left behind like a Mormon at the anti-rapture.

"Okay!" he claps. "Good question! Will! Offutt! Survive!? It all depends on how deep underground they are—what their ventilation apparatus looks like. They'll survive the heat and seismic turmoil, but no one knows about the ejecta. Who can describe ejecta for me?"

Carole Fergussin raises her hand. "It's the rocks and stuff the asteroid kicks up."

"Right!" Nguyen says. "Ejecta! There's evidence that the asteroid that killed the dinosaurs sprayed ejecta as high as the moon before it rained back down into our atmosphere. Our guess is that the rocks will be about the same temperature as volcanic lava, and about the size of aerosol particles. So, our friends in the shelters might survive underground, but we've got no idea for how long. It depends on the quality and pervasity of the ejecta and the apparatus they constructed in its anticipation."

"Couldn't we have done something before now, Mr. Nguyen?" Anais Bignault asks. She's crazy skinny, like she stopped eating a week ago but her skeleton insists on taking the rest of her out for strolls.

"Call me Fred," he says, and Jesus, I don't want to call him that.

"What if we all get together, everybody in Pigment. In the whole Colony? We dig a shelter?" Carole Fergussin asks. She's wiping the tears from her big, brown eyes. I feel like Carole and Anais ought to get an award for best sad puppy impressions on the eve of apocalypse.

Then I picture drowning them.

Nguyen shrugs. "I wish they'd selected me to engineer something like that. I really do. But with impact 36 hours away, can we build something that we can survive inside for ten years? Twenty? Ten thousand?"

"Can we?" I ask.

Nguyen points out the window at the refinery. It smokes above metal spires three miles away. "We'd need a lot of fuel. And a small population."

"Like Offutt," Carole says.

Nguyen nods.

I'm picturing Cathy in a dark, underground city. Picturing her safe and loved. Picturing the evolution of the survivors, people like my parents, over a thousand generations. I'm trying real hard to find the bright spot, here, but the future looks pretty monstrous.

"Did I ever tell you my parents' story?" Nguyen asks, then answers himself in a lower voice: "Of course I didn't. Why would I do that?"

"Tell us," Carole says through her sniffles. I consider throwing my desk and announcing that this is not group therapy. During my last hours on Earth, I do not want to hear anyone's crappy life story. I just want to hold my baby sister. Oh, yeah. And not die.

"It really was the last plane," Nguyen says. "My father bribed a town official for the spot. And here I am today. I never wondered about those other people left behind. Survivors don't do that kind of thing. But now I wonder. That's because we're not the survivors anymore. But we're still the heroes of our own stories. You understand?"

I don't. I want him dead. I imagine that I am Aporia, colliding. I am bigger than this whole planet, and my wrath is infinite.

"What I'm saying is, I always thought I'd be famous and my children would be rich. Why else would I be so lucky, born in America? But does dying make me less? I'm still Fred Nguyen, aren't I?"

He looks at me, "Some of you, your parents abandoned you. Some people sold their own children's tickets. That makes them villains, you understand? But you can still be heroes."

The kid in the back row who used to be Harvard bait spits a wad of chewed-up quiz. "Liar!" he says. "Human consciousness was a bad mutation. Aporia is Earth's self-correct. There's nothing after this."

Nguyen throws a piece of chalk at him and we're all totally shocked. "I'm not talking about God! Who cares about that idiot! I'm talking about the devil. You don't have to let him out. Scramble for some false promise of salvation; climb over your own neighbors for crumbs. I won't leave my family to live in some hole! I'm going to die with dignity!"

The bell rings.

We all kind of sit there. What the hell? Is he having a nervous breakdown? At least he picked a good day for it. Then I figure it out—clear as the open gates of heaven: Mr. Nguyen has a ticket.

• • •

Jules and I eat jerky in my shelter after school. I'm fantasizing about stealing Mr. Nguyen's ticket and saving Cathy from our idiot parents. I'll show up at their barracks, baby bunny in hand, and for the first time since the five days they've been gone, Cathy will stop crying and smile. Then I'll glare at my mom and dad until the guilt drops them dead. They'll resurrect again after Aporia, turning them into decent people instead of assholes. We'll live a few years down there, until I figure out the environmental cure for ejecta that will make Earth's surface habitable. Then everybody will elect me king and they'll all say how awesome it is to be gay.

We'll wear as much goddamned pink as we want.

It's the first happy fantasy I've had in a long time, and I wish I could keep it going. But the shelter's cold, and Jules is smacking her lips. We've got the crank-CB tuned to the scabs. They were worked up about a missing rig a little while ago. Somebody broke through a checkpoint with it during the night.

Then the call we've been waiting for comes in: The steel cage at the top of a catalytic reformer went smash.

"Wanna check it out?" Jules asks.

She's been kissing me and I've been letting her. Once, we tried to go all the way. The experience was miserable, which she tells me is normal.

"Okay. Let's go chase an ambulance." I start climbing the wooden ladder out. I built this shelter with my dad. We dug for more than a week, then realized that under any seismic stress, the whole thing would collapse. *Son*, my dad had said, looking down the twenty-foot hole. *Buried alive's an unaccountable way to go.*

When I was twelve, my dad found my Freenet porn. Nothing crazy—just guys on guys. He called me a perversion. It made me feel like I was covered in herpes or something, and I'm starting to think it's why they left me behind. And you know, with all these dead-puppy-skinned-meat-people fantasies I've been having, maybe he was onto something. Then again, maybe calling somebody a perversion makes them act like one. Or maybe everybody's having these thoughts, because the apocalypse sucks.

The truth is, my parents are the real perverts. They're love perverts. You're supposed to care more about your children than about yourself, and they messed it up. The whole fucking world of adults messed it up.

Jules and I get on our bikes and ride through Sacket Street. The grocery is dark. So's the pharmacy. It's blue-dick cold. We're over the tracks, racing just ahead of the supply train headed for Omaha. It's a thrill. The kind that makes you feel like Superman.

"Arm or leg?" Jules asks as we race, out of breath and too cold to cry.

"Arm?"

"Okay. Arm, your turn. Leg, I get to be the doctor," Jules says.

"Game on."

We drop our bikes and head for the crowd. The grass is long in spots, dead from spills in others. I want to take off my shoes and feel the cold, frozen earth. Squeeze it between my toes and tell it to remember me.

We push through. Catalytic reformers look like space needles wrapped in steel scaffolding. They're the size of Manhattan buildings. You've seen them, probably. They turn low octane raw material into high octane fuel. But unless you live in a refinery town, you probably had no idea what you were looking at. You just blinked, then checked your distance to Chicago.

About twenty eight-by-two foot beams have collapsed. As Jules and I approach, some rent-a-cops retract a jaws of life. They pull a guy out from the wreckage and amputate his leg, thigh down. Then they give it to him. He's holding his amputated leg, high on morphine. Jules and I clench hands. I wonder if this turns me on, touching her. Or if it's the suffering that has my erection going.

Thirty minutes later, the generators start cranking. Dirty smoke spouts all over again. Jules and I book after the ambulance.

• • •

There's nobody in admission or reception at Pigment Hospital, just this janitor mopping floors. He picks at this stuck-on bit of grime with his fingernail.

I'm Jules' bitch today, so I take the nurse coat, and she doctors up. We head to the ER, where they always take the scabs.

Some doctor is just closing the curtain on our lucky refinery scab. She's one of the last in this skeleton crew. I wonder why she comes at all. But then again, why not?

Jules walks with purpose. I've got my clipboard and Nguyen's Bic pen. I'm thinking about Cathy, who was born here. She smelled like milk and I loved her.

I love her still.

"How are you this morning?" Jules asks once the doctor is long gone.

The scab kind of blinks. He's pale from blood loss and won't let go of his leg. Does he think we're going to steal it?

"Not so good?" she asks.

I'm completely serious when I tell you that Jules would have made a great doctor. She's not squeamish.

She peeks inside his bandage. He bites his lower lip to keep from crying, but that doesn't help; he cries anyway. He's one of the rave guys. I can tell because he's got glitter on his cheeks.

"I've seen worse. Don't worry," Jules says with this big smile.

The guy calms down. "Do I know you?"

"We're gonna take great care of you, mister. That's what we do in here in Pigment," she says with this made-up hick accent and I grin because it's funny, this whole thing. It really is.

"Can it be saved?" he asks. He's talking about his stump, which he's holding like a baby.

"We'll try real hard," she says. Then she turns to me. She's smiling that angry smile from this morning. I'm a little scared of her, and a little turned on. What's wrong with me?

"You'll need to change his bandages every few hours," she says.

I scribble *Bandages x2hrs* because I'm a terrible liar, so it's important to make this as real as possible. When I play the doctor I just stare while Jules does the talking.

"And you'll need morphine every six hours. Three em-gees per."

I jot that down, too.

"Dwight here's from Kansas," she says, nodding at me. "Where you from, sweetness?"

The guy's sweating from the pain—morphine comedown. "Jersey," he says. "But really no place. Bopped around the rigs in Saudi a while…You sure I don't know you?"

"I'm sure," she says. "Any family? Because there's some experimental treatment for your predicament, but it's a hella lotta *dinero*."

The guy looks at her funny, shakes his head. "No family. I got six gold bricks, another coming tomorrow."

I'm waiting for the punch line, because Jules usually makes this game fun. We even help a little, make the guys feel better. Listen to them talk about their ex-wives and good times. *You'll be saved*, we reassure them. *We'll all be saved by the giant nukes in the sky*!

"Aw," she says. "Then I guess you'll just have to pray the fuckin' thing gets all spontaneous regeneration, you fucking cripple."

She's running out through the curtain and I'm just standing there, so it's me he grabs. He's sweating even more, and I'm wondering if he's shotgun-up-the-cooter-guy. I wish I was the type to ask, but I'm not.

"Let go of me!" I'm crying, even though this guy can't stand up. His detached leg rests in his lap. I swivel, leaving him with just the jacket.

Jules is waiting for me in admission, white coat gone, like it never happened.

"You ever think about killing a guy?" she asks.

"Yeah," I say. "All the time."

• • •

We're at Jules' house for dinner. It's some carrots her big sister dug up from their yard. Everybody munches. I used to pretend that I could trade these guys for my real family, but it doesn't work like that. My parents yanked me across every pipeline on six continents. I know French and Hindi. When I'm introduced to someone, I shake firm, look people in the eye, and repeat their name back at them. I've got three million dollars in a trust fund I'm not allowed to open until I'm twenty-one. Jules' family is dirt poor. They're mean and they laugh out loud when you make a mistake. They give their boyfriends free rein, which is one of the reasons Jules is so mad all the time. Every time she puts a lock on her door they take it right down. If she had an ounce of self-awareness, she'd probably understand that it's also why she only falls for men like me, men she can't have.

I can't wait to get out of this town, she told me the first time we met.

Jules' mom and sister want to play Gin Rummy after dinner. They're starting to realize that Aporia's real, which is making them pretend all the more desperately that it's not. "Did you see that the sale of crank-operated devices has gone up 2000%?" her mom asks. "It's a conspiracy, this whole asteroid business. Mark my words!"

"I gotta shove off," I tell them as I stand. Then I look at all three of them and realize they've all got Jules' dull marble eyes. "Take care of yourselves," I say. Then I'm out the door.

"The asteroid's a hoax!" Jules' sister shouts behind me. But it's right outside, big as the moon and in the opposite direction. It glows, making the night doubly bright.

I'm on my bike, headed I don't know where. Well, actually, yes. I do know. I've been thinking about it all day.

"Hey!" Jules calls after me, and she's riding, too.

It's biting cold. We're wrapped in Hefty garbage bags to keep warm. "You go ahead. I don't wanna rave," I tell her.

"Where else is there to go?"

"Omaha," I say.

She doesn't chew me out for a half-brained plan, like riding our bikes six hundred miles in below-freezing weather. She just pedals right along with me, fast as she can, like the whole world behind her is on fire.

We go past the center of Pigment, near the high school. I stop at this arts and crafts house with a hoop out front. It looks like gingerbread. Jules doesn't even ask whose house we're at.

I ring the bell. I'm so nervous I'm panting.

"Don't leave me," Jules whispers. She's sniffling. "You're my family."

But she's not.

A Hobbit opens the door. Mrs. Nguyen, I presume.

"I'm looking for Fred," I say.

Twin baby girls and a toddler boy crowd the mom's legs. Warm air gushes out. It's been so long since I felt radiator heat that I almost mistake it for magic.

Mrs. Nguyen brings us to a plastic-covered couch. The kids surround us, drooling. Out of habit, I pick one up and squeeze her thigh until she laughs. I'm going to murder Mr. Nguyen if I have to. This doesn't change that.

Mrs. Nguyen brings us blankets and steaming hot cocoa with little marshmallows. The sugar is so sweet that my mouth dries on contact, then waters all over again.

"Jesus God this is good," Jules says.

Mrs. Nguyen grins. "Don't tell the Militia about our heat!"

We fake smile back.

"Mr. Tom Crawford, Ms. Juliet Olsen," Mr. Nguyen says as he walks in. He's still in khakis and a dirty shirt. He seems pleased we've come.

"I want your ticket," I say. "I know you have one."

Jules squeezes my knee.

Mr. Nguyen sits on the arm of a La-Z-Boy. The kids squirm and roll like seals. Mrs. Nguyen brings out hot brie and crackers.

"I love food," Jules says as she scarfs. "I'm so happy about food!"

"Are you staying for dinner?" Mrs. Nguyen asks.

"I want a ticket," I say. "My sister needs me. She can't be raised by those people."

"You know your parents got four tickets, don't you?" Mr. Nguyen asks.

I'm holding a dull cheese knife, which should be funny but isn't. I'm also crying. Everybody looks horrified. Mr. Nguyen is standing between me and his kids. Mrs. Nguyen is holding the twins. Even crazier, Jules has the little boy.

"Give me your ticket!" I'm shouting, waving the damn cheese knife.

Mr. Nguyen opens his wallet. He pulls out this credit card-looking-thing and hands it to me slowly, and I want to yell, *Seriously? You think I'm going to cheese knife your stupid family?*

The ticket is clear with engraved writing:

Offutt Refugee Center, First Class
Thomas J. Crawford
109-83-9921

I'm holding both the card and the cheese knife, and for just a second, I'm happy. Fred Nguyen is a magician.

Jules leans over, babe in arms. "Why do you have his ticket? Did you steal it?"

Mrs. Nguyen kind of connipts. She's waving her hands, which happen to be full of kids. "His parents traded it for fuel to Nebraska! Dears, dears! It wasn't easy for them. You have to know. They had no other way of getting to the shelter. Without fuel they'd have frozen to death. They had to sell! But true, true. We could have given it away. That would have been Christian. Indeed, indeed. I wish we had, to be honest. I truly do wish we had. It was a bad idea."

Mrs. Nguyen runs out of steam. She's got big tears in her eyes. "Now, Tom, dear, may I have that knife?"

I'm looking at Mrs. Nguyen, who's holding these sweet baby girls who just happen to be the same age as Cathy. And I'm wondering if it would break her heart if I stabbed them.

"What are you people, the sultans of petroleum?" Jules asks.

"My husband prepared a year ago. They should have chosen us. We deserve to live," Mrs. Nguyen says.

"Honey, take the children into another room," Mr. Nguyen says, and Mrs. Nguyen starts to reach for the boy in Jules' arms but I stop her.

"Let me get this straight—My parents got four tickets? They kept three and sold mine, to you, my teacher, who's supposed to be a nice guy? Mr. Role model? Mr. Don't Let The Devil Out?"

Nguyen nods. "I meant to give it back to you. But I'd been hoping to acquire more, for the rest of my family," he opens his arms to signify his wife and three kids. "The clock ran out."

"That's really sad for you guys. As long as you're giving them away, you got another ticket for me?" Jules asks.

"Please put the knife down, Thomas," Mr. Nguyen says. "I'm very sorry. You know I am."

I'm looking at Jules and the boy in her arms. She kisses his cheek, because it's human nature to love children. But not for nut jobs like me, because all I'm thinking about is murder.

She turns to me. "Put the stupid knife down, you psycho! You're freaking me out."

• • •

We leave with eight gallons of gasoline and my ticket. It's more than enough to get me to Offutt. Jules helps me carry it to the back seat of Nguyen's Kia. They've also packed a lunch for us, white bread peanut butter and jelly. Because Jules is a mess, she's already forgiven them. She hugs Mr. Nguyen, his wife, and his kids good-bye.

"Should I drop you off with your family?" I ask once we're on the road.

"I don't want to die with them. I'll go with you as long as this goes," she tells me.

Which won't be long. There are four checkpoints between here and Offutt, and you need a ticket to get through every one.

Through static on the AM dial, a scientist is talking about how gravity's all messed up because of the asteroid. My crank-phone has stopped getting reception. We've got twenty hours and six hundred miles to go.

I stop at the hospital first.

"Wait in the car," I tell Jules.

"What's your plan, Sherlock?"

"I need to finish something." I shut the door and leave her in the warmth, then jog to the entrance. I grab a scalpel. That legless guy is in the same bed. There aren't any doctors around. Just that same janitor, scrubbing those same floors.

"You hurt my friend," I say to him.

The guy smirks. He's still got glitter on his cheeks. His stump rots in the corner. He was scared yesterday, but now it's funny. He's one of those.

I want to cut him up. Take my revenge on Jules' behalf. That way I'll have done right by her. I won't feel bad about leaving her to die in this town that she hates.

"You think you're so special," I say. "But that doesn't excuse you."

I'm not getting through to him. His smirk is horrendous. I squeeze the bandaged stump until the scab breaks open along with the stitches. Blood oozes. He writhes. Now is the time to slit his throat. Now is the time to be what I was always meant to be. Important.

But I'm not thinking about puppies and skinned people or all the bad things anybody's ever done to me. I'm trying to let the devil out, and I realize Nguyen wasn't a genius after all, because there's no devil in there. There's just fucked up me, and I'm nauseous.

I let go and I'm walking backward. "It's coming," I say. "And no one loves you."

• • •

We make it to Offutt. The checkpoints were abandoned by the time we passed through. It's a wonder my ticket didn't get stolen all over again. Makes me almost believe in God.

A storm is brewing—everything seems especially light.

We reach the final checkpoint—Offut. Here, there's lots of soldiers. I get an idea. Maybe it'll work.

They don't necessarily believe my story, but they pass it up the chain. We get to the final line. I can see the elevator to salvation about five hundred feet ahead. It's iron, with linked chain pulleys. It goes down three miles, where there's enough self-generating fuel to last 10,000 years. There are 200,000 people and fifty miles of tunnels down there. These are the facts we've learned from the crowd along the way.

"This is my sister, Alison Crawford," I tell the manager. He looks like he hasn't slept since 2010. "My father stole her ticket and gave it to his girlfriend. That's why we're so late. We were looking for it. He's inside."

The manager starts talking on his CB. He tells us to wait in a holding tank with a few thousand other people. Some of them are crying, some are sleeping. Most are too nervous to stand still.

You'd think they'd riot, but in the end, we're all lambs.

I work on my letter, this one right here that you're holding.

The asteroid in the sky is bigger than the sun.

It's minutes to impact.

A guard comes back. I can't believe he's still doing his job. They all are. "Nice try. Your parents are real beauts," he says. "They sold their baby's ticket for better sleeping quarters."

"Cathy? Where is she?" I don't know how I missed her. But I see her in an old woman's arms. And then I'm holding her, pressing baby bunny into her fat little fingers. I'm crying. Cathy is squeezing my face. I love her so much.

"Let us in," I beg.

"One ticket. One person," the manager says. "I'd do it, but then I'd get shot and the elevator would lock. The last men down are the guards. I gotta take care of my own skin."

Jules is crying and trying not to. She's still in that stupid cat-suit. I hate her, I really do. I give her my ticket.

"Naw," she says.

"Take it." It's funny. I finally feel like a hero.

"I love you," she says.

"I know," I say, like Han Solo. "Sorry about the toast thing."

The manager puts his arm around Jules and takes her to the elevator. The elevator won't go. They walk back to us, and I'm kissing Cathy so my lips warm her forehead.

"They changed the code," the manager says. "Dealing with overflow. It has to be the person whose name is on the ticket."

"I'll take care of Cathy. You go," Jules says. Her eyes are those same dull marbles. Like her whole life has been a disappointment.

I break the ticket. It's just plastic.

On his last trip down, I give the manager my finished letter. Cathy's sleeping in my arms. Jules is leaning into me. For once, she's not trying to kiss me. She's calm. And I think: This is my family. So I look to the sky, for the most beautiful night in three billion years.

And you, dear reader, are my witness. The survivor-hero of this story. In ten thousand years, your dirt-blind, rodent species of monsters will study this document, and wonder what all the fuss was about love.

ABOUT THE AUTHORS

Robin Wasserman is the author of several books for children and young adults, including *The Waking Dark*, *The Book of Blood and Shadow*, the Cold Awakening Trilogy, *Hacking Harvard*, and the Seven Deadly Sins series, which was adapted into a popular television miniseries. Her essays and short fiction have appeared in several anthologies as well as *The Atlantic* and *The New York Times*. A former children's book editor, she is on the faculty of the low-residency MFA program at Southern New Hampshire University. She lives and writes (and frequently procrastinates) in Brooklyn, New York. Find out more about her at robinwasserman.com or follow her on Twitter @robinwasserman.

Desirina Boskovich has published fiction in *Lightspeed*, *Nightmare*, *Realms of Fantasy*, *Fantasy Magazine*, and *Clarkesworld*, and in the anthologies *The Way of the Wizard*, *Aliens: Recent Encounters*, and *Last Drink Bird Head*. She is also the editor of the anthology *It Came From the North: An Anthology of Finnish Speculative Fiction* and is a graduate of the Clarion Science Fiction and Fantasy Writers Workshop. Find her online at desirinaboskovich.com.

Charlie Jane Anders' story "Six Months Three Days" won a Hugo Award and was shortlisted for the Nebula and Theodore Sturgeon Awards. Her writing has appeared in *Mother Jones*, *Asimov's Science Fiction*, *Tor.com*, *Tin House*, *ZYZZYVA*, *The McSweeney's Joke Book of Book Jokes*, and elsewhere. She's the managing editor of *io9.com* and runs the long-running Writers With Drinks reading series in San Francisco. More info at charliejane.net.

Ken Liu is an author and translator of speculative fiction, as well as a lawyer and programmer. His fiction has appeared in magazines such as *The Magazine of Fantasy & Science Fiction*, *Asimov's*, *Analog*, *Clarkesworld*, *Lightspeed*, *Nature*, *Apex*, *Daily SF*, *Fireside*, *TRSF*, and *Strange Horizons*, and has been reprinted in the prestigious *Year's Best SF* and *The Best Science Fiction and*

Fantasy of the Year anthology series. He has won the Hugo, Nebula, and World Fantasy awards. He lives with his family near Boston, Massachusetts.

Jake Kerr began writing short fiction in 2010 after fifteen years as a music and radio industry columnist and journalist. His first published story, "The Old Equations," appeared in *Lightspeed* and went on to be named a finalist for the Nebula Award and the Theodore Sturgeon Memorial Award. He has subsequently been published in *Fireside Magazine*, *Escape Pod*, and the *Unidentified Funny Objects* anthology of humorous SF. A graduate of Kenyon College with degrees in English and Psychology, Kerr studied under writer-in-residence Ursula K. Le Guin and Peruvian playwright Alonso Alegria. He lives in Dallas, Texas, with his wife and three daughters.

Tananarive Due is the Cosby Chair in the Humanities at Spelman College. She also teaches in the creative writing MFA program at Antioch University Los Angeles. The American Book Award winner and NAACP Image Award recipient has authored and/or co-authored twelve novels and a civil rights memoir. In 2013, she received a Lifetime Achievement Award in the Fine Arts from the Congressional Black Caucus Foundation. In 2010, she was inducted into the Medill School of Journalism's Hall of Achievement at Northwestern University. She has also taught at the Geneva Writers Conference, the Clarion Science Fiction & Fantasy Writers' Workshop, and Voices of Our Nations Art Foundation (VONA). Due's supernatural thriller *The Living Blood* won a 2002 American Book Award. Her novella "Ghost Summer," published in the 2008 anthology *The Ancestors*, received the 2008 Kindred Award from the Carl Brandon Society, and her short fiction has appeared in best-of-the-year anthologies of science fiction and fantasy. Due is a leading voice in black speculative fiction.

Tobias S. Buckell is a Caribbean-born speculative fiction writer who grew up in Grenada, the British Virgin Islands, and the U.S. Virgin Islands. He has written several novels, including the *New York Times* bestseller *Halo: The Cole Protocol*, the Xenowealth series, and *Artic Rising*. His short fiction has appeared in magazines such as *Lightspeed, Analog, Clarkesworld*, and *Subterranean*, and in anthologies such as *Armored, All-Star Zeppelin Adventure Stories*, and *Under the Moons of Mars*. He currently lives in Ohio with a pair of dogs, a pair of cats, twin daughters, and his wife.

Jamie Ford is the great grandson of Nevada mining pioneer Min Chung, who emigrated from Kaiping, China, to San Francisco in 1865, where he adopted the western name "Ford," thus confusing countless generations.

His debut novel, *Hotel on the Corner of Bitter and Sweet*, spent two years on the *New York Times* bestseller list and went on to win the 2010 Asian/Pacific American Award for Literature. His work has been translated into 32 languages. Jamie is still holding out for Klingon (because that's when you know you've made it). He can be found at www.jamieford.com blogging about his new book, *Songs of Willow Frost*, and also on Twitter @jamieford.

Ben Winters is the winner of the Edgar Award for his novel *The Last Policeman*, which was also an Amazon.com Best Book of 2012. Other works of fiction include the middle-grade novel *The Secret Life of Ms. Finkleman*, an Edgar Award nominee; its sequel, *The Mystery of the Missing Everything*; the psychological thriller *Bedbugs*; and two parody novels, *Sense and Sensibility and Sea Monsters* (a *New York Times* best-seller), and *Android Karenina*. Ben has also written extensively for the stage and is a past fellow of the Dramatists Guild. His journalism has appeared in *Slate, The Nation, The Chicago Reader*, and many other publications. He lives in Indianapolis, Indiana, and at BenHWinters.com.

Hugh Howey is the author of the acclaimed post-apocalyptic novel *Wool*, which became a sudden success in 2011. Originally self-published as a series of novelettes, the *Wool* omnibus spent time as the #1 bestselling book on Amazon.com and is a *New York Times* and *USA TODAY* bestseller. The book was also optioned for film by Ridley Scott and Steve Zaillian, and is now available in print from major publishers all over the world. Hugh's other books include *Shift*, *Dust*, *Sand*, the Molly Fyde series, *The Hurricane*, *Half Way Home*, *The Plagiarist*, and *I, Zombie*. Hugh lives in Jupiter, Florida with his wife Amber and his dog Bella. Find him on Twitter @hughhowey.

Annie Bellet is the author of the *Pyrrh Considerable Crimes Division* and the *Gryphonpike Chronicles* series. She holds a BA in English and a BA in Medieval Studies and thus can speak a smattering of useful languages such as Anglo-Saxon and Medieval Welsh. Her short fiction is available in multiple collections and anthologies. Her interests besides writing include rock climbing, reading, horse-back riding, video games, comic books, table-top RPGs and many other nerdy pursuits. She lives in the Pacific Northwest with her husband and a very demanding Bengal cat.

Will McIntosh is a Hugo award winner and Nebula finalist whose debut novel, *Soft Apocalypse*, was a finalist for a Locus Award, the John W. Campbell Memorial Award, and the Compton Crook Award. His latest novel is *Defenders* (May, 2014; Orbit Books), an alien apocalypse novel with a twist. It has been optioned by Warner Brothers for a feature film. Along with four novels, he has published dozens of short stories in venues such as *Lightspeed*, *Asimov's* (where he won the 2010 Reader's Award), and *The Year's Best Science Fiction & Fantasy*. Will was a psychology professor for two decades before turning to writing full-time. He lives in Williamsburg with his wife and their five year-old twins.

Megan Arkenberg lives and writes in California. Her short stories have appeared in *Lightspeed*, *Asimov's*, *Strange Horizons*, and dozens of other places. She procrastinates by editing the fantasy e-zine *Mirror Dance*.

Scott Sigler is the *New York Times* bestselling author of the Infected trilogy (*Infected, Contagious,* and *Pandemic*), *Ancestor,* and *Nocturnal*, hardcover thrillers from Crown Publishing; and the co-founder of Empty Set Entertainment, which publishes his Galactic Football League series (*The Rookie, The Starter, The All-Pro* and *The MVP*). Before he was published, Scott built a large online following by giving away his self-recorded audiobooks as free, serialized podcasts. His loyal fans, who named themselves "Junkies," have downloaded over eight million individual episodes of his stories and interact daily with Scott and each other in the social media space.

Jack McDevitt has been described by Stephen King as "The logical heir to Isaac Asimov and Arthur C. Clarke." He is the author of nineteen novels, eleven of which have been Nebula finalists. His novel *Seeker* won the award in 2007. In 2003, *Omega* received the John W. Campbell Memorial Award for best science fiction novel. McDevitt's most recent books are *The Cassandra Project*, a collaboration with Mike Resnick, and *Starhawk*, which follows the young Priscilla Hutchins as she seeks to qualify as an interstellar pilot. Both are from Ace. A Philadelphia native, McDevitt had a varied career before becoming a writer. He's been a naval officer, an English teacher, a customs officer, and a taxi driver. He has also conducted leadership seminars. He is married to the former Maureen McAdams, and resides in Brunswick, Georgia, where he keeps a weather eye on hurricanes.

Nancy Kress is the author of thirty-two books, including twenty-five novels, four collections of short stories, and three books about writing. Her work has won two Hugos ("Beggars in Spain" and "The Erdmann Nexus"), four Nebulas (all for short fiction), a Sturgeon ("The Flowers of Aulit Prison"), and a John W. Campbell Memorial award (for Probability Space). The novels include science fiction, fantasy, and thrillers; many concern genetic engineering. Her most recent work is the Nebula-winning and Hugo-nominated

After the Fall, Before the Fall, During the Fall (Tachyon, 2012), a long novella of eco-disaster, time travel, and human resiliency. Forthcoming is another short novel from Tachyon, *Yesterday's Kin* (Fall 2014). Intermittently, Nancy teaches writing workshops at various venues around the country, including Clarion and Taos Toolbox (yearly, with Walter Jon Williams). A few years ago she taught at the University of Leipzig as the visiting Picador professor. She is currently working on a long, as-yet-untitled SF novel. Nancy lives in Seattle with her husband, writer Jack Skillingstead, and Cosette, the world's most spoiled toy poodle.

Seanan McGuire was born and raised in Northern California, resulting in a love of rattlesnakes and an absolute terror of weather. She shares a crumbling old farmhouse with a variety of cats, far too many books, and enough horror movies to be considered a problem. Seanan publishes about three books a year, and is widely rumored not to actually sleep. When bored, Seanan tends to wander into swamps and cornfields, which has not yet managed to get her killed (although not for lack of trying). She also writes as Mira Grant, filling the role of her own evil twin, and tends to talk about horrible diseases at the dinner table.

Jonathan Maberry is a *New York Times* bestselling author, multiple Bram Stoker Award winner, and comic book writer. He's the author of many novels including *Code Zero*, *Fire & Ash*, *The Nightsiders*, *Dead of Night*, and *Rot & Ruin*; and the editor of the *V-Wars* shared-world anthologies. His nonfiction books on topics ranging from martial arts to zombie pop-culture. Jonathan writes *V-Wars* and *Rot & Ruin* for IDW Comics, and *Bad Blood* for Dark Horse, as well as multiple projects for Marvel. Since 1978 he has sold more than 1200 magazine feature articles, 3000 columns, two plays, greeting cards, song lyrics, poetry, and textbooks. Jonathan continues to teach the celebrated Experimental Writing for Teens class, which he created. He founded the Writers Coffeehouse and co-founded The Liars Club; and is a frequent speaker at schools and libraries, as well as a keynote speaker and guest of honor at major writers and genre conferences. He lives in Del Mar, California. Find him online at jonathanmaberry.com.

David Wellington is the author of the Monster Island trilogy of zombie novels, the 13 Bullets series of vampire books, and most recently the Jim Chapel thrillers *Chimera* and *The Hydra Protocol*. "Agent Unknown" is a prequel to *Positive*, his forthcoming zombie epic. He lives and works in Brooklyn, New York.

Matthew Mather is the author of the bestselling novel *CyberStorm* and the acclaimed Atopia Chronicles science fiction series. *CyberStorm* was optioned by 20th Century Fox in 2013 for a major film production, and his works have been translated into over a dozen languages worldwide. He started out his career working at the McGill Center for Intelligent Machines, and among other things is an award-winning videogame designer. He spends his time between Montreal, Canada and Charlotte, NC.

Paolo Bacigalupi is the bestselling author of the novels *The Windup Girl*, *Ship Breaker*, *The Drowned Cities*, *Zombie Baseball Beatdown*, and the collection *Pump Six and Other Stories*. He is a winner of the Michael L. Printz, Hugo, Nebula, Locus, Compton Crook, and John W. Campbell Memorial awards, and was a National Book Award finalist. He currently lives in Western Colorado with his wife and son, where he is working on a new novel.

Sarah Langan is the author of the novels *The Keeper* and *The Missing*, and her most recent novel, *Audrey's Door*, won the 2009 Stoker for best novel. Her short fiction has appeared in the magazines *Nightmare, Cemetery Dance, Phantom*, and *Chiaroscuro*, and in the anthologies *Brave New Worlds, Darkness on the Edge*,and *Unspeakable Horror*. She is currently working on a post-apocalyptic young adult series called *Kids* and two adult novels: *Empty Houses*, which was inspired by *The Twilight Zone*, and *My Father's Ghost*, which was inspired by *Hamlet*. Her work has been translated into ten languages and optioned by the Weinstein Company for film. It has also garnered three Bram Stoker Awards, an American Library Association Award, two Dark Scribe Awards, a *New York Times Book Review* editor's pick, and a *Publishers Weekly* favorite book of the year selection.

ACKNOWLEDGMENTS

Agents: John thanks his agent Seth Fishman, who supported this experiment and provided feedback and counsel whenever he needed it, and also to his former agent Joe Monti (now a book editor who he plans to sell lots of anthologies to), who was very enthusiastic about this idea when it first occurred to him, and encouraged John to pursue his idea to self-publish it. Hugh likewise thanks his agent Kristin Nelson for all of her support and for constantly playing out his leash.

Art/Design: Thanks to Julian Aguilar Faylona for providing wonderful cover art for all three volumes of The Apocalypse Triptych, and to Jason Gurley for adding in all the most excellent design elements that took the artwork from being mere images and transformed them into *books*. These volumes would not be the same without them.

Proofreaders: Thanks to Anthony Cardno, Kevin McNeil, and Bradley Englert. Any typos that made it past them are on us.

Narrators/Producers: Thanks to Jack Kincaid for producing (and narrating some of) the audiobook version of this anthology, and to narrators Tina Connolly, Anaea Lay, Kate Baker, Mur Lafferty, Rajan Khanna, James Keller, Lex Wilson, Ralph Walters, Roberto Suarez, Norm Sherman, Folly Blaine, Scott Sigler, and Sarah Tolbert for lending their vocal talents to the production.

Family: John sends thanks to his wife, Christie, his mom, Marianne, and his sister, Becky, for all their love and support, and their endless enthusiasm for all his new projects. He also wanted to thank his sister-in-law Kate and stepdaughter Grace who had to listen to him blab incessantly about this project as it was coming together, ruining many a dinner. Hugh thanks his wife Amber, who co-edits this wonderful life they have together. His chapters would be boring and lonely without her.

Readers: Thanks to all the readers and reviewers of this anthology, and also all the readers and reviewers who loved Hugh's novels and John's other anthologies, making it possible for this book to happen in the first place.

Writers: And last, but certainly not least: a big thanks to all of the authors who appear in this anthology. It has been an honor and a privilege. As fans, we look forward to whatever you come up with next.

ABOUT THE EDITORS

John Joseph Adams is the series editor of *Best American Science Fiction & Fantasy,* published by Houghton Mifflin. He is also the bestselling editor of many other anthologies, such as *The Mad Scientist's Guide to World Domination, Armored, Brave New Worlds, Wastelands,* and *The Living Dead.* He has been nominated for six Hugo Awards and five World Fantasy Awards, and he has been called "the reigning king of the anthology world" by Barnes & Noble. John is also the editor and publisher of the digital magazines *Lightspeed* and *Nightmare,* and is a producer for Wired.com's *The Geek's Guide to the Galaxy* podcast. Find him on Twitter @johnjosephadams.

Hugh Howey is the author of the acclaimed post-apocalyptic novel *Wool*, which became a sudden success in 2011. Originally self-published as a series of novelettes, the *Wool* omnibus is frequently the #1 bestselling book on Amazon.com and is a *New York Times* and *USA TODAY* bestseller. The book was also optioned for film by Ridley Scott, and is now available in print from major publishers all over the world. Hugh's other books include *Shift*, *Dust*, *Sand*, the Molly Fyde series, *The Hurricane*, *Half Way Home*, *The Plagiarist*, and *I, Zombie*. Hugh lives in Jupiter, Florida with his wife Amber and his dog Bella. Find him on Twitter @hughhowey.

COPYRIGHT ACKNOWLEDGMENTS

Cover Art by Julian Aguilar Faylona.
Cover Design by Jason Gurley.
Interior layout by Hugh Howey.

ALSO EDITED BY JOHN JOSEPH ADAMS

If you enjoyed THE END IS NIGH, you might also enjoy these other anthologies and magazines edited by John Joseph Adams.

Armored
Best American Science Fiction & Fantasy [Forthcoming, Oct. 2015]
Brave New Worlds
By Blood We Live
Dead Man's Hand [Forthcoming, May 2014]
The End Is Now [Forthcoming, Sep. 2014]
The End Has Come [Forthcoming, Mar. 2015]
Epic: Legends Of Fantasy
Federations
HELP FUND MY ROBOT ARMY!!! [Forthcoming, Jul. 2014]
Thes Improbable Adventures Of Sherlock Holmes
Lightspeed Magazine
The Living Dead
The Living Dead 2
The Mad Scientist's Guide To World Domination
Nightmare Magazine
Other Worlds Than These
Oz Reimagined
Robot Uprisings [Forthcoming, Apr. 2014]
Seeds Of Change
Under The Moons Of Mars
Wastelands
Wastelands 2 [Forthcoming, 2015]
The Way Of The Wizard

COMING SOON:

THE END IS NOW & THE END HAS COME

We hope you've enjoyed reading THE END IS NIGH. If so, be sure to keep an eye out for THE END IS NOW (September 2014) and THE END HAS COME (March 2015), volumes two and three of THE APOCALYPSE TRIPTYCH.

Edited by acclaimed anthologist John Joseph Adams and bestselling author Hugh Howey, THE APOCALYPSE TRIPTYCH is a series of three anthologies of apocalyptic fiction. THE END IS NIGH focuses on life before the apocalypse. THE END IS NOW turns its attention to life during the apocalypse. And THE END HAS COME focuses on life after the apocalypse.

Visit johnjosephadams.com/apocalypse-triptych to learn more about THE APOCALYPSE TRIPTYCH or to read interviews with the authors. You can also sign up for our newsletter if you would like to be reminded when the other volumes of the TRIPTYCH become available.

THE END...

...HAS ONLY BEGUN

9093280R00218

Made in the USA
San Bernardino, CA
03 March 2014